RACHEL
A Jewish girl, a gentile boy, and a world at war

Another historical Novel by Sid Rich

America Star Books
Frederick, Maryland

Softcover 9781682298275
PUBLISHED BY AMERICA STAR BOOKS, LLLP
www.americastarbooks.pub
Frederick, Maryland

DEDICATION

This work is dedicated to my friends and the staff at
The Jewish Community Center of Austin, Texas.

**YOU CAN ORDER BOOKS DIRECTLY
FROM THE PUBLISHER**
www.americastarbooks.pub

Books are also normally available from
Amazon and the Barnes & Noble websites

**TO LEARN MORE ABOUT SID RICH, HIS FAMILY, AND
FUTURE LITERARY PROJECTS, CONSULT HIS WEBSITE.**
www.sidrichonline.com

**TO COMMUNICATE DIRECTLY WITH SID RICH
YOU CAN EMAIL HIM.**
sidrich@austin.rr.com

BOOKS BY SID RICH
Standing on the Promises
Men in War
Picking up the Pieces
Two Tigers from Texas
Manila Gold
Chance Meeting
Willie John Mahoney
Ramblin Rose
The Lobbyist
The Game
The Promise
Duke Shannon
Battle of Britain
Rachel

PROLOGUE

German statesman and foreign minister Gustav Stresemann spoke of the new Germany after accepting the Nobel Peace Prize in June 1927. Surely he never envisioned a new Germany led by a sadistic, anti-Semitic madman like Adolph Hitler—a man who sought to conquer all of Europe—and exterminate the entire population of Jews. This story begins in 1933 in Berlin, Germany, during a time of general unrest. It's the story of a Jewish family named Rosenthal, of a Jewish girl, a gentile boy, and a world at war.

Rachel by Sections

PART ONE

TURMOIL IN GERMANY

1

The Year 1933

"EMIL, IS THERE anything else I can get you?"

"Yes, I would love some brandy."

She put a goblet in front of her husband and filled it half full, leaving the decanter on the table. "I guess I'd better clear."

"Not yet. Sit here beside me. We need to talk."

She frowned. Emil looked serious and she didn't know what was coming.

Emil took a sip of the brandy and placed the goblet back on the dining room table. She looked anxious. "Ruth, the legal measures taken by the new Nazi government in February and March mean that the government can legislate contrary to the constitution."

"What does that mean exactly, Emil?"

"It means they can do whatever they want to do. And it has started with the boycott of Jewish shops. I am very concerned about how far it will go and where it will end."

Ruth started to speak, but she stopped when Emil raised his hand.

"I have been exchanging letters with Saul in Buenos Aires. Business is good, life is good. He's pretty well set with his holdings, except for one thing, and we both agree it would be a good investment. Beef is huge in Argentina. He and I are going to buy a meat packing plant. I think we can do extremely well. Saul will be a part owner, but I will be the majority owner. That way our family will have a business that we control and that we can leave to the children. I would envision Dietrich running the company some day."

Ruth was speechless. "I never thought about leaving Berlin, leaving Germany. I'm a German, not an Argentinean."

"I understand, Ruth. Even after Meir and Saul left, I never considered it. But these are not ordinary times. I believe life for Jews is going to become more and more difficult. I don't know where it all will end but I don't want to leave it to chance, leave it to Adolph Hitler."

Tears began to slowly run down Ruth's face. Her voice broke but she concluded, "You are the head of this house. I don't like it, but I trust you to take care of your family."

He smiled and touched her hand. "I am going to Buenos Aires in two days so Meir and I can close the deal. I do not want anyone to know of my plans."

"What about the children?"

"We'll just tell Dietrich and Rachel that I'm going on a business trip. That's all they need to know for now."

There was more to the plan.

"When I get back, I want to get the children out of Berlin and to Buenos Aires. When that has been accomplished, I will liquidate our assets and then you and I will leave."

Emil had a second thought. "Ruth, I feel a real sense of urgency to get this done."

Ruth looked worried. Her sense of foreboding was not unfounded.

2

EMIL ROSENTHAL STOPPED in Barcelona on his way to Buenos Aires. The Barcelona stop was to purchase real estate on Front Street. At least Jimenez was led to believe that was his main purpose. Jose Jimenez was primarily in real estate, but a good business deal of any kind was always appealing. The German Rosenthal had called him from Berlin; he told him he had understood that he had the listing for that particular piece of property—a large apartment complex overlooking the ocean. The deal was made with little haggling and the German paid it all in cash.

I remember that the German wanted to close the deal quickly. There was a definite sense of urgency.

THE AFTERNOON AFTER the sale, Jimenez received a telephone call. The voice at the other end of the line wanted Jose to meet Herr Rosenthal for an aperitif at the Hotel Gallina bar at 6:30 p.m. Jose agreed.

The maitre'd recognized Jimenez as he entered the cantina and led him to a corner booth where Rosenthal was waiting. He took a seat and the maitre'd promised to send over a waiter.

"Thank you for coming, Mr. Jimenez," said Emil, in Spanish.

"Thank you for inviting me, and please call me Jose."

The waiter appeared. "What can I serve you?"

Both men ordered Scotch whiskey. They were alone and could talk privately. "Jose, I have a proposition for you and I hope it will be appealing. The apartment building I purchased today cost 500,000 American dollars."

"Yes, Herr Rosenthal."

"My people tell me you are not only a competent realtor, but you manage projects as well, and do a first class job of it."

"Thank you, Herr Rosenthal," touching Emil's glass.

"You are young, unmarried, career driven, and anxious to make big money. My information is correct?"

"Yes, definitely, Herr Rosenthal."

"It just may be possible for me to help you."

Jose was wide-eyed. He edged forward on his seat. "Please—tell me more."

"It would not take a very smart individual to recognize that the purchase of a large real estate project, by a German, all cash, in the present Spanish political climate, is a bit unusual, to say the least. Agreed?"

Jose smiled. "Agreed."

"I purchased the complex as a source of income should I decide to become a resident of this country. That may not happen, but having this project is like an insurance policy. It's nice to have it if I need it. I have no business office here and a wise investor realizes that operations are equally as important as the property itself. That brings me to the heart of the proposition. I want you to operate the business for me."

"Herr Rosenthal!" he exclaimed, with enthusiasm.

"I can offer you 20,000 pesetas annually for your management fee and a 25 percent interest in the business. You are a smart man. I think you can see that even if this depressed economy lingers, a debt-free project makes your 25 percent become even more profitable."

Jose Jimenez was momentarily speechless.

"So, my friend, what do you say? Can we be business partners?"

"Herr Rosenthal, I am honored and thrilled to be your business partner. Since we have our drinks, we can drink to it as well."

"Good. Now, I am aware that you are a pilot, and that you own a small plane, which you keep it at a small airfield outside of the city."

"What you say is true."

"The day will come when I may need your services. When that day comes, you need to respond immediately and without question or hesitation. Can you do that?"

"Without question, Herr Rosenthal."

"My wife and I and our two children will be leaving Germany in the near future and we will want to land at that little airfield outside of town. We will then board a ship. Further instructions will be given you by courier or telegram as to what will be expected of you. Now that you have heard the conditions, do we still have a bargain?"

"Yes, Herr Rosenthal."

"All right. I must impress you with the importance of confidentiality. No one is to know any of this. No one. If you act unilaterally to change these arrangements, your part of the deal will be legally terminated. If you betray me, you will be killed."

"We have a bargain, Herr Rosenthal. You have my loyalty and my trust."

"Then I have not misjudged you, Senor Jimenez. I have already made the arrangement for our partnership. It will all be legal and in writing. Our attorney at today's closing shall be your attorney and he shall provide you with wisdom, comfort, and advice. If you fulfill today's promise, it shall become a most fruitful, mutually beneficial relationship. Please remember all the words I have spoken to you today. Follow them to the letter."

He stood, followed by Jose. "Now, I shake your hand and with it the understanding that a bond has been established."

"Yes, Herr Rosenthal."

"All right, Jose, then let us go and sign the papers."

THE PAPERWORK WAS finally completed. "Buena suerte, Senior Rosenthal, you have a partner for life."

It is not about the money. I am moved by this man. I have just sworn allegiance to a Jewish man I have known for only a day.

3
The Weimar Republic

IN 1919, FOLLOWING World War I, a national assembly was convened in the city of Weimar, where a new constitution for the German Reich was written, and then adopted on August 11 of that same year. In its fourteen years, the Weimar Republic faced numerous problems, including hyperinflation, political extremists with paramilitaries (both left and right wing), and continuing contentious relationships with the Allied powers that had defeated them on the battlefield.

The Weimar Republic is the name given by historians to the federal republic and representative democracy established in Germany to replace the imperial form of government. It is named after Weimar, the city where the constitutional assembly took place. During this period, and well into the succeeding Nazi era, the official name of the state was the German Reich.

The Weimar Republic successfully reformed the currency, unified tax policies and the railway system, and eliminated most of the requirements of the Treaty of Versailles. Germany never completely met the disarmament requirements and only paid a small portion of the total reparations required by the treaty, which were reduced twice by restructuring Germany's debt.

4
The Year 1927

THUS BEGAN THE depression in Germany. The instability of investment behavior was one of the central features of the German economy after 1924. Cross-country comparisons revealed the instability of fixed investment in the public and semi-public sectors to be the most significant. This is traced unambiguously to capital market difficulties at home and abroad, both of which arose out of events internal to Germany itself and unrelated to Wall Street's share speculation.

. . . . .

"FATHER, I HAVE sold the last of my restaurants," said Saul.

"How did you do?"

"Very well. I'm very pleased with the total proceeds, particularly in this economy."

"What's next for you, Saul?"

"I plan to leave Germany."

Leopold frowned, "And go where?"

"Buenos Aires."

"Leave Germany for South America? Leave your family?"

"I hate that you put it that way, Father."

"I put it as I feel."

"Look, Father, you are an established businessman and you and mother have been Berliners all your lives. It would be hard for you to move even if you so desired. And you're smart, you have deep roots, and your business is stable. You will survive. But I'm young and, frankly, I wonder about Germany's future and where I might fit in."

"You have such little faith?"

"Father, we are in a depression. There are bankruptcies, instability in fixed investment, rising unemployment, millions of Germans out of work, and there is distrust of public officials. I want out!"

Leopold stared at his son.

He took up his pipe, packed it, lit it, and began to puff. He looked at it with satisfaction, puffed again, and looked Saul in the eye. "Why Buenos Aires?"

"I have been thinking about this for a long time, and I have done my due diligence. Argentina has had an open door policy on immigration for many years, including a long period where immigration, specifically from European countries, has been encouraged. Do you realize that the first Jewish Community was created in Buenos Aires as far back as 1862? There are probably 150,000 Jews in Argentina today. I find this a positive factor in my decision. I speak Spanish and I'm good at the food business. I plan to go to Buenos Aires and open a chain of restaurants, as I did here in Berlin."

"You have thought this out very well. I'm impressed."

"You should not be surprised that you raised a thoughtful and wise man."

Leopold smiled, still puffing on his pipe. "No, I should not."

"There's more, Father."

"Let's hear it."

"There are more than 20,000 miles of railroad tracks throughout Argentina, most of the lines being British-built and owned. I am encouraged that the government allows foreign investment and in such an important part of its infrastructure. The railroads have helped to further open up the country. It occurs to me, Father, that a smart fellow could find a way to invest in railroads."

Leopold smiled again.

"Beef is a big part of the economy and the railroads allow cattle and meat to be transported all over the country. It occurs to me that an entrepreneur might want to buy a ranch and go into the cattle business as well. That way I would serve my own beef. So, I think you can see that there are some attractive business possibilities in Argentina for a shrewd businessman, and this is why I chose Buenos Aires. I think I can do very well and become a wealthy and well connected man in a peaceful land with a good climate."

"Well, it will be a shock to your mother, and I will have a hard time dealing with it myself. But, go with my blessing. I won't stand in your way."

"You have Emil and Nathan. I don't think they will ever leave Berlin."

"I didn't think Meir would ever leave either, but he did. But I must admit he has done very well in America."

"Meir is a thoughtful and wise man as well."

Leopold laughed. "Yes, he is."

5

The Year 1928

GERMAN AGRICULTURE REACHED only its prewar level and remained stagnant, despite protective tariffs. The year before, German manufacturing had been at its postwar high: 22 percent above what it had been in 1913. But much of economic boom that Germany had enjoyed in the mid-1920s was built on foreign capital, with German entrepreneurs not accumulating enough of their own working capital. Germans were accumulating debts. Labor unions were forcing up wage rates, and a spiraling rise in wages and prices appeared. Modernization of equipment was resulting in a decreased need of skilled workers. In September 1928, Germany had 650,000 unemployed.

6
The Year 1929

THE US STOCK market had been on a nine-year run that saw the Dow Jones Industrial Average increase in value tenfold, peaking on September 3, 1929. Shortly before the crash, economist Irving Fisher famously proclaimed, "Stock prices have reached what looks like a permanently high plateau." The optimism and financial gains of the great bull market were shaken on September 18, 1929, when share prices on the New York Stock Exchange abruptly fell.

On October 24, known as "Black Thursday," the market lost 11 percent of its value at the opening bell on very heavy trading. Several leading Wall Street bankers met to try and find a solution to the panic and chaos on the trading floor. The meeting included Thomas W. Lamont, acting head of Morgan Bank; Albert Wiggin, head of the Chase National Bank; and Meir Rosenthal, president of the National City Bank of New York.

Over the weekend, the events were covered by the newspapers across the United States. On October 28, "Black Monday," more investors decided to get out of the market, and the slide continued with a record loss in the Dow of 13 percent.

The next day, October 29, 1929, about sixteen million shares were traded, and the Dow lost an additional 12 percent, primarily because of the anticipated effects of the pending Smoot–Hawley Tariff Act. Congress wanted the tariffs to protect American farmers, but the Act raised tariffs to historical levels, some as much as 50 percent. It backfired and provoked a storm of foreign retaliatory measures, which did not help America's depression. It also hurt Germany.

William C. Durant joined with members of the Rockefeller family and other financial giants to buy large quantities of stocks in order to demonstrate to the public their confidence in the market, but their efforts failed to stop the large decline in prices. Due to the massive volume of stocks traded that day, the ticker did not stop running until about 7:45 that evening. The market had lost over $30 billion in the space of two days. The volume of stocks traded on October 29, 1929 was a record, which was not broken for nearly 40 years.

After a one-day recovery on October 30, where the Dow regained 12 percent, the market continued to fall, arriving at an interim bottom on November 13, 1929. The market then recovered for several months, starting on November 14, and reaching a secondary closing on April 17, 1930. There would be many dark days ahead.

■ ■ ■ ■ ■

THREE MILLION GERMANS were out of work. In the wake of the great fall of prices on the US stock market, lenders from the US gave Germany ninety days to start repayment.

In Munich, Adolf Hitler, still a political aspirant, told US media that with Germany's economic troubles, especially bankruptcies, rising unemployment, and distrust of public officials, Germany was slowly, but surely, slipping into conditions of Communism.

The Communist reasoning was that a crisis in capitalism, and middleclass suffering, was supposed to produce a rise in class consciousness among working people and trigger revolution. The Communists did realize a modicum of support, but, rather than Germany moving to the kind of revolution the Communists yearned for, Hitler and the Fascists, railing against Communism, were steadily gaining strength. Journalists asked Hitler whether he would again oppose the government by force. Hitler replied that his movement was growing so rapidly that they had no need of other than legal remedies.

7
The Year 1930

FOLLOWING HIS ELECTION as governor of New York, Franklin Roosevelt began running for President of the United States. While the "great depression" severely damaged Herbert Hoover and the Republicans, Roosevelt's bold efforts to combat the economic decline in New York enhanced his reputation. Henry Morgenthau arranged a fund-raiser for Roosevelt at the Waldorf Astoria Hotel, attended by over 100 of the most prominent Jewish businessmen in the city, including Meir Rosenthal.

Meir had supported FDR for governor in 1928 and they became friends, as did he and Morgenthau. After his speech, FDR artfully worked the room and spoke personally with everyone who wanted to see him. Henry Morgenthau and Meir Rosenthal were some of the last to leave the event. "Meir, my old and dear friend, I am so glad to see you."

Oh how I wish I could pat this good man on the shoulder or give him a manly hug, FDR lamented. He had been in a wheelchair since he contracted poliomyelitis while vacationing at Campobello Island in 1921. *I guess we'll see if a cripple can be elected President of the United States.*

They smiled and shook hands.

"This country is in trouble. It is going to take an extraordinarily talented man to lead us out of this dilemma. I happen to think you are that man," said Meir.

Roosevelt laughed. "I think we have Meir's support, Henry."

"I think you're right, Governor."

"If we make it to the White House, I'm going to need the counsel of both you gentlemen."

"You have it, Governor," said Meir. "Just tell us where and when."

"All you have to do is ask," said Henry.

· · · · ·

BY SEPTEMBER 1930, Germany's unemployment had risen to three million and Germany's manufacturing had fallen seventeen percent from the 1927 level. Bankruptcies were increasing. Farmers were hurting. Some in the middle class feared sliding into the lower class. And some in the middle class blamed the economic decline on unemployed people being unwilling to work. Hunger was widespread.

The parliamentary coalition that governed Germany fell apart, and new elections were held. The biggest winner in these elections was Adolph Hitler's National Socialist Party. They increased their seats in parliament from twelve to 107, becoming Germany's second largest political party. The largest party was still the Social Democrats, who won 143 seats and 24.5 percent of the vote. Communist Party candidates won 13.1 percent of the vote and when they joined together with the Social Democrats, they constituted a large enough block to claim the right to form a government.

In spite of the coalition, Communists and Social Democrats remained hostile to each other. The Communist International, established in 1919, was opposed to their members working with reformers, and believed that a collapse of parliamentary government would hasten the revolutionary crisis that would propel them to power.

Instead of a left-of-center socialist government, the president of the German republic, Paul von Hindenburg, selected Heinrich Brüning of the Catholic Center Party to form a government. His Party had received only 11.3 percent of the vote—less than the Communists—and Brüning did not have the majority parliamentary support needed to rule the country. He was forced to operate under Hindenburg's emergency powers.

This was the beginning of the end of democracy in Germany because Hindenburg was willing to do anything but give the government back to the Socialists. Brüning attempted to restore economic equilibrium by a balanced budget, high interest rates, and remaining on the gold standard with no emergency deficit spending. But the economy continued to slide.

8
The Year 1931

ADOLF HITLER WAS looking better and better to many Germans because he seemed to be a man who believed in something and wanted radical change that differed from the alternatives offered by the Socialists and Communists. Hitler appeared to be truly devoted to Germany. He was. He was a sincere nationalist and, in addition to being obsessed by what he saw as enemies within and without Germany, he identified with Germans.

Hitler found his greatest support in traditionally conservative small towns. He campaigned with attacks on Marxism, making it clear that by Marxism he meant the Social Democrats. Hitler appealed to morality, attacking free love and what he inferred was the immorality of Berlin and some other major cities. He promised to stamp out big city corruption. He called for a spiritual revolution, a "positive Christianity," and a spirit of national pride. Hitler repeatedly called for national renewal. He and his National Socialists benefited from the upheaval in the Soviet Union and the rise in fear and disgust for Bolshevism. His party's message was, "If you want your country to go Bolshevik, vote Communist. If you want to remain free Germans, vote for the National Socialists." It worked.

Hitler called for a strengthened Germany and a refusal to pay reparations. He promised to restore Germany's borders. He appeared to be for the common man and critical of Germany's ruling class. To the unemployed, he promised jobs and bread. His party had the appeal of being young and on the move. Even disillusioned Communists joined his movement, as did many unemployed young men and a variety of malcontents.

In addition to finding support in small towns, he found support among the middle class. He found support too from some among the newly rich and among some aristocrats. He found support among a few industrialists and financiers who wanted lower taxes and the arrest of the labor movement. He was able to set up places where unemployed young men could get a hot meal and trade their shabby clothes for storm trooper uniforms.

Hitler's call for more territory for Germany did not win him many votes at the time because the country was in no mood to consider risking war. Appeals to anti-Semitism had not been much help to conservative candidates before the depression, and conservative governments after the arrival of the depression were making no moves to rescind the rights of Jews. But Hitler continued his attacks on Jews and continued to hammer away at what he described as the Jewish aspect of capitalism, appealing to those who believed the myths about Jews and believed in the socialism of his National Socialist German Workers Party.

9
The Year 1932

AT THE 1932 CHICAGO convention, Franklin Roosevelt won the nomination as the Democratic Party candidate for president. He broke with tradition at the time and flew to Chicago to accept the nomination in person. He campaigned energetically, calling for government intervention in the economy to provide relief, recovery, and reform. His activist approach and personal charm helped defeat Herbert Hoover in November 1932 by seven million votes. Meir Rosenthal became a valued banking and economic advisor and Henry Morgenthau became Secretary of the Treasury.

■ ■ ■ ■ ■

MORGENTHAU WAS BORN into a prominent Jewish family in New York City, the son of Henry Morgenthau Sr., a real estate mogul and diplomat, and Josephine Sykes. He attended the Dwight School and studied architecture and agriculture at Cornell University. He became friends with Franklin and Eleanor Roosevelt in 1913.

While American cities prospered, the vast migration from rural areas and continued neglect of the US agriculture industry would create widespread financial despair among American farmers and would later be blamed as one of the key factors that led to the 1929 stock market crash. Morgenthau, who operated a farm near the Roosevelt estate in upstate New York, became a champion of farming and became a voice for reclamation, conservation, and scientific farming.

In 1929, as Governor of New York, FDR appointed Morgenthau chairman of the New York State Agriculture Advisory Committee as well as the Conservation Commission. Morgenthau played a major role in designing and financing the New Deal, one of FDR's signature recovery initiatives.

After 1937, still in charge of the Treasury, he played a central role in financing US participation in World War II. Henry Morgenthau was an important man to know, and little did Meir Rosenthal know in 1930 just how important their friendship would be.

· · · · ·

THE DEPRESSION HAD been worsening in Germany and unemployment reached thirty percent—5,102,000. At age 84 years, Hindenburg ran for re-election, his major opponent for the presidency was none other than Adolf Hitler. Neither Hindenburg nor Hitler won a majority, and in the runoff campaign, Hindenburg won 19.4 million to Hitler's 11.4 million. But in the parliamentary elections held later that April, the National Socialists increased their seats from 107 to 162, becoming the largest political party in Germany. Hitler had lost the election for the presidency, but his campaigning had paid off.

Hindenburg had become dissatisfied with chancellor Brüning, and the hunt was on for a new chancellor. Brüning still lacked the parliamentary majority needed for democratic rule, and without Hindenburg's support, he was forced to resign. His last act as chancellor was to put a ban on Hitler's street force, his storm troopers, also known as the *Brown Shirts.*

The aristocratic Hindenburg disliked Hitler, seeing him as a rabble-rouser of working class types and believing that the Nationalist Socialists were indeed socialists. He was not about to select Hitler as his new chancellor while his aide, Kurt von Schleicher, was having difficulty putting together a governing coalition of national unity. Giving up on national unity, Schleicher put together a cabinet that was largely of aristocrats—to be known as *the cabinet of barons*—with himself as minister of defense and Franz von Papen as chancellor. It was another government that lacked a parliamentary majority, and it was unpopular across Germany. But the new government did have at least one success in foreign affairs—the cancellation of Germany's obligation to make reparations payments.

The crisis over establishing a government with a parliamentary majority continued, and in late July 1932, another parliamentary election was held. The results hurt the middle class and middle-road political parties, and the National Socialists increased their seats in parliament to 230 of a total of 670 seats. The number of seats for the Communists rose to 89. Schleicher believed that it was necessary to form a government that included National Socialists, and Hitler was buoyed by the thought that he was on the verge of being selected as chancellor. When parliament opened in September, the National

Socialists, seeking a government led by Hitler, organized a vote against the von Papen government. Von Papen responded by dissolving parliament, with new elections scheduled for November 1932.

In the November elections, the Communists won 17 percent of the vote, and their number of seats in parliament rose to 100, while Hitler's National Socialists lost 34 seats. This drop shocked the National Socialists, who believed, with some others, that their movement might have lost its momentum.

The National Socialists were in debt from all their campaigning. Hitler had borrowed money extravagantly for his campaigns, believing he could pay it back easily if he won and that the loans did not matter if he lost. Discouraged financial backers began withdrawing their support from the National Socialists, and opportunistic party activists began leaving the party. Hitler was distressed, and there was talk that some of those leaving the National Socialists were going over to the Communists.

Schleicher was alarmed by the growth of support for the Communists. This fear was shared by Frederick Sackett, America's ambassador to Germany. Schleicher forced von Papen's resignation. Papen was irritated with Schleicher and, buoyed by the decline of the National Socialists, he devised a scheme to head a coalition that included the National Socialists, believing that he and other respectable conservatives in his cabinet could control the humbled National Socialist party.

Schleicher formed an emergency government and tried to put together a coalition of many political parties, including some National Socialists that he hoped to split away from Hitler. Schleicher hoped to win the support of both moderate socialists and conservatives, but the reforms that he hoped would appeal to the moderate socialists were rejected by conservatives, and Schleicher's coalition failed to hold together. The unwillingness of these conservatives to compromise was paving the way for Adolf Hitler.

10
The Year 1933

"LET ME TOP off your drink, Saul," said Emil. "Is everybody else okay?"

They had put Leopold in the ground beside Sarai, his wife of 54 years, who had succumbed to pneumonia the year before at 85 years of age. Jewish law required the body be buried within a day or as soon as practical from the time of death. Exceptions could be made in certain cases: if there were legal issues surrounding the death, if the body had to be transported from one city or country to another, if close family members had to travel far distances to be present for the funeral, or to avoid burial on Saturday or another holy day. Emil and Nathan had to wait for Meir and Saul to arrive from America and Argentina.

Friends had voiced their condolences and had finally left Leopold's mansion and returned to their own homes. After the interment, there was normally a reception at a family home. Friends or the synagogue community would normally prepare a consolation meal. But Emil didn't want that. They had the reception, but he wanted the consolation meal to be just for the family. The women were preparing the food while the men talked and had their tobacco and brandy. Leopold Rosenthal had lived a long, prosperous, and healthy life.

"I think he died of a broken heart," Emil speculated.

"He was 91 years old, brother," said Meir.

"Yes, he was old but I think Meir is right," said Nathan. "I don't think he was ever the same after mother died. Emil and I were here, we could see it."

"They both had a long run," said Saul. "We should be so lucky."

"Sarai and I are moving to Poland," said Nathan.

"Where did that come from?" Emil questioned.

"Sarai is from Grojec and still has family there. I promised her we'd move there some day. Now that mom and dad are gone, we're going to do it."

"You won't have much of a medical practice in Grojec," reasoned Emil.

"My office will be in Warsaw, but I'll also take care of the people in the village who want me."

"Father got very upset with me when I left Germany for New York," Meir disclosed.

"He got over it, brother, and he was very proud of your success," said Saul.

"I never knew that."

"He mentioned it to me when I told him I was going to Buenos Aires," Saul confessed.

"Germany is a great country. Well, it was a great country," Emil declared. "You may be surprised to learn that I'm going to join the rest of you. I am preparing to take my family and leave as well. I don't think Germany is going to be a country where Jews will be welcome, or much worse. Mother and father are dead so they won't be hurt that all their sons are leaving."

"Where are you taking your family, Emil?" Meir asked.

"Argentina."

"Argentina?"

"Yes. Saul and I have purchased a meat packing plant. I have majority ownership and it will be my family business. Dietrich will run it someday."

"How is Argentina?" Meir asked.

"Things have worked out exactly as I planned," said Saul. "My restaurants are booming, and I have been able to invest in railroads. My cattle ranch is also growing and the meat packing plant is thriving. Life is good."

"That's great news, Saul," said Nathan. "And it will be nice to have Emil and his family there as well."

"It sure will."

"My God, we'll be scattered all over the world. That's the sad part. We'll never see each other," Emil lamented.

"You're probably right about that, Emil," said Nathan.

"How does Argentina feel about Jews?" a cynical Meir asked.

"Like everyone else in the world. Actually, it's been pretty good. But now not as good. But what the hell, lots of people in this world don't like Jews. But life goes on."

The room was silent for a time. Then Nathan broke the silence, "While we're still together, we need to discuss the estate."

"Well said. Since I will be the only one left in Germany, I'll have to see to it. The will calls for the four of us to share and share alike," said Emil. "Since I have taken over the management of Pop's real estate business, I have acquired additional holdings."

"Then sell off Pop's part and we'll divide that money plus whatever the house brings," Nathan suggested.

"Since Emil will be doing all the work, his share should be more. I think he should get 40 percent of Pop's part and we'll divide the difference," said Meir.

"That sounds fair to me," said Saul. "Emil, how do you feel about Meir's suggestion?"

"It is perfectly acceptable."

"Then we have a plan," said Meir. "Let's drink to it."

"Emil, we won't be able to stay for the *shiva*. We'll observe the mourning periods, but not in Berlin," said Saul. "I've got to get back to Buenos Aires."

"We've also got to leave," said Meir.

"And Sarai and I," said Nathan.

"As soon as I can liquidate all the property, we'll leave as well. The sooner the better."

Ruth stepped into the room and announced, "The meal is on the table."

■ ■ ■ ■ ■

EMIL TOOK MEIR aside before he left and handed him a briefcase.

"What's this, brother?"

"It's an investment my family is making in America."

"I'm sorry, Emil, you're not making this very clear."

"It's full on money, Meir, lots of money. I'd like you to establish an account for me and deposit all of it in your bank."

Meir smiled, "I'll take care of it, brother."

■ ■ ■ ■ ■

ADOLPH HITLER REJECTED any proposal that did not designate himself as the head of a new government. Von Papen went to Hindenburg and proposed a government with Hitler as chancellor and himself as vice-chancellor, with the majority of the cabinet to be conservatives from von Papen's Nationalist Party. Hitler met with some right-wing industrialists, reassuring them of his respect for private property. He told them that democracy led to socialism and that he would curb socialism and the socialist-led labor unions. The industrialists liked what Hitler said and in January 30, 1933, Hindenburg gave power to Hitler and his new coalition. The conservatives still believed that they could control Hitler. Hindenburg, of course, had no idea what a disastrous decision he had made.

It was not democracy that gave power to Hitler. He became Germany's chancellor, the equivalent of a prime minister, without ever having received more than 37 percent of the popular vote in the elections he had entered. His National Socialist Party had never received more than a third of the seats in parliament. Hitler had been appointed chancellor by a lone individual—von Hindenburg—who did not believe in democracy and had been maneuvering against the creation of a government that had majority support as the parliamentary system demanded. Hindenburg's purpose was entirely driven by denying power to Social Democrats. Moreover, simply as chancellor, Hitler's powers were limited. But those limitations were soon to be cast aside.

PART TWO

ESCAPE FROM BERLIN

11

The Year 1934

"COLONEL CHRISTIAN ALBRACHT."

"Yes, I'm Albracht."

"Your mother, Helga, lives at 13 Hannestrasse, apartment 7-C. She has been there for 18 years. She's a lovely woman."

"Who are you?"

"My name is Emil Rosenthal. Does that name, Rosenthal, mean anything to you?"

"I don't think so? How do you know about my mother?"

"I'm the current owner of her apartment building."

"And you want to raise the rent."

Emil smiled, "No, not at all."

"I'm sorry, Herr. Rosenthal, I am confused and this conversation is even more confusing. We are …"

"Indeed it is. I'm sorry, Colonel. Let me explain. Your father was wounded in the war. He made it back but died in 1918."

"That's right. I was eight years old. It was terrible on both of us. Mother had to go to work, but she didn't earn enough for us to pay the rent, utilities, food."

"How did you survive?"

"I'm not quite sure. All I know is that mother said I shouldn't worry about it. She said we wouldn't have to move after all. And we didn't."

"My father, Leopold Rosenthal, was the original owner. He waived the rent until your mother found a job and got established. He also provided food for your family. Then he fixed the rent at whatever she could afford."

Christian Albracht looked bewildered. "I never knew any of that. Your father was a good and generous man. We couldn't have made it without his kindness. And you own the property now and never raised the rent."

"No, I didn't. Leopold had a policy. Once he set a rent, it never changed for the people who lived there. New tenants paid the going rate in the market. I liked his policy. I kept the policy."

"Well, Herr Rosenthal, the Albrachts owe your father—and you, a great debt."

"Yes, you do."

Emil and Christian shook hands. "If I can ever do anything for you, just let me know."

"As a matter of fact, Colonel, you can."

Albracht was taken aback, even though he had just made the offer. He smiled. "What is it?"

"It has come to my attention that you make occasional solo flights to Madrid, Barcelona, and Lisbon."

"Herr Rosenthal, you know more than you are supposed to know."

"Yes."

Albracht laughed. Rosenthal smiled.

"I have a proposition for you."

"Very well, what is it?"

"Before I explain, let me say this. You are 34 years old, a graduate engineer from the University, married and have two children. You are a rising star in the military and an accomplished pilot. But military officers, unless perhaps a field marshal of aristocratic blood, don't make enough to give a family all that one would desire. Am I correct, Colonel?"

"Correct, Herr Rosenthal."

"My family will have occasion to leave Germany within the next six months. My son and daughter will leave first. Then, when I have attended to my affairs, my wife and I will leave. I will give you 150,000 marks for each person transported. I will give you the first installment when you depart. You will receive the remaining funds upon verification of their safe arrival at the destination point. This arrival will be verified by my agent. If everything has gone as planned, the remaining funds will be deposited in a blind account of your selection."

Before Albracht could speak, Emil had one more thought. "You say you owe my family a great debt and this is certainly true. Maybe you should do this service for me without compensation. But I want to do this for you and your family in the way I have described. I will have it no other way."

I believe in my heart that Christian Albracht is a good and honorable man, Emil thought, *but financial compensation is powerful motivation.*

Christian Albracht was overwhelmed. *Everything Herr Rosenthal has said is true. The money will help secure my family's future. And I do owe this man a kindness.*

"I'll do it, Herr Rosenthal. And you can trust me with your secret."

They smiled and shook hands. "Wonderful. Your destination will be a small airfield just outside Barcelona. When the time comes, I will supply you with a map and all the necessary information."

EMIL ROSENTHAL HAD learned well from Leopold; he had substantially increased the family real estate holdings. At age 43 years, he was one of the largest single owners of apartment housing in Germany. He was always in the "acquisition" mentality. It never occurred to him to sell any of his holdings. He bought judiciously and regularly, only in the best locations, sometimes paying a bit more in some cases to avoid property in secondary locations. He reasoned that the wealthy would pay for location and service. His reputation for fair rents and good management preceded him. Rosenthal buildings in Berlin became synonymous with good living.

Bankers loved doing business with Emil because his mortgage payments were prompt and his buildings were beautifully maintained. He was considered modest, respectful, honorable, frugal, hardworking, and intelligent. What the bankers and most people didn't know was that he had a good heart. He ignored his genius for business and marveled at his good fortune. Yes, he was Jewish, but he was never subjected to anti-Semitism. Thankfully, it had never been an issue.

·····

EMIL AND RUTH realized soon enough that Dietrich not only had extraordinary intelligence, but a physical capacity to match. He was outgoing, courteous, and respectful of authority and his elders. Rachel had no bent toward athletics, but was also highly intelligent, made good grades, and was kind and courteous. Neither of the children could comprehend the enormous wealth of their father. Emil and

Ruth did not spoil their children. They lived a comfortable, but rather modest life.

It is difficult for some to grasp the importance that Europeans attach to their sport of soccer. It cuts across social, financial, political, national, and in most cases, ethnic lines. In Europe, there is soccer— and then the other sports. The heroes of soccer are household names long after their careers are over. A budding star's progress was carefully noted. While still developing and far from his full potential, Dietrich Rosenthal's progress had been noted.

Emil marveled at Dietrich's celebrity. It was not in the least uncommon for a business acquaintance to stop him and congratulate him on some performance. It astounded Emil that it would be of such great importance. Emil, ever the intense and absorbed businessman, was known to cancel an appointment in order to see his son play.

It was clear that Dietrich was a superior talent. He definitely stood out among the team. Spectators were most effusive in their praise for Emil's young lion. Jews have always honored intellectual pursuit. Being migratory by perforce, excluded by many, and survival-oriented, little time was customarily afforded to games. Yet here was Dietrich, excelling like a gentile. But without question, there was little prejudice in a winning goal.

■ ■ ■ ■ ■

DEITRICH DONNED HIS uniform and ran quickly to the school soccer field for the intrasquad game. He had been unavoidably detained and was late to practice. The coach, Herr Allendorf, greeted him with enthusiasm. *I can't believe he's not mad.*

"Son, are you ready to play?"

"Yes, sir."

"Go in for Edward."

Frederick Hubermann was the second best player on the team. He was two inches less than six feet tall, blond, husky, and aggressive. He was a promising young player, who was sometimes prone to dirty play. He hated not being the best.

His jealousy of Dietrich Rosenthal often showed; he just couldn't help it. His father, SS General Franz Hubermann, was a soccer devotee of the first order. Because of his meteoric rise in the SS, he had the financial means to send his son to this exclusive private school located in a fine section of Berlin. Franz' appointment as head of the Berlin Unit was due to his solid police background, a fine military record—and his friendship with SS Chief, Heinrich Himmler.

Himmler has definitely helped advance my career, but I don't agree with the tactics and philosophy of these sadistic bastards dressed in black, particularity against the Jews.

Franz Hubermann never missed a game and he knew of Dietrich; he'd seen him play and knew full well how good he was. He spoke to his man, Captain Muller, "This boy's athletic prowess, his leadership, and his courage is contrary to my long standing beliefs about the sons of Abraham. I wonder if this boy may be adopted. I want you to find out about his family. His father is Emil Rosenthal and he's a very wealthy man."

His son Frederick frequently spoke ill of young Dietrich. He knew he was Jewish and let his raging anti-Semitism show. He loved his son but recognized that the disparaging remarks smacked of pure envy. Being honest with himself he thought, *My son is not of great intellect and I see in him the coarseness of his mother's brothers, loud, aggressive bullies. The boy is just bright enough to be dangerous to others and himself. He doesn't always think things through.* He had another thought, *On a number of occasions he has taken advantage of my station, the usual ploy of the ungrateful, spoiled, and inadequate. But his mother and I must share some of the blame for that.*

"GENERAL HUBERMANN, I have finished my inquiry into the Rosenthal family," said Muller.

"Good. Let's have it."

"You were correct about Herr Rosenthal. He is a wealthy man. He owns a considerable number of buildings in Berlin. He is considered a good credit risk, keeps his properties in top condition, and is easy to do business with. In fact, he is extremely well thought of by most everyone."

"Really?"

"Yes, sir."

"And his family?"

"He and his wife Ruth have two children, Dietrich and his younger sister, Rachel. They are not adopted."

Hubermann thought for a moment, "Very well, my curiosity has been satisfied. Thank you, Muller."

"Sir."

■ ■ ■ ■ ■

FREDERICK HUBERMANN'S PREVIOUS contact at the school with Dietrich had been uneventful. While Frederick had taken pleasure in bullying others, he had an instinctive wariness when it came to types like Dietrich. Frederick had seen, first hand, the agility and wiriness of the six foot two inch Dietrich, whose quiet, supreme confidence seemed to discourage confrontation from others.

Since Frederick had come to the Bohm School two years earlier, his jealousy of Dietrich had bordered on sickness. But he had masked his resentment thus far. It was all the more galling since Dietrich paid little attention to him at all.

A sudden clapping and yelling signaled Dietrich's entry into the game on the opposite side of the field from Frederick.

When Dietrich had possession of the ball, Frederick was guilty of holding, pulling, and tripping. He continued his unsportsmanlike conduct for the better part of thirty minutes. Dietrich took advantage of Frederick's poor positioning and scored two easy goals, making his detractor look foolish. The byplay escaped no one, especially Coach Allendorf. The coach felt that Frederick's selfish play in the past month had cost the team, which diminished his standing and elevated Dietrich's.

It was too much for Frederick, and suddenly in a fit of pique he rushed Dietrich from behind and bowled him over. Dietrich, off-balance, took a precarious fall. Action had come to an abrupt halt. Dietrich rose slowly, brushing off an elbow, and quietly asked, "Frederick, what's come over you? Why are you deliberately trying to hurt me—your fellow teammate?"

Frederick, drew close, shaking his finger, using pat phrases from recent Jew-baiting of lesser boys, he yelled, "Don't question anything I do you Jew-*kike*. Everyone knows your *kike* father gouges his tenants and your mother is a worthless, common Jew-whore."

Dietrich promptly nailed him with a left hook to his unsuspecting gut, followed by a right cross to his filth-spewing mouth. The forceful blows dropped him like a sack of potatoes. Frederick lay there on his back in pain, feeling his mouth where blood was beginning to drip from his cut lip. He could sense the two teeth that hung by a thread.

The other players began to murmur among themselves. And then one boy shouted, "He got what was coming to him."

Dietrich was not finished. He approached Frederick, yanked him to his feet by the shirt, blood spewing from the cut, and methodically slapped him front-hand side and back-hand side on the return. Frederick, was now a bloody mess, but there was more. Dietrich turned him around and soundly kicked him in the butt, sending him headfirst into the ground.

Dietrich left the playing field and slowly walked home. Rachel was upstairs studying and his mother had just returned from shopping. He told her the story and she promptly called Emil.

Frederick was taken home by Coach Allendorf. He had tried to clean the boy up, but he didn't look good. His mother was in a panic and called the general. He was home in twenty minutes. After the doctor treated Frederick, he said, "General, I've given him a sedative, and he should sleep several hours. He's going to be fine. He'll need to see the dentist. I'll leave you now and you can call me if you need me. But you should not have to call."

"Thank you, doctor Kaiser."

"Now, what happened, Coach?"

Allendorf was apprehensive. He wondered what to say, but decided the truth was the best, in spite of who he was addressing. He explained, "General, your boy played dirty with Rosenthal. Young Dietrich tried to talk to him about it, but when Frederick called his mother a common Jew-whore, young Rosenthal decked him."

"Thank you, Coach Allendorf, for bringing Frederick home and explaining what happened. It may be that young Frederick will learn from this. I have warned him about his attitude and his conduct, but I think that my status in the German army has given him a kind of arrogance that may have contributed to his conduct. Now, Coach, will you join me in a brandy?"

Allendorf's relief was unimaginable. "I would enjoy that, sir."

After a benign conversation about soccer, Allendorf said goodbye.

Hubermann closed the front door and proceeded to the kitchen to discuss the situation with his wife, Astrid. "My dear, our son apparently provoked the Rosenthal boy unnecessarily and paid dearly for the provocation. I should imagine he'll be more careful in the future. I've given him far too much rein lately because I've been busy. He needs more attention. I'm going back to the office for awhile now. When the boy awakes, tell him I want to speak with him before supper. I think today is a good day—perhaps a turning point for Frederick—an event that will shape his manhood."

Astrid did not reply. She would leave it to the general.

12
TWENTY-FOUR HOURS LATER

EMIL ROSENTHAL WAS in a panic. His boy had beaten up the only son of a well-connected SS general, with close ties to Himmler. "Ruth, we cannot take a chance with the children now that this has happened. These people act swiftly and without mercy. I have laid the plan; all I have to do is activate it."

Rachel had been told what had happened at school. Emil started, "Dietrich, what happened today at school is history."

Dietrich was confused; he frowned and tried to speak. "Dietrich, just be quiet and listen. That goes for you as well, Rachel."

"Yes, Father," said Rachel.

"It really doesn't matter what happened today, the why or how. If this had not happened at school, then it would have happened in another fashion to any one of us, your mother or me or Rachel. What you children must know is that it is no longer safe for Jews in Germany."

Rachel looked scared. Dietrich was solemn but staid.

"I have been making plans for all of us to leave Berlin. I did not want to worry you with it at the time. Anyway, your Uncle Saul and I have purchased a meat packing plant in Buenos Aires. I own the controlling interest, so that will be the family business in the future. This incident at school has triggered your immediate departure from Berlin tonight."

"Tonight!" screamed Rachel.

Dietrich stared at Emil. He frowned but said nothing.

Ruth put her arms around Rachel. "Don't be afraid or concerned. Your father will provide for his family."

"Yes, Mother."

"We do not have much time, so listen carefully, Dietrich. I'm counting on you."

"Yes, Father."

"I've tried to think of everything. Clothes for both of you are laid out on your beds upstairs. Don't wear anything other than what is on your bed. Understand?"

"Yes, Father."

"Inside your pea jacket, Dietrich, you will find more information in an envelope. Read it on the plane."

Dietrich and Rachel frowned.

"You and Rachel will leave Berlin by plane and be flown to Barcelona."

"The plane? Barcelona?" Dietrich questioned.

"Yes, please just pay attention."

"Yes, Father."

"After you have read the instructions in your jacket, tear up the envelope and the pages into small pieces and destroy them. Here is an inventory of everything that I put in your duffel bags. You should have no occasion to go into your duffel bag during the trip until such time as you actually get on the ship and are in your cabin."

"The ship?"

"Dietrich!"

"Sorry, Father."

"Here are three chocolate bars for each of you. They should quell your hunger. It could be awhile until your next meal.

"Secondly, and more importantly, you will answer to the name Rader. Until you are safely in Buenos Aires under Uncle Saul's protection, you are Dietrich and Rachel Rader. If someone should approach you, whom you don't know and who does not start the conversation with, 'Are you Dietrich and Rachel Rader from Hamburg?' then do not trust that person or give him or her any information."

"Yes, Father."

Emil shoved a brown clasp envelope over to Dietrich.

"Thirdly, in there are your birth certificates and passports. There are also copies of information on bank accounts and a safety deposit box. There are also two keys to the safety deposit box. That's one key for each of you. I set up these accounts at the Buenos Aires National Bank, *El Banco Nacional de Buenos Aires*. On the passports, your last name is the only change, other than a different address here in Berlin. That address is a small building that I used to own. It doesn't even exist anymore. It's been torn down. Your ages and everything else are exactly the same.

"Now, the fourth thing is the money belt."

Emil slid the custom-made money belt over to Dietrich. It had eight separate sections and each one of them was full. "This goes under your shirt. Don't let it out of your sight."

Dietrich looked puzzled.

"May I know what's in the belt, Father?"

"Sure. The belt contains money and diamonds. This is part of our family wealth. The belt also contains all of your mother's jewelry. Put the diamonds and your mother's jewelry in the safety deposit box and deposit the money in the bank account. Your name and Rachel's are on the bank cards. They will need your signatures in order for you to access the money, so take your birth certificates to the bank and get that done. Just so you'll know, we also have a handsome sum of money tucked away in Uncle Meir's bank in New York. Oh, and I have purchased an apartment complex in Barcelona. Jose Jimenez, will meet you there. Your Uncle Saul has the legal papers on that investment."

Dietrich smiled, "You've been busy, Father."

"Yes."

They smiled at each other.

Rachel had been sitting quietly, listening, somewhat in shock from the news of their immediate departure and separation from their parents. But Emil wanted her to know the information as well.

Dietrich shook his head. "Father, you seem to have thought of everything."

"Where my children are concerned, there must be nothing left to chance."

Emil paused for a moment. "Do you understand, Dietrich? What I mean is do you understand everything I have told you to this point?"

"Yes, Father."

"Rachel?"

"Yes, Father."

"You will be in another country. I will not be there for you. Trust no one except Saul and Pedro."

"You trust this Mr. de Vargas?"

"With my life, or maybe I should say with the life of my children."

Both the children smiled.

"Everything understood?"

"Yes, Father."

"Rachel, go get dressed and bring down your duffel bag."

"Yes, Father."

"Dietrich, you have been raised with certain values and moral principles. These things dictate behavior and decisions you make in life. But right now, survival is at stake. Survival may depend upon thinking in advance, using discretion, going against your convictions, and being strong. You may have to lie. Whatever it takes for you and that little girl to survive, that's what you will have to do. You are young, but you are highly intelligent, resourceful, determined, and strong. You can do this. You can do whatever it takes."

Emil sighed. He didn't want to say more but he had to do it. "Dietrich, survival could mean you have to kill."

My Dietrich did not react. He may be stronger than I ever imagined.

"Think carefully, think hard, and do whatever is necessary for you and Rachel to survive and arrive safely in Buenos Aires. Have I made myself clear?"

The two men stood. Dietrich was taller. *This young man is truly a formidable specimen. I wouldn't want to tangle with him.*

"We will survive, Father. Your son and daughter will eagerly await the arrival of their mother and father as soon as humanly possible. You can count on me."

Emil extended his hand, tears running down his face. "I believe I can, Dietrich. Now, go dress and bring down your things. You just have time to say goodbye to your mother. I will bring the car around."

THEY DROVE FOR about twenty minutes. Dietrich and Rachel were dressed entirely in black: black boots, black trousers, black sweat shirts, black pea jackets, and black stocking caps. Her hair was tucked underneath the cap. They didn't know where they were going. They paid little attention to streets until they came to a corner, turned, and stopped. The car that was running ahead of them stopped as well. "I love you both more than you can imagine."

"We know. We love you too."

"Now, take your things and climb in the car in front of us. God be with you," he whispered, tears running down his face.

When they reached the car, the passenger's side door opened. They didn't recognize the driver, but he was a handsome man wearing the uniform of a pilot. The man asked, "Are you Dietrich and Rachel Rader from Hamburg?"

Dietrich smiled, "Yes, we are."

"Good, put your stuff in the back seat. You sit up here and Rachel can sit in the back."

They drove for a half hour and then Albracht stopped the car and explained. "We are close now. When we are inside the gate at the base, I will go and check for final weather reports. You will both stay put. Rachel, right now you need to lay down in the floorboard. We'll put this blanket over you for the time being. When I return, we'll drive straight to the plane. Don't say anything to anyone, Dietrich. If anyone should come over to the car while I'm inside, tell him you're waiting for Colonel Albracht. Here, Dietrich, put on this black fedora and shove the stocking cap in the pocket of your jacket."

Albracht pulled up to the gate and honked his horn.

"We're in luck. Sergeant Hoffmann is on duty."

Hoffmann recognized Albracht, raised the gate, and saluted him through. It was not at all unusual for the colonel to be flying at night. He was the wing commander and the entire base knew he was a bit unconventional. It was also common knowledge that Germany had no better pilot—one who did everything with panache. It was also known on the base that he often reported on a Saturday or Sunday morning out of uniform, in a T-shirt, dungarees, and sneakers to take an airplane for a spin. In the military, he was known as an unpretentious, demanding, no-bullshit, leader of men. Pilots yearned to fly for him and he attracted the best and brightest. New airplanes came to Albracht's wing for testing and evaluation. He often embarrassed some poor engineer with a scathing evaluation. Herr Rosenthal had trusted the lives of his children to the best of the best.

Albracht entered flight operations and carefully pored over the flight conditions, routes, and weather, while Corporal Wolf squirmed nervously. He was not required to sign out for the airplane or account for his travel intentions. He was Colonel Christian Albracht. His preparation completed, he returned to the car, gave Dietrich a wink, and headed to the flight line.

He took the military passenger plane, which was already warmed up and waiting. He drove the car up near the door and Rachel exited using the car to screen her as she boarded. Dietrich put the duffel bags and the other luggage on board. Albracht yanked the chocks himself as no ground crew was present, by design. Then, he entered the plane and went immediately to the cockpit. Dietrich closed the door and joined him in the copilot's seat. Rachel took a seat in the passenger section.

Albracht taxied to the head of the runway, made a right turn, revved the engine for sixty seconds, released the brakes, and roared down the runway.

"The trip will take us across Germany, parts of France, and over Spain to Barcelona. Ever been to Barcelona?"

"No, Colonel, I've never been out of Germany."

"Well, now you're going. You can stay up here with me for a few minutes, but then you should go back and keep your sister company. And you may as well take a nap. It's going to take about four hours."

13

"WELL, RACHEL, WE'RE on our way."

"I'm sad to leave mother and father. However, since father was so afraid for us, I am relieved that we are on our way. When do you think they will join us?"

"It's hard to say. Father has to liquidate all our properties, and we have a lot of them. The Colonel suggests we nap. It's up to you."

The hum of the engines helped Rachel drop off to sleep.

Dietrich reached inside his jacket, retrieved the letter from his father, and began to read.

Considering all that had to happen, I would guess that you will be reading this at about 9:00 p.m.

Dietrich checked his watch. It was 9:13.

If I am correct, Barcelona should be about four hours away.

Dietrich smiled and slowly shook his head.

That would put you and Rachel in Barcelona about one o'clock in the morning, more or less. The airfield in Barcelona is actually a small strip outside the city, out in the country. Lights will be lit for your landing where you will be met by a man named Jose Jimenez. You and Rachel will be under his protection until you board the ship. I trust him completely, so do not be concerned. The identification question will be the same. Pampas Packing will be the new family business, and someday you will run it. You must be well educated, so you will go to America and get a bachelors and masters degree in business from Harvard. Uncle Saul and Uncle Meir will make the arrangements.

Dietrich was drowsy, and he dropped off to sleep.

ALBRACHT YELLED FROM the cockpit, "Dietrich, you want to fly this thing?"

Dietrich stirred. He looked at his watch. It was midnight.

"Dietrich," screamed Albracht.

"Yes, Colonel, I'm coming."

Unbeknownst to the colonel, Dietrich loved airplanes and secretly wanted to learn to fly and get a license. He was thrilled at the thought of taking the controls.

"Just keep the wings level. The instrument panel has a silhouette of the plane. Keep the wings congruent with the silhouette; that is to say, parallel. Keep the nose two points beneath the horizon. Try to relax, try not to fight it, lay gently on the wheel. The heading is 220 degrees. Try to maintain it."

It was hard at first, but soon he got the feel of it. Dietrich was good at everything. At 12:50 a.m. Albracht said, "You did well, very well. I think you could be a good pilot. But I must take the controls now because we are getting close."

They descended about 2,000 feet, looking for the landing lights of the runway. The strip was crudely illuminated by flaming barrels placed 100 feet apart on each side of the field. The weather was clear. Albracht descended more. "There, I see the field." He maneuvered for the landing. *There's no wind sock and no radio contact. It's crude, but I can handle it. After all, I'm damn well the best there is.*

He landed the precious cargo on the grass field without any difficulty. Dietrich looked at his watch. It was 1:20 a.m. Albracht helped Rachel off first, then Dietrich and the luggage. A small car approached and a man got out.

"Colonel Albracht, I shall take your passengers. The gasoline for your return flight will arrive shortly. We thank you."

The man turned to the passengers and said, "I am Jose Jimenez. Are you Dietrich and Rachel Rader from Hamburg?"

"We are," said Dietrich.

"Please get into the car."

"We will, but spare us a moment please. Thank you for everything, Colonel. It has been a great pleasure to meet you, and thanks for the flying lesson."

"You are a natural, son. I hope you will continue what we started."

"I will, Colonel."

"You have my thanks as well," said Rachel, kissing the handsome flier on the cheek.

"Good luck to you both."

"Toss your things in the trunk. Rachel can sit in the back seat and you can join me up front," said Jose. "In this brown sack you will find sandwiches and a thermos of good hot coffee. You've had a hasty departure and a long flight. I hope both of you can relax now. It will take us about an hour to get to your lodging."

"Dietrich, pass me a sandwich."

After they ate, they both dropped off to sleep.

THE NEWS REACHED Emil that the two packages had arrived in Barcelona undamaged. There was rejoicing when he told Ruth the news.

14

AT THE AGE of 27 years, unmarried, Jose Jimenez was no doubt a rarity. Most of his friends had been married for years and had four or five children. He was sure that Rosenthal's intrusion into his life was a sign.

It was 2:30 a.m. when Jose pulled up in the back of the three-story apartment complex. They were obviously in Barcelona. It was a clear night and they had seen much of the shipping silhouetted in the harbor as they drove down Front Street.

"Your father owns this building. I manage it for him and have a small ownership interest. Now, you won't be here long. We'll just leave your things in the car. They will be fine. Follow me, please."

Jose opened a back door of the complex and then the apartment to the immediate right. It had two beds. Why don't you and Rachel try to get some sleep? I'll wake you when it's time to go."

HE THOUGHT HE was dreaming. He felt pressure on his shoulder. The room was dark; he was disoriented. "Dietrich, it's time to get up. Wake up Rachel."

Rachel was a light sleeper. The talk easily awakened her. She sat up and swung her legs around and sat on the edge of the bed. "What time is it?"

"It's 4:00 a.m. At 4:30 a.m. we must meet Captain Werner at the pier where the ship is docked."

"Dietrich, I need the bathroom," said Rachel. "Are you okay for the moment?"

"Yeah, go ahead."

After answering nature's call, she washed her hands and face with cold water. "I think I'm back in my body now. It's all yours, Dietrich."

After a satisfying relief, he washed his hands. Bloodshot eyes looked back at him from the bathroom cabinet mirror over the sink. Cold water revived him as well.

Jose handed each of them a container of hot coffee. "This should help for the moment. We had better go."

As Jose drove, he explained, "Everything has been arranged with the captain. Dietrich, you are to be his cabin boy for the journey. You'll deliver his food, wait on him, clean, and make up his cabin each day. You may also be assigned work on the ship during daylight hours. Rachel, it is going to be boring for you. You'll have to stay in the cabin."

She sighed.

"It's necessary, Rachel, and seven days is not a lifetime. Then you'll be in Buenos Aires. Dietrich, you'll both eat in your cabin. You'll bring in the food. We don't want the crew to know about Rachel, so we don't want any of them in your cabin. You and Rachel will need to work out a secret knock so Rachel will know it's you at the cabin door.

"Dietrich, you should have as little contact with the crew as possible. Keep your wits about you. The ship is Argentine; the crew is Argentine. I understand you speak Spanish. That should help you. The captain speaks German and Spanish. You're in good shape, Dietrich; you can communicate with everyone. Now, your Uncle Saul and Pedro de Vargas will meet you at the pier in Buenos Aires. Questions?"

"No, we understand?"

Dietrich looked at Rachel. She nodded; she understood everything.

"One more thing. There won't be many, if any, crewmen about at this hour. Captain Werner will want to get you to your cabin quickly so no one knows about you, Rachel. Keep your hair tucked up under that black wool stocking cap, just in case some crewman is about. It's dark, there shouldn't be a problem. I believe that's all."

It was still dark when Jose's car pulled up to the pier. There was a small freighter lapping water parallel to the dock. Dietrich slung the duffel bag over his shoulder. Dressed in a black pea jacket, the large lad looked like a seaman. Rachel was all in black as well, wearing a pea jacket with the black wool cap pulled down just above her eyes and her hair tucked under it. She slung her smaller duffel bag over her shoulder. Dietrich looked at his sister. He grinned; *She's the one who looks like a cabin boy.*

They quickly walked down the wharf in relative silence until they reached the ship's ladder. There they were met by a short stocky man with a grey mustache and beard, pea jacket, hat with visor, smoking a pipe.

"Captain Werner?" Jimenez inquired.

"Yes."

He looked at the two people with Jose and asked, in German, "Are you two Dietrich and Rachel Rader from Hamburg?"

"We are," said Dietrich.

"Captain Werner," said Jimenez, "I leave the Raders in your safekeeping. Get them to Buenos Aires without incident."

"Thank you for everything, Jose," said Dietrich, with a firm handshake.

Rachel smiled and kissed him on the cheek.

"Now if you will forgive us, Mr. Jimenez, I must get my charges on board."

Jose saluted the Rosenthal children and said, "Buena suerte."

PART THREE

PASSAGE TO BUENOS AIRES

15
June 1934

THE SHIP WAS almost new, about three years old. It was one hundred eighty feet long, in excellent condition. For most of 1934, it had carried cargo between Barcelona and Buenos Aires. The owners of the ship were the Bustillo brothers. Emil and Saul Rosenthal intended to buy the vessel and add it to the small fleet of four ships they already owned. Ever the resourceful businessmen, they envisioned shipping meat to destinations outside of Argentina. And they'd carry other cargo as well, if it was profitable. All the ships were under the Argentine flag.

Considering the sudden departure from Berlin, it was indeed fortunate to find the *Alcantara* in Barcelona Harbor at exactly the right time. Although Barcelona was its principal away port, the odds were still long that it would have been in position to receive such unexpected but priceless cargo. It was also fortunate that the ship was almost loaded for its voyage. They were at sea the next day.

■ ■ ■ ■ ■

SPEAKING IN GERMAN, Werner carefully guided the two passengers aboard and into their cabin. No one saw them. "Make yourselves as comfortable as possible."

Comfortable, she thought, *that's a laugh.*

The cabin had a double-bunked iron bed, a single wooden chair, two footlockers, a small sink, a toilet, and a single porthole. That was it.

"The ship's crewmen are able seamen, but they are not gentlemen of stature and social graces."

Dietrich and Rachel smiled.

"Some of them have criminal backgrounds. Rachel, you will need to stay in this cabin. These men do not need to see you or even know you are here. That information would increase our security challenges and put you in potential danger. That's why we rushed you on board under cover of darkness."

She looked around and said, "I'll go stir crazy."

"I understand your concern." He sighed, "Here's the way it has to be. Dietrich will bring your meals to this cabin. Yes, the days will be long but you can go out on the after deck after 10:00 p.m. with Dietrich. You will wear your pea jacket and wool cap pulled down right above your eyes, hair stuffed under it like it is now. There shouldn't be anyone on deck. Even if there is, it'll be dark, and you won't be all that noticeable. The only people on duty are the helmsman and the look-out who will be on the bridge, looking forward. They couldn't possibly see you. That's the best we can do."

"It'll be seven days, Rachel, not a lifetime," said Dietrich, trying to minimize the situation.

"I'm going to sleep," said Rachel, smiling.

"We had less than two hours' sleep last night," said Dietrich.

Werner smiled and nodded.

"I need to show Dietrich around, Rachel."

"I understand, Captain."

THE CAPTAIN REMOVED his cap and pea jacket as they entered his cabin. He didn't know that his passengers were the children of Emil Rosenthal, but he was keenly aware that they were precious cargo and it was his responsibility to see that they reached Buenos Aires safely. He knew that failure in his responsibility was not an option.

He invited Dietrich to be seated on the other side of the table.

"I was under the impression that I would eat with Rachel."

"No, that won't work. You'll eat your meals with me."

"All right."

"Dietrich, I eat at 0800, 1200 and 1800 hours."

Dietrich frowned.

He's not familiar with my meaning.

"Let me be clear. That's 8:00 a.m.,12 noon, and 6:00 p.m."

Dietrich smiled, "That's better."

"Now, the galley is aft. The cook will have the food ready fifteen minutes before the hour. You pick up food for both of us. Bring it back here and eat with me. Then you'll go back to the cook and tell him I want seconds. Then you take that food to Rachel. When she's finished, bring the plate and utensils back here. Then take two plates and utensils back to the galley with no one the wiser."

"Won't the cook find it strange that you want seconds every meal?"

"It won't matter if he does. Anyway, after that, you are free to roam the deck. But you should stay away from the crew. Don't talk to them and don't try to make friends with them. Now, if you have any problems or questions, you come to me."

· · · · ·

THE NEXT MORNING, he appeared early to get directions and such.

"Good morning, Captain Werner."

"Good morning, Dietrich."

"Miguel is the first mate. I'll call him."

He stepped outside his cabin and yelled. "Miguel!"

Miguel appeared.

"Miguel, this is Dietrich Rader."

He nodded.

"He will be taking care of my meals during the voyage. Show him where the galley is located. Then orient him to the rest of the ship."

Miguel nodded, and he and Dietrich left the captain's cabin.

DIETRICH RETURNED TO his cabin at 3:30 p.m. He was through until 5:45 p.m. when he had to get the captain's food, then eat himself, then get Rachel's food and return the plates, glasses and utensils to the galley. Then he would be finished until 7:45 the next morning.

"How are you doing, Rachel?"

"I'm fine, brother. I slept most of the day."

She paused a moment. "I want the bottom bunk, Dietrich. Do you mind awfully?"

"Not at all, sis." He glanced at his watch. "I've got two hours before I have to leave again. Let's see what Father packed for us. We'll do mine first."

He opened the duffel bag and found the list of items. "Here, Rachel, you can see if it agrees with what's inside."

"Toilet articles," she announced.

Dietrich started, "Two toothbrushes, two tubes of tooth paste, four bars of soap, a comb, a brush, two small aspirin bottles, and a first aid kit."

"That agrees with the list," said Rachel.

"Towels and linen."

"Four hand towels, four bath towels."

"Check," she confirmed.

"Two pairs of dungarees, eight T-shirts, eight pairs of shorts, three black turtleneck sweaters, eight pairs of socks, a belt, two pairs of sneakers, four pairs of shoe laces, and two jackets: cloth and leather."

"Check."

"One flashlight, nine batteries, three flashlight bulbs, alarm clock, hunting knife, a ten-foot length of rope, can opener, poncho, Spanish dictionary, English dictionary, a map of Spain, and a map of Argentina."

"Everything checks," said Rachel.

"Okay, Rachel, let's see what's in your bag." Everything on the list was there including *Kipps* and *The History of Mr. Polly* by H. G. Wells.

"Rachel, Father is like no one I know. For example, who else would think to include extra bulbs for the flashlight?"

"I know what you mean. And he had to have prepared all this well in advance."

"Exactly. He couldn't have done this on the spur of the moment."

They transferred their things to the footlockers. Then they folded the duffel bags and put them under the beds.

16
Three Days at Sea

THE ALARM CLOCK rang at 7:30 a.m. *I'd like to break that thing into a million pieces.* Rachel stirred but didn't wake up. He turned on the light and ran the tap. He washed himself, dried his body, and put on fresh clothes. Suddenly, he felt a bit strange. Then he realized it was the motion of the ship, making his stomach feel a bit uneasy. He closed the door quietly, locked it, and dropped the key in his pocket. He climbed up two ladders and was greeted by bright sunshine and a beautiful blue ocean. He worked his way aft and soon entered the galley. The cook turned to see who had come in. He was stacking mountains of pancakes. *Fat, dumpy, bald, with lily white skin. I don't think he ever goes on deck. Oh, well.*

"I've come for the captain's breakfast."

The cook grunted and pointed to a tray that had already been prepared for the captain and then turned back to the griddle. There was an enormous helping of pancakes. Dietrich took a plate from the stack, additional utensils, and helped himself to a stack of pancakes. Then he was off to the captain's cabin.

"Breakfast, Captain," said Dietrich.

Captain Werner had his back to the cabin door as Dietrich placed the tray on the table. He glanced at his watch. "Ah, Dietrich, right on time. Good man."

Dietrich nodded.

"Have a seat."

THE CAPTAIN PUSHED back his plate, belched, and lit up his pipe. "Damn tasty. I'm partial to pancakes. You?"

"I like them myself, Captain."

"Well, time to feed your sister."

"Yes, Captain."

"How is she doing?"

"Bored. Sleeps a lot. Reads."

"Are any of the crew bothering you? Any problems or concerns?"

"No, Captain."

DIETRICH DID NOT return to their cabin until about 1:30 p.m. with Rachel's lunch. To his surprise, the door was ajar and he could hear grunting coming from inside. Alarmed, he opened the door to see a squat, dirty man on top of Rachel. He slammed the door, dropped the tray, and dashed forward. He put a head lock on the man and pulled him off Rachel, but he did not relax his grip. He tightened his grip on the intruder's throat. The man could not scream, could not make a sound. His struggling, his efforts to free himself from Dietrich's vise grip were futile at best. Soon his body went limp, and Dietrich relaxed his grip and the man's body hit the floor.

It's Esteban, the bastard.

Dietrich's blood was still boiling and he kicked the man several times in the gut and then bent over his body and spit in his face.

He opened the foot locker and pulled out the rope. He bent down to tie Esteban's hands and feet.

Dietrich felt the man's carotid artery and there was no pulse. Esteban was dead.

He sat silently for a time, his head swimming, his blood pressure elevated. *It feels like my eyes are bulging out.* Then he remembered his father's words, *You can do whatever it takes. Dietrich, survival could mean you have to kill.*

17

HE BENT OVER Rachel. Esteban had knocked her unconscious. Her pants were on the floor and her panties had been ripped off. Dietrich had interrupted him before penetration could take place.

He wet a wash cloth and washed her face.

"Rachel, sis, wake up."

She stirred and when her eyes opened she began to pound him, not realizing in the moment that it was not the intruder, but Dietrich. Then she grabbed him around the neck and began to weep.

"It's okay, sis, I'm here and Esteban will never hurt you again."

"Oh, Dietrich, it was horrible."

"I know, little sister, but you're okay."

She noticed Esteban's body on the floor. "You knocked him unconscious?"

He hesitated, sighed, "Not exactly."

"What do you mean?"

He hesitated. "He's dead. I accidentally killed him. I didn't intend to but he's dead, Rachel."

"Dead! My God, Dietrich, what will we do now?"

"I don't know, but I'll figure it out."

"Of course you will, Dietrich," her voice breaking. "You're smart, you'll figure it out."

"Here, sis, put your dungarees back on."

In time she calmed herself. "How did Esteban get in?"

"He must have had a key. I mean, how else could he have gotten in? I was sound asleep. It was hot, so I took my dungarees off."

"I don't know why Esteban came in or what he was looking for, but he was single-minded when he saw you like that."

She sighed.

"Look, I've got to take your tray back, pick up the Captain's, and return everything to the galley. Sorry about your lunch."

"Well—I'm not exactly hungry."

"I understand, sis. I'll work supper and get you fed. Once I have completed my chores, I'll figure out what to do with Esteban. I'm sorry you have to be here with the body, but we have no choice."

She sighed. "No, no choice at all."

Dietrich reached in Esteban's pocket, but there was no key. When he tried the other pocket, it was there. "Look, Rachel," holding up the key. He moved the body over against the wall and covered it up. "I'll lock the cabin door and since we have Esteban's key, you can put it in the lock. Then no one can enter, not even me. I'll knock when I return. Remember, one knock, pause, three in a row, pause, and another single knock."

"I'll remember."

"Will you be all right?"

"Yes, go."

18

NOW, WHAT TO do with Esteban? Dietrich had seen the intruder before.

I don't believe losing a man overboard is all that unusual. I've certainly heard of it. It would all be over. No body, no questions, no fuss, no nothing.

At 2200 hours, he went on deck to see if anyone was about. There was no one. *The railing is no more than four feet high. Pushing Esteban over the side should not be difficult.* He could make out, as his eyes became accustomed to the darkness, the huge wake made by the churning propellers. *Esteban's body will disappear in a matter of seconds.* He went back to his cabin and got Rachel.

"It's time. Put on your pea jacket and cap."

"Ready?"

"Ready."

They dragged Esteban out of the cabin. There was no blood, so they didn't have to worry about a trail. He knew the ladder route in the dark. He had practically memorized it that afternoon. Dietrich was large and very strong, and Esteban was a small man. *It won't be all that hard to do, especially with her help.* In no time at all, they had reached the main deck. He walked outside, looked around, and saw nobody. "Okay, let's feed Esteban to the fishes."

She grimaced, but grabbed his feet.

"That's that," said Dietrich. "Now we can both get some air."

My brother is a man. Father knew it and now I know it.

The freighter *Alcantara* was short a crewman.

19

DIETRICH WAS IN the captain's cabin having breakfast when Miguel came knocking.

"Captain, Esteban is missing."

The captain pondered the news. "Turn the ship upside-down and then report back."

"Yes, Captain."

After he had gone Dietrich asked, "Shall I help them look?"

"No, finish your breakfast and your mess duties and don't come back until lunch."

"Yes, sir."

At noon, Dietrich brought a tray with two plates of food and sat them on the table. The captain was writing in his log book.

"What of Esteban, Captain?"

"They found no sign of him."

The captain made entries in his log each day at 1100 hours. He was late today while waiting for the results of the search for Esteban. After years at sea and endless reports, he had developed his own unique style. The first entry was the day of the week, then the date, the hour, the ship's position, the days at sea, the estimated time of arrival, and the cargo.

Years of experience had taught him to be as brief as possible. That would serve him well in the event there was an incident and an investigation. Sometimes what seemed clear at the time the entry, became clouded during an investigation. He had learned a valuable lesson as a first mate. He would never make the same mistake as his captain had once made, almost losing his license for some innocent editorializing. Away from his ship and the sea, a skipper on land can become vulnerable before a suspicious Board of Inquiry. Anything out of the ordinary was entered as an addendum to his formal entry for the day. A few succinct lines signaled Esteban Dejesus' departure from the planet.

> Lost at sea, Seaman Esteban Dejesus, 19, Argentine. Buenos Aires, no permanent address. Absence noted at the beginning of the work day. The captain was informed at 8:15 a.m. and immediately instituted a

shipboard search. Crewman Dejesus was not found. It can only be concluded that Mr. Dejesus went overboard sometime last night. The exact time is not known.

Captain Ernst Werner

ALTHOUGH IT WAS not noted in the log, Miguel had reported to Captain Werner that Esteban had consumed many bottles of cerveza with his friends.

"Esteban was a fairly heavy drinker. He was from the Buenos Aires waterfront slums and told us he was an orphan. He seemed to be a fairly typical seaman. He drank, screwed the waterfront whores, blew his money, and shipped out again." Miguel laughed. "He was pretty much like the rest of us."

Werner laughed. "Thank you, Miguel. That will be all."

Pondering the information Miguel had just given him; he packed his pipe and lit it. Then he carefully removed the addendum to the log.

20

SOLID PERMANENT FRIENDSHIPS rarely developed shipboard. There was little to no bonding whatsoever. Consequently, Esteban's disappearance was no great moment for this crew. What the hell, it wasn't one of them. And, although Esteban was a human being, some woman's son, perhaps a brother, his life meant nothing to Captain Werner.

■ ■ ■ ■ ■

AFTER MIGUEL AND Dietrich had gone, Werner unrolled his charts and went back to his work. The rest of the voyage was uneventful. Werner, if not impractical or providentially hindered, preferred to dock in Buenos Aires between 0600 and 0700 hours. The harbor was usually quiet at that time and there was good light for docking. The crew was fresh for unloading and usually by 1400 hours, everything would be completed. Then they had the rest of the day off, plus any other free days, while they were preparing for the next trip.

Dietrich was awake. He looked at his watch. It was 0600 hours. The lack of ship motion, after being at sea, was as strange now as the motion was in the beginning. He heard the clanking of the chains setting the gangway in place. He leaned over the side of his bunk. "Rachel, we've arrived! We're in Buenos Aires."

21

THEY WERE GETTING their things together, getting ready to leave the ship.

"You know what I'm looking forward to, brother?"

"No, sis, what are you looking forward to?"

"A bath. I can hardly stand myself."

Dietrich roared with laughter. "The escape from Berlin, Barcelona, the crossing, Esteban; and all you can think of is a bath?"

"That's true. Maybe it's a girl thing." She paused and seriously said, "Dietrich, you are quite a man. I love you, brother. You are my hero."

They embraced. "I love you too, sis. We're here, we're safe. Father and Mother will join us soon and our family will start a new life."

"Yes."

· · · · ·

CAPTAIN WERNER GREETED Saul Rosenthal and Pedro de Vargas as they came aboard.

"Any problems, Captain?" de Vargas asked.

"None at all, Pedro."

"My niece and nephew are safe and sound?" Saul asked, anxiously.

"Absolutely."

"Thank you, Captain. My brother and his wife will be overjoyed."

"Miguel, you know where Dietrich's cabin is."

"Yes, Captain."

"Then go get them and bring them here."

Go get them? Miguel thought. *Did he mean that?* He shrugged, "Yes, Captain."

"As Dietrich and Rachel came on deck, she removed her black wool cap, shook her head, and released her long black hair. Then she removed her pea jacket which revealed her substantial endowments. Crewmen in the area, who didn't even know she was on board, gasped at the sight of this stunning, raven-haired beauty. She laughed. She enjoyed the moment.

Captain Werner had only seen her once, when she boarded, with her cap on. *My God, she's ravishing.*

Uncle Saul extended his open arms and she ran to meet him. They hugged and he kissed her. "You're here, you're safe."

Dietrich smiled and shook his hand.

"Dietrich, my boy."

"Uncle Saul."

"Dietrich, Rachel, meet Pedro de Vargas. He is our plant manager and a trusted friend and confidant."

Greetings were exchanged. "Let's go," said Saul.

Soon they were in the black Mercedes, headed for Saul's hacienda.

22

SAUL STARTED HONKING his horn as the big black car neared the house. Soon all the servants and Aunt Pilar were gathered outside to greet Dietrich and Rachel.

"Look, Dietrich, I guess that's our welcoming committee," said Rachel.

"Yes, I see them," he said, laughing.

"We wanted to show you how pleased we are to have you here," said Saul.

As soon as the car stopped, Pilar opened the door. Rachel, smiling, stepped out. Pilar smiled, spread her arms and hugged Rachel. She pushed back and said warmly, "Welcome to our home, my dear."

"Thank you, Aunt Pilar, thank you very much."

Dietrich came around from the other side of the car. Pilar hugged him as well. "My dear Dietrich, what a man you have become. Welcome to Buenos Aires and our humble hacienda."

Humble hacienda, that's a laugh, thought Dietrich.

A sumptuous breakfast had been prepared for the family and Pedro. Servants took Rachel's and Dietrich's duffels to their respective quarters, which had a sitting room, study, bedroom, a separate bath with tub and shower, and a balcony with a beautiful view of the gardens, tennis courts, and pool.

"I couldn't eat another bite," said Rachel. "It was all wonderful, Aunt Pilar, but I haven't had a real bath since we left Germany."

"Oh, my dear," she exclaimed. "Take her to her room, Maria, and make her comfortable. We'll go shopping tomorrow, Rachel."

"Thank you, Aunt Pilar."

"I could use a bath too, Uncle Saul, and some sleep—like for a week."

Saul laughed. "Take him to his room, Mario, and get him whatever he needs."

"Right away, sir."

23

The Year 1934
Berlin, Germany

WALTER REICH HAD been Emil Rosenthal's attorney from the beginning. He had been recommended by Herr Spellmeyer, his bank's vice president. Actually, it was more of a behest. Emil was constantly expanding his holdings and needed continuous financing.

Reich had worked out well. He did his work thoroughly and in a timely manner. Emil did not need vision or creativity, he had that. He just needed an attorney for the legal basics. But Reich had something else. He came from a proper German family and their social acceptability was a major asset for Emil since Jews were not welcomed in certain transactions, business or otherwise. Adolph Hitler accelerated anti-Semitism, but it had always been there.

Reich and Rosenthal were strange bedfellows. They were polar opposites ethnically and personally. Rosenthal was a private person while Reich was outgoing and gregarious. While the authorities were increasingly more hostile to the Jews each succeeding day, Rosenthal had not been at all inconvenienced, and being Jewish had not been an issue. Even though he enjoyed a good reputation, he suspected that Reich was the only reason he had not been arrested. Things were changing rapidly in Germany.

The recent volume of property sales had brought Rosenthal a tidy sum of money, which he mailed to Saul in Buenos Aires in the form of cashier's checks. Emil paid his banker, Herr Spellmeyer, two percent of every transaction to buy his silence.

Taking assets out of Germany was against the law. Reich pocketed a tidy sum in legal fees.

On the morning of Monday, September 10, 1934, Reich was to come to Emil's house for a meeting. Emil was going to his office less and less. Reich had been able to dispose of about 75 percent of Emil's properties. There was less management required under the circumstances, and Emil simply felt safer at his residence these days. He desperately wanted to avoid any street incident. He and Ruth had become, by their own choosing, virtually housebound. The climate for Jews in Germany was getting ugly.

"Come in, Walter," said Ruth, "Emil is in the study. Coffee?"

"Yes."

"How are you, Walter?" Emil asked.

"I'm fine, just fine," he replied, ambivalence in his demeanor, even a tinge of disrespect. Or was it disinterest? Emil didn't press the issue.

Ruth entered the study, gave Walter the coffee, and left without a word.

"Walter, I think it's fair to say that you have benefited quite well from being my lawyer on these real estate deals."

He shrugged.

"Well, today is really your lucky day. I have decided to deed over the remainder of my properties to you. When all of the sales have been completed, you can keep 60 percent of the proceeds."

Reich's manner changed with the news. "I must say, Emil, I am overwhelmed with your generosity. It's not necessary, you know. I have profited handsomely, as you said, from our relationship."

"I have thought long and hard about it, and this is what I want. You are my friend and legal counsel. Just see that we are protected for just a little bit longer. I am also providing you $100,000 in cash in the event there is some difficulty that comes up about Ruth and me."

Small talk continued until Reich finished his coffee. Then they voiced their goodbyes and Reich left. He didn't even remember the drive back to the office, not a street nor a traffic light. The enormity of the gift Rosenthal had given him was staggering, even to a man who had already done quite well. He instructed his secretary to reschedule all his remaining appointments for the day. He needed to think.

Walter Reich lit a cigarette, took a satisfying drag, and stared alternately at the deeds and the cash box. He put the deeds and the money in the safe. He put on his hat and coat and considered the afternoon. "Helga, I'm leaving for the day. Tell callers I'm in meetings outside the office. I'll see you in the morning."

"Very well. Herr Reich."

I think I'll call Else. We'll have drinks and make love for the rest of the afternoon. A nice way to celebrate my very good fortune. With the extra money, I can move her to a better apartment and buy her more pretty things. She will be very grateful to me.

Reich did not return home until 10:00 p.m. He had called his wife, before his matinee orgy, to tell her he had to meet with a new client who lived outside the city and that he would not be home for dinner. Actually, his wife had not been feeling well and told him she planned to retire early. Walter had a nightcap before going upstairs. He wanted to savor the remains of the day. As he sipped the amber liquid it came to him. *Why shouldn't I become a millionaire? I can keep the property, keep the tenants, and the rents will just keep rolling in. I'll raise the rents. That's exactly what I'll do. And I get a cash bonus for being clever. I don't even have to practice law anymore. I'll be Herr Reich, the rich property owner.*

■ ■ ■ ■ ■

NIGHTS AT THE Rosenthal home were lonely and boring. There was no Dietrich or Rachel to brighten the place and no real work for Emil to do anymore. They were no longer having friends over for dinner, coffee, or dessert. They were living on the edge. Truth be known, they were frightened. The bright part of their existence was the thought of being united with Dietrich and Rachel and Saul and Pilar. They would be a family again, reunited in Buenos Aires, beginning a new life in a neutral country.

They were packed and ready to go at a moment's notice. Emil had contacted Colonel Albracht. They were waiting for him to tell them the day and time.

"My beautiful home, all my beautiful things," Ruth lamented.

"I know how you feel, my dear. But we can replace things once we get to Buenos Aires."

She frowned as she looked around the drawing room, touching this piece of furniture and that. He frowned as well. He knew the sadness she was feeling.

They were having a late cup of tea when the doorbell rang. It startled them. They were expecting no one and no one visited anymore. Most of their friends had left the city voluntarily—some involuntarily. Emil pushed back his chair and went to the door. He opened it to two German soldiers in grey topcoats and caps with silver skulls on them.

"Yes?"

They flashed their identification and the tallest man asked, "Are you Emil Rosenthal?"

"Yes, I'm Rosenthal."

"I am Lieutenant Schneider. This man is Sergeant Weber."

"What do you want?"

"I will be direct, Herr Rosenthal. You and your wife will have to come down to headquarters for questioning. Certain charges have been made against you."

Emil was scared but also angry. "We have done nothing wrong. I do not understand. What charges?"

"You have committed crimes against the State."

"Who makes such charges?"

"Your attorney, Walter Reich."

24

GENERAL MARTIN HUBERMANN received an internment list each Friday. Most were Jews; some suspected communists and people classified as enemies of the State. Enemies were usually people who, in civilian life, had inconvenienced or had a dispute with one of the thugs who was now in charge. They constituted mostly petty vendettas, but not much was considered petty to the Nazis.

Hubermann rarely read the list. As chief of the Berlin Garrison, he had carried out his duties superbly. In fact, the only time he had been reprimanded was when he overruled one of his subordinates and released a Jew who had been arrested on a trumped-up charge. He knew the family. He knew the charge was bogus.

It was rare that anyone reprimanded General Hubermann, whose excellence was highly recognized. He had no issues with the Jews but decided to become blind to the Jewish question in deference to his career.

But for some reason, he glanced at Friday's report. *Emil Rosenthal. Ruth Rosenthal.* The names jumped out at him. He rang his adjutant.

"What can I do for you, General?" Major Richter asked.

"Bring me the files on the Rosenthals, Emil and Ruth."

"Right away, General."

What's the big issue here? It's just another Jew arrest, Richter wondered.

The file was delivered within the hour by Lieutenant Schneider, who waited in Richter's office while Hubermann read the file.

> *Rosenthal, Emil and Ruth – Jews*
> *Subjects were picked up at their home, 15 Gross Street, Berlin at 1930 hours, 10 September 1934. A complaint was filed by Walter Reich, attorney. Subjects are his clients.*

Hubermann read the charge.

> *Subjects disposed of real property in Germany for cash and jewels and have transferred the same illegally to foreign countries. These acts constitute crimes against the State.*

"That sonofabitch Reich," he screamed out loud.

He rats on his clients, but we don't know why. I know the man. He comes from a proper family and has plenty of clout. I shall warn some of my unsuspecting friends to look out for this fellow. It's ridiculous. The Jews are persecuted here in Germany. The Nazis don't want them here but won't let them leave. It's nonsense. We call their acts illegal, yet we are the ones who initiate the illegality. What a charade!

The General returned to the report. The next part genuinely saddened him.

> *At headquarters, while being questioned by Lieutenant Schneider and Sgt. Weber, subject, apparently under severe stress, suffered a massive cerebral hemorrhage and died. This was confirmed by the medical report signed by Dr. Beck. Ruth Rosenthal, the subject's wife, was assigned for internment to Dachau.*
>
> *Lieutenant Helmut Schneider*
> *Attest: Sergeant Albert Weber*

GENERAL HUBERMANN RANG Richter and asked that Lieutenant Schneider come in. Schneider entered the office, stood at attention in front of his desk, and saluted smartly.

"At ease, Lieutenant. I've read your report. Now tell me what really happened. How did Rosenthal die?"

Schneider was sweating. *What the hell is going on here? We killed a Jew, so what? Is the general a Jew lover? Was Rosenthal a friend of the family? My father always told me that when all else failed, just tell the truth. So I'll do that and take my chances.*

"We brought him in for questioning. I mean, it's standard procedure when a complaint has been filed. It came across my desk, and I carried out my duty as my job dictates. I did my duty."

"Listen Schneider, I don't give a shit about your duty. Tell me how you killed Rosenthal."

He sighed, looked down, and didn't answer right away. He sighed again, looked up, and began his explanation. "We took him in the interrogation room and left his wife in the cell. He was really angry about being here, about being turned in by his attorney. He was difficult, General Hubermann, and wouldn't answer any of our questions. He called us scum and riffraff. But when he called us rat shit, Weber lost control and hit him in the temple with a truncheon."

Schneider gulped. He dreaded the last words. "The blow killed him instantly."

"I am appalled, Lieutenant."

"I do regret it, General Hubermann. Weber really hates Jews, sir. He lost control."

Neither one of the men spoke for what seemed to be an eternity. That unnerved Schneider even more. Urine puddled on the floor by his shoes.

"And Mrs. Rosenthal?"

"She left the next day for Dachau."

"I knew the Rosenthal family. They were nice and respectable people. This came as a huge shock to me. The sight of you, Schneider, disgusts me. Now take the file and get out of my office."

"Yes, General."

Damn, Hubermann thought. *Now that she's been sent to Dachau, there is nothing I can do.*

As Schneider walked to his car, he became nauseous. He stopped by his car and leaned against it, trying to calm down and collect himself. He went over the meeting with Hubermann. *I told the truth. I did not lie. I can only hope I will be spared any punishment. I don't know about Weber. What I couldn't admit was that we raped Mrs. Rosenthal.* They took turns violating her inside the cell while the other watched. *She was a beautiful Jewess. She was regal, elegant, the kind of woman who always held me in contempt when I worked in hotels, restaurants, and dress shops. Forcible entry wasn't all that difficult. After Weber busted her lip, she didn't resist anymore. She was a really pretty woman and she had a great body. I will never forget how she excited me, how stimulating it was. Weber enjoyed himself as well.*

He opened the car door, threw his briefcase in the back seat, and drove away.

GENERAL HUBERMANN WAS fed up with the SS and its policies. *They are barbaric bastards without honor. I've got to get out of this job.* Even so, he had the garrison well organized and functioning well.

I need to command one of Erwin Rommel's infantry divisions. I'll speak with my old friend while he is here in Berlin.

25

ARGENTINA HAD ENORMOUS possibilities. Money could eliminate most any obstacle and, unlike a developed country such as America, there were enormous financial opportunities and Saul had tapped into them. The first issue for Dietrich and Rachel was citizenship. With the Rosenthal money and his well earned connections, Saul was able to obtain Argentine citizenship for his niece and nephew in short order. He also knew that money could transcend prejudicial lines and, if carefully manipulated, could insure a person's safety. That was extremely important.

They had seen the value of investing in railroads for moving cattle and beef around the country. But shipping was an area that Emil and Saul had not thought about initially. But as the winds of war grew stiffer, they realized there might be an opportunity to export beef, and they purchased two refrigerated ships. With their ships flying an Argentine flag, a flag of a neutral country, their ships would be safe from German U-boat attacks.

The deal to purchase ships was put together by Ruben Cohen, a little balding Jewish man, but a giant in the legal profession. He was recognized as the leading corporate attorney in Buenos Aires. In fact, Cohen had helped them get the meat packing plant and Saul's railroad investments and the ranch on the Pampas. Like most of the Rosenthal's closest associates, he was given a share in the enterprises he helped put together. He had also become a friend as well as an investor and legal adviser.

Pedro de Vargas negotiated shipping markets in Spain, Portugal, England, and France. He also arranged for runs up and down the coast of South America. He worked out two runs a month for each ship.

"Saul, the ships are busy and profits are rolling in," said Pedro. "We need to begin to make plans for plant enlargement."

"I agree, but let's get young Dietrich involved in the discussions so he can begin to understand what we have here. Someday, he'll run the show."

· · · · ·

AS THEY DROVE to Pampas Packing, Saul said, "Dietrich, you have been accepted at Harvard and you'll start in September."

"I understand that my primary goal is education, but I am a very good soccer player."

"You'll just have to contact the coaches when you get there. They won't be able to get any recommendations from Berlin."

Dietrich laughed, "You're right about that."

"When the time comes for you to leave, you'll fly to New York and your Uncle Meir will meet you and take you to Boston and get you settled in. But Pedro and I want you to tour the plant. Then we want you to participate in the conversation about plant expansion. Someday, you'll be the boss; you'll run the company."

"Thank you, Uncle Saul, I appreciate being included."

THERE WERE EIGHTY butchers, standing amidst sawdust, blood, and animal parts, busily engaged in boning out the various cuts of meat. Dietrich was fascinated by the swift skillful work of the men dressed all in white. Pedro answered his many questions.

"The tour of the plant was very impressive, Uncle Saul," said Dietrich. "You and Pedro have done a great job."

"As you know, your father has the controlling interest, but Pedro and I have a financial interest. We have been granted permission to make business decisions until your father arrives."

Dietrich smiled and nodded.

"Here is a folder for each of you," said Pedro. "Inside you will see the plans for plant expansion. I think in five years we could be one of the five largest meat packing companies in the world."

"In the world?" questioned Dietrich.

"In the world."

"Your father Emil and your Uncle Saul are real visionaries. I'm just glad they gave me a chance to be a part of this grand venture."

"We're glad too, Pedro," said Saul.

"Most definitely," echoed Dietrich.

"All you need now is a woman," said Saul, with a laugh.

Pedro laughed as well, but said nothing.

■ ■ ■ ■ ■

PEDRO de VARGAS did not have need of a woman. He didn't need a constant companion or a wife. He could have women when he wanted them, but always on his own terms. When they got serious, and particularly demanding, he dropped them and got someone else. Besides, at least in his own mind, he could take care of himself better than anyone else. Anyway, Pampas Packing, the ranch, and the ships kept him very busy. He preferred not to have the distraction of a woman. His only concession to his success was a comfortable home on a hill not far from the waterfront, a house girl, and a cook. Oh, and Jaime Zapata, who was his chauffeur, valet, and anything else Pedro needed.

■ ■ ■ ■ ■

"RACHEL, WE'VE GOT to get you registered for next term in The Hebrew School," said Pilar.

Rachel thought for a moment. "Aunt Pilar, I've been going to Jewish school all my life. I'm in a new country, I'll be a senior, and I think I'd like my final year to be in a secular school."

"Let me talk to your Uncle Saul, but I don't see why not. I think you should be able to do that. In fact, I think it would be good for you."

■ ■ ■ ■ ■

THE JEWS WHO arrived in Argentina in the first waves of immigration at the end of the nineteenth century were as concerned about their children's education as about earning a livelihood and organizing their community. Those who moved to the cities usually found the state education system open to all residents. Argentine law stipulated that state education was compulsory, secular, free, and co-educational.

In 1917, with JCA (Jewish Colonization Association) assistance, the Congregación Israelita de la República Argentina, the oldest Jewish organization in the country, established a national network for the support and organization of Jewish education.

However, according to established custom, perhaps due to the influence of the Catholic Church, separate schools were established for girls and boys in places where this was permitted. Despite the law, in certain districts where Jewish agricultural settlements were established under the auspices and management of the JCA, the central federal government, or the provincial authorities, were unable to set up schools that would provide the education obligated by law.

With children of Jewish residents in danger of growing up without formal education, the JCA, after some hesitation, decided to establish schools for the settlements that would provide general and Jewish education in accordance with the ideology of the Alliance Israélite Universelle, where boys and girls studied together.

■ ■ ■ ■ ■

"IT'S OCTOBER, PEDRO, and we've lost contact with Emil and Ruth. Frankly, I'm frightened," said Saul.

Pedro frowned. "I share your fear. Let me contact Jose Jimenez. He knows how to contact Colonel Albracht. The colonel can look into it."

"Good, let's do that right away."

26

The Year 1935
The Company Airplane

DIETRICH ROSENTHAL HAD always wanted to fly, although it was second to his love of soccer. Pampas Packing had been able to purchase a Antonov An-2 for Dietrich. The An-2 was a Russian designed and manufactured craft and was one of the best biplanes in the world. Saul found a German pilot living in Buenos Aires to give Dietrich lessons. They kept the airplane at Saul's ranch on the Pampas. They could have purchased Dietrich any number of airplanes, but the An-2 made business sense as well. It was used as a light utility transport as well as for agricultural work and many other tasks. Its slow flight and good field performance made it suitable for short unimproved fields, and it performed well in cold weather and other extreme environments. It seemed like the perfect airplane.

"So, Dietrich, what do you think?"

"It's a fine machine. I am excited to learn to fly it."

"Well, Herr Heinz will teach you."

· · · · ·

MANFRED HEINZ was the last pilot interviewed by Saul Rosenthal. He carefully studied his resume, *A degree in aeronautical engineering, Luftwaffe pilot, veteran of the Spanish revolution. He should have had a great career in the German air force. Why is he here?*

"You have an impressive resume, Herr Heinz."

"Thank you, sir, but please call me Manfred."

Saul laid down the folder and lit up a cigarette. "Very well, Manfred, why are you in Buenos Aires?"

Manfred Heinz knew exactly why Saul was asking the question. He hesitated and then explained. "My mother, whom I never knew, was a maid in an aristocratic household in Berlin. The head of the house impregnated her but, of course, took no responsibility for it. She was subsequently dismissed from the household and delivered me in a facility run by Catholic nuns. My mother was beautiful, sir."

He hurriedly dug into his wallet and pulled out a picture of her.

"You're right, Manfred, she is beautiful. How old do you think she was?"

"About 22, I am told. This picture is all I have of her."

Saul immediately took note of the change in Manfred's expression. "That problem is, sir, she was Jewish."

Saul gulped and shook his head in disbelief.

"I was put up for adoption. A prominent Jewish family took me. She was barren and they wanted a child, a boy. They loved me and educated me. But they didn't give me their name. Heinz is the name of my father. It may be that they thought I would have a better chance in life with a German name. I don't know how the authorities found out, sir, but they did. That's the new Germany, sir. Being pure Aryan is important in Germany these days. Of course, not only did this put a damper on my career, but I felt that it put my life in jeopardy. So, I got out of Germany while I could. I knew a lot of Jews had immigrated here."

"What happened to your mother?"

"Sadly, I do not know."

"My brother Emil and his wife Ruth were not so lucky. We do not know what happened to them either but we do know that they never made it out of Germany. We told Dietrich and Rachel that their parents died but didn't speculate."

"You mentioned Rachel. Who is Rachel?"

"Oh, that's Dietrich's sister."

Heinz nodded.

"Well, back to business. I have a meat packing company to run, plus a chain of restaurants, an interest in a railroad, and a ranch on the Pampas. An airplane will help me manage all the enterprises and, naturally, I need a reliable pilot who will have to be on call seven days a week. But there will probably be periods when you won't fly for days. If your work is satisfactory, you'll be well taken care of. And I'll want you to teach my nephew Dietrich to fly. His father and I started Pampas Packing, but my brother has the majority interest and Dietrich will take over management of the business when he is old enough and wise enough to handle the responsibility."

There was a moment of silence.

"How does all this sound to you, Manfred?"

"Just fine, sir, but we haven't discussed a salary."

Saul laid his cigarette in the ash tray and wrote a number on a blank piece of paper. He smiled and shoved the paper toward Manfred Heinz. He picked up the paper, looked at it, smiled, and asked, "When do I start?"

27
The Year 1935

DIETRICH ROSENTHAL HAD taken to flying like he did to soccer. He was a quick learner and was soon licensed to fly.

"He's a natural, an excellent pilot," said Manfred Heinz.

"I can't say that I'm surprised," said Saul. "He seems to be good at everything."

Dietrich tried to fly at least several times a week. He took Rachel with him from time to time. "I like flying, but I am not interested in piloting a plane myself," she told Dietrich.

"That's okay, Rachel. It's not for everyone."

■ ■ ■ ■ ■

ON FEBRUARY 26, 1935, Nazi leader Adolf Hitler signed a secret decree authorizing the founding of the Reich Luftwaffe as a third German military service. In the same decree, Hitler appointed Hermann Goering, a German air hero from World War I and the second-ranking Nazi, as commander in chief of the new German air force.

The Versailles Treaty that ended World War I prohibited military aviation in Germany, but a German civilian airline, Lufthansa, was founded in 1926 and provided flight training for the men who would later become Luftwaffe pilots.

The Luftwaffe was to be unveiled step-by-step so as not to alarm foreign governments, and the size and composition of Luftwaffe units were to remain secret. However, when Britain announced it was strengthening the RAF, Hitler revealed his Luftwaffe, which was rapidly growing into a formidable air force.

28
August 1935

"HE MUST HAVE headed out to sea. There is no evidence of an airplane crash anywhere on land," said Heinz.

"Why would he do it?" Saul asked.

"He's good and he knows it. His confidence level was enormous. If he did go out over the ocean, he did it because he hadn't done it before. He wanted to experience everything. That's the way he was," said Heinz.

"Would flying out to sea be dangerous?"

"Oh, not particularly. But a pilot could get disoriented because of a lack of landmarks. But I don't think it was pilot error. He was young, but he was good. I think the machine failed in some way and he couldn't make land."

"We'll probably never know. That's the hard part, never knowing exactly what happened," said Saul.

He was silent for a time, staring into space. "I'm glad his father didn't have to deal with this. He worshiped that boy. This would have killed him."

"What now?" Heinz asked.

"It's time to call Rabbi Lepavsky and tell the family. I may have the Rabbi tell Rachel."

· · · · ·

"I HAVE NO one left," Rachel lamented. "My parents never left Germany and now Dietrich is gone."

"You have your Uncle Saul and his family here in Buenos Aires. They love you very much. And you have family in New York and Poland," said Rabbi Lepavsky.

"I know, I know, but surely, Rabbi, you can see my point about my immediate family."

"Yes—I can."

"This is the first time I have had to deal with the loss of someone close. I mean, there were my grandparents, but I was young. They explained very little to me and Dietrich, and we asked even less.

My mother and father died, but they were in Germany. With them, you know, there was no funeral for me to deal with. I'm a Jew but I don't really know the details about Jewish funerals and what we do."

"Well, shall I tell you about Jewish funeral traditions?"

"Yes, Rabbi, I would very much like to know."

"While there are many denominations within Judaism that hold differing views, Jews commonly believe that holiness can be attained through following the laws and commandments laid out in the Torah. Though there is no explicit afterlife in Judaism, many of us Jews believe that after death, the soul of the deceased is judged and those who led perfect lives are let into the World to Come, while those who did not must wait for a year."

He paused for a moment. "That is what I believe."

"Come on, Rabbi, who can lead a perfect life?"

"I can understand why you would ask that question. Some Jews also believe that when the Messiah comes, every person will be resurrected."

"Do we know when to expect the Messiah? Does the Torah tell us?"

"I'm afraid not, my dear."

There was a moment of silence.

"When a Jew dies, those who mourn the death should recite the prayer *Dayan HaEmet*, recognizing God's power as the true judge. A rabbi or funeral home should be contacted immediately. According to Jewish law, the body must be interred as soon as practical from the time of death, which means that funeral planning begins immediately. From the moment of death until the moment of burial, a Jewish body should not be left unattended, and the rabbi or funeral home can help designate a *shomer.*"

"I like that tradition, but what does *shomer* mean?"

"A *shomer* is a guardian for the purposes of staying with the body. In addition, the funeral home will begin to make arrangements for the funeral service and burial, coordinate with the family's rabbi or assist the family in identifying an appropriate rabbi, and put the family in touch with the local *chevra kadisha* or burial society if one exists. Questions so far?"

She hesitated for a moment and then said, "No."

"The *shomer* may be a family member, a friend, or a member of the congregation or *chevra kadisha.* As the *shomer* may be required to stay with the body for an extended period of time, it is not uncommon to have more than one *shomer* or people taking turns acting as the *shomer.* While the *shomer* may simply sit with the body, it is traditional for the *shomer* to recite *tehillim*, which means psalms.

"I already told you that Jewish law requires that the body be buried within a day or as soon as practical from the time of death. However, exceptions may be made in some cases, including if there are any legal issues surrounding the death that must be investigated, if the body must be transported from one city or country to another, if close family members must travel far distances to be present for the funeral, or to avoid burial on Saturday or another holy day."

"Do we believe in organ donation?"

"Good question. Organ donation is generally acceptable in Judaism and is often viewed as a *mitzvah,* a good deed. Likewise, it is generally acceptable to donate a body to medical research."

"Do you think that will be common practice some day?"

"Could be. Routine autopsies are not acceptable in Judaism as they are seen as a desecration of the body. In most cases, the family of the deceased may refuse to have a routine autopsy performed. Should an autopsy be necessary for legal reasons, a rabbi familiar with the procedures may be present while the autopsy is performed if possible.

"Embalming and cosmetology are not generally used by Jews unless required by law."

"I like that custom. To me, embalming and all that is disgusting."

"I agree with you."

"Oh, do we believe in cremation?"

"Cremation remains taboo among most Jews. Both Orthodox and non-Orthodox rabbinical authorities frown on cremation. Jewish law bans the practice. For Orthodox Jews, cremation is not acceptable and the body should be buried, intact, in the ground. Still, both the Conservative and Reform movements within Judaism let their rabbis officiate at the funerals of people who will be cremated. Orthodox groups don't allow any such leeway. For Reform Jews, however, cremation is becoming an increasingly common practice, and most Reform rabbis will willingly perform a funeral and interment for someone who has been cremated."

"Where do you stand?"

"I am Orthodox."

"So you find cremation unacceptable."

"Yes."

They did not speak for a moment. Then he asked Rachel, "Do you wish me to continue?"

"There's more?"

"Yes."

"Then I want to know. I want to know all of it."

"To prepare the body for burial, it must be washed, purified, and dressed. This process is called *taharah*, which refers to both the specific act of ritual purification and the general process of preparing the body. The body should be washed, a process called *rechitzah*, by members of the *chevra kadisha*. Men should wash the body of a man and women should wash the body of a woman. Once the body is washed, the body must be purified with water. This act is executed either by fully submerging the body in a *mikvah*, ritual bath, or by pouring a continuous stream of water over the body. The body is then fully dried and dressed in a simple white *tachrichim*, a shroud, which should be made out of a simple fabric such as linen or muslin. Men may also be buried in a *yarmulke* and a prayer shawl, also known as a *tallis*.

"Once the body is fully prepared, it is placed in the casket. Jewish law prescribes that the casket, known as an *aron*, must be a simple wooden box, commonly made out of pine, without any metal. In this way, the casket and the body can decompose. Some Jewish caskets may have holes drilled into the bottom to accelerate the rate at which the body will decompose, thus fulfilling the principle stated in the Book of Genesis, "for dust you are and to dust you shall return." The casket should remain closed at all times with the exception of viewing for identification purposes."

"I very much like that rule. I do not like the idea of people standing around staring at the deceased."

"Me neither. There is generally no viewing, visitation, or wake in Jewish tradition. Before the funeral service, the family will gather and participate in a rite known as *keriah*, in which a visible part of clothing—such as a lapel, shirt collar, or pocket, for example—is torn as a symbol of mourning. In many communities, the practice has shifted from tearing a piece of clothing to tearing a black ribbon attached to a lapel, shirt collar, or pocket. When mourning the death of a parent, clothes should be torn or a torn ribbon should be affixed on the left side of the chest over the heart; when mourning all other family members, clothes should be torn or a torn ribbon should be affixed on the right side of the chest. This torn item of clothing or the torn ribbon will be worn throughout the week-long mourning period."

"We'll wear a torn ribbon on the right side of our chest."

"That's right."

"The Jewish funeral may be held in a synagogue, at the gravesite, or at a funeral home. If the funeral will be held in a synagogue, pallbearers may carry the casket into the sanctuary for the service and out of the sanctuary after the service. The funeral consists of prayers and the reading of psalms. The prayers that are traditionally recited at a Jewish funeral include the Memorial Prayer, called *El Maleh Rachamim*, and the Mourner's Blessing, called *Mourner's Kaddish*, among others. There may be one or more eulogies delivered at the funeral service, and they may be delivered by family members or by the rabbi. All eulogies should seek to both praise the life of the deceased and express grief over the death.

"Flowers are traditionally not present at the funeral service. Instead, donations are often made to an appropriate charity in the name of the deceased.

"After the funeral service, all mourners should follow the hearse to the cemetery or place of interment. At the burial or interment site, the rabbi will say a few prayers, all will again recite the *Mourner's Kaddish*, and the casket or urn will be interred. If the body is being buried in the ground, it is traditional for all mourners to place dirt into the grave, either with hands or with the back of a shovel.

"After the interment, there may be a reception at a family home or at the synagogue. Friends or the synagogue community should prepare the consolation meal. Eggs are traditionally served as a reminder of the cycle of life.

"There are two periods of mourning in Judaism. The first, called *shiva,* meaning seven, takes place over the seven days immediately following the funeral. During *shiva,* the family gathers every day in a family home to mourn and pray. For seven days, family members do not go to work or participate in the routine of their normal lives.

Guests are received during this time. On the first day of *shiva*, a *shiva* candle is lit, which will burn for the duration of the week.

"The second period of mourning is called *shloshim*, meaning thirty, and lasts until the thirtieth day after the funeral. During *shloshim*, mourners will resume many of their daily routines, but will continue to recite the *Mourner's Kaddish* daily. *Shloshim* marks the end of the formal mourning period and a full return to daily life, except in the event those mourners are mourning the death of a parent. If a parent has died, the formal mourning period lasts an entire year.

"There are two specified memorial events in Judiasm. The first, called *yahrzeit,* is observed on the anniversary of the death, according to the Hebrew calendar. Every year, the night before the anniversary of the death, a *yahrzeit* candle is lit, which will burn for 24 hours, and the mourner recites the *Mourner's Kaddish.*

"The second memorial event, called *yizkor,* takes place on Yom Kippur, the Day of Atonement, as well as on the holiday of Shemini Atzeret, and on the last days of the holidays Passover and Shavuot. *Yizkor* is a memorial prayer service, and mourners will go to the synagogue to mourn with the community."

"Thank you, Rabbi."

"We plan to have a memorial service for Dietrich at the synagogue," said Rabbi Lepavsky.

29
Senior Year in Buenos Aires

"MRS. ROSENTHAL, RACHEL is doing splendidly in school," Mrs. Vega reported.

"I'm not surprised," said Pilar, "but it's good to hear. She's been through a lot in her personal life, which could have been a huge distraction."

"She is far from distracted. She's quite focused. Her acclimatization to our school has been remarkable. She speaks and writes Spanish as well as anyone in the school. Her vocabulary is not as large as some of our students, but I believe we can attribute this to the fact that she has spoken German for most of her life and her hesitancy in using a Spanish word she is unsure is correct. But this will come. Her Latin and math teachers tell me that she has not made a single error on a quiz to date. This is quite remarkable. She does not volunteer in class, but when she is called on, she answers quickly and correctly. Her history and science teachers regard her as superior."

"Once again, I am so pleased. I can't wait to tell my husband."

"She is going to college in the United States?"

"Yes. Radcliffe College. She doesn't even know yet."

Vega smiled, "She should have no trouble, Mrs. Rosenthal."

30
The Year 1936

"RACHEL, THE CONTROLLING interest in Pampas Packing is with your family. Your father and I set it up that way. He envisioned that after he retired, Dietrich would take over and run the company."

"I thought you ran the company."

"Pedro and I were to manage the business until your father got here. Someday, Dietrich was to take over. I have money in the company, so I have a dual interest in making sure that the company is a success. Since Dietrich is gone, you are next in line to be president of Pampas Packing."

Rachel was taken aback. She never knew how the company was put together.

"The Rosenthals are strong. You are a young girl, this is true, but some day you will be a woman—and a strong woman. What we need to do now is make sure you are an educated woman."

"The University of Buenos Aires?"

"No, Radcliffe College, in Cambridge, Massachusetts."

"The United States."

"That's right. I wish you could go to Harvard, but right now, females are not able to attend. Radcliffe is the next best thing. I have talked to your Uncle Meir in New York City and he and Lea will help. We'll send you there, and they will take care of you and get you admitted to Radcliffe."

She was silent for a time. Then she smiled. "I've always wanted to visit the United States. Now I'm going to live there and get my education. This will be an adventure for me."

"An adventure? Yes, I suppose it will."

* * * * *

SAAR VOTED TO return their coal-rich territory to Germany and voted for annexation to the Reich. This was Hitler's first geographic expansion. He defied the Treaty of Versailles and no country called him on it. Hitler delivered a speech to the Reichstag claiming he had not the slightest thought of conquering other nations.

Max Kohn, a Jewish student, died in Dachau, the first Jew to die there in 10 months. Anti-Jewish riots continued in Berlin, and Jews were severely beaten. Nuremberg Laws redefined citizenship, and Jews were declared to not be of German blood. The Minister of the Interior called for codifying laws that would impose legal restrictions on Jews taking part in trade and industry.

PART FOUR

RACHEL AT RADCLIFFE

31
The Year 1936
Radcliffe College

MRS. CROMWELL, DEAN of Women at Radcliffe, called Rachel into her office. Meir and Lea were asked to wait outside.

"Sit down, my dear." *She's beautiful. I would never have suspected that she was one of them.* Cromwell opened Rachel's file where her admission application and other required information was located.

"Why do you wish to attend Radcliffe College, my dear?"

This bitch is such a phony. "I am expected to run the family business some day. I need an education from an elite school, and Radcliffe is my first choice."

"Well, my dear, I must say you are straightforward."

Rachel shrugged.

"Your grades in high school are top notch."

"Yes."

"How did you come to be in Buenos Aires?"

Rachel paused for a moment before she answered. "When Adolph Hitler became chancellor of Germany, it became obvious to my wonderful father that life as a Jew was going to change dramatically. He feared for the very worst. So he arranged to send my brother and me out of the country. That was a priority. Then he planned to liquidate his assets so he and my mother could join us."

"Why Argentina?"

"My uncle was there, and he and my father had a business in Buenos Aires."

"What kind of business?"

"Meat packing."

"Are your parents in Buenos Aires or have they moved to the states?"

Rachel sighed, "They are both dead."

Cromwell frowned. *I'm not going to ask her how it happened. I'm afraid to find out.* But she was genuinely touched. "I am so sorry to hear that, my dear."

Rachel took a sip of water. Cromwell took a moment to collect herself.

"You speak German and Spanish."

"That's correct, but I also speak Polish and Hebrew."

"That's impressive." *I wonder why that wasn't on her application? This young woman has been through a lot. I'm not going to add to her woes by turning down her admission because she's a Jew.*

Cromwell closed the file and smiled at Rachel. "You are well qualified and I suspect you will do well at this institution and do us all proud. If I can ever be of assistance to you, please don't hesitate to get in touch."

"Thank you, Mrs. Cromwell, you are very kind." *Maybe she meant it. I don't know.*

• • • • •

MANY SCHOOLS REASONED that a large Jewish attendance would make their institutions less attractive to the sought-after white Anglo-Saxon Protestant students. They created departments of admissions whose representatives would evaluate the personal background, leadership, and potential of prospective students. Ranking students by applying a set of subjective criteria enabled college administrators to "weed out" Jewish applicants who generally came with higher marks and scores than their non-Jewish counterparts, but who nevertheless were considered inferior enrollment material.

• • • • •

RADCLIFFE COLLEGE, FOUNDED in 1879 in Cambridge, Massachusetts, was Harvard's coordinate institution for female students. It was also one of the Seven Sisters colleges, amongst which it shared with Bryn Mawr College the popular reputation of having a particularly intellectual and independent-minded student body. Radcliffe conferred Radcliffe College diplomas to undergraduates and graduate students. The course of study included 51 courses in 13 subject areas, an impressive curriculum with greater diversity than that of any other women's college at its inception.

Throughout most of the college's history, residential life and student activities at Radcliffe remained separate from those at Harvard, with separate dormitories and dining facilities, newspapers, radio stations, drama society, student government, yearbooks, athletic programs, and choral associations.

Dances were popular features of undergraduate life. At different times there were class dances, club dances, junior and senior proms, sophomore tea dances, Christmas dances, and spring formals. Dormitory-based dances, known as "jolly-ups," were also frequently held.

The Radcliffe Choral Society became a particularly popular and influential student group. Started in 1899 and conducted by Marie Gillison, a German-born singing teacher, the group cultivated an interest in sophisticated classical music at a time when many collegiate choral groups were devoted to college songs and more popular ditties.

32
Jewish Women in College

THE MASS IMMIGRATION of Jews to the United States between 1881 and 1924 occurred at precisely the same time as the development of public education for the masses. Newly arrived families were far more interested in their sons' chances of attending college than they were their daughters.' Conventional wisdom was that a girl's chance of earning a living, even with a college education, appeared slight. The help provided by daughters within the household and the wages secured from outside work represented important contributions to the family in terms of putting food on the table and even paying college tuition for their brothers.

In spite of the bent toward the boys, Jewish daughters often pursued an education while also holding down jobs and helping with family chores. A study of night school attendees in 1910 revealed that although Jews comprised only nineteen percent of the population in New York City, forty percent of the women enrolled in night school were Jewish. Still, this high number of women willing to pursue an education, even after a long day of work, did not translate into a significant Jewish female presence in college during the decades preceding and following the beginning of the twentieth century.

Amelia D. Alpiner, a student in the class of 1896 at the University of Illinois at Urbana-Champaign, was the first Jewish female collegian to be identified by religion. A prominent student on campus, she was visible in many campus activities and served as a charter member of Pi Beta Phi sorority. Two years after she graduated, another identifiable Jewish female, Gertrude Stein graduated from the Harvard Annex, later Radcliffe College. Other than these two prominent women, the Jewish females who attended college during the latter decades of the nineteenth century and the first decade of the twentieth century did so in relative anonymity.

Because of their small numbers and relative invisibility as a group, Jewish students, and particularly the females among them, attracted little notice in terms of their religion from either their fellow students or outside society. Jewish members of the community, however, at times helped the few Jewish collegians to maintain their religious identities by inviting them to their homes for Passover and to share other celebrations with them. In some places, members of the Jewish Ladies Circle or other social organizations in the community helped Jewish students to take on their new collegiate identities without losing their sense of themselves as Jews. In other places, young Jewish women struggled alone to make their way through the intricacies of higher education, often finding it easier to forgo or suppress their Jewish identity to fit in better with the small number of female collegians surrounding them.

A 1916 survey found that Jewish men attended college in a higher proportion than did their non-Jewish counterparts, while female Jewish students comprised only one-ninth the number of Jewish males and attended college in numbers less than half of their non-Jewish female counterparts. While the study located only a tiny number of Jewish women enrolled at colleges nationwide, it found that at the women's colleges such as Barnard, Radcliffe, Smith, Wellesley, and Vassar, Jewish women occupied a mere five percent of the enrolled places.

Having few Jewish sisters accompanying them in their collegiate experience both hampered and aided Jewish women in the decades surrounding the turn of the twentieth century. While often spared the outright anti-Semitism directed at their male counterparts, Jewish women tended to face their struggles alone and had to combat more tacit forms of anti-Semitism. According to a Menorah Intercollegiate Association survey, Jewish women participated along with other students by hiding or simply not declaring their religious and cultural heritage.

The year 1916 saw Jewish girls also do well academically. At Smith College, for example, the three percent won nine percent of the Phi Beta Kappa keys awarded. At Bryn Mawr College, the Jewish four percent of the senior class earned more than twice that percentage of the cum laude degrees awarded.

IN THE 20-year wave of immigration up to 1917, the Jewish population expanded from less than one million to more than 3.3 million, with the bulk of the new arrivals emigrating from Eastern Europe. These new arrivals were poorer, less educated, and less cultivated than their German predecessors.

By the 1920s, the children of these immigrants began to arrive in numbers on college campuses and their presence attracted greater societal and institutional notice and comment than had the earlier Jewish students. The 1920s has been called a period of democratization in higher education, a time when the gates of Ivy League schools opened en masse to students of less privileged and more racially and ethnically diverse backgrounds. Jewish women participated in this wave of expanding enrollment, joining the collegiate ranks in greater numbers and with increased visibility. Jewish women at Radcliffe College formed a Menorah Society, whose mission included spreading Jewish culture and ideas. Increasingly made aware by their fellow students and institutions of their identities as Jews, female students, buoyed by their strength in numbers, began to form organizations to aid themselves and their Jewish sisters in responding to and combating the rise in anti-Semitism and discrimination that accompanied their increased presence on campus.

Societal paranoia and fear of foreigners mixed with institutional concerns regarding the expanding number of Jewish students enrolled on campuses produced an elevated level of anti-Semitism during the 1920s and 1930s. During these two decades, students, alumni, and administrators of many institutions, eager to preserve the so-called "Anglo-Saxon superiority" of their colleges, instituted explicit and tacit policies both to limit Jewish enrollment and to restrict Jewish participation in campus activities. Drawing on racial theories to justify their discriminatory policies, many administrators of higher education across the country created screening techniques to "weed out" Jewish applicants for admission. These institutional efforts to maintain an exclusive and "homogeneous" student body hurt Jews more than they did other ethnic and religious groups. This is because Catholics and African Americans developed and maintained colleges specifically for their own students. Jews, on the other hand, preferred to enter the American mainstream through the same avenues as non-Jews.

Jewish women experienced the policies of quotas and other practices for manipulating admission procedures to curb or even prevent the entry of Jewish students. Ivy League "sister" schools, such as Barnard and Radcliffe, and the all-female institutions of many other schools began to copy the more prestigious male institutions with their anti-Jewish stances.

While technically forbidden by state and national laws from imposing admission quotas based on race, religion, or ethnicity, the women's branches of many major state universities in the east and Midwest devised strategies to address a situation they labeled the "Jewish problem" by limiting, in a tacit manner, Jewish attendance at their institutions.

The policies against Jewish female applicants proved effective. Between 1928 and 1932, Jewish female enrollment declined by more than a third, from seventeen percent in 1928 to eleven percent in 1932. Radcliffe College introduced screening policies to weed out Jewish candidates from admissions. Between 1936 and 1938, the college reduced the number of Jewish women it admitted by almost half, and cut the percentage of Jewish students enrolled among its ranks from 24.8 to 16.5 percent despite the fact that applications for admissions from Jewish women rose during the same period.

At Radcliffe and other institutions, deans of women and other powerful administrators adopted the practice of interviewing every student who applied and evaluating each on the basis of intellectual ability, character, personality, health, and background. This practice enabled administrators to single out for rejection the students whom they considered "undesirable," "crude," and "lacking in refinement," a high proportion of whom were often Jewish.

Hounded by the knowledge that in order to fit in, they had to hide their religious affiliation, yet conscious that such action would separate them from their own families and communities, Jewish female students struggled to find a way to make themselves belong on American college campuses in the early decades of the

century. All of this happened to Rachel Rosenthal, but she didn't
hide anything.

33

"RACHEL, I WANT you to pledge Delta Gamma," said Katie, sitting on her bed in their dorm room.

"Why do you care?" asked Rachel.

"Because we're friends, roommates, soul mates."

"Soul mates?" she questioned, with a grin.

"Yeah, and you know it," said Katie, playfully swatting her with a pillow.

"Of course I do," said Rachel, leaning over and giving her a hug.

"Okay, can I put your name up?"

"Sure, but I don't think they'll approve me. Come on, Katie, I'm a Jew. That's why the Jewish sororities were developed. You know, I just want to be an average college student, not a Jewish college student."

Katie frowned.

Rachel sighed, "Do you know what I'm saying? Do you know what I mean?"

"Yes—I do."

"I was interviewed by Dean Cromwell, did I ever tell you?" Rachel lamented.

"No," said Katie, "why did she do that?"

"Are you serious, Katie, you really don't know?"

She frowned, "No, I don't."

"All Jews are interviewed to see if they are suitable for admission. I knew what was happening, but I wanted to go to this school. I didn't have any choice."

Katie frowned. She was getting the picture.

"Look, friend, roommate, soul mate, I'd love to be a Delta Gam with you. But not if it means that the Jew girl has to be subjected to some sort of unusual scrutiny. Not if it means that you have to wage a war with the Delta Gamma girls on behalf of the Jew girl."

"Oh, Rachel," said Katie, tears running down her face. "I love you so much. I hate that your religion has caused you pain. I guess gentiles have no idea what you are subjected to. I guess we just don't see it."

"Yeah, it's different when you live it."

Both the girls were quiet for a few minutes. Tears were running down Rachel's face. "I'm a young woman who will live the rest of my life without parents because of anti-Semitism, because the Nazis killed them."

"Oh, Rachel, how horrible. I'm so sorry."

"It's interesting because no one told me. But I know. Dietrich and I figured it out. I'm not in any danger like my parents were, but I may never be treated like everyone else; and all because I'm a Jew."

There was no more talk of Delta Gamma or Judaism. The conversation had taken an emotion toll on both girls. They both dropped off to sleep.

· · · · ·

DELTA GAMMA, founded in 1873, was one of the oldest and largest sororities in the nation. The "DG" mission was to offer women a rich heritage based on principles of personal integrity, personal responsibility, and intellectual honesty. Its primary purpose was to foster high ideals of friendship, promote educational and cultural interests, create a true sense of social responsibility, and develop the finest qualities of character.

They wanted Katie Mulligan to pledge very badly. She had been a cheerleader, a beauty queen, senior class favorite, and a National Honor Society member in high school. It also helped that her mother had graduated from Radcliffe and had been a Delta Gam. It probably didn't hurt that her father Ben was a well-connected northern liberal Democrat and a successful restaurateur, who owned a chain of 12 successful pubs in Boston called Mulligan's. He had given substantial sums of money to the school and was a friend, supporter, and contributor to President Roosevelt. The Delta Gammas wanted Katie Mulligan, and Katie Mulligan wanted Rachel Rosenthal. Rachel reluctantly went through rush.

· · · · ·

"WELL, YOU'RE IN," said Katie.

"No kidding?"

"No kidding. They saw in you the quality young woman that you are. You were approved unanimously."

The truth was that the application, because Rachel was a Jew, had to be referred to the national office, but Katie saw no reason to mention it.

"Not a single black ball?"

"Not a one," said Katie, jubilantly hugging her best friend. "This will be fun."

They laughed and jumped up and down.

■ ■ ■ ■ ■

FOR MANY JEWISH women, the religious-based sororities, created and developed by sisters of their faith in the 1910s, provided opportunities for campus involvement that might have been closed to them otherwise. The Jewish organizations served as an entrée into mainstream collegiate society, in part because of a deliberate mission to counter negative Jewish stereotypes. Teaching etiquette, manners, dress, sports, and upper-middle-class activities and mores, Jewish sororities and fraternities were driven to make their members ideal college students.

Jewish women argued that their sororities could help them reach parity on campus with their non-Jewish counterparts. By placing a high level of emphasis on school loyalty and patriotism and on dispelling myths about Jews by virtue of their deportment and behavior, members of the Jewish Greek system sought to use their organizations as vehicles for personal as well as collective advancement. Rachel Rosenthal would have gladly pledged a Jewish sorority, but she didn't have to.

34
The Year 1936

RACHEL AND KATIE had a morning freshman English class together. They were both trying to make the adjustment from high school: tougher studies, boys, living away from parents and adult supervision. They bonded immediately.

"These class essay assignments are killing my grades," Rachel confessed. "I don't have much trouble telling a story, but I do have trouble spelling English words. It is overly complicated. For example, the word *metal* has four different spellings and meanings."

Katie laughed, "I don't find English all that easy myself."

"Well, I need English for my degree, so I think I'll get a tutor."

"I think you should."

"I will."

"Listen, we have a dance next month. There is a boy at Harvard that's sweet on me. His name is Paul Adams and he'll be my date."

"This is the first I've heard of the boy," Rachel said.

"That's true. He's the son of close family friends."

Rachel smiled, "Tell me more."

"His father is a Boston banker. I guess Paul will get a degree in business and go to work for his daddy."

"You sound like you don't have a lot of respect for him. I mean, the way you said daddy."

"We dated before and he just does exactly what his daddy tells him. I think he's weak and I don't like that."

"Katie, he's young, we're young. Don't you think we have to do as we're told until after college?"

"I guess."

"Maybe you are a bit too hard on him."

"Maybe."

"What else about him? Is he good looking?"

"Yes, he's good looking, but he's not a great kisser."

"Something to work on." They laughed.

"I'd like to go, but I don't know any boys," Rachel said.

"I can fix that."

"You can?"

"I'll ask Paul to bring his best friend as your date."

"Who is he?"

"His name is Brick Hansford. His family is very well off. He's a football player."

"What's he look like?"

"He's also good looking. We wouldn't stick you with an ugly boy."

"I would hope not."

"Well, look, are you up for a blind date? You know, really, it's one evening in your life. If you don't like him, then that will be the end of it."

"That's true. I think I need to take a few dancing lessons. I wouldn't want to embarrass myself. I've lived in Germany and Argentina, not exactly hot beds of the fox-trot."

"Yeah, I see what you mean. So, you're agreeable to the blind date?"

"So long as he's not blind." They laughed.

"Goody. I'll tell Paul. I'm excited. It will be fun."

* * * * *

IN MARCH OF 1936, Hitler took a huge gamble. He ordered his troops to openly re-enter the Rhineland, breaking the terms of Versailles Treaty once again. But he made it clear to his generals that the troops should retreat out of the Rhineland if the French showed the slightest hint of making a military stand against them. This did not occur. Over 32,000 soldiers and armed policemen crossed into the Rhineland. This emboldened the little Austrian paperhanger.

France was going through an internal political crisis at the time, and there was no political leadership to oppose Nazi Germany. Britain generally supported the view that Germany was only going into her own "backyard" and that this section of Versailles did not need to be enforced in the mid-1930s. It was believed that Germany was behaving in a reasonable and understandable manner. Therefore, no action was taken. Hitler's later commented that the march into the Rhineland had been the most nerve-racking 48 hours of his life.

35

"CLIMB IN, OLE Buddy," said Brick.

"My, my, aren't we uptown," Paul remarked.

"Dad delivered it this morning so we'd have it for tonight."

"It's a fine car, my man. It should be good girl bait."

"I certainly hope so," said Brick, laughing as he climbed in the driver's side.

"A 1936 Auburn 852 Cabriolet," said Paul, "am I correct?"

"You know your cars."

PAUL AND BRICK picked up Rachel and Katie at their dorm. They were waiting patiently. Soon they spotted the girls coming down the stairs.

"My God, she's beautiful," said Brick quietly. *She could be Spanish or Italian.*

"She sure as hell is. You lucked out, my friend, some blind date. What a contrast. Katie's a blue eyed blond and Rachel's a brunette with black eyes."

"And both of them well endowed."

"Very well endowed."

The boys hurried to the bottom of the stairs. Paul took Katie's hand and Brick took Rachel's. *He's very handsome,* Rachel thought, *I hope he's fun to be with.*

"Rachel, I'm Brick Hansford."

"Pleased to meet you, Brick. And you would have to be Paul."

"Guilty as charged." They laughed.

"Are we ready?" Paul asked.

"Ready," was voiced in unison.

Brick opened the passenger side door and Katie and Paul climbed into the jump-seat. He helped Rachel in and carefully closed the door.

"Nice car, Brick," Rachel commented.

"Thanks, Rachel," he replied, with a huge smile.

When they arrived at the dance, Brick hurried around and opened Rachel's door.

They entered the hall and checked their wraps. The band was playing *A Fine Romance*, and both couples took to the floor. "This song was introduced by Fred Astaire in the movie *Swing Time* with Ginger Rogers," Brick informed her.

"I didn't know that. How did you know that?"

"I saw the movie. I'm a real movie buff. How about you?"

"Not so much.'

The band followed with Cole Porter's *Easy to Love* and *I've Got You Under My Skin*. They danced every dance until intermission.

"The band is pretty good."

"They're not Count Basie, but they'll do. By the way, you follow very well."

"You lead very well." They laughed.

"That was fun, but I could stand a break," said Rachel.

"How about some punch?"

"I thought you'd never ask." They laughed and he got the punch.

"Why don't we step out on the terrace?" Brick suggested. "It's a nice night."

"Sure."

They tipped their cups. "Cheers," he said.

"I wonder where Katie and Paul are?"

"Does it matter?" he asked.

"No, just wondering."

Brick took a flask from inside his coat pocket and asked, "May I add a bit of this fine bourbon to your punch?"

"No, thank you."

"Mind if I do?"

"No."

"Katie told me you were living in Argentina before you came to Radcliffe."

"That's right."

"But you're a …"

"A Jew?"

"Uh, yeah, I guess."

"Do you really want the story?"

"Yes, of course."

Rachel told him everything.

"Wow, I don't know what to say."

"You don't have to say anything. But from what I have observed, people in America don't have any idea what's coming. The pot is boiling in Europe. Time will tell, of course, but there may very well be some bad times ahead."

"Europe?"

"The world."

36

THEY STARED AT each other for a short time. It seemed longer. Brick went to get more punch.

"Here you are."

"Thanks. Now it's time for you to tell me your story. Katie tells me you play football."

"That's right," he replied, as he poured more bourbon in his punch.

"My brother played football. He was one of the best young players in Germany."

"You mean soccer."

"Yes."

"Well, I'm afraid there has been a misunderstanding. I don't play soccer, I play American football. I'm the Harvard quarterback."

"You're right. I didn't understand, and I do not know about American football."

"Maybe you would like to come to some Harvard football games?"

"I might like that. We'll see. Now, tell me more about you and your family."

"My father graduated from Harvard as did my grandfather."

"Sounds like you didn't have much choice in colleges."

"I don't really know what my father would have said if I had wanted to go to Yale, for example. Harvard's a great school and he's paying for it. I knew they wanted me to go there, so I just went. We never discussed other schools. You may find it interesting to know that my mother went to Radcliffe."

"I was interviewed by the Dean of Women before I was admitted."

"Why was that?"

"You really don't know? Think about it."

He frowned, deep in thought. "Oh, no, it wasn't because you're …"

"Jewish. That's exactly the reason."

Brick frowned, "I'm so sorry to hear that."

"I made the cut. So go on with your story."

"My dad Martin owns Hansford Motors, a chain of eight automobile dealerships in Boston. My mother, Samantha, was a Mortimer, old money. Dad was a captain in World War I, was wounded, but not seriously. He has no lingering effects from it. That should give you a pretty good idea about us."

"Yes, it does. What do you plan to do with your education?"

"I'll run one of the dealerships so I can learn the business, Then I'll move into the corporate office. Anyway, that's the plan. That's what Dad has said."

"But what do you say?"

"Well—I mean, what is there to say? It's the family business."

"Brick is not your real name, is it?"

He laughed, "No, it's short for Brickley."

"Brickley Hansford."

"Yeah, that's me."

"What religion is your family?"

The question caught him off guard. He thought for a moment. "I don't really know. We don't go to any church at all."

■ ■ ■ ■ ■

"DID YOU HAVE a good time, Rachel?" Brick asked.

"Yes, I did."

"Good. I'm pleased."

"Hey, Paul, Rachel and I will ride back in the jump-seat. That way you'll get to drive this fine car. I know you are anxious to get behind the wheel."

"That's a deal. Let me help you in, Katie."

They laughed and talked on the way back to the girl's dorm. Brick finished off the bourbon. Shortly, he grabbed Rachel around the neck and kissed her hard while running his hand up her skirt to the sweet spot. She tore herself loose from his grasp and belted him in the mouth. "Paul, stop the car and let me out!" Rachel screamed.

"What's the matter," said Katie.

"Yeah, what's going on back there," said Paul, as he abruptly brought the car to a stop.

Rachel got out and started walking. "Rachel, please get back in the car," Brick pleaded. "I'm so sorry."

After a few minutes of negotiating, the boys were sent to the jump-seat and Katie drove the rest of the way to the dorm. Rachel got out, slammed the door and, without another word, walked toward the entrance to the dorm. When they were both back in their room, Rachel explained what happened.

"That sonofabitch!" Katie yelled.

■ ■ ■ ■ ■

GERMAN REARMANENT MOVED forward at an alarming rate. Britain and France protested, but failed to keep up with German war production. The German air fleet grew dramatically, and the new German fighter, the Messerschmidt-109, was far more sophisticated than its counterparts in Britain, France, or Russia. Luftwaffe pilots received combat training during the Spanish Civil War. They tried out new aerial attack formations on Spanish towns such as Guernica, which suffered more than 1,000 killed during a brutal bombing in April 1937.

The Luftwaffe was configured to serve as a crucial part of the German blitzkrieg, or "lightning war"—the deadly military strategy developed by General Heinz Guderian. As German panzer divisions burst deep into enemy territory, lethal Luftwaffe dive-bombers would decimate enemy supply and communication lines, cities, and cause panic.

37

"RACHEL, IT'S YOU know who again. He's not going to stop calling so you may as well talk to him. This is driving me crazy."

Rachel frowned, sighed, and grabbed the telephone. "What do you want, Brick?"

There was a moment of silence. Then he said, "Rachel, I'm sure you never want to see me again, but may I please come over to the dorm and apologize in person. Then you never have to see me again."

She was silent for a moment. She sighed; he could hear it, "When did you want to come?"

"I could be there in 30 minutes."

She looked down at her watch. "That would be at 6:00."

"Uh, yes."

"All right, I'll meet you in the downstairs living room."

"You weakened," said Katie.

"Well, watching him grovel might be satisfying. And then I don't have to ever see him again."

"Paul is put out with him. I mean, they're best friends. He's embarrassed about it."

"Some friend."

RACHEL WAS WAITING in the living room of the ladies dormitory when Brick arrived. He slowly walked over and stood humbly in front of the couch. "May I?"

"Sit down."

He swallowed hard, squirmed, and began. "First. let me say that I'm sorry. For better or worse, I am not one to say I'm sorry very much: hardly at all. But I am saying it to you now. I was tipsy, no excuses. I insulted you and made a fool out of myself."

"You planned it, suggesting that Paul would like to drive your new car so we would sit in the jump-seat."

Brick turned red, raised both arms in surrender, "Guilty as charged."

"Look, I had a good time. You're a good-looking boy and you had been a perfect gentleman. I would have kissed you. But you lost control and ruined an otherwise enjoyable evening."

"Rachel, I have no defense. I was guilty of very bad form, and I have offended a beautiful and classy young woman who didn't deserve my offensive and obnoxious behavior. I don't know what else I can say."

Brick stood, "I just hope you will give me some credit for trying to make it right and not think too badly of me. Thanks for seeing me. Thanks for letting me tell you in person." He sighed and looked sad. "I'll just go now and leave you alone." Brick turned and started walking toward the front door.

"Brick!"

He stopped and turned around.

"I haven't eaten supper and I'm hungry. A burger and chocolate malt would really taste good. And *Born to Dance* is showing downtown. It's got Eleanor Powell, Jimmy Stewart, Frances Langford, and Buddy Ebsen. It should be good. So what do you think? Do you have anything better to do?"

Brickley Hansford looked stunned. He was having difficulty coming to grips with what he just heard. Then the words sunk in.

"What about it, Brick?"

He smiled, "Yes, I mean no. I don't have anything better to do. We, we can go. I'd love to do that!"

She laughed.

He held out his hand and helped her up. They stood for a moment, holding hands, smiling at each other.

■ ■ ■ ■ ■

THE AUBURN 852 came to a stop outside Rachel's dorm.

"I had a great time," said Rachel.

Brick was relieved. He thought it had all gone well.

"So did I, Rachel."

"Walk me to the door?"

"Yes." He almost fell down as he hurried around to open her door. They held hands as they walked to the door. "You don't have to go in."

Rachel gave him a tender kiss on the mouth. The hair on his neck stood on end.

"Call me sometime," she said, matter-of-factly. Then she climbed the front steps, entered the door, and proceeded to the stairs without another word or a look.

He returned to the car, lit a cigarette, leaned over the cab and tried to make sense of what had just happened. When he had finished his cigarette, he climbed in the car and drove back to Boston.

It was dark when she opened the door. Then a bedside lamp came on and Katie sat up. She positioned her pillow behind her and said, "What happened to you? You went downstairs to hear his apology and you're gone for the next three hours. I want to know what happened."

Rachel put on her pajamas, climbed up in bed, put her legs under her and told Katie everything.

■ ■ ■ ■ ■

PAUL ADAMS HAD made dinner reservations at the Union Oyster House.

"I like this place," said Rachel.

"Well, Rachel, it's the oldest restaurant in Boston and the oldest eating establishment in continuous service in the United States," said Paul. "It opened its doors for the first time in 1826."

"No kidding?' said Rachel

"No kidding."

The waiter arrived. "Bring this man and me a very dry martini," said Brick. "Rachel, what do you and Katie want to drink?"

The girls ordered Coca Cola.

"We'll order food when you return," said Paul, seated beside Katie with Brick beside Rachel at an upstairs booth.

"Very good, sir."

"Well, Rachel, are you and Katie feeling pressure at school?" Paul asked. "Brick and I sure did when we were freshmen."

"I think we did at first," said Katie, "but I think we are both settling in now. Right Rachel?"

"Yeah, we struggled for a time, that's true. But we're fine now."

"That's good," said Paul. "I think all freshmen struggle at first. There is a huge difference between high school and college."

"There sure is," said Katie.

"Imagine coming from Germany by way of Argentina," said Rachel.

"Frankly, I can't imagine it," said Brick.

"We better look at the menus," Paul suggested.

"Yeah, I think you're right," said Katie.

"Get whatever you want, Rachel," said Brick.

"And what was it that made you think I would not?"

They all laughed.

"Okay, folks, here are your beverages. Have you decided on your dinner selections?"

"What do you all think about us getting the Oyster House Sampler for the table? It has grilled oysters, baked stuffed cherrystones, clams casino, oysters Rockefeller, and shrimp scampi," Brick asked.

"Great idea," said Paul. "Are you girls okay with that?"

"Sure."

"All right—we're doing good so far. I want a cup of clam chowder, a Caesar salad, and the 12 ounce center cut sirloin medium rare."

"You're not having seafood?" Paul inquired, with a slight frown.

"Nope. I want meat and besides, we're having the sampler."

"The man knows what he wants," said the waiter with a smile, "and for the ladies?"

"Let's see, I'll have the onion soup and the cold lobster salad platter," said Rachel.

"And for you?" he asked Katie.

"I'll have a Caesar salad as well and the seafood Newburg."

"Excellent choices so far. And you, sir?'

"The seafood platter."

"Now, sir," talking to Brick, "you have a choice of potato or rice."

"I'll have the rice."

"Now, I'll get some butter and our fabulous corn bread. How about those drinks?" Rachel and Katie ordered more Coca Cola and the boys ordered another martini.

"I think there are rice families and potato families," said Brick.

"What?" Katie asked.

"Here's what I mean. When I was growing up, we ate far more rice than potatoes. I think there are others who will eat more potatoes than rice."

They were all in thought. Finally Paul said, "I think you're right about that. We definitely ate more potatoes."

"We ate more rice, "said Katie.

"I'm German, what do you think?'

Brick smiled. "Got it."

The waiter returned with butter, corn bread, salads, and onion soup. Another man brought the Cokes and the martinis.

Brick raised his glass, smiled and said, "Here's to happy times with the two best-looking girls at Radcliffe."

"Happy times," echoed everyone.

Brick looked admiringly at his martini and said, "This is awfully good."

"Yes, it is," said Paul, touching his glass to Brick's.

"What are you going to do when you graduate, Katie?" Brick asked.

"I'd like to be an executive assistant to the president of a large company in Boston or New York."

"Here's the main course," said the waiter. "Bon appétit."

"Boy, this food looks great," said Paul, "and I'm hungry."

"It does look good," said Rachel.

"Look at that piece of meat," said Brick, cutting into his steak, "and cooked to perfection."

"I guess football players don't eat much fish," Rachel speculated.

"I can't speak for all football players, but I eat fish—just not a lot of it." They all laughed.

"How is your lobster, Rachel?" Brick asked.

"It's very good."

"What are you going to do with your degree, Paul?' Rachel asked.

"My father is a banker. I'll go to work for him."

Rachel looked at Katie and smiled. Katie smiled back. Paul frowned, "What?"

"Nothing," said Rachel. He looked confused.

"Nothing at all," said Katie.

"Before you ask," said Brick, "Dad has auto dealerships. I'll start out selling, then I'll manage one of the locations, and I'll eventually move over to the corporate office. It will all be mine someday. I'll run the company."

"Hey, you girls could work for us," said Brick.

The girls laughed. "Why is that funny?" Paul asked.

"Anyway, we haven't heard from you, Rachel," said Paul. "Have you thought about the future?"

"I've got a few years to decide. I sure don't have to do it tonight."

There was more eating than talking for the rest of the meal. The boys had paid out and they were all having coffee. Paul looked at his watch. "We've got time to make the movie."

"Let's do it," said Katie.

38
The Year 1937

RACHEL AND BRICK, Katie and Paul were inseparable. There were dances, and burgers, malts, movies, and football games. The Radcliffe Choral Society was a popular and influential student group, and Katie and Rachel were members.

"PAUL KEEPS PRESSURING me to have sex with him," Katie confessed.

"What have you told him?"

"I've told him no, of course."

"The fact that you're telling me makes me think you're wavering, that you're considering it."

"Well …"

"Well, nothing. Are you?"

"I guess. He says he loves me."

"Boys say that to soften girls up."

"You think?"

Rachel laughed, "Yeah." Then she asked, "Do you love him?"

"I think so."

"So you've gotten over the disrespect part, that he's a daddy's boy."

"Yeah, I guess. And besides, you told me that I was being too hard on him, that we all had to pretty much do what we are told until after college."

There was a moment of silence.

"You disappoint me, Katie. Hasn't it ever crossed your mind that if you let him have sex with you, that he might then disrespect you, and maybe even drop you?"

"You think so?"

"Of course I do. And what if you get pregnant? Think about explaining that to your family. You'd have to drop out of school. I mean, it could ruin your life."

"I guess I never thought it through like that."

"Sister, sister, it's time you did. The next time he pressures you, tell him if he doesn't cut it out, you'll never see him again."

"Okay, I will. I won't mean it, but it might work. He loves me very much, I can tell. He wouldn't want to lose me."

"Okay. I'm counting on you."

"Has Brick ever asked you?"

"Since that episode in the jump-seat of his car, he has been a perfect gentleman. He wouldn't dare."

• • • • •

AS PART OF a speech covering four years of economic, national, and foreign affairs victories, Adolph Hitler addressed the Reichstag and called for withdrawal of the German signature from the Versailles Treaty. Germany began overt and outright preparation for war. Fascist Italian dictator Benito Mussolini visited Germany. After Hitler showed off his military assets, Mussolini returned to Italy certain that his alliance with Germany was the right decision to make. Hitler detailed a broad plan for war preparedness against France, Britain, and Russia. An exhibition in Nuremberg portrayed Jews as the leaders of international Bolshevism, dedicated to destroying Germany. Buchenwald concentration camp was established. Many of the Germany military became concerned about Nazi policy and selected General von Fritsch to try and dissuade Hitler from his aggressive course of action toward war.

• • • • •

RACHEL AND Brick, Paul and Katie, were having a Coke and a burger at Porky's in Cambridge. "What do you think of American football, Rachel?" Paul asked.

"I don't like it as much as soccer, but I enjoy it."

"She's seen all the games," Katie reminded him.

"I know."

"Look, she comes to support her boyfriend," said Brick.

"Yes, I do."

She started to grin, looked at Brick, and said, "It's too bad you had to lose to Dartmouth and Army. It would probably help if you had a better quarterback."

She laughed and so did the others, including Brick.

"That hurts. That cuts to the bone. My girlfriend has no respect for my game. I am crushed."

"Cheer up, Brick, you're really okay."

"Just okay. I'm your classic triple threat."

"You are?" questioned Rachel. "What's that mean?"

"That means he can run, throw, and kick," said Paul.

"That's true, I guess. But it's good to know what you are." They laughed.

"It's your line that needs help," said Rachel.

"Can we quit with the relentless criticism of the Crimson," said Brick, playfully. "Now, regardless of your opinion of our skills with the pigskin, Rachel, you have to come to *The Game*."

"Okay, I'll take the bait. What is *The Game?*"

"The Harvard-Yale rivalry, consisting of two of the most well-known universities in the world. It's the oldest college rivalry in American sports," said Paul, who knew his Harvard facts as well.

"The Harvard–Yale football game," inserted Brick, "is known as The Game by many followers and sports writers. The Game is always played in November, the last game of the football season, with the venue alternating between Harvard Stadium and the Yale Bowl."

"Well, isn't that special," said Rachel, with a smile and a giggle.

"Rachel, will you quit it," said Brick, playfully.

"Okay, is there more?"

"Well, how about this?" said Paul. "Before the 1916 Game, Yale coach Jones inspired his players to a 6-3 victory when he unequivocally asserted, 'Gentlemen, you are now going to play football against Harvard. Never again in your whole life will you do anything so important.'"

"In all seriousness, I'm shocked that you guys give so much weight to a sporting event," said Rachel.

"Well, to be fair, that statement was made in 1916, before we entered the war," said Brick.

"Good point," said Rachel.

"I have another important bit of information about The Game."

"All right, let's get it all out so we can eventually talk about something else," said Rachel.

"Not only is The Game historically significant for all college sports, but also many students and alumni of Harvard and Yale consider The Game one of the most important days of the year. The schools are located only a few hours' travel from one another, and perhaps because they are among the nation's most prestigious and oldest universities, the rivalry is intense."

"Seriously, Rachel, these rivalries are fun for people," said Brick. "I suspect that soccer teams in Europe have rivalry games as well."

She smiled, "You may be right."

"Beating your rival is often considered more important than the team's season record," said Brick.

"You're a player," said Katie, "do you feel that way?"

Brick smiled, "No, but it's damn well important."

"The first meeting between the teams occurred on November 13, 1875, at Hamilton Field in New Haven. The Harvard–Yale football rivalry is the second oldest continuing rivalry and also the third most-played rivalry game in college football history," said Paul.

"You guys are driving me crazy," said Rachel.

"Well, include me in that," said Katie.

"Okay, okay, just one more thing," said Brick. "Prior to The Game in 1933, Handsome Dan II, Yale's bulldog mascot, was kidnapped, allegedly by members of the Harvard Lampoon. Then, the morning after a 19–6 upset by Harvard over Yale, hamburger meat was smeared on the feet of the statue of John Harvard that sits in front of University Hall in Harvard Yard. A photo was snapped of Handsome Dan licking John Harvard's feet."

Brick and Paul laughed wildly.

"Is that it?" Rachel questioned.

"Yes," said Brick.

She looked at Paul, "Yes."

"Now, I want to tell all of you and the world, if that's necessary, that I plan to attend the Harvard-Yale football game. I won't do it because of the rivalry but to support my triple threat boyfriend who just happens to be the quarterback of Harvard."

Brick grinned, "Now, ain't that sweet."

39
The Year 1938

IN THE EARLY hours of September 30, 1938, leaders of Nazi Germany, Great Britain, France and Italy signed an agreement that allowed the Nazis to annex the Sudetenland, a region of Czechoslovakia that was home to many ethnic Germans.

Adolf Hitler had threatened to take the Sudetenland by force. The Czechoslovakian government resisted, but its allies Britain and France, determined to avoid war at all costs, were willing to negotiate with Hitler. On September 29, Hitler met in Munich with Prime Ministers Neville Chamberlain of Britain, Edouard Daladier of France, and Benito Mussolini of Italy. The meeting was intended to reach a final settlement.

Czechoslovakian leaders were not included in the talks, having been given a choice by Britain and France: accept the terms or resist the Nazis on their own. *The New York Times* reported on October 1 that Czechoslovakia accepted the Munich terms. Premier Syrovy angrily responded, "We've been abandoned."

The Times also reported: "Mr. Chamberlain met a great demonstration when he arrived in London, and a similar one was accorded to Premier Daladier when he reached Paris." The British prime minister famously declared in a September 30 speech that the agreement ensured "peace in our time."

40

"HEY, IT'S THREE and a half hours from Boston to New York City. It's no big deal to drive it. I think it's a better plan than flying or taking the train. And dad will let us have a nice new four-door car from one of his lots," said Brick.

He looked at Rachel and Katie and asked, "Can we leave after your classes are out on Friday? That way we can maximize our time in the city."

"Sounds okay to me," said Katie.

"Yeah, fine," said Rachel.

"Paul, did your father make the reservations at The Plaza?" Katie asked.

"Yes, he did."

RACHEL FELT HER excitement grow as the car moved closer to Manhattan.

"When I came to America, I flew here from Buenos Aires and my Uncle Meir picked me up. Since I had never met my aunt and my cousins, we stayed around their home to get to know each other. We really didn't do anything. Then it was time to take me to Cambridge. So, this is my first real chance to experience New York City."

Rachel could hardly contain herself as they arrived at The Plaza. The snow was falling lightly as they prepared to go inside.

"Paul Adams checking in."

The manager, Andre, was talking with a staffer when he heard the name Adams. He turned to greet him. But Mason Adams was not there.

"Adams?"

"Yes, Paul Adams."

"Are you Mr. Mason Adams' son?"

"Yes, sir."

"I was under the impression your father and mother were staying with us. They have been faithful patrons for years."

"Sorry about the confusion."

"Well, now, Morris, what do we have for young Mr. Adams?"

Katie glanced at Rachel who was sporting a coy grin. Then she glared at her friend, but it didn't change her expression.

"We have two suites reserved."

Andre turned to young Paul for instructions.

"Uh, my friend here, Brickley— Brickley and I will stay in one, and, and, these girls, these ladies, will stay in the other."

"All right then. The gentlemen will be in 1321 and the ladies in 1323. If we could have each of you sign the register. Please sign all your charges to the rooms. We have been instructed to send the bill to your father's office in Boston. His credit is good with The Plaza."

"Well … well, thanks," Paul replied.

"All right then, Morris will take it from here. I hope you enjoy your stay."

"I'm sure we will," said Paul.

"Good. Give my regards to your father."

"Here are your keys. I'll have your bags taken right up. Don't worry about a thing."

"Thank you, Morris."

"Before you go, I thought I would mention that we have High Tea in The Palm Court every afternoon. It's something a great many of our guests enjoy. I thought the ladies, in particular, would enjoy it. I mention it now because if you are interested, you need to make a reservation."

"I'd like to do that," said Katie.

"Rachel, how does that sound to you?" Brick asked.

"I think I would enjoy it as well."

"Okay, let's go over and make the reservations."

THEY HAD JUST put away their clothes when there was a knock on the door.

"What do you think of your suite?" said Paul. "Daddy knows what to ask for."

"It's quite lovely," said Rachel, taking the lead.

"Yes, very nice indeed."

"We were just thinking," said Paul, "that we should go to the Stage Deli for lunch. Daddy and Mother just love it. They recommended it. The snow is falling lightly, so we could walk. Then we've got High Tea here this afternoon, dinner at the Russian Tea Room, and then the theatre."

Rachel sighed. "This is going to be quite a first day. The plan sounds wonderful. Please thank your daddy for all the arrangements," said Rachel, glancing at Katie with a coy grin. "Since this is my first time to really see New York, it will all be new to me and a surprise. But if this hotel is any clue, it's sure to be memorable."

"Paul, it does sound great," said Katie.

"Then what are we waiting for?" said Brick.

They laughed and held hands as they walked. "It is quite a city, isn't it?" said Rachel.

"Yes, it is," said Brick. "But you lived in Berlin. Isn't that quite a city too?"

"I was a very young girl at the time. It was gay all right, but I couldn't appreciate it, particularly the nightlife."

"I understand."

"I'LL HAVE A roast beef sandwich and a beer," said Brick, closing his menu.

"Rachel?"

"I want the corn beef hash with the poached egg on top and black coffee."

"The lady and I are having the pastrami," said Paul. "She'll have a Coke and beer for me."

The waitress took the menus and turned in the order.

"Tell me about the Russian Tea Room," said Rachel. "Has anybody been there?"

"I've been there with my parents," said Paul.

"Okay, so what can you tell me … tell us?"

"Well, it was founded by the Russian Imperial Ballet in 1927."

"No kidding?" said Katie.

"It has become a place where actors, writers, politicians, and executives plan deals and celebrate with their friends after Carnegie Hall and Broadway performances. You enter through antique revolving doors and are greeted with Russian style décor fit for nineteenth century aristocrats."

"Wow," said Katie, "I'm excited."

Rachel was smiling broadly. She looked excited as well.

"I'd like to tag along, if that's okay?" said Brick.

Rachel squeezed his hand and smiled, "I'm planning on being on your arm as we enter that fine establishment."

He smiled and gave her a quick kiss.

THEY ALL HAD cheesecake before they left. Then they walked down to Rockefeller Center and had a coffee while watching the skaters. "Do you skate, Rachel?" said Brick.

"No, I don't."

"Me neither."

"But I'm an accomplished skier. My brother and I skied a lot while we were growing up in Germany."

They stopped at St. Patrick's Cathedral before returning to the hotel in time for High Tea. Rachel felt a bit strange inside the church, but said nothing. Brick looked at it like another tourist site in New York City. Paul and Katie lit candles and crossed themselves. They were Catholics.

"I'd like to put my feet up for a few minutes," said Katie, when they returned to the Plaza. "I'm tired from walking."

"I agree," said Rachel. "You boys can knock on the door when it's time to go down for tea."

THEY WERE SEATED at a nice table. The waiter, dressed in black slacks and shoes, a starched white waist coat and shirt, black tie and white gloves, was eager to please. "Ladies and gentlemen, my name is Conrad and I'll be taking care of you. As the Palm Court is a formal setting, formal table service is indeed appropriate. We have thirteen premium quality, loose leaf white, green, oolong, and black teas. Herbal and Rooibus infusions are served in a two-cup teapot, fully decanted. The decanting of the tea keeps the leaves from stewing in the pot. Your second cup should be as good as the first. As no detail is too small, milk for your tea may be served warm on request."

Rachel, hands clasped under her chin, arms against her chest, was beaming from ear to ear. "This is just great," she said.

Katie giggled, "I love it."

"Shall I continue?" said the waiter.

"Please do, Conrad," said Brick, grinning at the girls' reaction.

"Very well. There are many challenges when serving afternoon tea in a large venue. The Palm Court has once again reverted to the traditional English self-service, three-tier stand. We serve the scones on top, sandwiches in the middle, and pastries on the bottom."

Brick and Paul were grinning as well.

"Whether in the kitchen making certain that every piece of bread is fresh, every cookie crisp, every plate artistically arranged, or the wait staff who seem to be in constant motion, all of us have great pride in what we do to make your experience as perfect as possible. Now, you can choose from The Classic or The New Yorker. Take a look at the choices and let me know your decision. I will be right back."

"We don't want to spoil our dinner tonight, so I recommend that we go with The New Yorker. I mean, The Classic is really heavy with the lobster and roast beef," said Brick.

"I agree with Brick," said Rachel. "I'm looking forward to a great dinner."

"Anybody disagree?" Brick asked.

Paul and Katie looked at each other and said, "No."

"Have you folks decided?"

"Yes, Conrad. We'll all have The New Yorker. And Conrad, bring us your favorite tea, and I'm sure we'll love it."

"All right then."

"Before you leave, Conrad," said Rachel, "can I ask you about the Palm Court? It is just spectacular. I grew up in Europe. It reminds me of Europe."

"It has European splendor, that's for sure, which is not accidental. From the moment the Plaza opened in 1907, it became a venue of choice as a world destination point. The Palm Court is the heartbeat of the Plaza. Aside from the European style furnishings, who could escape the grandeur of the 1,800 square foot stained glass laylight above us?"

"Okay," said Rachel, with a contented smile.

"We haven't talked about the theatre," said Katie. "Tell us about it, Paul."

"Okay, we're really in luck. It's Thornton Wilder's *Our Town.* It's set in the fictional American small town of Grover's Corner. It takes place between 1901 and 1913, and tells the story of an average town's citizens in the early twentieth century as depicted through their everyday lives. It's the hottest show on Broadway, but daddy pulled some strings to get us tickets."

"I must say that your Daddy has gone out of his way to put this weekend together for us and pay for most of it. Not all parents would have gone to so much trouble and expense," Rachel concluded.

"I agree," said Katie. "This weekend is shaping up to be incredible."

41

May 1939
Graduation from Radcliffe College

RACHEL AND KATIE were piled up in bed, in their dorm room, in their sweat pants and comfortable school t-shirts. "Can you believe we are actually seniors, soon to graduate from this fine college?" Katie asked.

"Yeah—ain't we something special?"

They both giggled.

"Sometimes it seems like we've been here forever, and sometimes it seems it has gone really fast," said Katie.

"I agree. Look, we deserve a reward for all our hard work, don't you think?"

"I certainly do. What shall we do?"

"Let's go somewhere."

They both thought for a moment. Katie pulled her legs up under her and said, "Hey, let's go to Paris. My brother is there studying art. He can show us around and be our chaperone. What do you think?"

"I love it," said Rachel, bouncing up and down on the bed.

"I think my brother would keep my parents from objecting."

"Let's make the arrangements," said Rachel.

"I just had another thought," said Katie.

"What is it?"

"What about the boys?"

"What about them?"

"They have the money. Well, their parents do. They could go with us."

"I don't want them to go," said Rachel sternly. "I want to go with my sister. You know, Katie, this is probably our last fling. After graduation everything changes. Things will never be the same again. I want to enjoy this time with you."

"You're right. I'll explain it to Paul"

"You mean you need his permission?"

"Well, no, not exactly. But we are going to get married."

"That's the first I've heard about that and I'm your best friend. At least I thought I was."

"You are! You are! It's just that …"

"What?"

"Our parents have been long time friends. They want it, they have always talked about it."

"Please tell me this is not the reason."

"He's a nice boy, well educated, and he'll always have money. We'll have a comfortable life with no surprises."

"Please tell me this is not the reason."

"I love him."

"Of course you do, Katie. Now, I like the idea of going to Paris. I'm going alone if I have to. Are you going with me or what?"

"Yes."

"Is this settled?"

"Yes."

"Then let's make the arrangements."

■ ■ ■ ■ ■

"UNCLE MEIR HELPED me work this out. We're flying to England on Pan American's *Dixie Clipper*," Rachel reported with excitement.

"We're not sailing?"

"Are you kidding? Not when we can fly the *Clipper.*"

"I must confess that I don't know a lot about it, but I didn't think Pan American flew to Europe?"

"They haven't, but listen to this, my girl. Pan American flew mail from Port Washington to Marseilles in 29 hours on May 20."

"No problems?"

"No problems."

Rachel could hardly contain her excitement. "On June 28, the *Clipper* will make its inaugural passenger flight from New York to Southampton and we're booked on it."

Katie was speechless.

"Katie, we're gonna make history."

Katie was grinning broadly. It was beginning to set in. "How long will it take?"

"I'm not sure exactly, but I do know that the mail run took 29 hours."

"Do they have sleeping accommodations?"

"Yes. Let me tell you," said Rachel, fidgeting with excitement. "First of all, only twenty-two privileged people will be on this maiden flight."

Katie started clapping and giggling. "And Katie Mulligan and Rachel Rosenthal are among the inaugural few."

"That's right. And it took more than the price of a ticket to be on this flight. My Uncle Meir has important contacts within the Roosevelt administration. It is amazing what he can get done. Now, that's not something we need to talk about, but I wanted you to know.'

"Well, I'm glad your uncle is so well connected. You mentioned the price of a ticket. What's this going to cost us?"

"Okay, the deal was that I would take care of the expenses at the Ritz and you would take care of everything else."

"That's right."

"I don't think it would be fair for you to pay for the *Clipper*. So, let's pay for our own tickets. They are $375.00 one way."

"That's a good idea. That makes sense. And that is a lot of money."

"Hey, we've worked four years for this little outing—and we have the money."

"We do. This is going to be great."

"You asked about sleeping. Let me just finish telling you about this flying hotel."

"Okay, shoot."

"It has plush seating for 74 people, sleeping berths for 40 …"

"That means all 22 on this flight will get a sleeping birth," said Katie, interrupting.

"That's right," said Rachel, with a smile. "I'm not finished. There is a separate dining room where full-course meals are catered by four-star hotels, separate men's and women's bathrooms, a deluxe compartment for VIPs, dressing rooms, and a dedicated lounge."

"All the comforts," said Katie.

"All the comforts."

"Then we'll take the train from Southampton to London and then British Airways from London to Paris."

"Sounds like a plan," said Katie.

"I can hardly wait," said Rachel, with a huge grin.

■ ■ ■ ■ ■

THE MUNICH AGREEMENT did not, in fact, bring about peace. The Nazis seized the rest of Czechoslovakia in the spring of 1939. It is often argued that the reluctance of Britain and France to stand up to Hitler emboldened him in his quest to conquer Europe. In fact, the Munich Agreement is held up as the prime example of the dangers of appeasement.

PART FIVE

PARIS AND POLAND

42
Paris

THE SOCIAL AND cultural features known as the "Roaring Twenties" began in leading metropolitan centers, especially Chicago, New Orleans, Los Angeles, New York City, and Philadelphia. But they also spread to London and Paris. Frenchmen called them the *années folles*, the "Crazy Years", emphasizing the era's social, artistic, and cultural dynamism. From the 1920s to 1940, Paris underwent a creative fever that brought artists, writers, musicians, film-makers, and intellectuals from around the world to the City of Light. The Bohemian charms of Montparnasse attracted artists such as Cezanne, Picasso, Chagall, Braque, and Giacometti. A vibrant café culture provided a forum for disputes between proponents of Cubism, Dadaism, and Surrealism and gave rise to a group of expatriate writers including Ernest Hemingway, Gertrude Stein, and F. Scott Fitzgerald. The jazz craze attracted many black musicians such as saxophonist Sidney Bechet. In architecture, the geometric shapes created by Le Corbusier changed the modern building. The creative energy was all-encompassing, establishing Paris as the epicenter of new trends in the arts.

Famous entertainers of the 1930s in Paris included Maurice Chevalier and the famous black dancer and singer Josephine Baker. Jazz music continued to be enormously popular, and there were many jazz clubs. The popularity of African American musicians, to the consternation of their French counterparts, caused the government to pass a law in 1933 stating that only 10 percent of musicians could be foreigners.

Nevertheless, jazz continued to be the rage and most musicians were American. Restaurants and cabarets that lost American musicians lost business as well. That opened the door for other styles of music, and dance and music from the Caribbean became popular, to the chagrin of French jazz musicians who hoped to benefit from the law.

When the law was lifted, black American musicians found work again and ended up joining forces with musicians from Cuba and Martinique, all of whom were fixtures in the Paris music scene. Musicians from the Antilles promoted a Creole folk dance called the *beguine* and its popularity was ensured by Josephine Baker who added it to her revue. Cole Porter wrote a song about it.

■ ■ ■ ■ ■

BEN MULLIGAN WAS not pleased that his son Billy had dropped out of Harvard. Billy did odd jobs to save money to go to Paris. He would get no help from his disappointed father. Billy Mulligan was not concerned with the politics in France. As far as he was concerned, it was still *années folles,* and he wanted to be a part of it—and become a painter. Montparnasse, on the left bank of the river Seine, was the perfect spot. The area was known for cafes, bars, dance halls, and cabarets. Financially challenged painters, sculptors, writers, poets, and composers came from around the world to thrive in the creative atmosphere. Billy Mulligan had an apartment there.

43
Paris
The Year 1939

RACHEL AND KATIE went straight to the Ritz upon their arrival in Paris. Although they could have lived in a fine hotel in Cambridge, they wanted the college experience and remained in the dorm for the entire four years. They both had access to money, and now it was time to spend some of it.

"Wow, this is a great hotel, Rachel."

"Yes it is, Katie, and this suite is every bit what I would expect."

"We deserve it and we can afford it."

"This is going to be fun."

Billy Mulligan met them at the Ritz for dinner at the L'Espadon and then he insisted on showing them the Paris nightlife.

"We're tired from the trip, Billy, let us get some rest," said Katie. "We're in no hurry. We have plenty of time."

. . . . .

THE HOTEL RITZ, a grand palatial hotel in the heart of Paris, overlooks the octagonal border of the Place Vendôme at number 15. The hotel, ranked highly among the most prestigious and luxurious hotels in the world, was the preferred getaway for young twentieth century socialites.

The hotel was founded by the Swiss hotelier, César Ritz, in collaboration with the chef Auguste Escoffier in 1898. The new hotel was constructed behind the façade of an eighteenth century town house, overlooking one of Paris's central squares. It was reportedly the first hotel in Europe to provide a bathroom en suite, a telephone, and electricity for each room. It quickly established a reputation for luxury, with clients including royalty, politicians, writers, film stars, and singers. Several of its suites were named in honor of famous guests of the hotel, including Coco Chanel and Ernest Hemingway who lived at the hotel for years. One of the bars of the hotel, Bar Hemingway, remains devoted to Hemingway, and the L'Espadon quickly became recognized as a world-renowned restaurant. It continues to attract aspiring chefs from all over the world who come to learn at the adjacent Ritz-Escoffier School. The grandest suite of the hotel, called the Imperial, has been listed by the French government as a national monument in its own right.

■ ■ ■ ■ ■

IN SPITE OF Billy's insistence on showing them the Montparnasse, they had their own plan. They took the Seine River cruise, Vedettes du Point-Neuf, which was spectacular at night with all the lights. They visited the Musee d'Orsay; the Musee Rodin; the Arc de Triomphe; the Eiffel Tower; the Notre Dame Cathedral; the Luxembourg Gardens; the fabulous Musee de Louvre, where Mona Lisa proudly hung; and the unforgettable Versailles Palace, located 10 miles southwest of Paris.

"Katie, did you know that the French government was housed here during the reign of Louie XIV?"

"No, I did not. Really, Rachel, how do you describe this place?" she wondered, as they walked among the indescribable gardens.

Rachel smiled and shook her head, "I can't find the words, and the Hall of Mirrors. Ole Louis sure knew how to live."

"He sure did, and I don't think money was a problem."

They laughed.

AFTER THEY RETURNED to the city, they ordered wine at a sidewalk café on the Champs-Elysees. "It's pretty spectacular, isn't it Rachel? I mean, the trees along the boulevard, the colorful banners …"

"You know, when you see the Arc de Triomphe there in the distance, it's as if it is standing guard over the city."

"I hadn't thought about it like that, but I see what you mean. The shops, the cafes, the couples holding hands as they stroll, it's an enjoyable place to sit and relax and just watch the people."

"It's worth the price of a ticket," said Rachel, touching her wine glass to Katie's.

The people-watching eventually gave way to the growl of their tummies. "What do say we eat at Les Deux Magots?' Rachel asked. "I was reading about it in this brochure."

"What's it say?"

"I'll read it. *This historic café on Place St. Germain des Pres has been around since 1914 and was a favorite of the likes of Picasso and Hemingway. Sit at one of the outside tables and order a Croque Madame, a glass of wine, and while away the hours. You won't regret it.*"

Katie laughed, "If it's good enough for Pablo and Ernest, it's good enough for me."

"Then let's get a cab."

44

RACHEL AND KATIE had done all the traditional things that most tourists do—maybe even a little more.

"Well, Rachel, I guess we have to give Billy some time."

"Yeah, I think we've put the lad off long enough. We'll meet him at his apartment."

BILLY SHOWED THE girls more of the Montmartre. Then he explained, "Tonight we're going to Bricktop's on Place Pigalle."

"Where?" asked Katie, with a laugh.

"Yeah, this sounds interesting," said Rachel.

"I need to give you some background. The lady called Bricktop was born Ada Beatrice Queen Victoria Louise Virginia Smith in 1894."

"Come on, Billy, how do you know this stuff? Or better yet, why do you know this stuff?" Katie asked.

He laughed. "Well, she's just such a compelling character that I was just interested in finding out about her. She is the child of a black father and a mulatto mother. Her red hair, for some reason, earned her the nickname of 'Bricktop' and it stuck. She got her first job in show business as a teenager on Chicago's Southside and ended up as a headliner in Harlem's top Jazz Age cabarets. She eventually made the jump from Harlem to Paris, then to Montmartre."

"That was some jump," Rachel reasoned.

"It was, but it worked."

"Have you met her?" Katie asked.

Billy smiled proudly, "Yes, I have, and if she's there tonight, I'll introduce you."

"That should be interesting," said Katie, smiling and looking at Rachel.

"She has several places and they are all the rage, and have been for a decade. All the top jazz musicians have played at her clubs."

PARIS WAS BRICKTOP'S magic charm. The glitterati of the 1930s knew her places for ultra-chic, café society and a beacon for Parisian nightlife. The international set gathered there to bask in her hospitality and enjoy each other's company. Earnest Hemingway and T. S. Eliot wrote about her; Cole Porter gave her gowns and furs and even composed a song for her.

"As I said, tonight we're going to her place in Place Pigalle," said Billy.

"You said that before, but explain," Katie insisted.

"Okay, Place Pigalle is located between the Boulevard de Clichy and the Boulevard de Rochechouart, near Sacre-Coeur, at the foot of the Montmartre."

"I'm sorry I asked," said Katie, laughing.

"Place Pigalle is a hot spot. You'll see. Her place is a combination nightclub, neighborhood bar, bank, and mail drop. I hope you can meet her. It's not unusual for her to leave the stage and walk among the tables, smoking a cigar, stopping to rub a bald head, kiss a cheek, or tell a joke."

"Maybe she will tonight," Rachel speculated with a grin.

■ ■ ■ ■ ■

"THIS IS ONE hell of a joint," said Rachel.

"It sure is," said Katie. "I can see why people are drawn to this place."

TWO HOURS LATER

"BRICKTOP, THIS IS my sister Katie and her friend Rachel."

The girls stood and shook her hand.

"Is this your first trip to Paris?"

"Yes, it is," said Katie. "We just graduated from college in America and we came here to celebrate."

"Well, isn't that fine."

"Billy has been telling us about your clubs and about you," said Rachel.

Bricktop laughed, "Has he now? Well, I'm 100 percent American Negro with a hair-trigger Irish temper."

Billy, Katie, and Rachel laughed as well.

"I like your voice," said Katie.

"I always said I'm no a singer, but I do have a style and I make it tough on singers who have to follow me."

"You're way too modest, Bricktop," said Billy.

"Thank you, darling," she said, kissing him on the cheek. "Have a good time and thanks for coming in."

45

"WELL, KATIE, IT'S our last night in Paris. We've pretty well done this town except for one thing."

"I don't know what it would be?"

"Well, Katie, we haven't been to Maxim's."

"Maxim's, I guess you're right."

"What do you think?"

"I'm game. I mean, I've heard the name but I don't know much about the place."

"It's just about the most famous restaurant in Paris. But I've got this brochure. Let me read what it says.

> *Maxim's is the name of a restaurant in Paris, France, located at No. 3 of the rue Royale. It is known for its Art Nouveau interior décor.*
>
> *Maxim's was founded as a bistro in 1893 by Maxime Gaillard, formerly a waiter. It became one of the most popular and fashionable restaurants in Paris under its next owner, Eugene Cornuché. He gave the dining room its Art Nouveau decor and made sure that it was always filled with beautiful women.*
>
> *In 1913, Jean Cocteau said of Maxim's: "It was an accumulation of velvet, lace, ribbons, diamonds and what all else I couldn't describe."*
>
> *In 1932, Octave Vaudable bought Maxim's. He started selecting his clients, favoring the regulars, preferably famous or rich, beginning a new era of prestigious catering under the famous Vaudable family, which lasted more than half a century. Famous guests included Edward VIII, Marcel Proust, and Jean Cocteau, a close friend and neighbor of the Vaudables.*

"Sounds interesting. But being the last night, we need to include Billy."

"He can't dress like a penniless artist. They wouldn't let him in the front door," Rachel mused.

"I know. He does have one suit. I saw it in his closet. I guess Mother insisted he bring it."

Rachel laughed. "I'll make a reservation for three."

· · · · ·

"THE DINNER WAS spectacular," said Billy. "I don't have the money for lobster tails with veal medallions."

"It was spectacular," said Katie. "Billy's right about that."

"It literally melted in my mouth," said Rachel.

"I'm glad you suggested this for our last evening in the City of Lights," said Katie.

"What about dessert?" Billy asked.

"So, you have a sweet tooth, do you brother?"

"Yeah, I do."

"Well, we're going all out so I suggest we order Crepes Suzette," Rachel said. "When I was coming back from the ladies room, I asked a waiter about what he was doing. He said Crepes Suzette."

"So they make them table-side?"

"Right."

"That's does it as far as I'm concerned, " Katie said.

AT THE RITZ they said their goodbyes.

"You take care of yourself, brother."

"You and Rachel take care. I don't know about you going to Poland."

"We'll be fine," said Katie.

"How long do you plan on staying in Paris, Billy?" Rachel asked.

"I don't really know, Rachel, but as of this moment, I have no plans to leave."

"I sure would like to think that our family will be united again."

"Did Mom and Dad ask you girls to bring that up?"

"No, not at all," said Katie.

"Well, goodbye, sis." He hugged her and kissed her on the cheek.

"Goodbye, Billy."

Rachel extended her hand to Billy, but he grabbed her and kissed her on the lips. It was more than a peck and she was taken aback. "Goodbye, Rachel."

What was that about? Rachel thought.

Wow, my brother may have been fantasying about Rachel. It's easy to see why.

"Goodbye, Billy, you take care," said Rachel, with a confused smile.

"How much more to take this man to the Montparnasse?" Katie asked the cabbie. She paid the driver, and he drove away with Billy.

"I was surprised by the kiss," said Rachel, biting her lip.

"So was I," said Katie.

46
August 1939

RACHEL AND KATIE flew from Orly Field in Paris to Warsaw. They were met by a staffer from the American embassy. He greeted them as they exited the plane.

"You must be Rachel and Katie."

They were taken aback. "Yes, we are, but who are you?"

"I'm Leo Russell from the American embassy." *They are two very pretty young women, but there's got to be more to this than looks. Washington was quite clear. Take good care of them.*

"I was told to meet you."

The girls looked at each other, grinned, and then back at Russell. "Well, how nice of you, Mr. Russell."

"It's my pleasure, and please call me Leo. Let's collect your luggage and get you to your hotel."

As the car moved into the city, Russell inquired, "Just out of curiosity, what are you doing here? The winds of war are definitely blowing and the little German paperhanger is really strutting his stuff here in Europe."

"Well, I haven't seen my cousin in six years and have never met some of my Polish relatives. We were vacationing in Paris when I got a wire from New York that my cousin is getting married on August 27 in Grojec. So, it seemed like a good time to come."

Immediately after he sent the wire, Meir Rosenthal exercised his considerable influence with the Roosevelt State Department in order to insure that Rachel and Katie were well taken care of in Poland.

Russell sighed. Rachel and Katie noticed. Rachel was not ignorant of world affairs. In fact, she was well informed. "Look, a lot of pretty smart people have analyzed the situation here in Europe. The Munich Pact was signed in 1938. Hitler has gotten pretty much what he wanted without firing a shot. But I don't think he can do another Munich. The French army is the most formidable in Europe and if Hitler wants to start shooting, he'll also have the British to contend with. You are a professional diplomat and you can tell me I don't know what I'm talking about, but I think I'm right on this, and I don't think there is going to be any fighting. We don't feel threatened.

Anyway, after the wedding we'll leave and return to the States," said Rachel.

"Hitler has a lot of people wondering. But truthfully, I can't really argue with you. You could be absolutely right," said Russell.

"My Uncle Nathan will pick us up tomorrow."

"That's fine. Where are you staying?"

"The Hotel Bristol."

A historic luxury hotel. Vacationing in Paris. These young ladies are not only well-connected politically, but their parents must have money, he reasoned.

"The Bristol is very nice. You'll enjoy it. It was finished in 1900. Some of its interiors were designed by the noted Viennese architect Otto Wagner. The property was opened on November 19, 1901."

"Excuse me," said Katie, "but how do you know all this?"

He laughed, "I have always been drawn to old historic buildings. And there are lots of them in Warsaw."

"Maybe you should have been an architect instead of joining the diplomatic service," said Rachel.

He laughed. "Maybe so. Shall I continue?"

"By all means," said Katie.

"After Poland gained its independence in 1919, Jan Paderewski became the Prime Minister and held the first session of his government at the hotel. Paderewski and his partners sold their shares in the hotel in 1928 to a local bank, which renovated the property in 1934 with modern interiors by Antoni Jawornicki."

"Well, you certainly know your buildings," mused Rachel. They all laughed.

There was small talk the rest of the way. "Here we are," said Russell.

A bellman greeted them and took the luggage inside. They crossed the lobby to the front desk.

"Can you have dinner with us tonight?" Rachel asked.

The question caught him off guard.

"I believe I can," he stammered, blushing.

"Good. Eight o'clock in the lobby?"

"Perfect."

UNCLE NATHAN PICKED them up the next morning. "All the family is happy, particularly Hagar, that her American cousin in coming to her wedding."

"Imagine us being in Paris at this very time. I can't comprehend such luck," admitted Rachel.

"Perhaps it was meant to be."

"Perhaps it was."

"Young lady," said Nathan, speaking to Katie, "have you ever visited Poland?"

"Not hardly, sir, but I am pleased to be here and looking forward to meeting more of Rachel's family."

"Good."

"Uncle Nathan, we were so sad to hear of the passing of your beloved Sarai."

"Thank you, Rachel. It was a shock, too young. It has been hard on me—hard on all of us."

"Katie, Uncle Nathan met Aunt Sarai in Berlin. They fell in love. She had lived her entire life in Grojec and did not want to stay in Germany."

"This is true," said Nathan. "Sarai and Grojec went together. If I wanted to keep Sarai, I had to return her to Grojec."

"And you wanted to keep Sarai," said Katie.

"I wanted Sarai."

They arrived after dark in Grojec, a historic village in Oswiecim County.

Rachel and Hagar, the same age, cried and embraced at their first meeting since 1933. Many family members were gathered at Nathan's house to greet the Americans. During the meal, Rachel told them of her and Katie's stay in Paris, how she got out of Germany, of Dietrich's death, news of her parents' deaths, life in Buenos Aires, in America, and at Radcliffe. They were graciously interested in Katie as well, and she filled them in on her life. Each family member spoke—it was a lovely welcome. They talked well into the night.

47
The Wedding

SIMON POSNER WAS Rabbi Weizenbaum's assistant. He was quite taken by Katie and was more than willing to explain what was going on and what everything meant. It was a nighttime event with perfect weather.

"I love the look of everyone with their candles. It gives me a wonderful feeling," said Katie.

Posner nodded and explained, "In traditional Jewish literature, marriage is actually called *kiddushin*, which translates as sanctification or dedication. Sanctification indicates that what is happening is not just a social arrangement or contractual agreement, but a spiritual bonding and the fulfillment of a *mitzvah,* a divine precept. Dedication indicates that the couple now have an exclusive relationship, which involves total dedication of the bride and groom to each other, to the extent of them becoming, as the Kabbalists state, 'one soul in two bodies.'"

"Interesting," said Katie, with a smile.

"The very first stage of a traditional Jewish marriage is the *shidduch*, or matchmaking. This means that the process of finding a partner is not haphazard or based on purely external aspects. Rather, a close friend or relative of the young man or woman, who knows someone whom they feel may be a compatible partner, suggests that they meet. The purpose of the meeting is for the prospective bride and groom to determine if they are indeed compatible.

The meetings usually focus on discussion of issues important to marriage as well as casual conversation. The Talmud states that the couple must also be physically attractive to each other, something that can only be determined by meeting. According to Jewish law, physical contact is not allowed between a man and a woman until they are married, and they may not be alone together in a closed room or secluded area. This helps to ensure that one's choice of partner will be based on intellect and emotion as opposed to physical desire alone."

Katie, smiled, "It's quite different for us Gentiles."

Simon smiled as well. "Yes, I imagine."

"When the families have met and the young couple have decided to marry, the families usually announce the occasion with a small reception, known as a *vort*. Some families sign a contract, the *tenaim*, meaning conditions that delineates the obligations of each side regarding the wedding and a final date for the wedding. Others do this at the wedding reception an hour or so before the marriage."

"What have Hagar and Jules done?"

"They have already done it. Now, one week before the wedding the bride and groom, the *chosson* and *kallah,* stop seeing each other in order to enhance the joy of their wedding through their separation."

"Okay, the canopy, what is the significance of that?" Katie asked.

"Good question. The *chuppah,* the canopy, is a decorated piece of cloth held aloft as a symbolic home for the new couple. It is usually held outside under the stars, like we are doing tonight, as a sign of the blessing given by God to the patriarch Abraham that his children shall be as the stars of the heavens."

"Here comes the groom."

"This is exciting," said Katie, with a smile.

"The groom is accompanied by his parents and usually wears a white robe, known as a *kittel,* as Jules is doing. This symbolizes the fact that for the bride and groom, life is starting anew with a clean white slate since they are uniting to become a new entity without past sins. In fact, the bride and groom usually fast on the day of the wedding until the *chuppah*, since for them, it is like Yom Kippur, the Day of Atonement."

Musicians played as they led the groom and his parents to the canopy. Katie pointed to them with excitement. "I like the music. Is that a usual practice?"

Simon smiled, "Yes, it is."

"Look, Simon, here comes the bride to the *chuppah* with her parents."

"Yes."

Everyone gathered around the canopy. A cantor sang a selection from the "Song of Songs," and the groom prayed that his unmarried friends would find their true partners in life. Hagar circled the groom seven times with her mother and future mother-in-law while the groom continued to pray.

Simon whispered in Katie's ear, "This symbolizes the idea of the woman being a protective, surrounding light of the household, that

156

illuminates it with understanding and love from within and protects it from harm from the outside. The number seven parallels the seven days of creation and symbolizes the fact that the bride and groom are about to create their own new world together."

Katie smiled and nodded.

Under the *chuppah,* Rabbi Weizenbaum recited a blessing over wine and a blessing that praised and thanked God for giving them laws of sanctity and morality to preserve the sanctity of family life and of the Jewish people. The bride and groom then drank from the wine.

"Wine is symbolic of life," said Simon. "It begins as grape-juice, goes through fermentation, during which it is sour, but in the end, turns into a superior product that brings joy and has a wonderful taste. The full cup of wine also symbolizes the overflowing of divine blessing, as in the verse in Psalms, 'My cup runneth over.'"

Jules took a plain gold ring, placed it on Hagar's finger, and recited, "Behold, you are betrothed to me with this ring, according to the Law of Moses and Israel."

"The ring symbolizes the concept of the groom encompassing, protecting, and providing for his wife," Simon explained. "The *ketuvah* will now be read aloud by Rabbi Weizenbaum, after which it is given to the bride."

"I love your traditions, I really do," said Katie. "What's next?"

"The *sheva brachos,* or seven blessings, are recited, by the Rabbi. The blessings will be recited over a full cup of wine. The blessings begin with praising God for His creation in general and creation of the human being, and proceed with praise for the creation of the human as a two-part creature, woman and man. The blessings express the hope that the new couple will rejoice together forever as though they are the original couple, Adam and Eve in the Garden of Eden. The blessings will also include a prayer that Jerusalem will be fully rebuilt and restored with the Temple in its midst and the Jewish people within her gates."

The couple again shared in drinking the cup of wine, and the groom broke the glass by stamping on it.

"This custom dates back to Talmudic times and symbolizes the idea of our keeping Jerusalem and Israel in our minds even at times of our joy," said Simon. "Just as the Temple in Jerusalem is destroyed, so we break a utensil to show our identification with the sorrow of Jewish exile."

Then the Rabbi recited the verse, "If I forget thee, O Jerusalem, let my right hand forget its cunning: If I do not raise thee over my own joy, let my tongue cleave to the roof of my mouth."

With the breaking of the glass the band started playing and the guest broke out into dancing and cries of "Mazel tov! Mazel tov!"

"Now that the couple are married, they are accompanied to the *cheder yichud*, the room of privacy. They may now be alone in a closed room together, an intimacy reserved only for a married couple. In fact, according to many Jewish legal authorities, the very fact that they are alone together in a locked room is a requirement of the legal act of marriage," said Simon.

"What happens in that room?" Katie asked. "Do they have sex?"

Simon laughed. "No, not yet. There is food for them in there because they have been fasting all day. But we don't have to wait for them. As you can see, the guests are beginning to sit down to eat a festive meal."

"Rachel, come and join Simon and me."

The meal was preceded by ritual washing of the hands and the blessing over bread.

"That was a very moving ceremony, Rachel."

"Yes, it was. And the fact that it was my cousin made it even more meaningful."

THE BAND ANNOUNCED the arrival of the bride and groom. "For the very first time, Mr. and Mrs. Jules Weiss."

Everyone joined in dancing around the bride and groom. The dancing, in accordance with Jewish law, required a separation between men and women for reasons of modesty; hence there was a *mechitzah*, or partition, between the men and women.

"Rachel, I love the traditions except for this one. I'd like to dance with a man."

"Well, it's not like it's your last dance ever."

Katie laughed, "You're right."

"Or mine either."

The main focus of the dancing was to entertain and enhance the joy of the newlyweds. Large circles were formed around the "king and queen," and different guests performed in front of the seated couple.

"It is not unusual at all to see jugglers, fire eaters, and acrobats at a wedding," said Simon.

The meal ended with the *Birchas Hamazon,* grace after meals, and again the seven blessings were recited over wine, shared afterwards by the bride and groom.

■ ■ ■ ■ ■

THAT VERY NIGHT Adolph Hitler issued an order to the German army.

"Execute Case White." That was the invasion of Poland.

48
September 1, 1939
Escape from Poland

IT WAS VERY early in the morning. News of the German invasion spread rapidly.

"They've crossed the Czechoslovakian border," shouted Nathan, "and are headed for Krakow. We are loaded, me, Jules, and Hagar. Rachel, you and Katie bring your luggage. I can fit them on top of the car."

"Okay, but where are we going?"

"Warsaw."

The village was in a general panic. They were loading what they could on whatever means of transportation they had. They had to leave. They had to leave quickly.

THE ROADS WERE packed with refugees. There were cars, horse drawn wagons, trucks, tractors, carts, cattle, horses, and dogs. There were old people, young people, babies, and Polish soldiers on horseback.

"Such a honeymoon," Jules lamented.

· · · · ·

UNCLE NATHAN DROPPED Rachel and Katie at the American Embassy, where they were met again by Leo Russell. Uncle Meir Rosenthal had again used his substantial political influence with the Roosevelt administration to make the arrangements.

Rachel took Leo aside, "Can't you take my family?"

"No, Rachel, they are Jews. They could jeopardize everything for us and the other neutrals. I understand your concern, but I can not do it."

Rachel was distraught. She said her tearful goodbyes to her family as they continued their attempt to leave the country.

Rachel and Katie were tired, frightened, and hungry. Russell dealt with their immediate needs and arranged for them to have lunch at the embassy.

"My God, we are in the middle of a war," said Leo.

"We were strafed by German fighter planes," said Rachel, in a quiet voice.

"German bastards!" screamed Katie. "They killed a lot of people."

There was a long period of silence.

"So much for your theory about Hitler's intentions, Rachel." Russell lamented. He rubbed his temples with the fingers of both hands and stared at the dining table for a moment. He sighed, "Look, all the senior staff left for Stockholm. I drew the black bean."

"What?" Rachel asked.

"I'm in charge here now. I've got to stay here. I can't leave, so why don't you two use my apartment?"

"Okay," Rachel said.

"Mr. Russell, how do Rachel and I get out of Poland?" Katie asked. "We're scared to death."

"That's understandable," said Russell. "The plan is for you to leave with me and the embassy staff and a few other Americans who got caught in this unholy mess. The German army will have the city surrounded by the end of the week. Adolph Hitler has decreed that if the Poles don't surrender, Warsaw will be leveled." He paused, thinking. "And I believe that Kraut sonofabitch means it."

Rachel glanced at Katie and shook her head. They all looked a bit bewildered.

"The Swedish ambassador is trying to negotiate a safe conduct out of Warsaw for all neutrals. That's how we'll get out of here, I hope."

"You hope!" Rachel exclaimed.

"You're not sure?" Katie asked.

Russell sighed, frowned, and said, "I'm sure, I'm sure."

Katie looked at Rachel and thought, *Russell does not give me comfort.*

RACHEL AND KATIE took a damaged trolley to the building where Russell's apartment was located. There was rubble everywhere and the streets were a mess. He had sent along an embassy security guard, and he helped them take their luggage up two flights of stairs to the apartment. They were surprised when they opened the door.

"Dark mahogany paneling, expensive furniture, ornate chandeliers, Persian rugs, antique clocks, bookcases filled with well known editions, and impressive paintings. Nice," said Katy.

"Nice, indeed. I had no idea embassy employees lived so well," said Rachel.

They continued the apartment tour.

"Flip a coin for who gets the bathroom first," said Rachel, playfully.

Katie frowned, "No need for that. You go first."

"Are you sure?"

"Yes."

As Rachel began to take her clothes off, sirens began to wail. Bomb blasts shook the apartment, the chandelier swung perilously, parts of the ceiling fell, and dust filled the rooms. They didn't know what to do as they sat in a corner and huddled against the wall. Thankfully, there were no direct hits on the building. It seemed like an eternity, but soon the bombers were gone. They rushed to an open window and witnessed the awful sight below.

"My God," said Katie, "bomb craters, dead animals, dead people, cars and trucks destroyed, and fires raging."

Through her tears, Rachel said, "I never expected to see anything like this."

They hugged each other tight, "Neither did I," said Katie, "it's horrible!"

"I am so sorry I got you into this," said Rachel.

Katie frowned, "You couldn't know."

Soon, Leo Russell rushed through the door. "I wasn't suppose to leave the embassy, but the telephones are down and I had to know if you were alive or dead."

"We're fine," said Rachel.

"I am relieved, of course. But now we have been informed that the Russians have crossed the Polish border," said Russell, "and are marching in this direction. Things are looking grim for Warsaw."

"The Russians!" Rachel exclaimed, "Why are the Russians involved with Poland?"

"The bad news is we don't know. But the good news is that the Swedish ambassador has worked out something for the neutrals. I've got to have all my people ready to go. Okay, you're safe. I must get back, but I'll be in touch."

Rachel and Katie looked at each other, a bit relieved at Russell's news.

"I hope he's right," said Katie.

"Yeah," said Rachel.

NATHAN ROSENTHAL AND his daughter and son-in-law were waiting at a Warsaw checkpoint when the German bombers came. Their car suffered a direct hit. There was nothing left after the explosion.

49

THE NEXT DAY, it was time to leave Warsaw. Important embassy papers, cables, and correspondence had been burned. Everyone gathered on the grounds of the complex. All they could leave with was one bag per person. Embassy staffer Marvin Mark was beside himself.

"Leo, I thought we were going to be flown out of here on US Army planes. But we're not. We're going to the Germans."

"Calm down, Marvin, we'll be safe."

"My passport says Mark, but I'm from Queens and my father's name is Markowitz. You get it?"

"Marvin, you have a US passport. How will they know?"

"Easy for you to say."

Most of the embassy staff, families, and other neutrals were loaded on large trucks. The Swedish ambassador's vehicle led the convey. Leo, Rachael, Katie, and Smitty, the driver, followed in the embassy car.

As the vehicles drove away from the compound, the people were laughing, singing—happy to be leaving Poland. But the main road was cluttered with refugees, horse drawn carts and wagons, cars, trucks, and Polish soldiers coming and going to the front. Travel was hectic, but not dangerous until they reached the expansion bridge over the river. The singing and laughter changed to screams as German artillery rounds began hitting in the water close to the bridge. When a shell hit the bridge, people on foot began to scream and run and motor traffic hurried as much as possible. Polish artillery was returning fire.

The embassy convoy finally reached the point of debarkation where a "cease fire" had been established. The neutrals walked forward carrying white flags.

"I don't like this at all," said Katie, quietly.

All too soon, they reached German lines. Tanks, troops, and artillery pieces lined both sides of the road.

"The Germans are a daunting sight. I hope this safe passage is for real," Leo said. "I'm glad the ambassador is still with us."

"It is quite unnerving to see these brutal bastards up close," said Rachel.

They finally arrived at a checkpoint. Russell had furnished the Germans with a list of the neutrals and was active in helping the German soldiers at their registration tables identify the people. The ambassador stood by his side. After being checked off, soldiers helped the people load on trucks once again. But this time they were German trucks.

Marvin Mark pissed in his pants. Rachel squeezed Katie's hand.

50

September 1939
Poland to Stockholm

IT WAS A three-hour drive to where they were to be transferred to a train that would take them to Stockholm and safety. The Swedish ambassador was again at the front of the convoy followed by Russell's embassy car. But this time, they were accompanied by German soldiers on motorcycles with sidecars and machine guns.

"I find it hard to relax and feel that we are truly safe," said Russell.

It was nighttime when the trucks finally reached the train station. The vehicles stopped and backed up to the loading docks. German soldiers with machine guns stood by each of the large doors. The people were quickly hustled out of the trucks and into what seemed to be a kind of dimly lit holding area. Large red banners with black swastikas on a circular white background hung around the perimeter. Armed German soldiers faced them, which added to their overall anxiety. There were groans and murmurs. *They are going to kill us, for sure*, thought Marvin Mark.

An SS officer entered from a side door. He stared at the nervous group for a moment and then threw a switch, which lighted the area. To their astonishment, beyond the line of soldiers were long tables loaded with platters of sumptuous food—sausages, sauerkraut, roasted chicken, potatoes, fresh fruit, and loaves of good bread. Young girls dressed in peasant outfits entered the area from every door, carrying mugs of beer. As the person responsible for the safety of the group, Russell's tears were a testament to his enormous relief. Rachel and Katie hugged each other. The signs of joy were everywhere as they plunged into the food. Loudspeakers blared with festive music. They swayed, laughed, ate, and drank their fill. Even some of the German soldiers joined in.

"I don't know what to make of this," said Russell." I hope it's not the prisoner's last meal."

Rachel elbowed him. "Don't talk like that."

After the meal, the people were moved to the boarding area. Their jubilance continued. "We'll soon be on that train and on our way out of Poland," said Rachel.

"And not a moment too soon," echoed Katie.

Their mood changed abruptly when an SS officer and some Gestapo men confronted them. Captain Reinhardt demanded, "Who is in charge here!"

"I am," said Leo Russell. "I'm a diplomatic officer from the American embassy in Warsaw. These people are neutrals. The Swedish ambassador has arranged, through your government, for them to leave the country."

Reinhardt stared at Russell and then his steely eyes searched the crowd. "How many Jews do you have?"

Marvin Mark turned white.

Russell turned red, "I don't know. We don't care about people's religion. It's not noted in any of our records."

"But you do have Jews?"

"Even if we did, I would not tell you."

Reinhardt turned red, "Who are the Jews?"

"I honestly don't know if we have any Jews."

Reinhardt pressed on, "My government's policy is to maintain separate records for Jews."

"As I said, I just do not know."

Reinhardt put his hands on his hips, "I am instructed to separate out the Jews. Everyone will form two lines, Jews in one line and all others in another." The Jews in the area, who were not in Russell's group, complied with Reinhardt's demand. Russell shook his head at his group. Everyone stood fast.

Reinhardt stood nose to nose with Russell and screamed, "You are in the custody of the German army, in a combat zone, under strict martial law. Do you understand?"

Russell did not back down. He defiantly answered Reinhardt, "Then my answer is that we are all Jews."

The silence in the group was shattered when a frightened woman shouted, "I'm not a Jew and I'm not going to be classified as one!"

"Me neither," said a man.

Reinhardt smiled as he approached the blond woman. Leaning in close he asked, "Who are you and where are you from?"

The woman swallowed hard but got it out, "I'm Clara Kennedy, and I'm an Irish Catholic from New York City."

Reinhardt exhibited a sinister smile, "Point out all the Jews in your group."

She gulped, but called up a modicum of courage, "I don't know of any."

Reinhardt turned red and engaged the man. "What is your name?"

"Mike Stanley from Ashville, North Carolina."

"Well Mr. Mike Stanley, did you know that your group will not be allowed to board the train until I carry out my orders."

"I sure would like to cooperate with you, but as far as I know, there are no Jews in our group."

Russell had had enough. He confronted Reinhardt. "If this continues, your government will receive an official protest from the United States of America. And may I remind you that we are a neutral country."

Reinhardt smiled, which irritated Russell. "There is no reason for a protest. The officials from other governments are cooperating with our policy."

"That does not include the United States!" Russell retorted.

Marvin Mark was on the front row. Reinhardt approached, stood in front of him, and stared at him. Mark looked nervous. "And what is your name, little man, and where are you from?"

Mark was seemingly paralyzed for a moment. "I'm Marvin Mark, and I'm from Minnesota."

The familiar sinister smile came over Reinhardt's face. Before he could continue his questioning, a superior officer approached and said, "Reinhardt, what is the delay?"

"I'm trying to identify the Jews in this group."

"They are Americans from the embassy, they're neutrals. You're wasting time, Reinhardt, now get on with this. Let these people board the train."

Reinhardt turned red, clicked his heals, and saluted smartly. Then he walked away.

"All right," said Russell, "we can board now. Make sure you don't leave anything on the landing."

"I wet my panties," said Rachel. "After all, I am Jewish."

"So did I," said Katie, "and I'm not."

They smiled, but there was no laughter.

51

September 1939
Life after Poland

"THE EXPERIENCE IN Poland, was unnerving, to say the least," said Katie. "Frankly, I was scared to death. I'm so glad to be here in Stockholm, and I can't wait to get back to Boston."

"And marry Paul Adams."

"Yes, the wedding is planned for December."

"Well, that's wonderful. I hope you'll be happy, I really do."

"Brick is in love with you."

"He never told me."

"He told his parents. He was serious about asking you to marry him."

"And what did mommy and daddy say?" Rachel asked, sarcastically.

"When he told them you were Jewish, his father told him he'd be on his own. They would have nothing more to do with him, and he could forget the family business or any inheritance"

"How do you know that?"

"Paul told me, but I didn't see any reason to tell you at the time."

"And he caved, of course."

"Of course."

"It doesn't matter. I'm not in love with him, and I would have never considered marrying him. Look, in an all-girl school like Radcliffe, it hard to meet boys. Brick is a nice boy and I enjoyed dating him. He was there, he was around, and he wanted to date me, you know what I mean."

"Yeah, I do. Will you be my maid of honor?"

"I can't, Katie. I'm not going back," said Rachel, with resolve.

Katie was stunned. "You can't be serious, Rachel."

Rachel took her time responding. "My father was a wise man. When most Germans were caught up in the Hitler euphoria, my father was not deceived. He saw where Germany was headed, and he wanted no part of it. His first priority was to get his children out. Dietrich and I didn't understand the danger at the time. We did what we were told.

Father was to liquidate his assets, and then he and mother were to join us in Buenos Aires."

Tears came to her eyes. Her voice cracked. "My father and mother never left Germany. I'll always believe those Nazi bastards killed them."

"Oh, Rachel, I know. I am so sad about that."

There were no words between them for what seemed like an eternity. "After Poland, I can't go back to America or Buenos Aries and pretend life is just the same."

"What will you do?"

"I love America, but they are sitting on the sidelines, a neutral. England has declared war on Germany. I'm going to London."

"And what do you expect to do?"

"I don't know. I might try for a position at the foreign office, parliament, the RAF—I don't really know. But I'm going to do something to help the war effort."

Tears were streaming down the faces of both young women. "God bless you and keep you, Rachel."

PART SIX

FOR KING AND COUNTRY
1942

52
The Year 1942

"OKAY, BOYS, WE'RE coming into enemy territory, so call out those bandits as soon as you see them," said Captain Brick Hansford, the commander of the B-17, *Rachel*.

"Oh, crap, they're here," said Gifford. "Bandits at one o'clock."

"Hold your fire, boys, until they're in range. Don't waste ammunition," said Hansford.

"Two 190s at twelve o'clock high!" Carter yelled.

"Three fighters at nine o'clock coming around! Keep your eyes on 'em, Tony."

"Top turret at eleven o'clock!" shouted Hansford.

"Got him in my sights, Skipper. I got him, I got him!" screamed Gifford.

"Bogey at four o'clock, you see him?"

"Two more at 12 o'clock. Damn, they love to come at us head on," said Bud Carter, co-pilot of the *Rachel*. "It sure would be nice if we had some 50s on each side or just under the nose that we could fire by remote control from up here."

"You're dead on about that, Bud. We need to mention it at debriefing. Help me remember," said Hansford.

"Look at that sucker come apart," said Carter, as a Messerschmitt-109 fighter plane exploded outside his window. "Yee-ha! *Mom's Apple Pie* actually got that bandit. Can you believe it?"

"It's beginner's luck, but I hope they keep it up," said Hansford.

"My God, they're like fireflies," said Carter, observing the German fighters coming in from every direction.

"I know what you mean. And it seems like every one of our positions is firing," said Hansford.

"That's because they are," said Carter.

Looking out his window, Carter observed, "*Monkey Business* is on fire. Why don't they get out?"

Hansford took a look, frowned, and sighed, "I don't know, but they better..." At that moment, Brick and Bud were horrified as *Monkey Business* exploded before their reluctant eyes.

During this mission the 91st suffered the loss of 12 ships, 120 young men. I'm just glad it wasn't us, thought Brick. *Daylight bombing is going to kill a lot of brave young men before this war is over.*

53

"RACHEL, THE AMERICANS are having a dance at their air base in Bassingbourn, Saturday night," said Scarlett. "I'm dating a handsome young pilot from that base and I'm going. Why don't you go with me?"

"Oh, I don't know."

"Come on Rachel, it'll be fun. You never go anywhere or do anything."

Rachel looked at her, frowned, but didn't respond.

"I think my boyfriend Bud can get his buddy to be your date."

"I haven't had a blind date since I was at Radcliffe."

"Will you do it? Please? We'll have fun."

"Okay, find out if Bud's friend is available and willing. Then let me know."

· · · · ·

SCARLETT WAS EXCITED. "I talked to Bud and his friend is available. So you'll go?"

"Yes, I'll go. May I know the fellow's name?"

"It's Brickley Hansford. He goes by Brick, and he's a captain and the aircraft commander. Bud's his co-pilot."

Rachel looked like she had seen a ghost. "Rachel, what's wrong?"

Rachel frowned, bit her lip, and shook her head back and forth. "Rachel!"

"I dated Brick Hansford when I was in college. He was in love with me, but when he told his parents, they threatened to disown him."

"Why?" Scarlett exclaimed.

"Because I'm Jewish."

"Oh, no, are you kidding?"

"I'm not kidding. My friend Katie told me."

"Does that mean you won't go?"

"No," she replied, with a sinister smile. "This should be interesting."

"Rachel?"

"He's handsome and a nice boy. We had some great times. But I wouldn't have married him in any event. I wasn't in love with him. But I will look forward to the dance. I haven't seen him since May of 1939."

She thought a minute. "I've got an idea. Tell him the girl's name is Margie McMillan. When we arrive we'll say Margie was ill, and I volunteered to come in her place."

Scarlett giggled, "I like it. This should be interesting."

54

"HERE THEY COME," an anxious member of the ground crew shouted. All eyes turned toward the skies and everyone started counting. The brass in the tower raised their binoculars to get a better look. *Rachel* had been badly shot up on a previous mission and the ground crew was finishing up repairs. She had not been to Lorient, France to hit the submarine pens, but she would fly tomorrow if there was a mission. Today the crew was relaxing and playing touch football when the squadron returned.

"Eighteen," some one shouted.

"Nineteen, and there's twenty," said another man. One by one the Fortresses were coming home, and then they stopped.

"Where's *Lucky Lady*?" their crew chief asked, apprehension in his tone. Everyone was frantically searching the sky when she was finally sighted as she barely cleared the trees at the end of the runway. Everyone saw it, but nobody said a word. Finally, Destafano blurted out the obvious, "Oh no! She's only got one landing gear down."

Everyone with a view of the field was transfixed on the crippled B-17, limping in on two engines, badly ravaged from flak. Finally, she touched down and began the long skid. Smoke was pouring out everywhere.

"Get out of there, you guys," screamed Thibodeaux, fire engines screaming to others on the base that the boys were home and some of them were in trouble. As the ambulances and emergency vehicles frantically raced toward the cripple, flames engulfed the entire fuselage and a deafening roar accompanied the explosion. Luck had run out for the *Lady.* The fire engines poured water on to the raging fire, but the war was over for the ten brave crewmen. They had flown the mission, done their jobs, and paid the ultimate price.

MEN IN COMBAT learn to deal with tragedy, the loss of life, the loss of buddies, and get on with the work at hand. Any kind of pleasurable experience that took their minds off combat was always welcomed. Flight crews were issued 48 to 72 hour passes only twice a month due to the uncertainty of when missions would be ordered from Division, which made it difficult to let men leave their duty stations. To alleviate the situation, military bands would play for dances on base, and British women were bussed in to dance with the boys.

"Did you remember about tonight?" Carter asked.

"The dance. Of course I remember. What exactly do you mean?" Brick inquired.

"Did you hear that tonight's USO show features Artie Shaw and his big band with that pretty blond Frances Langford doing the vocals."

"I had not heard that. Wow! I hope my blind date can dance."

"I don't think Scarlett would pick someone who couldn't dance. Anyway, I hear she's good looking, so there's that."

"This should be interesting, and it's just one night in my life."

"I love your attitude, Skipper," he joked.

DANCING TO AMERICAN music, celebrities from the States, drinking, and enjoying the company of women was a welcomed event for the men who took to the hostile skies over Europe.

55

THE DANCE WAS held in a large hanger, with a B-17 directly behind the bandstand. A number of the men had girlfriends who came, but many of the British girls who were bussed in for the dance were unattached.

"I need to go to the head," said Thibodaux.

"I'm right behind you," said Gifford.

"You know something, Giff," said Thibodaux, "these limey girls like American music, particularly the jitter-bug. You know what I mean?"

"I do, and they love to dance with us uninhibited young and dashing captains of the clouds," said Gifford.

"You're mighty right about that, Giff. With so many of their boys away in other theaters of war—I mean ..."

"They definitely find us intriguing. They love to date the Yanks," said Gifford.

"I feel like a fox in a chicken coop," said Thibodaux. They both laughed wildly.

BRICK HANSFORD AND Bud Carter were waiting by the hanger entrance for the girls to arrive.

"Here's another bus," said Bud, excitedly.

Brick lit a cigarette, "Maybe this will be the one."

As the girls came off the bus, some were collected by waiting boyfriends while others hurried to the hanger, excited to hookup with a dashing Yank.

"There they are," said Bud. "Let's go meet them."

Oh, my soul, it can't be, but it is. Rachel Rosenthal.

"Captain Hansford, this is Rachel Rosenthal," said Scarlett.

Tears were running down his face as he took both her hands.

"Margie McMillan couldn't make it so you're stuck with me."

He hugged her tight as Bud looked bewildered.

"Let's walk, Bud," said Scarlett, "they'll catch up." On the way to the hanger, Scarlett filled in the blanks for Bud.

Brick whispered in her ear, "Not a day of my life has gone by that I didn't think of you."

Tears were in her eyes now as they kissed passionately. "You didn't contact Katie or any of us. We assumed you were here, but that's all we knew. How long has it been?"

He hesitated but a moment, "About three years, I guess?"

She smiled and nodded.

Bud and Scarlett were waiting at the hanger door having a smoke. "Are they coming?" Bud asked, impatiently.

"Bud—they haven't seen each other in years. We can give them a few minutes together to reconnect."

"Okay, okay."

"You're not a college girl any longer. You're a woman now, and more beautiful than ever."

"And you're no college boy. Just look at you, a captain and an aircraft commander—more handsome than ever. Maybe I should also add dashing."

They kissed again, tears in their eyes.

"Shall we go in?" Brick suggested.

She smiled, "Sure."

"Scarlett filled me in," said Bud, "this is gonna be great."

"Lieutenant, it's your job to find us a table."

"Yes, sir. Wait with the girls and I'll be right back."

■ ■ ■ ■ ■

BRICK TOOK RACHEL in his arms, and they smoothly glided along the dance floor.

"You're still a great dancer, Brick."

"You remembered."

"Sure I did, silly."

They continued to dance, and smile, and laugh.

"When do you fly again?"

"It will probably be tomorrow morning."

"Do you know where you're going?"

"I couldn't tell you if I did—but I don't, not a clue. We never know until the briefing. And then we go directly to the flight line, climb in our ships, and fly."

"Oh, Brick, I know. Your losses are enormous."

"How do you know that?"

"I'm sorry, but I can't tell you. I can't tell you where I work or what I do."

Brick frowned. He was annoyed and thoroughly confused.

• • • • •

RACHEL WORKED AT Bletchley Park, England's code-breaking centre, in Buckinghamshire. The secret organization had a cast of 12,000, ranging from mathematicians to Egyptologists. They were a bit different. Dillwyn Knox, a Cambridge classical papyrus expert, worked in his pajamas, while Alan Turing, the pioneer of the computer age, liked to take his cat on walks. When Churchill, an avid supporter, visited, he said to the head of MI6, "When I told you to leave no stone unturned, recruiting for this place, I didn't expect you to take me literally."

Bletchley women, who outnumbered the men by four to one, included WRENS, WAAFs, linguists, a handful of code breakers, and a smattering of dutiful debutantes. Sir Henry Bettencourt grunted and laid down Rachel's resume, "My dear, you graduated from an elite college in the colonies, speak five languages, escaped Nazi Germany, and survived the invasion of Poland. We are delighted to have you in England and we'd like to have you join us as a linguist. If you accept our offer, you cannot tell anyone where you work or what we do. Do you understand? Can we count on you?"

"Indeed you can, Sir. Henry."

"Jolly good."

"Can you start tomorrow morning?"

"I can, Sir Henry."

• • • • •

BRICK SIGHED, "I only have to survive twenty-five missions. But I try not to think about it."

Brick had a good voice and he had a habit of singing softly in the ear of the women he danced with. He sang along with Frances Langford, *"I'll be seeing you, in all the old familiar places, that this heart of mine embraces, all day through."*

Rachel squeezed the back of his neck and kissed him tenderly.

"I think you're happy to see the ole Harvard quarterback."

"Yes. I must admit I am."

"Good," he smiled. "That song is a good omen, do you get it?"

"I don't know, I ..."

"The lyric, I'll be seeing you," he pulled back, smiled and looked her in the eye. "Hey, I'm indestructible! Nothing's going to happen to me. I'll be seeing you, just as the song says."

His quiet confidence and easy manner had a calming affect on Rachel.

The truth is that unless you are in the airplane, Brick thought, *you cannot possibly comprehend the danger or the sheer terror that grips the crews as they struggle to fend off enemy fighters with bullets tearing into the airplane. When we're on our bombing runs, we must hold altitude and course, purposely flying directly into blankets of black metal flak that we can actually see directly ahead of us before it tears jagged holes in the fuselage of our ships. All through the formations, our friends are blowing up, spinning out of control, and going down in flames. Sometimes we see parachutes and sometimes we don't. No, you couldn't possibly know without actually being there.*

In most cases the boys were able to present a calm and unassuming demeanor. Most of them did not outwardly exhibit the stress and fear that they felt.

Brick perspired heavily and at the end of the tune, it was time to sit for a few minutes, cool down, and take a break. "I'll be right back. We're running on empty and we need fresh drinks," he said.

"Where are Scarlett and Bud?"

"I don't know. I don't see them."

Before he left the table, he bent down and kissed her soft lips tenderly.

"Listen, don't let these flyboys flirt with you while I'm gone."

She laughed, "I'll try to save your seat."

He laughed.

FRANK MCGUIRE FROM Tennessee, *Rachel's* ball turret gunner, was talking to a "tomato" named Marsha. She was a cute blond, short, with blue eyes, and a nice figure. McGuire, who fancied himself a ladies' man, was feeding her a line. It was what he called his pity approach. "We're flying tomorrow. My life could be snuffed out in an instant. I volunteered for all this; I thought it would be fun. Well, those other people shoot at us, they're trying to kill us, and it's no fun at all.

"When I think that I might never see the stars again, or a sunset, or listen to good music, or dance the jitter-bug, or be with a beautiful dish like you, I get depressed," he feigned.

Marsha stared at him, puffing away on one of the Camel cigarettes from the pack he had given her. Her eyes narrowed; she wasn't buying it.

"I'm sorry, you need a drink. I need a drink. I'll be right back," said McGuire, off for more booze and to rethink his approach. On the way to the bar, he bumped into George Gifford, *Rachel's* top turret gunner. "Hey Giff, you see that blond I was talking to?" he asked.

Looking in that direction, he replied, "Yeah, what about her?"

"She loves me, she's crazy about me, you know what I mean? She's gonna jump me any minute now," McGuire boasted.

Gifford laughed, "Dream on, Frankie boy, dream on."

McGuire was short but well built for his size, with blue eyes, a pug nose, and curly brown hair. He had always had good luck with the ladies.

ITALIAN TONY DESTAFANO, the waist gunner from Brooklyn, had a short fuse and was not a man to be trifled with. Built low to the ground, he was a powerfully built fellow with a barrel chest and massive arms and legs. Some of his buddies thought he looked somewhat like a gorilla, but they weren't about to say so to his face. He had picked out a well-endowed brunette named Maude, from North Pickenham.

I think he's cute, she thought. They were having a beer while Tony was dreaming of home.

"Honey, there's no place like New York City. I mean, we got great food, Broadway, major league baseball, professional football, the Rockettes, the Empire State Building—it's swell, you know what I mean?"

"No, I don't, but I'd sure like to see it someday."

"I hope you can, baby."

"But London is quite nice as well, don't you think?"

"Yeah, it ain't bad, but it ain't New York," said Tony. He sighed, starring into space.

GEORGE GIFFORD, THE well-built red-headed former running back from the University of Pittsburg, was doing a single, working alone, working the house, dancing with every girl who would oblige him. *I'm another Fred Astaire,* he said to himself with a laugh, *I want to give all the girls a chance to dance with a master.*

56

"YOU EVER FEEL like your number is up?" asked Lt. Clark Clifford, *Rachel's* nervous navigator from Durango, Colorado. He was a lean but well-developed athletic looking man, expert skier, with a blond crew cut and an engaging smile.

"No, Clark, I never do. I expect to make it," said Lt. Wilson Wyman, *Rachel's* steady bombardier.

Clifford shook his head and threw down a shot of whisky.

"Clark, get a hold of yourself, will you!" said Wilson impatiently. "Let's get a couple of girls and dance. Besides, this bar is like bumper cars. I'm sick of being knocked around."

"What do you think is going on out there at the dance floor?"said Clifford.

"At least I'll be looking at a babe and not your ugly puss," said Wyman. "You're depressing me."

As Wyman turned away, Clifford grabbed his arm, "Seriously, tell me the truth, aren't you ever scared? Don't you wonder what's going to happen to us, how it's all going to turn out?"

Wyman was a fellow of medium build, a rather pleasant looking young man with nice features except that one of his ears was flat against his head while the other one stuck out. That resulted in an occasional double take. He put his hands on his hips in disgust. "I don't wonder and I don't know. Do I look like Nostradamus? Listen, Clark, you've handled things fine up until now. What the hell's got into you?" Before Clifford could respond, Wyman admonished him, "Nine guys are depending on you to get them to the target and back home. Snap out of it."

GLENN GREGORY was the other waist gunner on the *Rachel,* from Flagstaff, Arizona. The skinny kid with wavy brown hair, green eyes and a horse-laugh, was sitting with a red-headed chic named Maureen. She was born in Scotland but had moved to London to help in the war effort. She was a hostess in a canteen for service men. "You've never had a hamburger? It's my favorite food in the whole world."

"I don't know what that is," Maureen confessed.

"Well, it's made with a patty of ground meat."

"I don't know when I've had meat," she confessed, with a sigh.

"I go to this place back home in Arizona. A man and his wife own it and they specialize in hamburgers. It's funny because they don't have any ham in them. I don't know why they call them hamburgers. Anyway, the owner uses fresh ground chuck, real lean. He mixes in Worcestershire sauce, garlic, a little thyme, salt and pepper, and then he hand molds the meat into individual patties. Then he pops the patty on a hot griddle."

"Glenn, you're making me hungry," said Maureen with a grin.

"I don't like my meat cooked to death because it loses its flavor, so I tell them not to overcook it. Now, they put both sides of the bun on the griddle so the bread gets hot and it soaks up the meat grease, which adds a nice touch. Then you tell them how you want it. I mean, you can have onions, lettuce, tomatoes, pickles, mayonnaise or mustard. It tastes soooooo good. Maureen, I couldn't begin to make you understand."

"Well, you've done a pretty good job of it."

"Then you add fried potatoes and chocolate malt and, brother, you're in heaven," he said with a sigh.

"Quit it, Glenn. You're driving me crazy," said a frustrated Maureen.

"I'm sorry. After the war, I want to open a chain of hamburger places. We're not gonna have a big menu, we'll keep it simple. We're going to specialize in burgers; hamburgers and cheeseburgers, with fries or hash brown potatoes, malts and pop, icebox pie and coffee. That will be it. But what we do, we'll do it well. I thought I'd call it Burger Heaven. And I want all my places to look the same and have the same menu."

"That sounds very nice, Glenn. But let's dance. No more talk about food," Maureen said, frustrated.

BRICK WAS AT the bar when First Lieutenant Thomas engaged him in conversation. Thomas was the new skipper of *Gone Fishing,* a B-17 and a crew that had not yet seen combat. They would get their baptism of fire on the next mission. "What's it like, Captain, to command a B-17?" Thomas asked.

"Well, first of all, you have nine men who are depending on you. Personally, when we're up there, I feel responsible for them. I remind them to pay attention, put on their oxygen masks, call out the enemy fighters, wear their flak helmets, not touch metal with their bare hands … all that stuff. It's not enough that the United States Army Air Corps expects me to reach the target and bomb it, those nine men expect me to get them back alive. So what's it like? It's one hell of a lot of responsibility!"

"Do you get scared?" asked Thomas.

Brick sighed, stared at him for a few seconds, frowned, growled, and said, "Oh, for God's sake, Lieutenant, of course I get scared. Anyone who tells you different is a liar and an idiot!"

Thomas looked confused, not a hint of confidence was evident.

"Look, Thomas, just fly the missions and rely on your training and common sense."

Hansford patted Thomas on the shoulder. "You'll be fine."

Thomas forced a smile, "Yeah, sure."

Brick picked up two scotch and waters and returned to the table where Rachel was waiting.

"You were gone so long," she lamented.

Brick smiled and kissed her. "Well, look, this guy at the bar…"

"Never mind."

BUD CARTER WAS an excellent dancer and Scarlett loved dancing with him. On the way back to the table, Scarlett squeezed his hand and looked longingly into his eyes. "I think I'm falling in love with you," she confessed.

He frowned, "Oh Scarlett, Scarlett." He kissed her tenderly.

"You two have not missed a dance," Rachel commented.

"That's right," said Brick. "I hope your toes are okay."

Scarlett laughed, "Bud's a good dancer. My toes are fine."

They all laughed.

"I'm dry," said Bud. "Come on Brick, let's get some drinks."

He looked at Rachel. He had just gotten back.

She smiled, "Go ahead, Brick."

PAUL THIBODEAUX from New Orleans had a great voice and could play a mean piano. Women were definitely attracted to the young Cajun with the coal-black hair and olive complexion, who resembled the actor Tyrone Power. The radio man on the *Rachel,* he was engaged in conversation with his counterpart from *Gone Fishing.*

"We've done some practice runs, but I don't think anyone on the crew, and that includes the pilot and co-pilot, feels comfortable or confident," Bob Simpson confessed.

"Incidentally, were you an athlete?" Paul asked, changing the subject.

"Well, yeah, actually I was. But what prompted you to ask?"

"Well, you look like a jock."

"I played quarterback at Villanova," he revealed.

"No kidding?" said Paul.

"No kidding. Why is that so surprising?" said Simpson.

"Because I played quarterback at Tulane," he said.

"Well, to use an old cliché, it is a small world," said Simpson.

"How did you feel before you went in and took that first snap?" Paul asked.

"Nervous, very nervous."

"How did you feel after the first play?"

"The butterflies left and I was fine."

"Well, that's how it will be tomorrow. You'll all feel a bit queasy during the briefing and until you get in the air. But I suspect once you're up there, you'll all be fine," Paul predicted with a smile. "You're busy doing your job. You won't have time to think about anything else."

Simpson sighed, but said no more.

JOE MORGAN, *RACHEL'S* tail gunner, had latched onto a tall slender brunette named Vanessa. He was long and lean himself and they made a good pair. With so many men away, she was working as a conductor on a double-decker bus. Morgan was from the small town of Gruene, home of the oldest dancehall in Texas.

"You talk funny," she said, "Not like the other boys."

"I'm from Texas and I guess we talk different from everybody in the whole world, and we're damn proud of it. But you're a fine one to talk. You Brits don't really speak English. It's awful hard to make out what you mean."

"Enough about our language difficulties, luv, we don't have any problem communicating when we dance."

190

"That's for sure, that's for dang sure."

She laughed as she pulled him toward the dance floor.

"IT'S BEEN A wonderful evening," said Rachel. "I haven't been going out much, hardly at all. Scarlett insisted and then when I found out it was you, I had to come."

"There is no one here in England?"

"No one at all."

"Now there is?"

"Now there is, Brick."

I really can't believe how good it is to see Brick and how tender I feel toward him.

He took her in his arms and kissed her tenderly.

As the band played the final number, hundreds of red, white and blue balloons were released from nets in the ceiling of the hanger, much to the delight of the boys and girls.

PART SEVEN

OBJECTIVE OF ALLIED AIR POWER

1943

57

January 23, 1943

AT THE CASABLANCA Conference, the objective of the strategic air forces was established as the "destruction and dislocation of the Germany military, industrial, and economic system, as well as the undermining of the morale of the German people to the point where their capacity for armed resistance is fatally weakened."

. . . . .

"ATTENTION!" WAS CALLED, as Col. Caldwell, the Squadron Commander, entered the room followed by the Air Executive, Major Cliff Harper. The curtain was pulled back, revealing the coast of France.

"Well, gentlemen, we're going to hit the submarine pens at Lorient. You went to St. Nazaire on the first, and I'm pretty sure that bomber command is going to continue to schedule these raids. As you know, U-boats are playing hell with Atlantic shipping, vital to sustaining the war effort here in Europe, not to mention everything in and around the Channel. These pens are constructed of thick concrete and are highly resistant to bomb damage. Many of the raids on these pens have been scrubbed due to bad weather; the raids we did conduct were often inaccurate because of poor visibility over the target. I have a farm boy's mentality. I don't like to plow the same rows over and over—and I don't like losing airplanes and fine men on failed opportunities. So when conditions are favorable, as they are today, we've got to make our strikes count." He strolled up and down with his arms behind his back and then continued.

"Bomber command has given us a new strategy, a new technique in the hopes of improving our accuracy. It's called bombing-on-the-leader. Instead of each plane dropping its bombs individually, all bombardiers will release their bombs when they see the bombs leave the bay of the lead aircraft. Command reasons that this will result in better accuracy because the most skilled bombardiers are in the lead ships. Captain Hansford, *Rachel* will have the lead for this mission. Lt. Wyman, you're the key man today. This will be a great help to some of you mullets—Lowenstein—who can't hit a football field, much less a pickle barrel." There was laughter. "Just kidding, Lowenstein, but some of you bombardiers have been off the mark.

"Now, another thing I want to emphasize is your formations. Keep them tight. Keep those wing tips close. When you do, you increase your defensive capabilities and maximize your group firepower. You also limit the ability of the enemy to dive through your formations, which will severely limit their striking power.

"Okay, gentlemen, I'm going to turn the briefing over to Major Harper to give you the details. Good luck today, men."

■ ■ ■ ■ ■

ON FEBRUARY 14, they hit the marshalling yards at Hamm, Germany; on February 16, 1943, the U-boat pens again at St. Nazaire; and the sea port at Wilhelmshaven on February 22, 1943.

58

"IT SEEMS LIKE forever since we've had a pass, time away from missions—and dying," said Brick.

"I can appreciate what you say. Hopefully, I can help." said Rachel, tenderly tugging his arm.

"This Dorchester is quite a hotel, isn't it?"

"It's one of the most prestigious hotels in the world."

"And one of the most expensive too, I'll bet. How can you afford to stay here?"

"The work I do is essential to the war effort. When the Battle of Britain started in July 1940, my superiors got me a room here. There is a cadre of us."

Brick frowned, "I don't understand."

She smiled, "The strength of the hotel's construction makes it one of London's safest buildings. Many foreign officials, political and military luminaries have taken up residence here, not to mention people like me."

"Are you telling me the British government pays the tab?"

"That's right."

He laughed, "That's a hell of a deal."

"Yeah, it is."

"But Rachel, the Battle of Britain ended in the Fall of 1940. But you're still here."

"And so are the others. I guess they were too embarrassed to ask us to leave. And the Germans still bomb."

"That's true."

"But, our team is really critical to the war effort. They want us safe."

Brick knew not to ask about her work.

"It has quite a history. It opened in April 1931. I have to admit that the ole girl has been closely associated with the rich and famous. During the 1930s it became known as a haunt of numerous writers and artists such as poet Cecil Day-Lewis, novelist Somerset Maugham, and the painter Sir Alfred Munnings."

"So ole Al hung out here, did he?"

She laughed, "Are you interested in what I'm telling you?" she asked with a laugh.

He laughed as well, "Oh, yes, darling, I'm hanging on every word."

"Shall I continue?"

"By all means."

"Very well. It has hosted prestigious literary gatherings, notably the Foyles Literary Luncheons, an event the hotel still hosts today. The hotel has 250 rooms and 49 suites. Some British cabinet members live here as well as displaced European royalty, generals, and admirals from all over the world. General Eisenhower had a suite here."

"Incidentally, how do you know these things?" he asked, his exasperation on display.

She smiled and touched his arm. "You know I can't tell you."

He sighed, "Let's eat."

"All right."

Brick got a waiter's attention and they ordered champagne, strawberries, oysters, and smoked salmon. The hotel had it all.

In no time at all, they were tipping their glasses and sipping the bubbly.

"The orchestra is marvelous. Dance with me, darling," said Rachel.

59

HANSFORD AND CARTER were in their quarters, taking it easy.

"Brick, what do we know about Colonel Birdwell and Major Ellis? They seem okay, but I was just wondering about their background."

"I checked them out—they've paid their dues."

"Then enlighten me."

"They both graduated from West Point the same year and have served together at several places. I think they're both competent, but in those situations, one usually has a bit of an edge over the other."

"Birdwell."

"Exactly."

"Anyway, they were together at Mitchell Field, New York, in the Fifth Aero Squadron. They were pilot and co-pilot on one of the planes of the Pan American Flight which made a goodwill trip around South America. They were together at Bolling Field, Washington, D.C., and at March Field, California, where they were in the 34th Pursuit Squadron."

"I get the picture," said Bud.

"Yeah, they're flyers. They're the real deal and they flew missions over here before we arrived."

"It's funny to see them together. You know, Birdwell is tall and Ellis is short," observed Bud.

"How about Gregory Peck and James Cagney?"

Bud laughed, "Brick, you nailed 'em."

THE LAST MISSION in February was a strike on the U-boat pens at Brest, France.

· · · · ·

ON MARCH 2, the Group was alerted for a mission to attack the marshalling yards in the French city of Rennes, a key railway center whose lines fed the principal German submarine bases in the Brest Peninsula. All preliminary steps necessary for this mission were completed before daybreak, and the combat crews were awakened just before 0500 hours. After a hurried breakfast, briefing began at 0545, and at 0730 hours, the men began to taxi the aircraft towards the end of the runway for a 0800 takeoff. Just before the last of the aircraft had positioned themselves, word was received from Wing Headquarters that the mission had been scrubbed. No reason was given.

Little effort was made to work on the ground training schedule and a majority of the combat crews were permitted to return to their quarters and catch up on the sleep they had lost during the early morning.

On his way to his own quarters, Bud dropped in on his friend Clark Clifford. "I thought you'd be in the sack already," said Clark.

"I'm headed that way, but I thought I'd drop by and see you first and give Brick a chance to fall asleep."

"Speaking of roommates, where is Wyman?"

"Oh, he'll be along. Listen, Bud, how are you and Scarlett getting on?"

"We are getting along beautifully. I think she's a keeper."

"You never said how you all met."

"I didn't. Well, it happened by the hospital as she was coming down the steps to the street."

"So, it was quite by accident."

"Yes, it was. I was the big man on campus in high school and college, if I do say so myself. I was a jock and had no trouble attracting girls. I had dated lots of 'em. But there was never anyone special. That's why I was so surprised when I saw Scarlett. Attraction is a crazy thing. It's often unexplainable. I say that because I'm not sure exactly what it was, but she nailed me in my tracks."

"I know what you mean about attraction," said Clifford. "It was that way with me and Kathy."

Bud walked over to the window sill where Clifford proudly displayed a picture of his wife and his little girls, Suzi and Stella. He picked up the frame and smiled at the sight of such a beautiful family. "How old are the kids?"

"Suzi is four and Stella is two."

"They're swell looking kids and Kathy is so pretty. You're a lucky man, Clark."

He took the frame from Bud, looked at their faces and sighed, "Yes, I am a lucky man. I just pray I'll make it back."

"Piece of cake, Clark, we're all gonna make it. Hey, the *Rachel* is a lucky ship."

"I hope you're right."

"Tell me, Clark, how does it feel to have a wife and two kids, the responsibility and all?" Bud inquired.

"I kind of like it in a strange sort of way." He smiled as he thought about being home with his family again. "I've just got to make it, Bud. I can't leave Kathy alone to raise those little girls."

Bud patted him on the shoulder, "We'll get our 25 and all go home heroes."

"I don't care about medals and heroics. Brick Hansford can have all that. I just want to finish my part of this war and go home to Durango, love Kathy, and teach my kids to ski."

"Sounds like a plan to me." Bud looked at his watch. "Gotta run, Clark, catch you later."

"Yeah, see you Bud."

60

BY THE TIME Bud reached his own quarters, Hansford was fast asleep—dead to the world.

Bud lit a cigarette and lay back on his pillow. He should have been sleepy, but his mind was wandering and his thoughts turned to that first meeting with Scarlett. His conversation with Clifford was still on his mind. He remembered it well, the circumstances, the situation, the conversation, everything.

I watched her all the way down the steps, my heart beating faster with every step. Wow, this is one great looking girl and so cute in her nurse's uniform. She stopped at the street and started to rummage through her purse. When she pulled out the cigarette, I had my opening. I drew my Zippo with the bravado of Douglas Fairbanks drawing his sword and presented myself with my tiny flame at just the moment when she needed it. She was a bit startled, glanced at me briefly, and then lit up. She took a long and satisfying drag, exhaled slowly, and asked me where I came from. I told her I was just walking by and saw her.

Soon we were at Queen Ann's Tea Room. Inside it was quaint with paneled walls with lamps on the wall above the side tables for two. In fact, most of the tables seemed to be for two. They were petite with tiny lamps on white embroidered table clothes. The waitresses were wearing dark blue dresses with white aprons and little white net hats. We were seated and she ordered for us.

She's quick; I like that, a short brunette, with big expressive brown eyes, a tiny waist, perfect rear and large breasts. She was definitely my type. Not all men have types, but I do, always have, and am always attracted to the same type woman. But she was the epitome of what I consider perfect. Of all the women I've come in contact with, to find this one in London in the midst of a world war. What are the odds of that? I can't begin to do the math.

I told her I was the co-pilot on a B-17 with the 91ˢᵗ Bomb Group flying out of Bassingbourn. She didn't want to talk about the war. I didn't blame her. She wanted to know about America. I told her about life in Austin, Texas. She told me about her family. Soon she had to go and I pitched some money on the small table, too much probably, and hurriedly followed her outside.

It was dark when we reached the street. All of a sudden all hell broke loose. Bombs started exploding everywhere, people were screaming, in panic, running in every direction. Another blast hit nearby, which knocked me to the ground, dazed, my face cut and bleeding. When I finally regained my senses she was gone. I saw civil defense workers pulling bodies from wreckage. A bus, one of the red double deckers, was on its side burning, buildings were burning, and there was the scream of sirens blaring. I scrambled to my feet and ran like hell as the front of a building collapsed, covering the spot where I was laying. As I huddled inside a doorway, it hit me that this is what we are doing to them. God help us all.

I searched frantically, but she was nowhere. Once I panicked when they lifted up a dead nurse on a stretcher, but it wasn't her. The raid was over and firemen were pouring large streams of water into burning buildings in a near futile attempt to put out the fires. The unnerving scream of ambulances could be heard coming from everywhere.

As I sat there on the train, I was in a state of total despair. She was a dream come true. And there had been an emotional connection for both of us. I was sure of it. But before we could play it out it was over. I didn't get her phone number. I didn't even get her last name. I remember thinking that she was probably dead.

BUD CARTER DROPPED off to sleep. The boys who flew airplanes never got enough shuteye.

61
Bletchley Park

THE ARRIVAL AT a mansion house in the Buckinghamshire countryside in late August 1938 was to set the scene for one of the most remarkable stories of World War II. There was an air of friends simply enjoying a relaxed weekend together at a country house. They even brought one of the best chefs at the Savoy Hotel to cook their food. But the small group of people who turned up at Bletchley Park were far from relaxed. They were members of MI6 and the Government Code and Cypher School, a secret team of individuals, including a number of scholars turned codebreakers. Their job was to see whether Bletchley Park could work as a wartime location, well away from London, for intelligence activity by GCCS as well as elements of MI6.

The GCCS mission was to crack the Nazi codes and ciphers. The most famous of the cipher systems to be broken was the *Enigma System.* There were also a large number of lower-level German systems to break as well as those of Hitler's allies. At the start of the war in September 1939, the codebreakers returned to Bletchley Park to begin their work in earnest.

THE POLES HAD broken Enigma in 1932, when the encoding machine was undergoing trials with the German Army. But when the Poles broke Enigma, the cipher altered only once every few months. With the advent of war, it changed at least once a day, giving 159 million possible settings to choose from. The Poles decided to inform the British in July 1939, needing help to break Enigma with the German invasion of Poland imminent.

As more and more people arrived to join the codebreaking operations, the various sections began to move into large pre-fabricated wooden huts set up on the lawns of the Park. For security reasons, the various sections were known only by their hut numbers.

The first operational break into Enigma came around the January 23, 1940. The team working under Dilly Knox, with the Cambridge mathematicians Alan Turing, John Jeffreys, Peter Twinn, and Gordon Welchman unraveled the German Army administrative key that became known at Bletchley Park as *The Green.*

Encouraged by this success, the codebreakers managed to crack the 'Red' key used by the Luftwaffe liaison officers co-coordinating air support for army units. Gordon Welchman, soon to become head of the Army and Air Force section, devised a system whereby his codebreakers were supported by other staff based in a neighboring hut, which turned the deciphered messages into intelligence reports.

SECRECY SHROUDED THE fact that Enigma had been broken. To hide this information, the reports were given the appearance of coming from an MI6 spy, codenamed *Boniface,* with a network of imaginary agents inside Germany.

While this was pure fiction, there was a real network monitoring the Germans' every move. The 'Y' Service, a chain of wireless intercept stations across Britain (and in a number of countries overseas), listened into the enemy's radio messages. Thousands of wireless operators, many of them civilians but also WRENS, WAAF personnel, and members of the ATS, tracked the enemy radio nets up and down the dial, carefully logging every letter or figure. The messages were then sent back to Bletchley's Station X to be deciphered, translated, and fitted together like a gigantic jigsaw puzzle to produce as complete a picture as possible of what the enemy was doing.

The codebreakers began working around the clock to send the intelligence they were producing to London. Special Liaison Units and their associated communications specialists, the Special Communication Units, were set up to feed the Bletchley Park intelligence to commanders in the field, first briefly in France in May 1940 and then in North Africa and elsewhere from March 1941 onwards.

THE PROCESS OF breaking Enigma was aided considerably by a complex electro-mechanical device, designed by Alan Turing and Gordon Welchman. The *Bombe,* as it was called, ran through all the possible Enigma wheel configurations in order to reduce the possible number of settings in use to a manageable number for further hand testing. The Bombes were operated by WRENS, many of whom lived in requisitioned country houses such as Woburn Abbey. The work they did in speeding up the codebreaking process was indispensable.

In October 1941, after receiving a letter from some of the senior codebreakers decrying the lack of resources being afforded them, Prime Minister Winston Churchill stated most emphatically, "Make sure they have all they want, extreme priority, and report to me that this has been done."

From that moment on, Bletchley Park began receiving a huge influx of resources, and a major building program ensued to create the space necessary to house the ever increasing workforce.

THE INTELLIGENCE PRODUCED by deciphering the Naval Enigma was passed to the Admiralty via the Z Watch in the Naval Section. However, in the early days, they struggled to get the naval commanders to take it seriously. A series of spectacular successes turned things around for the codebreakers. Throughout the First Battle of the Atlantic, they helped the Admiralty to track the U-Boat wolf packs, considerably reducing the German Navy's ability to sink the merchant navy ships bringing vital supplies to Britain from America.

In 1942, the codebreakers' many successes also included the North Africa Campaign, when they enabled the Royal Navy to cut Rommel's supply lines and kept Montgomery informed of the Desert Fox's every move. Early 1942 brought serious difficulties with the German Navy's introduction of a more complex Enigma cipher. But by the end of 1942 they had mastered it as well.

· · · · ·

"SIR HENRY, I just wanted to thank you for hiring me in 1939," said Rachel.

"My dear, how could we have known what a top notch individual we were getting?"

"You know my story."

"Yes."

"I came to England to do something for the war effort."

"Yes."

"How could I have known or fully understood what our mission was or how important it was? It gives me such pride and satisfaction to know what we are doing here."

"Does that flier ask you about your work?"

"He did at first, but he's given up now. He doesn't ask me anymore."

"That's good."

"I'll never forget that first operational break into Enigma."

"January 23, 1940," said Sir Henry, without hesitation.

She smiled. "A rather important date."

"Rather."

"That was quite the team working under Dilly Knox, with Jeffreys, Twinn, and Turing."

"You didn't mention Rosenthal. You were a big help to Dilly, and he is quick to acknowledge it. I hired you as a linguist and you wound up being one of our codebreakers."

"Well, Sir Henry, I did major in mathematics."

Smart and beautiful. If I was a younger man I'd ...

"I guess at the time I was intrigued by your vast language skills."

"They got me the job."

"They did at that," he replied, with a smile, puffing on his pipe. "How is that boyfriend of yours?"

"He's fine. His co-pilot tells me he is one of the best pilots in the 91st Bomb Group and often leads missions. He says the men love him." She frowned. "But I can't help but worry. The losses are staggering."

Sir Henry reacted in a positive way, "The Yanks by day and the RAF by night. We'll bomb the bastards out of business."

"And not a minute too soon."

"That's the ticket, my girl. And until then, we'll give the Allies the critical information they need. The value of the work we're doing here has given the Allies an edge. I dare say, our efforts will definitely shorten the war, perhaps by a year or two."

"That's good to know, Sir Henry. I'll be here until we win."

"Indeed you will, my dear, indeed you will."

62
March 1943

ON THE FOURTH day of the month, the 91st Bomb Group was alerted to fly what proved to be one of its most successful and costliest missions since its arrival in the European Theater of Operations. The target was the railway station and marshalling yards at Hamm, Germany, one of the most important railroad enters in that part of Hitler's Europe. The field orders for the attack arrived shortly after dinner and the work of making the necessary preparations began immediately.

No force of American heavy bombers had yet penetrated very far into enemy territory, and some felt consternation as preparations for the mission continued. The combat crews were awakened much earlier than usual, and after breakfast proceeded to the briefing room. The preliminaries were completed according to schedule, and 20 aircraft took off shortly after 0730 hours.

Mechanical failures caused four of the B-17s to turn back before they had reached the English coast, but the remainder of the formation proceeded in accordance with the preconceived flight plan.

The 91st Group was the leader of the Eighth Air Force effort on this mission. Major Ellis would fly the lead ship for this mission. Captain Bruce Banner from Mississippi, a veteran skipper and winner of the Distinguished Flying Cross, would lead the low squadron, and Captain Brick Hansford would lead the high squadron.

"IF THE WEATHER conditions over the North Sea are any indication," Bud speculated, "I'm just wondering whether or not it will be possible to continue on to the primary target."

"I was thinking the same thing," echoed Brick.

"Talk to me about the weather, Clifford."

"We've got three cloud layers extending from approximately 13,000 to 17,000 feet, which together constitute a 10/10 undercast."

Carter sighed, "Damn weather."

"Another layer of clouds extends from approximately 21,500 feet with tops at between 25,000 and 26,000 feet."

Major Ellis led the B-17 formations between two layers of clouds. As they approached the Dutch coast, some confusion developed among the leaders of the two groups that were following behind. Shortly after crossing the Dutch coast, these two groups decided that it would be impossible to reach the primary target and, instead of continuing on in the wake of the 91st Group, they turned south to bomb the target of last resort at Rotterdam. Meanwhile, the fourth group in the formation had either aborted as a body or had given up the mission. In any event, they returned to their base without having dropped their bombs on any target.

"Well, Bud my boy, it looks like this unhappy course of events has left the 91st Group with no support from either friendly bombers or fighters to assist us with the mission."

"It does look that way, Captain Hansford."

"Our orders were to bomb Hamm," said Brick, "and we know Major Ellis."

"We're gonna bomb Hamm," said Bud with a grin.

"That's what we're going to do," Brick concluded.

AS THE 91ST Group flew on alone towards Hamm, Clark Clifford, the navigator, said, "Skipper, weather conditions have substantially improved."

"It's Europe."

"It's really unbelievable," said Clifford, "we've reached the German frontier and the undercast is breaking up beautifully. Wyman, it looks like good shooting."

"You're magic, Clark. I don't know what I'd do without you."

"Oh, yes, it's definitely me."

SOMETIME BEFORE THEY reached the target, they had left all the cloud formations behind them, but other problems had developed.

"So much for your magic, Clark," said Wyman.

"Like the skipper said, it's Europe. This layer of haze will reduce visibility to between five and twenty miles, depending upon the direction you're looking."

"Bud, I'm concerned that the Luftwaffe is going to try to take advantage of the isolated position of our small group formation."

"I was thinking the same thing, Skipper."

Sometime before Major Ellis reached the initial point, formations totaling about 60 enemy aircraft made determined attacks.

"Well, this is a new twist," said Wyman. "The Germans are attempting to cover the target with a smoke screen."

"You don't blame 'em do you, Wilson? After all, they've got the 91st Bomb Group to contend with."

"There it is up ahead," said Carter, referring to the flak.

"Wow—it's intense and relatively accurate," said Hansford.

"There goes *Smoky Joe*," said Carter. "He's on fire and dropping out of formation. His goose is cooked."

"The smokescreen ain't working. We can bomb the primary target just as briefed. Bombs away!" yelled Wyman.

Brick looked at Bud and winked, "What do you say we get the hell out of here?"

"My exact thoughts, Skipper."

"I'm a killer," said Wyman, "the Krauts ought to put a bounty on my head."

"What do you mean?" said Carter.

"Well, all of you gentlemen with a view should take a look. We're striking all along the railroad tracks and yards with direct hits on the station buildings, on the locomotive-engine sheds, and on the platforms."

"You're right, Wilson," said Brick, "and hits on industrial buildings that were grouped in the vicinity of the railroad installations. But if you've noticed, there's other B-17s up here and they're dropping bombs as well."

"I can't speak for them, you know, their accuracy. I can only speak for myself and I did a hell of a job today."

"Your modestly is showing, but it's okay. In fact, I think I'll keep you."

"Gee, thanks, Skipper."

"The brass ought to be happy with this one," said Carter.

"Yes, they should," said Brick. "Now, let's look alive. Call out those bandits as soon as you see 'em. They ain't gonna let us fly home without a fight."

63

DURING THE MISSION debriefing, Brick Hansford reported, "Shortly after leaving the target area, while still in formation, we were subjected to another series of attacks by many enemy fighter planes. What would you say, Bud?"

"At least seventy-five bandits. Hell, the pilots of many of the Kraut planes continued their attacks until we'd passed the German coastline and the Frisian Islands and were well on our way across the North Sea towards England."

"One of the 91st Group pilots, who had formerly flown with the Royal Air Force," said the debriefing officer, "reported that the enemy fighter pilots were really crazy to have pressed their attacks as closely as some of them did during this mission."

"It was bad!" said Brick. "Both going and coming was worse than a naked man in a swarm of hornets."

"The Skipper really knows how to explain things," Bud mused. There was laughter.

The briefing officer said, *"Step'n'fetchit* lost their co-pilot shortly after leaving the target area. It had part of its instrument panel destroyed and its pilot was wounded in one eye and one hand. He successfully landed his aircraft without other assistance and with only two engines. It was little wonder that he was unable to stop his plane after it hit the runway. Fortunately, he ran off the end of the runway and into a field of Brussels sprouts and no one was seriously injured."

"Saved by Brussels sprouts," said Wyman, "that's a good one. I'm glad to know what they're good for."

Many of the enlisted men proved themselves during the running battles of that unforgettable mission. The Distinguished Flying Cross was awarded to Major Ellis very shortly after the completion of this almost historic mission.

THE COMBAT CREWS agreed that the mission, though costly, was one of the finest jobs of bombing they had seen. Captain Clovis Ridley, of the European Theater of Operations news section, rode with the 91st on the mission in order to get photographs for the Public Relations Office. He said, "I've not seen bombing results any more perfect than those I observed this morning. There were direct hits on the banks of the canal and on other industrial buildings. Minimal damage was done to residential and other property of a non-military value. Practically all of the bombs struck the targets."

▪ ▪ ▪ ▪ ▪

"LOOK AT THESE photographic reconnaissance reports, Cliff," said Col. Birdwell. "They not only confirm the interrogation reports of the combat crews, but also show conclusively that a tremendous amount of damage was done to the enemy installation."

When the photographs were taken three days after the attack, several of the main lines had not yet been returned to service, and one of the chief locomotive sheds, with its turntable, appeared to have been abandoned as unrepairable. Even the photographic interpreters admitted that the results of the attack had been unusually good.

IN SPITE OF the successes, officials in Washington still questioned the soundness of the American theory of high-altitude precision daylight bombing in a theater of operations as strongly defended as the skies over Germany, and in a climate where weather conditions provided so many obstacles. However, much of the skepticism subsided when they reviewed the reports of the achievements of the Fortresses of the 91st Group in their mission against the strongly defended target at Hamm, which was flown without fighter escort or supporting fire of other bomber formations.

AT THE OFFICERS Club, following the debriefing, the men of the *Rachel* were throwing down a series of adult beverages. "The crew of the *Rachel* performed well as usual," said Carter.

"You know something, there are no shortcuts. It takes a bunch of missions for everybody to get up to speed, but I think we have rounded into a very well-disciplined and effective crew. I'm proud of everyone," echoed Hansford.

Clark Clifford shook his head, gulped down a swig of beer, and said, "It was tough as hell up there today. *Easy Rider* had some of the most vicious attacks by German fighters as any plane in the formation. By the time they reached the German coast on the way out, three of their engines had been shot out and the remaining engine wasn't sufficient to keep them in formation."

"They ditched in the North Sea," said Carter.

"You sound a little jumpy, Clifford."

"Hell yes I was jumpy. I was scared to death."

Hansford laughed. "So was I, Clark. We're members of the war's largest club."

"Somebody in the debriefing said Captain Cushing and the co-pilot, Lt. Lawrence, were the last ones to leave the airplane after it began to break up," said Bud. "They refused to save themselves until after the other crew members had safely entered their dinghies. The high winds carried the dinghies out of reach of Cushing and Lawrence, and although the other crewmembers attempted to save them, they didn't make it."

"*Easy Virtue* exploded over the target and *Crimson Tide* had most of one of its wings shot off. It went down in flames just after leaving the target area," said Hansford.

"Thibodaux told me he saw *Party Animal* going down in a distressed condition in the vicinity of Texel Island," said Wyman, who added, "and the crew of *Rocky Top* was picked up by the Air-Sea Rescue in the Channel."

"It's safe to say that a lot of crew members were wounded and some could die later in the hospital," said Carter.

"I'd still rather be doing this than carrying a rifle," said Hansford.

"I agree with you on that, Skipper," said Carter. The others nodded.

"I counted a total of seven parachutes over enemy territory," said Hansford.

"Other crewmembers may have bailed out at lower altitudes," said Wyman.

"I hope that at least a good proportion of those who are missing in action will be returned as prisoners of war," said Wyman.

"I think the Germans treat our flyers okay," said Carter.

"Look, we had our share of losses, but I believe it's no exaggeration that this mission has brought both officers and men to a realization that the 91st has achieved the level of a veteran organization.

I think we can accomplish any mission that might be expected from any group in the United States Army Air Corps," said Hansford.

64

SINCE THE 91ST was standing down for awhile following the raid on Hamm, Col. Birdwell had turned loose with 72-hour passes for those who wanted them. The crew of the *Rachel* headed for London. Brick Hansford had money in his pocket, was in an amorous mood, and was looking forward to seeing Rachel.

. . . . .

"HERE WE ARE, folks," said the cabbie, "the Savoy."

"After the Dorchester, I guess the Savoy won't be very special," Brick lamented. "But I wanted to do something on my own for you."

"Quit it, Brick. I am very excited to be staying here and with you."

He beamed, "Well, good."

The Savoy had become a favorite hotel of Eighth Air Force B-17 drivers out of Bassingbourn, England. The flyboys especially enjoyed dancing at the popular hotel.

"The Savoy's entrance is one of London's landmarks," said Rachel.

"I can see why," said Brick, squeezing her hand and smiling. The Savoy was located on the Strand and its famous riverside front overlooked a classic sweep of the Thames, which had been famously captured in a painting by Claude Monet.

As they crossed the lobby on the way to registration, Rachel told Brick, "I've never stayed here. In fact I've never been inside—but I've certainly dreamed of it."

Brick smiled at her, "Neither have I. We'll be discovering it for the first time together."

"I'm ready to get started," she exclaimed.

"They tell me it's in a great location. The theaters, opera, ballet and shopping on the West End and Covent Gardens are located nearby. The Thames is just a short walk away."

Grinning from ear to ear, she said, "Captain Hansford, I'm very excited."

"HERE WE ARE folks," said the bellman, as he opened the door to their suite. Brick was ready to play and planned to show Rachel a good time.

He's an interesting little guy, our bellman, Rachel thought to herself, *and really cute with his bald head, handlebar mustache, and pot belly. But he looks more French than English.*

He put the suitcases on the bed and began to open them. "That's okay, Jeffrey, we can do that," said Rachel.

"Very well, milady. If there is anything that you require, just call for Jeffrey. But if I might take a moment, let me say that I have worked here since 1928 and I just adore the old girl."

Rachel looked at Brick, and he smiled back and shrugged.

"The Savoy was designed to a very high standard. You'll see— and you'll enjoy it here. We have a lovely view over the Embankment Gardens and the River Thames. Our very fine River Restaurant features contemporary and classical dishes. The atmosphere is relaxed with live music in the evenings, piano music Monday through Thursday, and a band for dancing on Friday and Saturday. You'll have a lovely time, depending on the Germans, of course. They're a bit of a bother from time to time."

A bother, thought Brick, *how funny.*

"We're looking forward to the dancing, Jeffrey. All the American boys talk about dancing at The Savoy."

Jeffrey lit up like the lights around the Thames after dark. "Oh, the Yanks love dancing at The Savoy, guv, and you will as well; you and the lovely lady. I meet some of them." He frowned and shook his head. "Many of the poor blokes don't make it—but we give 'em a time, sir, yes we do."

"I'll bet you do, Jeffrey," said Brick.

"The Savoy Grill's menu reflects the chef's fondness for modern European dishes. The Upstairs Restaurant has large windows overlooking the front entrance and offers a menu of Mediterranean cuisine as well as a variety of light to heavy contemporary dishes."

"I'm getting hungry," said Rachel, smiling and clasping her hands together.

"Before I go, l should mention that we also have an exchange, room service, shopping arcade, laundry and cleaning services, safe deposit boxes, porter services, as well as an indoor swimming pool. If you need anything at all, the name is Jeffrey."

Brick slipped him five dollars American.

"THAT JEFFREY'S A character, isn't he Rachel?"

She laughed, "Yes, he is, but good at his job."

"And one hell of an ambassador for the Savoy."

"Indeed."

THEY SHOWERED AND dressed.

"What's the plan, Brick?"

"I suggest we have a nice dinner at the River Restaurant, here in the hotel."

"Yeah, okay, Jeffrey likes it. It should be good."

"After dinner I thought we might walk a bit and have a drink at one of the pubs. The rest of it we'll make up as we go. How does that sound?"

"Just lovely, milord."

"Brick smiled and said, "I feel more like the gamekeeper."

They both laughed.

■ ■ ■ ■ ■

"WHAT WILL YOU HAVE, Yank?" said the bartender, with a smile.

"Two mugs of ale."

"Here you are."

He paid the tab and carefully carried the drinks to the table.

"Cheers," said Brick, gently touching her glass. They smiled at each other and both took a sip.

The pub was lively and crowded. A group of locals and British sailors were drinking beer and playing a friendly, but competitive, game of darts.

"Looks like the boys are enjoying themselves."

"Yes they are, and don't you go and challenge the winner."

"I'm good at darts."

"According to you, my darling Brick, you're good at everything."

"That's true, but I just can't help it."

She laughed and shook her head. "You're different than that boy at Harvard. Even though you were the hot-shot quarterback, you're different."

"War changes everything. Nobody dies on the football field."

"Yeah."

After a few moments of silent reflection, Rachel spoke up.

"This is fun, don't you think?" .

"As a matter of fact, I do. Nobody is shooting at me, but my job is rather intense. I mean, all of us are under enormous pressure."

"Tell me about it."

"You know I can't."

"That's right."

"Mr. Churchill came by and gave us a pep talk. I got to shake his hand."

"Well, that's swell, isn't it?"

"It sure is."

"You know, these pubs are rather an institution over here—a place where the locals gather for some fellowship and relaxation."

"That's very true."

"When Americans go to a bar, they're just there to drink—and get drunk."

THEY LEFT THE pub and walked and talked. Later on they ducked into a cabaret, the Fox and Hound, below street level. It was lively with lots of drinking, laughter, and dancing.

"I always enjoyed dancing with you, Brick."

"You're quite light on your feet, Rachel."

"I guess we're just quite the dashing couple."

"I always thought we were."

They laughed.

They ordered a round of drinks and continued to dance for another two hours.

"Captain Hansford, I'm starting to crash. I think you better take me to the house."

"You know, the ole gamekeeper is beginning to drag as well."

65

SATURDAY WAS A leisurely day. They slept late, which caught them up on their lost sleep, particularly Brick. Then they lunched at the Captain Morgan's.

"Darling, I've been by here on many occasions but never went in."

"Yeah? Jeffrey recommended it."

"If Jeffrey recommended it, it's got to be good."

He laughed, "Well, I guess so."

They looked over the menu and soon the waiter appeared and inquired as to food and drinks.

"Have you decided, Brick?" Rachel asked.

"Yeah, I'll have the liver, bacon, and onions."

"Liver and onions?"

"Yeah, why?"

"I don't know, I just thought ..."

"I grew up eating liver and onions. It's one of my favorite things."

She laughed.

"And for you, milady?"

"I'll have the Lancashire Hotpot," said Rachel.

"What's that," Brick asked.

"It's a meat and vegetable casserole. It's a favorite over here. I've been here so long now that I'm a Londoner. I've gotten used to the food and most everything. So, do you want to change your mind?"

"No. And two mugs of ale," said Brick.

"Right away, sir."

AFTER A THOROUGHLY delightful lunch, they took a cruise on the Thames. "I'm glad we decided to do this, Rachel. It gives you a perspective of the city and a great look at these wonderful old bridges."

"Yes, it does. I enjoy it every time."

After the cruise they strolled over to Westminster Abby, the great old church with so much history, and quietly stepped inside. Rachel was intrigued by the large painting of Jesus knocking at a door.

They stopped for a coffee at a sidewalk cafe and enjoyed watching the people. Brick had been talking reverently and fondly about the British Prime Minister.

"You're really taken by Winston Churchill, aren't you ?"

"Yes, I am. He just may be the most important man of the twentieth century."

"Really? I would have thought you'd have said Mr. Roosevelt."

"Roosevelt is my Commander-in-Chief and we all love and respect him. But if Churchill had not become Prime Minister when he did, I'm not sure Britain would have survived."

"Explain."

"Well, when officials in the government wanted to make a pact with Hitler, he resisted and convinced the people that they could survive and that they could ultimately win. And he made some really tough and gutsy calls early on. For example, when the super battleship *Bismarck* broke out into the Atlantic Sea lanes to attack convoys, he ordered an all-out effort to sink her, and they did. He knew that his country's lifeline was tied to the merchant fleets getting supplies from America.

"When the French government capitulated, there was the real chance that the Nazis would seize the French fleet. So Churchill ordered his navy to destroy that fleet, which was a very important strategic move and a gutsy one as well. But the action killed many French sailors, provoking an outcry. But it had to be done. Here's the deal. If England had fallen, then the Germans would have had a base for their submarine fleet, their war ships, and their air force. It would have been impossible to approach the European continent with them in control of England.

"And if they had defeated the Brits, they would have seized their ships and all their other military assets. I wonder what on earth we would have done for a staging area to mount our build up for the invasion of the European Continent? Because the British Isles are so critical to winning the war in Europe is why I give the nod to ole Winnie."

Rachel laughed, "The next time he comes by my office, I'll tell him how impressed my boyfriend is."

A CABBIE TOOK them to Madame Tussaud's Waxwork Museum. It was fun and they were eager to see who was there. "Oh my, Rachel, it's the entire royal family and all the prime ministers. Here's Disraeli, an interesting figure in history. I read a book about him one time."

"I see them."

"And over here are some of the past world leaders. I swear to goodness, Rachel, any minute I expect one of them to say something."

"I know what you mean."

"How can they make them so real looking?" he questioned.

"It beats me."

After the wax museum they walked a bit and then returned to The Savoy for a nap.

BRICK AND RACHEL had a drink at the hotel bar before departing for dinner at Patterson's Restaurant in Central London. She was hungry for a steak and they had good ones.

"Waiter, we've got tickets for *Brighton Rock* at Garrick, so be sure to get us out in time and get us a cabbie."

"Never you mind, guv, I'll see to it."

"I heard about this play from a co-worker," said Rachel.

"It a thriller, a murder mystery. It was recommended by another pilot on base."

"The star is an up and coming young actor, Richard Attenborough," said Rachel. "They say he's quite good, with a promising future ahead of him."

"I never tire of the theatre. It's always exciting to me," said Brick. "And, I wanted to show you a good time."

Rachel laughed, "You're good at that. You always have been."

■ ■ ■ ■ ■

THE FOLLOWING DAY they hit a few famous landmarks: Royal Albert Hall, Kensington Palace and the area's splendid museums, Knightsbridge, Big Ben, St. Paul's Cathedral, and the Changing of the Guard at Buckingham Palace. After lunch at a local pub, they rode a double-decker bus and turned a few stops on the subway for good measure and were still in time for the perfect English afternoon with high tea at Harrod's.

"Thank you for humoring me. You know, the touristy stuff like the bus and subway," said Brick.

"Thank you for humoring me with high tea," said Rachel.

"You're quite welcome, my darling. Remember that time at the Plaza when we were in college?"

She smiled, "I sure do. I remember it well."

He thought for a moment and then said, "Everything is old over here, you know, you've got major history all around you. That's fascinating to me."

Brick dipped his scone in his tea. She laughed. "They don't dip their scones in Boston. Not your crowd anyway. Where did that come from?"

"I don't know, but I like doing it."

She laughed.

"I'm having a swell time."

"And so am I, my darling."

They returned to the hotel for a nap before the evening activities.

THEY ATE DINNER at the Savoy and then took in the performance of *It's Time to Dance* at the Winter Gardens Theatre. All in all, it had been another spectacular day. "Thank you for a fabulous weekend, Brick. I've loved every minute of it."

He took a late train back to Bassingbourn.

66

THE WELCOMED REST for the 91st Group didn't last very long. The night before, they were alerted to attack the submarine base at Lorient. The aiming point was the power station and transformer installation upon which the entire submarine base was dependent for light, power, and other facilities. The secondary point was the railroad bridge situated very close to the transformer station. Preparations for the mission were completed early in the morning. The combat crews were aroused at 0430 hours for a 0515 briefing. Each step in this mission went smoothly, and the aircraft took off shortly after 1000 hours and joined the other groups of the wing at the rendezvous.

"Well, they changed up things quite a bit this time," observed Brick. "This mission is different from the earlier missions they dispatched against Lorient."

"That's true. It's an over-water route all the way out and back," said Bud.

"Meaning that we have to fly in a southwesterly direction in order to avoid the Brest peninsula, hoping to mislead the German defenses situated on that particular part of the continent," said Brick.

"Flying at a relatively low altitude during much of this flight should be welcomed by most the combat crews, who won't suffer nearly as much from cold and won't be compelled to use their oxygen masks until just a short time before reaching the target area," said Bud.

"But, it will lengthen the flight by approximately one and one-half hours. That could be a problem, so I don't know about it."

"I agree, Skipper. It's kind of a crap shoot."

Weather during this part of the mission was variable. Cloud layers with varying densities were encountered over the southern part of England, the English Channel, and the Brest peninsula. However, the cloud masses broke up completely as the formation approached the target area. Visibility at Lorient was at least 15 miles and there were no clouds to interfere with the bombardiers.

"A flak ship anchored in the harbor is extremely active and appears to be directing its fire at the group ahead us," Carter observed, "so we are fortunate in that practically no anti-aircraft fire seems to be directed at us."

"We can use a break," said the Skipper.

The German fighters did not appear in any strength. Combat crews reported having seen from eight to ten FW-190s and Me-109s, but only two or three of them approached within range. The only attacks witnessed by the 91st were directed against the lead group. This enabled the bombardiers to concentrate on getting their bombs right on the aiming point. The reports of excellent bombing made during the interrogation were later substantiated by strike attack photographs. Bombs were seen bursting on the transformer station, the railroad, and the powerhouse. None of the three targets escaped extensive damage.

67

Brick wrote to his folks in Boston.

Today was clear and warm, one of the first real spring days to be enjoyed by our group since we arrived in England. This was a Sunday that turned out to be a genuine day of rest.

With no flying or training activities, and with great weather, a majority of the officers and men had an opportunity to pursue a variety of individual diversions. Bud Carter got us some bicycles and we enjoyed the English countryside. In fact, a good many of the men went for bicycle rides into various parts of the surrounding countryside. Some of the other fellows played softball, touch football, and other outdoor sports.

We had a large number of civilian visitors, who came to have lunch with their friends on the airdrome and to tour the base.

This air war is a crazy thing. It's a combination of extreme boredom, bad weather, delays, frustration, bureaucratic crap, and rescheduling—mixed with episodes of sheer terror. But, as I've said so often, it beats carrying a rifle and spending the night in a hole in the ground.

Well, if Mr. Roosevelt calls, tell him we're kicking the hell out of the Krauts and not to worry. We're going to win.

Love until later,
Brick

68

ON MARCH 8, 1943, the 91st Group hit the marshalling yards at Rennes, France.

On March 9, 1943, they were alerted to attack the marshalling yards and engine sheds just outside of Amiens. However, the weather interfered and the entire mission was scrubbed about one hour before take-off.

During the night, the group was alerted to attack the harbor and dock facilities of the German city of Emden on March 10, 1943. Combat crews were awakened at 0300 hours for a briefing at 0345 hours. Just before take-off, this mission was also scrubbed.

Lots of missions were scrubbed, many because of bad weather or overcast skies over the target. "These stops and starts are driving me crazy," said Carter.

TWO ENTIRE TRUCKLOADS of back mail arrived at Bassingbourn. It had been diverted to Africa and had been two to five months en route. Nearly every officer and man on the station received from 10 to 40 letters.

Receipt of this back mail did a good deal to improve the psychological hang-over from the raids. Mail was one of the most welcomed commodities combat men could ever receive. Unless it was a Dear John letter, it was an instant morale booster.

69

BUD CARTER USUALLY received one or more letters at a time from his loving mom. And men in combat could always count on the fact that their mothers were praying for them. Lenora Carter was no exception.

Dear Bud,

Well, I hope this letter finds you in good spirits and well. I know you must be having trouble adapting to that wet and cold climate. Not like Austin, Texas, is it? Oh, well, you always adapted well, so I know you'll be fine.

You ought to see our Victory Garden we've started out back. Mr. Roosevelt encouraged all of us to help with the rationing by growing some of our own food. It's actually kind of fun. I do most of the work, of course, because Dad is busy at the station. We've planted tomatoes, okra, green beans, and Indian corn so far. The corn was your dad's idea.

It's funny what you get used to. You remember how much we all loved the sweet cream butter. Now we get a chunk of lard, some yellow coloring, and mix it all with some salt to taste. We've gotten to where we kind of like the stuff. But it's no real sacrifice. We live in the greatest country in the world. To sacrifice a bit so we can support all you fellows who are fighting Mr. Hitler is a privilege.

Take care of yourself, my son. We all pray for you at church. We pray for all the boys.

Love,
Mom

70

ON MARCH 12, 1943, the 91st Group was alerted to carry out an attack on Rouen. Combat crews were awakened at approximately 0300 hours and after breakfast and the usual briefing, they proceeded to their dispersal areas. Eighteen aircraft participated. Weather conditions were favorable and the aircraft took off shortly after 0900 in rapid succession. The 91st Group led the other three B-17 groups that participated in the mission, one of the first in which a diversion was carried out with considerable success.

The formation flew a rather large triangular course over the English Channel before crossing the French coast. As the target approached, the cloud cover receded and they had no difficulty in dropping their bombs.

The light German defenses enabled the *Rachel*, who was leading, to make a bombing run that lasted approximately 90 seconds. The result was an almost perfect attack by the group.

"Look at these strike photos, Cliff," said Col. Birdwell.

"Outstanding!" said Ellis, looking through the special magnifying glass. "These prove conclusively that all bombs of the 91st Group landed right in the marshalling yards. There's no question that this attack ranks among the best three or four that we've made so far."

"THE SPITFIRES DID a really great job," said Brick.

"You're not kidding, Skipper," said Bud. "Kraut fighters were unable to make any concentrated attacks."

All of the aircraft completed the mission exactly as briefed, with no aborts and no mechanical failures or other malfunctioning of equipment when the time came to release the bombs. All 18 of the aircraft dropped their bombs as a group. This may be why the effectiveness of the attack was so outstanding.

THE RETURN TO base was also made without incident. Not a single one of the 18 aircraft of the 91st Group left the formation after becoming airborne, and all 18 returned to the base and landed in their designated order. None of the aircraft were seriously damaged, no one was killed, no one was wounded. From the point of view of the 91st Group, this mission from beginning to end, was as near perfect as any mission flown by any group in the Eighth Air Force.

The group received a special letter of commendation from General Moreland, commander of the 1st Bombardment Wing. The positive effect on morale from this mission quickly spread from the combat crews to the ground echelon. Spirits were higher than they had been in several weeks.

71

RONNY HAD ALWAYS said that Maggie was attracted to Bud. But what he didn't know was that Bud was also attracted to her. Bud chose not to tell him because his best friend was also a meddling busybody, and he just didn't want to deal with his questions and persistent probing for details that were none of his business. He knew all too well what Ronny was like.

Bud had made it a habit of going by Dirty Martin's after school for a burger and a couple of cold beers. It was not out of the ordinary for him to stop by on Saturday as well. He made sure he always parked in Maggie's service area. They were developing a relationship although they had not seen each other save for the outside of the popular drive-in.

"Anything else you want, Bud?" Maggie asked.

A coy grin crossed his mischievous face, "Well, yeah, but this ain't exactly the time and place for it."

She grinned, but didn't take the bait.

"Listen, do you ever get any time off? It seems like you work all the time. I mean, it seems like you're always here."

"Of course I get time off, silly, why do you ask?"

"I was thinking about asking you out."

She scrunched up her face, cocked her head, and put her hands on her hips. They were very shapely hips, just below a small waist. Maggie was short and very well-endowed with big expressive brown eyes and honey blond hair pulled back in a pony-tail.

"Oh, come on, Bud, you know you're not serious."

"Do you have some sort of special powers?"

She frowned, "What are you talking about?"

"You seem to be able to tell what I'm thinking and what I mean, so I was just wondering."

"What?"

"You just told me I wasn't serious about asking you out, so I was just wondering how you could possibly know that."

Her hands were still on her hips, "You're really serious? You're really asking me out on a date."

"Yes, Maggie, I most certainly am."

She squealed, startling the people in the next car, quickly circled his car, and hopped in on the passenger side. She giggled and then threw her arms around Bud's neck and kissed him.

He couldn't help but laugh. "Does that mean you'll go, Maggie?"

"Yes, it does, Mr. Bud Carter."

"Well, good. Listen, you better get out of here before you get in trouble with the management."

Soon enough she was standing by the window on the driver's side.

"Give me your number and I'll call you tonight. Better yet, when do you get off?"

"Ten o'clock."

"I'll be here at ten to take you home."

"Goody," said Maggie, clapping her hands.

She is a living doll, he thought to himself.

"See you at ten."

"BUD, TIME TO wake up!" said Brick. "We have a mission today."

He sat up, stretched, and said, "Damn, Brick, I was having a great dream about a swell girl back home. It was quite a change since I get killed in most of them."

"Well, after all, they're only dreams."

72

"SCARLETT, HOW ARE you and Bud getting on?"

She smiled, "Just bloody wonderful. Why do you ask?"

"Because you're my friend. I'm interested."

"He's a lovely boy. He's good looking and fun. I love to be with him?"

"You love him?"

"Maybe. Given some time, it could happen."

"Does he love you?"

"I don't know." She scrunched up her face. "We don't talk about serious stuff."

"Like him being blown to bits over Germany."

Scarlett sighed, "Yeah. I didn't want to say that. But, I mean, with the war and all, everything's uncertain."

She had another thought. "With the pressure the fliers are under, they need to be able to relax and have fun when they're with us."

"I couldn't have put it any better."

"What's with you and Brick?"

"He's been in love with me since college. But you know that."

"Yes."

"He's different now. But they all are. A world at war, nobody's the same. The main thing is he's a man now."

"I didn't know Bud before, but I'm sure that's true with him— with all of them."

"Yes, I think it is. Brick and I are much the same as you and Bud. I mean, we keep it light and fun. Like you say, they are under so much pressure and strain."

"Do you love Brick?"

"I didn't back then, but I feel different about him now. I know that for sure. Is it love? I don't know. But then I don't have to decide right now."

73

AN ATTACK ON the marshalling yards at Amiens was ordered for the 13th of March. After breakfast at 0430 they attended a 0500 briefing.

"Doesn't Col. Birdwell understand that nothing important should ever be considered before 1000 hours?" Wyman quipped, as the officers walked toward the briefing hut. "It's still night, still dark, for crying out loud."

"Hey, you work for the Eighth Air Force. We go to work early," said Clifford.

Weather conditions were questionable, but they finally got into the air shortly after 0930 hours. "Skipper, I know I'm just one of hundreds of lowly bombardiers, but I think they should have cancelled this mission," said Wyman, speaking over the *Rachel's* communication system. All the crew heard it.

"You're one of many, this is true, but you're far from lowly. You're the best damn bombardier in the Wing—but I happen to agree with you."

"FRANKLY, I'M A little superstitious," said Carter. "After the excellent results of yesterday, I think it's down right foolish to attempt another mission today."

Brick agreed, but didn't want to unnerve the crew. But he thought to himself, *From the time of take-off, everything seems to point in the general direction of a fiasco. Then we had trouble making rendezvous with the other three groups. Then the 306th insisted on flying at the altitude and in the position assigned to the 91st. When we reached the English Coast, the Wing formation began to fly one of the diversionary triangular courses, but the flight plan was not followed. That caused us to almost miss making rendezvous with the Spitfire squadrons, which had escort duties. I hope to hell things get better.*

"Skipper, I want to strangle the navigator in the lead ship!" screamed Clifford. "He's leading the force across the French coast at Dieppe rather than at Cayeux."

"And so now the Germans are throwing up an anti-aircraft barrage, which we should have avoided," said Carter.

"I know, Clifford, I know," said Brick, his eyes narrowing, grinding his teeth in anger.

"Here we go again," said Clifford, "we're taking a heading other than the one outlined in the flight plan. I hope we find the target."

"I want to hurt somebody!" screamed Hansford, "The 306th Group is moving in at the altitude and position assigned to the 91st for the second time today."

This produced an embarrassing situation for the 91st. Rather than contest the position with the 306th Group, the 91st made a left turn after the aircraft of one squadron had dropped their bombs on the primary target.

The remainder of the Group flew northwestward to Abbeville, which had been assigned as their secondary target at the briefing. The message to cancel the mission, sent out by higher headquarters, was received just after the bombs had been dropped on the primary target. This was the chief reason why the formation of the 91st Group did not make a second bombing run on the target of Amiens, but proceeded to the secondary target. That allowed the remainder of the aircraft in the formation to be able to bomb the secondary target.

"Well, needless to say," said Clifford with disgust, "the weather conditions continue to deteriorate. There are varying amounts of thin cloud formations at approximately 20,000 feet, just under our formation."

"Heavy and persistent condensation trails are adding to the difficulties of the *Rachel* flying in the high position," Brick concluded.

"This haze is annoying," said Carter.

"It is for a fact," said Brick, "visibility at times is probably no better than one or two miles."

"The winds are different from those that were forecast by the Weather Section," Bud remarked. "Well, it is what it is, and we'll just have to deal with it."

"You ready to take the airplane, Wyman?" Bud asked.

"Do it, Skipper."

In a few minutes, Wyman spoke the magic words, validating why they were there. "Bombs away!"

The *Rachel* hit the Abbeville/Dreucat airdrome—and that's where the best results were achieved by the 91st Group. Runways, a dispersal area, and gun positions were hit with considerable effect. At least two bombs cut the railroad tracks just outside of town. However, results attained by the bombs dropped at Amiens by one squadron of the Group were questionable. Two aircraft of the group returned early because of mechanical difficulties.

"The Kraut fighters didn't want any part of the 91st Group," said Destafano."

"A piercing observation, Tony," said Gregory.

"I saw five or six of the sorry bastards, but the Spitfires changed their minds. They furnish excellent cover."

"And for the whole time," said Tony.

"Anti-aircraft fire at Abbeville was inaccurate," Carter commented. "I'm surprised. I don't think they caused any serious damage to our aircraft."

"This mission was poorly executed from beginning to end, and yet we did our jobs. The 91st Group was lucky not to have suffered serious damage," Hansford concluded.

74

BRICK WROTE HIS parents. The families of servicemen knew very well the dangers their young men were facing. They didn't need reminding, and the airmen couldn't give them any combat details anyway. But in spite of that, most men tried to write about things that were of a benign nature.

Hello, Mom and Dad,

I bet you just can't wait for the exciting news from merry old England. The war is still on, of course, and we're participating in it. Funny, right? The problem is I can't tell you anything that's really meaningful, so I'll just stick with the useless crap.

Here's a situation that you may think is funny, we certainly do. A shortage of ignition keys for motor vehicles has suddenly developed on the station. All personnel were advised to turn in ignition keys in their possession. It was also rumored that this order came as a result of two past incidents in which unauthorized personnel had slipped out through a station gate to take a joy ride to the nearby town of Royston. Some of these enlisted men just kill me.

Some 29 officers in the group have been cited for failure to pay their club dues on time. I am completely up to date. The 323d Bombardment Squadron had the dubious honor of leading the list. Those guilty of this minor infraction were restricted to the limits of the station for a week. But they never send officers to bed without supper. Ha-ha.

A few decorations for the combat crewmembers arrived at the station, but no formal presentation of awards was made. Several of the combat crews of the

Group have completed 15 missions. At the present rate, a good many of the older combat crews are likely to complete their tours of operations during the next six weeks to two months.

Carter and I were sent on temporary duty for a week to attend a course of instruction in blind-approach training. The idea is that when we complete this instruction, we can share what we've learned with the other pilots of the 91st Group. It speaks well for Bud and me that we were the ones chosen.

The officers of the station held their regular dance in the senior officers' mess. These things are lots of fun and we look forward to each one of them. We probably had 250 guests in attendance. Most of the girls came from Cambridge and other nearby towns, although quite a few were invited from London. These English girls really like us Americans. I think part of it is because we are less inhibited than their own men. Of course, most of the young ones are not around. They're in North Africa, Burma, and places like that. The music was furnished by the Jive Bombers, the name adopted by the 91st's own dance orchestra. They are really very good.

We were short on booze, so the event had a rather tame atmosphere although most everybody said they had just as good a time as at previous Saturday night affairs.

Love to you both,

Brick

HE NEVER MENTIONED that he was seeing Rachel Rosenthal.

75

THE 91st GROUP was ordered to hit Rouen. Bombs were loaded on the aircraft, armament personnel had all guns ready to install, and a plentiful supply of ammunition had been furnished to each aircraft. The weather was still good, and it was anticipated that the mission would go through without any delay.

"Can I have more sausage, corporal?" Bud asked.

"Sure thing, Lieutenant Carter, and more eggs if you'd like?"

"I'd like."

"Bud, you're a real chow hound," said Wyman.

"I've always loved breakfast. On Saturday morning, we'd have pancakes, eggs, sausage, biscuits, gravy, grits, orange juice, milk and coffee. Mom's a great cook."

CONDITIONS OVER THE continent deteriorated during the early morning. Word came from Wing Headquarters that the mission was scrubbed.

"We'll have ground school, that's for sure. Nobody likes it, but I guess it's justified. I understand that some of the crews have been absent from ground school classes during the past several weeks. Colonel Birdwell is not happy about it, and there's gonna be hell to pay if it doesn't stop. All aircraft commanders got the memo," said Brick, waving it in the air.

Two outstanding features of the training program were the special lecture and training film for all gunners and a code check for all navigators and radio operators.

76

AFTER BREAKFAST, Bud Carter went back to quarters and wrote a letter to his folks while he had the time to do it.

Hey, Mom and Dad,

It's your favorite bomber pilot, taking the war to Uncle Adolf every chance I get, but not today. I've just come from the officer's mess. Mom, I thought about your Saturday morning breakfast extravaganzas. I can't wait to put my feet back under your table.

Let's see, two combat crews reported to the 91st Group from the 11th Combat Crew Replacement Center, although they were not assigned to the squadrons as crews. Several of the older crews needed men, so it was decided to use the personnel to complete the older combat crews that had arrived initially in the theater with the group.

The medical section, Headquarters VIII Bomber Command, has initiated a testing program for all sections of the ground and air echelons. Various types of Royal Air Force and United States Army Air Forces winter flying clothing are being tested under actual combat conditions. We definitely appreciate the continued efforts to give us the best of equipment and techniques. Notes are being kept on the opinions of combat crewmembers, failures of individual pieces of equipment, incidents of frostbite, and other factors that will later be used to determine the value of each piece and type of equipment. Those conducting the tests want to find out which type of equipment will afford the greatest protection with a minimum of maintenance and replacement. Some of the officers are *convinced that proper clothing, along with adequate instruction in the use of this equipment, would reduce the incidents of frostbite. I think they're right.*

It seems that some of the officers and enlisted men have been careless and have lost or misplaced some of their personal equipment. I guess their mothers didn't teach 'em very well.

Some of the men have left camp without their passes or their identification tags. Some of our rules are wacky, but this kind of stuff is serious.

It is not uncommon for Bassingbourn airdrome to be covered by a ground fog early each morning due to the fact that the airdrome is on relatively low, flat, land. On occasions, we are covered with fog when all of the surrounding territory is relatively clear. Isn't that crazy? This condition has caused considerable difficulty on several occasions when aircraft were attempting to take off on early morning missions. It is also anticipated that the situation will become worse as the temperature variations between night and day become greater as the warmer season advances.

Think of us often and pray for us always.

Love,

Bud

77

THE 91st GROUP was alerted to attack Rouen. Take-off was scheduled for 1150 hours, but just as the aircraft began to taxi to the end of the runway, the mission was cancelled by higher headquarters. To the flyboys, it was definitely a SNAFU, which led the men to utter the popular Eighth Air Force refrain, "Situation normal, all f---ed up!"

THE MARCH 18th mission was the submarine building yards at Vegesack. As the briefing concluded, Major Ellis said, "You'll have 27 B-24s from the First Bombardment Group join you on this one."

"I guess they don't get to play with the grown ups very much, do they, sir?" Grabowski shouted.

Ellis didn't normally tolerate any idle chatter or shouting out during a briefing, but this time he allowed it. He even laughed, "I think you're onto something, Ski. But if they screw up, we'll have to make them stay after school." There was laughter.

"But seriously men, the Liberators will bring our force to 100 aircraft. And for your information, you're going to make history. This will be one of the largest American bombing missions of the war."

Ellis' remark created a buzz in the room. And while this was significant, history was being made on a regular basis.

"Well, good luck, fellows," said Col. Birdwell. "Put the hurt on 'em."

THE GROUND FOG did not clear and was much too heavy for the scheduled 1030 take-off, and the time of departure had to be postponed twice. However, by 1200 hours the visibility was increasing rapidly and the first of the Fortresses cleared the end of the runway at approximately 1215 hours. It was no "walk in the park," but the big bombers did their job.

78

BRICK HANSFORD HAD to admit that it was nice to be able to take advantage of the Dorchester Hotel.

"It's a bit strange, actually," said Brick.

"Strange how? What do you mean?" Rachel asked.

"Unlike London, you can get just about anything you want at the Dorchester. I would think you'd be a little embarrassed."

"Why? I'm not British. Look, I could have gone back to America after Poland, where it was safe. But I didn't. I came here and I've lived through the blitz and endured everything the citizens of London have. When you're not in town, I just work and come back to my room. At least I feel safe here. No, Brick, I don't feel embarrassed or guilty."

He looked embarrassed. "I feel terrible about what I just said."

"You want to leave and go to a pub?" she ask, sarcastically.

"No, baby, please forgive me."

She stared at him for a moment and then smiled, "Dance with me."

He almost turned over the table getting to her.

"You see that couple in front of us?"

"Yes."

"That's Averill Harriman, the American Lend-Lease director. He has a ground floor suite here."

"Who is the babe?"

She laughed, "The babe, Captain Hansford, is Pamela Churchill, the prime minister's daughter-in-law."

"Oh, my God, are you serious?"

"Deadly serious. It's hardly a secret anymore in this town. She works at the Ministry of Supply and also has a room here at the Dorchester."

"That helps a lot, doesn't it?"

"Indeed it does."

"What about her husband?"

"Randolph's regiment was sent to Egypt, and Pam was finally liberated to enjoy the erotic frenzy of wartime London."

"And she took advantage of it."

"Indeed she did."

79

EMDEN WAS ONE of the most important German ports through which Swedish iron ore flowed to the Nazi war machine, and it was the desire of the high command to inflict as much damage on these installations as possible.

After an hour in their planes and two postponements, the mission was cancelled. To the crew of the *Rachel*, it was another SNAFU!

"Well, the good news is that we don't have to do ground school," quipped Destafano.

"I'm surprised at you, Tony," said Gregory, "don't you want to be the best that you can be?"

"Don't you want to kiss my ass?"

"No, but I'll kick you ass."

"All right, knock it off," said Sgt. Gifford. Delays, postponements, and scrubbed missions did tend to put some of the men on edge. But, this was fairly typical.

"For what it's worth, fellows, today's training schedule will be carried over to tomorrow."

"Thanks for the reminder, Sarge," said Destafano.

THE PLAN WAS to hit Emden on March 20, 1943. Preliminary information arrived shortly after 2100 hours, but the mission was scrubbed again. The scrub order arrived just before time to awaken the crews, and they got to sleep in.

The kitchen force was probably more annoyed by this turn of events than any other section on the airdrome. They had all but completed a fine breakfast for the combat crews and members of the ground echelons.

■ ■ ■ ■ ■

NEWS REACHED HEADQUARTERS, Eighth Air Force, that the pocket battleship *Admiral Sheer* and the cruiser *Admiral Hipper* were at the naval base at Wilhelmshaven. The commanding general was very anxious to attack the ships. All available aircraft of the Group were loaded with the heaviest bombs available and the 18 combat crews were awakened at 0515 hours to begin the routine for the mission. After a series of delays, the mission was scrubbed. Combat crews taxied their aircraft back to the dispersal areas and arrived at their quarters for a late lunch.

"Did you hear from your wife, Clark?" Wyman asked.

"Yeah, I did. She's better at writing than I am. God—I miss them so much. One of my little girls had chicken pox, but she's okay now and no scars on that beautiful little face. Otherwise, everything's fine in Durango."

"I guess I'll get married," Wyman said. "But I'll have plenty of time to worry about that. I think Carter is pretty serious about the girl he's met over here. Wouldn't that be something if he married a Brit?"

"It happens," said Clifford.

80

Hey, Mom and Dad,

It's almost springtime here in merry ole England. Too bad we can't enjoy this beautiful country. Well, we can enjoy it but I'm sure you know what I mean. I like it a lot, and I hope to come back here after the war and see it in the proper way.

Here's a news flash from Bassingbourn. Drivers have been speeding on the base. It's funny in a way, you know. Our mission, our only reason for being here, is to bomb Germany into submission. But we're concerned about speeding on base. Sometimes I don't know whether to laugh or cry. Sometimes I do both. The truth is that the main job of some of the members of this fighting force is administrative crap! Anyway, vehicle drivers were warned about exceeding the speed limit of 20 miles an hour, which is in force on this station.

A USO show played Bassingbourn last night and about a 1,000 officers and men attended. This kind of thing is very important for morale, you know, to take your mind off war if only for a short while. This show was much better than many of the shows we've had lately.

Here's something else I can talk about. About 48 cadets of the Air Training Corps visited Bassingbourn. The Air training Corps is an auxiliary organization designed to give preliminary training and military indoctrination to boys between the ages of 15 and 17. This training is preparatory to the real training *for the Royal Air Force. The cadets are from the Hertford Grammar Flight School. They were really excited to see our Flying Fortresses, in particular. The commanding officer of the Flight was very appreciative of the opportunity. He stated that it had done more to stimulate interest in the Royal Air Force than any project in which they had engaged in several months.*

All combat crew members who have joined the group during the past month were given their regular weekly dinghy drill. Don't laugh. The boys who were not up to speed were given special instruction. This part of the training program has been emphasized during the past month. All combat crews are now being impressed with the importance of knowing their part in the dinghy drill. All of our missions involve flights of from 50 to several hundred miles over water, and all combat crewmembers have to be acquainted with the intricacies of the dinghy drill.

On a personal side, my girl Scarlett is part of the reason I remain happy and upbeat despite the war and the missions and the danger. When I'm with her, I can actually forget all of this. It still amazes me that no girl in the States ever came close to stacking up to this little British honey. She is wonderful.

I'd better hit the sheets. We'll probably fly tomorrow and if we do, they'll wake us very early.

Love to you both.
Bud

81

THE ATTACK ON the pocket battleship *Admiral Sheer* and the harbor installations at Wilhelmshaven was rescheduled for March 22, 1943.

Weather conditions improved greatly after morning ground fog burnt off, and 21 aircraft of the 91st Group rendezvoused with three other B-17 groups. The 91st Group took the lead, executed two maneuvers in order to allow the rear of the formation to close, and then set a course for the target.

The bombardiers had no difficulty in identifying their target and made their bombing runs with great precision. Strike photographs showed that bombs inflicted rather severe damage. Only three of the 21 aircraft dispatched by the group failed to bomb the target, but the remaining 18 more than upheld the record that the 91st had established.

CARTER AND CLIFFORD dropped by the officers club before going to their quarters. They figured a little alcohol would help them relax after a mission like they had just flown.

"Bud, if I get it, I want you to promise me that you'll be the one to inventory my belongings."

"Clark, I promise, but this 'death wish' is really getting to be a drag. You're obsessed with the idea that you're going to die, and I'm really getting sick and tired of hearing about it."

"It's not a death wish, but I just can't escape the feeling and I worry about my wife and kids," Clark Clifford lamented.

Bud Carter frowned and shook his head, "As I've told you a jillion times, you're a crewman on a really lucky ship. We've got one of the very best pilots in the 91st Bomb Group and a great group of fellows. I don't want you to mention this crap to me again."

82

"YOU GOT A girl back home, Tony?" asked Thibodaux.

"Yeah, I got a tomato and she's a swell little Italian girl. Actually, her parents came over from Sicily in the 20s. But she's all-American, you know—smart, good looking, fun. And she loves baseball. If you live in the Bronx, you gotta love baseball, you gotta love the Yanks."

"Well, you don't gotta, but it's swell when your girl likes sports. Sounds like you're pretty hung up on her."

"We'll get married when I get back."

"What's her name?"

"Maria. Maria Gambino. Her brother Artie's my best friend. He introduced us. What about you, Pat. You got a girl pining away for you back there in New Orleans?"

"Oh, hell yes, Tony," said Thibodaux, "but it's more like a half a dozen. They all want me, you know."

"Seriously, there's nobody special?"

"Nobody special. There are a lot of women in New Orleans, Tony. I hope to continue in music, playing piano and singing. Musicians attract women—all you want and you can just take your pick. So I'll just have a good time. I have no interest in marriage anytime soon—maybe never. I'll just see how it goes."

"We've heard you play and sing, Pat. You're good, you're damn good. I don't know if we're any judge of talent, but we all love your stuff. Any chance a guy like you could make records someday?"

"I don't know, maybe. Boy, that would be swell, wouldn't it?"

"It sure would. I can just imagine a Saturday night in the Bronx. Marie and I have just finished a big Italian dinner and we're having some vino and listening to Thibodeaux records. Man, what a deal."

"It sure as hell sounds good to me."

"You want another beer?" asked Tony.

"I sure do."

"You ever think about not making it, Tony?"

"Not for one damn second. You?"

248

"No, not a all. The only person on this crew who ever seems to worry about it is Lt. Clifford. I don't know, Tony, maybe if I had a wife and two kids, I'd worry."

"That's possible. It's hard to know how you'd feel. You know, when you're not in that other guy's shoes."

"True. So you like the Yanks?"

"Oh, yeah, that's true love. But I'm also pretty fond of the New York Giants." He shook his head. "It's just great to have all the sports that we have."

"You are really lucky. We'll never have professional teams in New Orleans."

"The truth is, you're probably right."

"Funny, you're for the American League because of the Yanks. I've always been a National League fan and my favorite team is the St. Louis Cardinals. I played shortstop in school and I really liked Marty Marion. But my favorite player of all is Stan Musial. Ole number six is just one of the best, and he seems like such a nice guy."

"That's interesting," said Tony.

"But guess what, my favorite professional football team is the Giants."

"No fooling," said Tony, with a smile. "So you're a Giants fan."

83

SHORTLY AFTER THE mission to Rotterdam had been scrubbed, a B-17 of the 322d Squadron caught fire and was all but destroyed.

"Did you hear about *Miss Lulu?*" Hansford asked.

"No, I didn't," said Bud.

Hansford shook his head, "It seems that a specialist in the ground crew was repairing an oxygen leak in the nose of the aircraft and was being assisted by two other men. In the middle of his work, Tuttle decided to light a cigarette while the oxygen was draining from one of the connections under repair. For some reason or other, the oxygen ignited and, in an instant, the whole nose of the aircraft was a mass of flames."

"What about the men?" Bud asked.

"All three of the men received serious first-degree burns and had to be evacuated to the station hospital at Diddington. A board of inquiry has been set up to investigate the accident."

BRICK WROTE HOME.

> *Dear Mom and Dad,*
>
> *Not much changes over here. You know, missions, bad weather, bad weather, bad weather. Did I mention that we have bad weather? The large volume of scrubbed missions causes more tension than flying the damn things. But, if we can't fly, we can't fly. There's really no good answer to this problem.*
>
> *Our big Skipper, Col. Birdwell, presided over the presentation of awards and decorations today. I have written you before about the problem of the men not getting their awards when they earn them. In the past, we always had some general officer or higher commander from Wing Headquarters do it. That was part of the problem also, you know, getting them down here. Okay, now we got a new regulation that the presentation of*

awards can be made by the commanding officers of stations unless some special occasion warrants the appearance of an officer of a higher rank or position. We are very fond of Col. Birdwell, and we would rather have him make the awards anyway. Colonel Birdwell awarded 14 Air Medals, three Oak Leaf Clusters to the Air Medal, and one Purple Heart. It was a good day.

The Special Service Department got its spring athletic program underway. The SSD, there's a bunch of warriors for you. I just need an attitude adjustment. Not everybody can fly in a B-17. Anyway, our heroes have established an inter-unit softball league on the station, and nine teams are competing for the base championship. They also established programs in volleyball, horseshoes, and touch football. Most all units on the station are participating in one or more parts of the program.

A regular hard ball team was also organized to represent the 91st Group during the coming summer months. I'm going to play third base, and that's a pretty big deal because we have several veteran semi-pro ball players stationed here at Bassingbourn and we expect the team to make a good showing when we meet the teams from some of the nearby airdromes.

Four of the six tennis courts at Bassingbourn were conditioned while the two in back of the senior officers' mess were already being used. Several officers and men have purchased tennis rackets and that includes Captain Brick Hansford and Lt. Wilson Wyman. We've had trouble getting tennis balls, but so far, enough have been found for a good number of people to play.

For several months, the pantry in officers' number one mess has been left open for the convenience of those individuals who have to work at night. Both officers and enlisted men have been guilty of abusing the privilege. Some property was destroyed and a good bit of food was wasted. As a consequence, an order was published placing all kitchens and pantries out of bounds to all unauthorized personnel. Now, no officers or enlisted men are permitted in these areas unless they're on official business. Somebody always has to screw things up for the others.

A message was received from General Hap Arnold, Commander of the Army Air Corps, congratulating the 91st Group on the brilliancy and effectiveness of the attack on the marshalling yards at Hamm, Germany on March 4, 1943. That's a big deal to us and very appreciated.

Take care of the home front. We'll try to keep the Krauts from taking over the world.

Love you both,

Brick

84

THE WEATHER AT Bassingbourn was dismal—something that had come to be routine, but annoying and stressful nonetheless. No mission was scheduled, and practically everyone on the station enjoyed a night of unbroken rest. Ground school emphasized aircraft recognition.

"Cliff, I want us to put more emphasis on all aspects of the ditching procedure," said Col. Birdwell. "The loss of Captain McClellan's aircraft in the North Sea on the last mission to Wilhelmshaven was unacceptable. We've just got to have better discipline and gain more knowledge in this phase of training."

"I'll see to it, Jack," said Ellis. "You don't need to be worrying about that kind of thing."

Birdwell frowned, "I worry about everything that jeopardizes the safety of these men. The enemy is brutal enough. I don't want to lose any of 'em on things like inadequate ditching procedures."

"I'll take care of it."

"Good."

"The commendation from General Eisenhower should help overall morale," said Birdwell. *It would have been more special if the man had actually commanded troops in combat.*

"Very definitely," said Ellis. "For the Supreme Commander of Allied Forces in Europe to congratulate us on our performance is damn special."

"The truth is that it was intended for all the members of the Eighth Air Force on their successes in recent operations," said Birdwell. "But," with a large smile on his face, "I'll slant it toward the 91st when I break the news to the men."

"I know they'll appreciate it," said Ellis, with his own large smile.

"Jack, we've received a precautionary warning over the signature of General Moreland."

"What's it say?" said Birdwell.

"Well, sir, he stated that it was altogether likely that the Germans might carry out retaliatory attacks against the airdromes of this command. He directed that each airdrome adopt every possible method to insure that defenses are in operation and manned, that personnel be thoroughly instructed with regard to their various duties in case of attacks, that adequate and proper dispersion be carried out, and that black-outs be strictly observed."

"Okay, get the message out to the men over my signature."

"It's as good as done, sir."

"Cliff, unfortunately, we still have to deal with the mundane around here. This base is beginning to look like a combination junkyard and privy. We have an accumulation of dirt, waste paper, scrap lumber, and other assortments of crap on various parts of the airdrome. I think maybe the look of the base has contributed to some laxness in discipline and especially in military courtesy. And we may soon have some distinguished visitors visiting the base. So, let's get her shaped up."

"We'll get squared away, sir."

"I know you will."

85

CLARK CLIFFORD WROTE to his wife in Durango.

Dear Kathy,

I think of you and our little girls constantly. I fell in love with you the first time I saw you and nothing has changed. I love you more each and every day. It hurts not being with you and being able to hold you and make love to you. It bothers me that I am not there to help you with the girls. I hope they will remember me. I'm the only member of the crew with children; so it's different with me.

While we were on a mission, one of life's many comedies took place at the airdrome. It was not intended as a comedy at all, but rather was designed as an exercise to prove the group as an organization. We're so self-contained that we should be able to defend ourselves and our base without much difficulty. Like I said, while we were in the air, the base conducted a sham battle. Apparently, it turned out to be sham from start to finish. But, they'll get it fixed.

There have been problems with guests who come over to visit their American friends at Bassingbourn. An order was published stating that all guests must be duly registered at the main gate upon arrival. This directive also pointed out the fact that Bassingbourn possesses very limited facilities for guests who wish to remain on the station over night. All officers and men were warned that proper arrangements must be made at least 24 hours prior to their arrival. I wish I had that problem for you and the girls.

This is funny. We got this directive from headquarters which stated that enlisted men in the area have been purchasing and wearing non-regulation items of clothing. The military is really strict about wearing the uniform properly and I agree with that. I mean, you can't have part of a uniform mixed with miscellaneous civilian clothes. I don't know exactly what to say except that some GIs are just a little crazy. The directive ordered station commanders to take steps to insure that all enlisted personnel will be properly dressed before they are permitted to leave the station. The directive didn't mention it, but if they want to stop this stuff, they better check how the guys are dressed when they return to base.

Now this is exciting, it really is. They have been testing some of the various types and combinations of winter flying equipment here at Bassingbourn. Electrically heated clothes and shoes have been accepted as necessary to deal with the temperatures at high altitude. An electrically heated flying suit has been recommended for adoption by the Eighth Air Force. The officers conducting the tests have stipulated that the flying suit, shoes, and gloves should be connected separately to the source of electrical supply and that the shoes and gloves should be connected in parallel so that they would be independent of each other in their operation. Further tests on other types of equipment will be conducted over the next two or three weeks. Combat crews, who have participated in the tests, are enthusiastic about the interest being shown in our problems. It's when they know, and do nothing, that really gets under our skin.

I've got to hit the sack, Kathy. But pray for all of us and give my little girls a big hug and kiss from me.

Love you, darling,

Clark

86

"COL. BIRDWELL, WE have a communiqué advising us that the Queen of England plans to visit Bassingbourn," Major Ellis advised. "Since it's also a permanent RAF base, she can kill two birds with one stone: visit her own troops while also saying hello to us Yanks."

Birdwell grinned and leaned forward, "Make no mistake about it, Cliff, Winston Churchill and the Crown are extremely happy to have America in the war. And they love to have the Eighth Air Force pounding enemy installations and factories during the day. You know, they quit the practice themselves because of unsustainable losses, but they love that we're doing it."

"Well, Skipper, don't you think that part of the Brit's problem is their aircraft and their formations?"

"Yes, I do. They gave up fire power for bomb load."

Cliff smiled, "And with the B-17, we have both."

"We sure do. Yes, the Yanks are mighty welcome over here in spite of unpleasant incidents from time to time. Cliff, when we get the details, you can alert everybody about the Queen. Then we'll turn out the Group and have them in formation for inspection for the First Lady of Great Britain."

"Good deal, Skipper, and we'll do it right."

"We better," said Birdwell, with a sly grin.

■ ■ ■ ■ ■

"I SAY, COLONEL, your boys are a handsome lot. Some of them look like movie stars," said the Queen.

Following the review of the troops, Birdwell took Her Majesty to the flight line to see the B-17s, the pride of the Eighth Air Force. They had purposely put the *General Ike* up close for her to see. The Queen took one look at the big plane and with hands on hips bellowed, "Where are the pin-ups? I want to see the pin-ups!"

Col. Birdwell was taken aback, but recovered his wits quickly and hollered, "Captain Hansford and Lt. Carter, front and center on the double!"

The boys broke formation and reported to the colonel, clicking their heels and saluting smartly.

"At ease, gentlemen. The Queen wants to see the *Rachel*. And take her inside the airplane, if she's interested, and show her everything."

The Queen smiled warmly and stuck out her hand. Brick and Bud looked at each other quickly and then glanced at Birdwell who frowned and nodded. They soon caught on and both bowed slightly and shook her hand. Then they climbed into her Rolls Royce and off they went.

Col. Birdwell and Major Ellis smiled at each other. "Are you sure we can trust them with the Queen of England?" asked Ellis, jokingly.

"Oh, yeah, they'll charm her completely."

DURING MARCH 1943, the 91st Bomb Group participated in nine missions against the enemy. Some were exceptionally good, while others ranked down at the bottom of the scale. The attack on the Hamm marshalling yards on March 4 and on Vegesack on March 18, although costly, had proved the value and potentialities of high-altitude, daylight precision bombing.

87

"SIR HENRY, MAY I have a word?"

"By all means, my dear, come into my office."

"Yes, sir."

"What can I do for you?"

"I was at the bar at the Dorchester when a man approached me and ask if he could buy me a drink," said Rachel.

Sir Henry frowned. Rachel noticed.

"Sir Henry, you know my background."

"Yes."

"Well, you should know I can take care of myself. If a man wants to spend his money buying me a drink, I'll let him. If he gets too pushy, he'll find out how useless it is and how foolish he's been."

Sir Henry smiled. He understood. "Please continue."

"Well, it was small talk for awhile and then he wanted to know where I worked and what I did. Needless to say, I wouldn't tell him and he seemed perturbed. I turned down his second drink offer, and after awhile he left. I didn't think any more about it until last night, when it happened again. The same fellow offered to buy me a drink again and I accepted."

Sir Henry frowned again.

She noticed. "Look, I was toying with him. I'm good at that. I figured he wanted to connect, you know, ask me out on a date."

"Or take you to his flat," Sir Henry interjected.

She grunted, "No matter. I would have turned him down, but as I said, I wanted to play with him."

"That could be dangerous."

"I'm a big girl, Sir. Henry. I can handle myself. But—you may have a point. Anyway, he eventually got around to my work and what I did. He pressed me more than the first time. That made an alarm go off."

"That kind of questioning is not normal or logical," said Sir Henry.

"Exactly, that's why I'm telling you."

"Were you able to get his name?"

"Yes, it's Willard Whatley."

"Of course, that may not be his real name."

"Here, he gave me his card. It says he's a sales representative with the Norwood Trading Company. When I pressed him for more information about what he did and what his company did, he just brushed it off by saying they just traded in things. Anyway, I think something's not right, Sir Henry."

"You're a smart girl, Rachel. It may be nothing, but then again, your suspicions may be valid. I mean, for him to press you about your job is suspicious, particularly since it happened twice. And that could mean someone at BP may have loose lips and could be guilty of violating the Official Secrets Act."

"The Official Secrets Act?"

"Yes. You signed a pledge not to divulge anything about what you are doing here at BP."

"I remember that, but I don't think it was explained to me that it was part of the OSA."

"I'll look into that. Anyway, people working with sensitive information are commonly required to sign a statement to the effect that they agree to abide by the restrictions of the act. This is popularly referred to as signing the Official Secrets Act. Signing this has no effect on which actions are legal as the act is a law, not a contract, and individuals are bound by it whether or not they have signed it. Signing it is intended more as a reminder to the person that they are under such obligations. To this end, it is common to sign this statement both before and after a period of employment that involves access to secrets."

Rachel nodded.

"I'll see that the right people get this information. You were right to come to me with this."

88

BY LATE SPRING, the United States Army Air Forces in the British Isles had become a relatively well-organized military force. Supplies and replacement parts, which were almost impossible to obtain a few months earlier, were now beginning to arrive in satisfactory quantities. This turn of events made operations much easier than the latter part of 1942.

The arrival of replacement combat personnel furnished a solution to a situation, which had threatened to become acute six weeks earlier. Although by no means ideal, their presence carried the promise that even greater improvements would be forthcoming.

"The attitude of the men has shown a remarkable improvement," said Col. Birdwell. "In the beginning, I'm quite sure that 25 missions seemed literally impossible to many of the crews."

"I know you're right, Skipper, and it was perfectly understandable," said Cliff Ellis. "The damn rain and aborted missions, mechanical difficulties, lack of replacements, heavy loses. All of it together made the completion of an operational tour and return to the United States seem next to impossible."

"Cliff, I'm sure you realize that many of the crews have passed the halfway mark, while several are approaching their twentieth."

"I do realize it, Skipper. The United States seems much closer than it did on the first of last month. You gotta really be happy for the original crews. They might even complete their assignments here in Europe and make it back to the States in time for a 4th of July celebration."

"True, it's very possible. You know, Cliff, they have learned so well. They realize that their experience in combat and knowledge of German tactics, together with their ability to fly a good defensive formation, have gone a long way toward their chances of successfully completing their tours."

THE CREW OF the *Rachel* had completed seventeen missions. None of them had been seriously wounded and, although the *Rachel* had taken a beating on occasions, the ground crews had always patched her up and sent their lady back out, looking and acting her best.

"Eight more missions to go, Brick, and we can all go home," said Bud Carter, excitedly. "I actually think we're gonna make it."

Brick Hansford lit up a Camel cigarette, repositioned his pillow, and laid back on his bunk. He took in a satisfying draw, exhaled, and said, "I'm gonna stay until the war's over. That is, unless they won't let me. But I think they will. Hell, why wouldn't they want to keep the best damn pilot in the Eighth Air Force?"

Carter sat upright on his bunk. "You can't be serious?"

"Why the hell not?" he quipped, a sinister smirk on his face.

"You are serious."

"I like the work, man, it's the most exhilarating thing I've ever done. And you gotta admit, I'm very good at it."

Carter frowned. "Most of us, me included, are here because someone had to do it—to stop the Nazi takeover of Europe—maybe the world. We do it because we're trained to do it. That's the difference between you and me, Brick; you do it—because you love it!"

Brick grinned, "I absolutely do, and that's a fact. But remember, Rachel is here. She's going to stay until it's over. I don't want to lose her. I did once, but it won't happen again if I can help it."

89

THERE WAS THE usual chatter in the briefing room when suddenly Col. Birdwell burst in followed by Major Ellis and the other briefing officers.

"Pull the curtain, Major Ellis, and let the boys see where they're headed."

"Germany!" one crewman blurted out. Then they saw the exact destination. "Oh, no, not Wilhelmshaven again!" said another man in disgust.

Birdwell just put his hands on his hips, thought Bud. *He always does that when he wants to get our attention or say something profound.*

"We don't pick 'em, gentlemen, we just fly 'em. But that sea port is plenty important to the German war effort, and that's why we have to keep hitting it. So stow the crap, and let's get down to business. I'll lead the group on this one. Captain Hansford will lead the high squadron and Captain Kennedy will lead the low squadron. Major Ellis, give the men the details."

Ellis began the countdown, "Okay, stations at 0700, start engines at 0710, taxi at 0720..." and so on it went until all the briefing information had been shared with the crews.

$$\bullet\ \bullet\ \bullet\ \bullet\ \bullet$$

THE GROUND CREWS were waiting anxiously. Some played pitch and catch, but most just sat on their vehicles or on their rear ends, looking to the skies. Cliff Ellis and the other officers on the tower were looking through their binoculars for a glimpse of the returning warriors.

"Got a cigarette, Captain Mullins?" asked Ellis, showing his anxiety.

"Sure thing, Major, and here's a light."

While Ellis was lighting up, another officer tapped on the window behind him. "They're heading in, Major. We just got a reading."

"How many?"

"Don't know that yet."

"There they are," said Ellis, pointing, "they're circling."

Crews of the crash vehicles and ambulances climbed aboard, started engines and moved toward the tarmac. "There's eight … nine …," said Ellis.

"Fourteen … 15 …16 …," said Mace Mullins.

"Mace, I'm going out to meet Col. Birdwell."

ELLIS DROVE HIMSELF out to where Birdwell's lead ship, The *Upperhand,* had stopped and cut engines. He walked toward her and stood by the forward hatch. In a minute it opened and Birdwell dropped out.

"How was it Colonel?" asked Ellis.

"It was rough. They were waiting for us, but we did our job. What's the count, Cliff?"

"It was 16 when I left the tower."

"Okay, Cliff, let's get over to interrogation."

Mullins was waiting at interrogation when Birdwell and Ellis burst through the door. "Twenty-two in safely," he reported. "Two ditched in the Channel, but both crews were picked up, drenched, of course, but all in good shape."

Birdwell clasped his hands in delight, "That's great news."

After Birdwell finished in interrogation, he and Ellis walked out and headed for headquarters. "Cliff, the next phase of the war against Germany is going to be the destruction of its aviation industry. A critical part of the strategy will be the elimination of German ball-bearing production since just about every machine that has moving parts requires ball-bearings. Business is going to pick up, and these major industrial targets are going to be well -defended and dangerous. Cliff, it looks like we're gonna stand down for several days. Let's cut loose for some passes to London before the shit really hits the fan. The boys have earned it."

"I'll take care of it, Skipper."

90

THE OFFICERS OF the *Rachel* were in the same railroad car with one additional passenger, a parson.

"How are we doing on time, Clifford?" Brick asked.

"We're about 12 minutes from the station."

"Thanks, Clifford."

"I assume you're seeing Scarlett, Bud?" Wilson Wyman asked.

"That would be an affirmative, Wilson."

"Oh, yeah, what's the program?"

"We're going to see a film and then get a bite to eat and probably throw down a few. The rest of the time, we'll just figure it out as we go. Are you seeing Millie?"

"Millie and I have split the blanket. I've got to find another girl, but there's plenty of them."

"What are you up to, Brick?" Wyman inquired.

"Rachel's meeting me at the station. It seems like forever since we've seen each other."

"Time to catch up."

"That's an affirmative."

The parson, sitting next to Brick Hansford, opened up a box lunch that contained two sandwiches, an orange, and a cookie.

"Hey, Padre, those sandwiches look good," said Brick.

"I'd be happy to share my food with you, Captain."

"No, no, I wouldn't think of it. It was just a comment."

The padre smiled as he took a bite of his sandwich.

"We're almost there," said Clifford.

"Yes, we are," said Bud, with a smile.

Brick stood up, stretched, and put on his hat. "I can't wait. Have fun fellows." And with that, he left the group. On his way down the passageway, he poked his head into the compartment where the enlisted contingent of the *Rachel* was riding.

"How's it going, fellows?"

"Just fine, Skipper," said Gifford.

"Say, can you tell us anything about what we'll be doing when we get back?" questioned Destafano.

266

"I don't have any idea, but don't even be speculating about destinations while you're here in London. Do you understand?"

"Yes, sir," Morgan replied.

"Now, enjoy yourselves. For God's sake, quit thinking about missions. Enjoy this time while you have it. And that's an order," said Brick, with a smile.

Brick stood anxiously in the doorway. He couldn't wait for the train to stop. Soon enough it did, and he rushed to the newsstand where he and Rachel had agreed to meet. She saw him, but ducked behind it in order to surprise him. When he didn't see her, he looked around anxiously. She came around behind him and grabbed him around the waist, laughing wildly. Then she faced him, grinning from ear to ear.

"Hey, you," he said with the broadest of smiles, and then took her in his arms and kissed her. He kissed her for a long time. "It seems like forever since I've seen you. You look good, you smell good, and you taste good!"

"I'm pretty glad to see you too, Capt. Hansford, in the remotest chance that you couldn't tell."

THE MEN HAD a 72-hour pass and they needed it.

Some of the crew were enjoying themselves at The Dove, 19 Upper Mall. King Charles II used the pub as a place to meet his mistress Nell Gwynne. The composer of "Rule Britannia" lodged in the rooms upstairs, William Morris lived next door, and Ernest Hemingway was a regular visitor.

Lt. Wyman was playing darts with McGuire and George Gifford. Soon he became bored and wanted to have some fun.

"Hey, McGuire, you wanna play the William Tell game?" Wyman asked, with a sheepish grin and mischievous laugh.

"I don't know LT, what is it?"

Wyman grabbed McGuire and stood him with his back against the dart board, holding a beer bottle on top of his head. Then he took a boiled egg from the container on the bar and placed it carefully on top of the bottle. He planned to toss darts at the egg. At that moment, McGuire decided to chicken out. Wilson bribed him with a ten dollar bill. McGuire closed his eyes as Wyman prepared to make the first toss—while crew members screamed and hollered at the top of their lungs. Wyman pieced the egg with the first toss to the cheers of his admiring crew, other patrons, and to the great relief of McGuire.

"It just like when I drop my bombs. Always right where I aim."

"McGuire, you wanna go again?"

"That's it, Lt. Wyman, no more William Tell."

"Oh, hell, McGuire, I bet you'll do it again for fifty dollars."

"Not a chance, LT."

No amount of money could get McGuire to give Wyman a second toss, and there were no other volunteers.

The fun and games were interrupted by the sirens announcing another enemy air raid. The owner of the pub came out from around the bar and broke the news that was painfully obvious, "The German bombers, they're back again. Follow us," he said, holding out his hand for his wife. "There's an air raid shelter just down the street."

Everybody left the pub but Wyman. He stayed around and drank free liquor while the others took cover. Some of the bombs hit close by, but no damage was done to the little pub, and besides, close didn't impress Wilson Wyman. He even went outside to look at the fireworks.

When the bombing ended, he put on his hat and left the bar. He was on to something else. He looked left, then right, and then started walking. He didn't know where he was going. After about ten minutes of wandering, he bumped into a girl. "Hi there, Yank, aren't you the dashing one?"

Nice, Wyman thought to himself. *She's a hooker all right but a real dish. I ought to know the type and the look. I've been with plenty of them.*

"How far is your place from here?"

"About 5 minutes by taxi," she relied. "It's cozy and comfy."

"Breakfast?" he asked with a grin.

"Hot tea, toast, marmalade, and me," she said.

"What's the price for being dashing?"

"You can afford it, luv."

Brick raised his hand and shouted, "Cabbie!"

91

"WHAT CAN I do for you, mate?" said the bartender, wiping the area in front of Brick with his bar towel.

"I'd like a sherry and a half and half."

He set the beer in front of Brick and asked, in reference to the sherry, "Sweet or dry?"

"Sweet."

They had just gotten out of a film and wanted a night cap before he took her home.

He paid the tab and took the drinks to the table. "Cheers," said Brick, lightly touching her glass. They smiled at each other and both took a sip.

"I don't know how the Brits drink warm beer."

"They put the mug to their lips and tilt it slightly," said Rachel.

"Funny," he replied with a smile.

The pub was lively; several locals were at the bar, several other couples in booths, and a group of GIs and British soldiers were drinking beer and playing a friendly, but competitive, game of darts. "Looks like the boys are cohabitating nicely."

"Cohabitating? Well, they look like they're getting along."

"A man at the bar cursed me under his breath, something about 'damn Yanks over here throwing around money…'"

"You have to realize that the Brits have had heavy restrictions on them for quite awhile now, and the British government introduced a system of rationing."

"We have that in the States now."

Rachel smiled, "Yes, America's in it now. The American people will have to do with less to support the war effort—but not to the extent they are doing it here. So, it's understandable that some are a bit bitter at seeing the Yanks flush with cash."

"I think you're right about that. Still, my men have been treated very well here."

"That's good to hear. Anyway, at least the government officials recognized that children should be treated differently from adults and entitled to extra food considered essential for growth, such as milk and eggs," said Rachel.

"That's good."

"People have been encouraged to provide their own food. The government has a program called *Dig for Victory* that calls for every man and woman to keep an allotment. Lawns and flower-beds are turned into vegetable gardens. Chickens, rabbits, goats, and pigs are reared in town gardens."

"My parents told me they are doing some of that at home," said Brick. "Mr. Roosevelt has asked people to plant gardens, Victory Gardens. But they're probably not doing it on the same scale as they are doing it here."

Rachel laughed.

"What's funny?"

"What's funny is that I don't see the Boston Hansfords tending a garden."

Brick laughed. "Yeah, you're right. I think that they were talking about some parts of America."

She giggled, "Yeah, I think that's it. They've been rationing clothes here since June, 1941. A point system allows people to buy only one completely new outfit a year."

"That policy would not be well received in certain neighborhoods in Boston."

"No kidding," said Rachel, with a grin.

"To save fabric," Rachel continued, "men's trousers are now made without cuffs, and women's skirts are short and straight. Women's magazines are packed with handy hints on how, for example, old curtains might be cut up to make a dress."

"That reminds me of Scarlett O'Hara in *Gone with the Wind*."

She took a sip of her sherry and continued. "Stockings are still in short supply, so girls color their legs with gravy browning. Sometimes a girl will draw a line down the back of her leg with an eyebrow pencil for a seam. Well, you get the picture."

Bud laughed.

"I'm not kidding," she insisted, "but I don't have to do that."

They laughed.

"Well, I think that's quite enough about hard times in England. But it does explain why the men resent the Yanks. Well, some of them. It's just that you boys have so much more money, you know, to spend on the ladies. They seem to think it puts them at a disadvantage."

"Do you believe that?"

"It's true to some extent. I work with these girls and they talk to me. But there is absolutely no question that the British girls are extremely attracted to American boys."

"So they're just after our money," said Brick, playfully.

"And you're just after their panties," said Rachel.

They stared at each other for a moment and both started laughing.

He leaned over and kissed her.

"That was nice," she said.

"Have I ever told you how soft your lips are—and what a dynamite smile you have?" asked Brick.

"You have, but I always like hearing it."

"The fact is, Rachel, you're a knockout."

"A knockout?"

"Yes."

"You're very sweet."

He pulled out a pack of Camels and offered her one, "Smoke?"

"Yes, thank you." After packing the tobacco tight, he lit her cigarette and then his own.

"Hey, that was a swell film, don't you think?" said Brick.

"Yes, it was, and I'm very pleased you liked it. I was afraid that you were just going to see it to please me."

"I was going to please you, but the thing is, I really like those romantic comedies. You think Clark Gable is good looking?"

"Of course I do, silly. I'm a girl."

"But he's not here, and I am."

She laughed, "That does give you an advantage."

They laughed.

"What do you think about Claudette Colbert?" she inquired.

"She's cute and very popular, but she's not my type."

"What is your type?" she asked playfully.

"Maybe you'll figure it out in time," he said. They both laughed again.

"That film, *It Happened One Night,* won the American Academy Award in 1934."

"I can't believe you know things like that," she remarked.

"Come on, Rachel, you know I'm a big movie fan."

She thought for a minute, "Come to think of it, I do remember that. Listen, I was thinking it might be fun to double date with Bud and Scarlett sometime," she suggested.

He grinned, "We could do that, but I sure like having you all to myself."

She smiled.

"Incidentally, what happened to your buddy Paul Adams? Is he in the service?"

"Paul and I were going to join up together, much to the consternation of our parents."

She frowned, but didn't comment.

"During his physical exam, they found that he had a heart murmur. A lot of these are benign and of no significance, but some signal cardiac pathophysiology."

"That's a mouthful."

"It is, and it's also a disqualifier. He was crushed."

"He really wanted to go?" she questioned.

"Well, yeah. Think about it. America at war, and you're in that eligible age group, and everybody wondering why you are at home."

"I hope it was more than embarrassment."

"It was, Rachel, he really wanted to serve."

"Do you hear from him?'

"Yeah, we correspond."

"Speaking of old friends, have you gotten in touch with Katie at all?"

"No, I have not."

"I mean, you girls were soul mates. I think that's strange."

"Well, I came to England to help with the war effort. I got a position almost immediately. And it's the kind of post that consumes you. I just poured myself into it and ignored the rest of the world." She sighed, "Katie is not serious minded. She's immature. She's still in a sorority getting ready for the dance. Do you know what I mean?"

"Yes, I do. What about your family in New York, Buenos Aires, and Poland?"

"I'll take Poland first. There has been no word from them since they dropped Katie and me at the American Embassy in Warsaw. There is no confirmation, but I can assure you, they are dead." Her eyes narrowed. "Nazi bastards! We've got to wipe them out, Brick."

272

"I know, baby."

"I drop a line to New York and Buenos Aires occasionally to let them know I'm alive."

He nodded.

92

"WHAT DO YOU want to do when all this is over?" she inquired.

"I could always go back and work for Hansford Motors. But you know, I might just want to stay in the Army Air Corps and make it a career if I make it and have some rank by the time it's over."

Rachel did not react at all. She was curious to see what he was thinking.

"But I don't have to decide right now. What about you?" He was curious as well.

"It's pretty much the same for me. This war is going to go on for quite awhile, and I'm staying until the end. That's been my plan all along. And I'm doing some very important work."

She has that look. I've seen it before. He laughed, "But you can't tell me anything about it."

"That's right, Brick. And if you knew the target of your next mission, you couldn't tell me."

He smiled. "Fair enough."

"You mind if we walk?" Rachel asked.

"Not at all," he replied, smiling and taking her hand.

"We never know when they're going to bomb, so when we can walk a bit, it's quite nice." They weren't sure how long it had been, but the Germans came again. The bombing was not near by, thank God, but it still gave them pause.

"Let's duck in here," Brick suggested, leading her down to an apartment below the street level. "This is about the best we can do for the moment."

She cuddled up close to him, and he put his arms around her. *This man makes me feel safe,* she thought.

They stood under the overhead from the steps leading to the apartment above. She looked up at him with a lost kind of look, "It's hard to get used to this," she lamented.

He thought for a minute. "Somewhere in Germany, some girl is probably having the same conversation."

"Does it bother you?"

"No, not really. They started this thing."

He had another thought. "It's not up close and personal like with the ground troops. There's killing, but at 20,000 feet you just see explosions. And we do our best to just hit the industrial targets. But I don't know about the Brits."

She didn't respond.

They stood there for a time just looking warmly at each other. "I think it's over now," said Brick, glancing up at the sky.

"Yes, I believe they've gone. I wonder how many they killed tonight?"

They walked up to the street level, a bit tentative, as if it might not have come to an end. He took her hand, and they started to stroll again. The streets in the neighborhood were deserted.

"I think I'm ready to go home."

"Okay," he smiled, and started looking for a cab.

"DORCHESTER HOTEL," he said to the cabbie.

She leaned in close again and kissed him.

93

BACK AT BASSINGBOURN, Destafano was lonesome for the Bronx. He said so in a letter to his folks back in New York City.

Hey there, Mom and Dad,

We didn't fly today. We got a bum starboard engine, but they'll have it purring like a kitten by tonight. I'm sure we'll be up tomorrow. Anyway, I had some time after ground school and decided I better write to you before you got sore.

I sure wish I was back home, right now, sitting at Yankee Stadium with a couple of dogs and a cold beer. Hey, let me know how the team is doing. I miss you two and my friends, you know, hanging around talking and checking out those beautiful tomatoes.

Speaking of tomatoes, tell Marie she owes me a letter. I sure do miss her. She wanted to get married before I left and I said no. I wish we'd tied the knot, but it's my fault.

Boy, I get tired of the food on the base over here. But it's good compared to the limey grub. They don't know how to cook anything. I'm so hungry for a big rare steak from Destafano's I don't know what to do. I dream about that juicy meat and a baked potato with all the trimmings. That's another thing, they can't even cook potatoes.

We've been flying a lot, but that's what we do. I just want this thing to be over. We're piling up some missions, so maybe it won't be so long. With better weather, we'll fly more with fewer scrubbed missions. And we really have a swell crew, good guys who know what they're doing.

How is that punk little brother of mine? Tell Georgio to study hard and keep his nose clean. And tell him if I hear that he gives you any trouble, I'll kick his ass when I come home.

Well, that's all for now. Light a candle for me and ask Father Murphy to read my name at Mass.

Tony

94

IT WAS FOUR o'clock in the morning and very quiet. Brick was awake and thinking about the day ahead. *Would they have a mission?* He was tempted to pull back the curtains and look out the window, but decided against it. He was just going to roll over and try to go back to sleep. The next thing he knew, there was someone coming in their room. The corporal said, "Sir, it's time to get up. Breakfast is in 30 minutes, briefing in an hour. Your crew is in today.'"

Yes, they were in. They would fly a bombing mission today—kids who had worked at the corner drug store, kids who had thrown the Sunday newspaper, scored the winning touchdown, or failed algebra. Captains of the clouds, they would take the huge B-17 bombers deep into enemy territory, higher than men could breathe. They would endure subfreezing temperatures, hostile fighter planes, and deadly flak, fastened to life by short hoses of oxygen.

"Thank you, corporal, I think," said Brick. He put on his robe and house shoes and woke Bud. The corporal woke Wyman and Clifford, who were in a room across the hall. Someone else would wake the rest of the enlisted crew who were quartered in another building.

Breakfast for flight crews consisted of hot biscuits, bacon, fresh eggs, and lots of hot coffee. Bud glanced around the mess and said to Brick, "The nerves of some of the fellows are on edge while other men are as calm as can be. Some men eat like they're in their mother's kitchen, others pick at their food, some can't eat at all while others stuff food in their flight jackets for later. It's quite a scene."

Soon they were all together. The briefings held the most importance for the officers because they were directly in charge of flying, navigating, and dropping the bombs. But all the crew members had a right to know where they were going and what to expect.

The extensive instructions about survival are excellent, Brick thought. *If we have to bail out or crash land in enemy territory, the fellows will know what to do. Once we take off, Bud and I are way too busy to cover all the details of survival or other intelligence issues. Being in on the full briefing makes everyone better prepared.*

Everyone was provided a survival kit that contained candy bars, detailed maps on silk, a compass, and pictures of every man wearing a dark suit and tie. "The pictures are supposed to be used by the underground for making up papers of identification for the downed flier," said Brick. "But I'm told that the Germans have caught on to what we were doing."

"I've heard the same thing," said Carter. "Well, hell's bells, the clothing in every picture looks exactly the same."

"This is not the time or place to bring it up, but I'm going to talk to Major Ellis about it," said Brick.

As the chairs squeaked and groaned, they sat and stared at that infamous black curtain that had been deliberately pulled over the huge map of Europe.

"What waits behind the sheet?" Bud questioned. "That's what everybody in this room wants to know."

At one point, Brick looked at Bud but neither man said a word.

Suddenly, the side door to the briefing room opened. "Attention please, gentlemen!" was shouted as the meteorologist, the intelligence officer, and the other briefing officers followed Col. Birdwell and Major Ellis into the room. Birdwell spoke first as usual.

"Gentlemen, today the Eighth Air Force will assemble the largest B-17 force to date, and you'll make your deepest penetration into enemy territory. This raid, and the others like it, will take the war to the Krauts' own backyard and begin to put a stranglehold on their ability to wage war. Gentlemen, this raid today is big. The Eighth Air Force will assemble 376 crews for this combined operation."

There was a noticeable buzz in the room along with some groans. The men knew the stakes were high and the dangers great. The B-17 Flying Fortress bomber carried a crew of 10 men, which meant that 3,760 boyfriends, husbands, fathers, brothers, nephews, and sons would be sent to fight a determined enemy who was hell-bent on killing them.

" Tonight, some of the boys will still be in Germany," Brick sighed.

"Gentlemen, it gives me goose bumps to be a part of it—to lead it. Major Ellis, show 'em where they're going."

Ellis pulled the curtain and someone shouted, "Schweinfurt!" On the map, there was a bright red tack with red yarn extending from

Bassingbourn and trailing over the IP then to Schweinfurt and the homebound route all the way back to base.

Ellis wheeled around and confirmed it, "Yes, Schweinfurt, the ball-bearing factories."

The briefing officers discussed the target in detail, bomb load, weather, anti-aircraft, flak, enemy fighters, and the rest. The last briefing officer to speak, Captain Nash, had never flown a mission. He rubbed his hands together in deep thought and said, "Do a good job today men, and maybe we won't have to go back." Everyone in the room groaned.

AS THEY LEFT the briefing room, Clark Clifford had a thought that kept nagging at him. *Will I come back today? Does this one have my number on it?*

He gathered himself, as he had done on so many occasions, and thought, *No, I am going home to see my wife in just seven more missions. I can't die today; it won't be me!*

Loading quickly into the 6 x 6 vehicles that would take them to the flight line, their minds now turned to the mission.

Brick thought about what they had to do to make the mission a success. *It's a team effort. Every man in the crew has to perform well.*

Everyone climbed aboard the *Rachel* except Hansford and Sergeant Mahoney, the ground crew chief. They walked around the giant aircraft and did a visual inspection. "She's ready to kick ass, Captain Hansford," said Mahoney, reassuringly.

Brick smiled, "Okay, Mahoney." And with that, he swung up into the forward section of the *Rachel*.

95

ONCE ON BOARD, each man made sure everything was ready at his station. Everything had to be checked and rechecked. The mission and their lives depended on it. The emergency equipment, the radio equipment, the oxygen pressure, bomb load, and fuel load. This mission and the ones to come would require B-17s to fly thousands of miles. Although some of the diversion routes had challenged their fuel loads, in most cases they were fine. With a range of 1,850 miles, this airplane could do it.

Brick and Bud started the checklist prior to starting the engines; then, the tower advised that there would be a delay in departing.

Bomber crew members, even though they were going in harm's way, always wanted to get on with it. Delays drove them crazy and the ball turret gunner, Frank McGuire, reacted with disgust. "Oh no—not another delay. Just once, I would like to get in this airplane and go."

He voiced the standard response, "Situation normal!"

And the other crew members responded in unison, "All f---ed up!"

"Oh well," said McGuire, "I'll just work on my turret; it was sticking a little on the last mission. There's the problem, a handkerchief. I can't believe that someone on the ground crew dropped his handkerchief in the works."

With time to burn, Bud was thinking of home. "I wonder what the folks did? I sure could use some of Mom's hot cakes and sausage. Nobody can cook like her. Dad and I are two pretty lucky guys. I just wish the flight order would come down so we can get the mission over with."

"The take-off orders are coming in now," announced Brick. "Ball turret, are you ready?"

McGuire responded, "Yes, sir, I'm all checked out."

"Pilot to Morgan, is your tail gun position ready?"

"My tail guns are ready and the camera hatch works fine. I'll just wait for the take-off. Boy, these waits are worse than the real thing." Morgan's mind was also drifting to more pleasing thoughts. *I wonder what's happening back home? I'll bet Jane is having a date every night and has forgotten all about me. No, Mom said she was over and asked about me and how I was doing. Maybe I'll just write her when we get back from this mission. I wonder if she still has that cute little puppy I gave her?*

Hansford checked with all the other positions, and every crew member was ready.

"Pilot to Destafano, how do those engines sound from the waist gun position?"

"Sir, they sound good this morning. I guess we have about the best ground crew in the entire Eighth Air Force."

"Mahoney can really fix this sweet girl, and the patches from the last mission don't even show," said Gregory.

"Glenn, you remember when we came in on two engines with half the tail shot off?"

"I remember. Two days later it was like a new B-17. They are good."

Gifford asked, "Sir, may I come forward for takeoff?"

"Come on up, Giff."

Joe Morgan was day dreaming, *Lynn is even prettier in that dream than I remember her. I wonder if she's writing me a letter every day as she said she would? No mail now in four days. If any comes today, I may be too tired to read it. One of these days when this war is over, we'll go on a long vacation up at the lake where we can sleep until we want to get up. Then we'll swim over to the little café and eat breakfast, no rush, take time to play the pinball machine and swim back to the cabin. Maybe we'll take the boat and fish or just drift with the wind until we are tired of relaxing. I hope she still wants to marry me.*

"Hey, there goes the first plane," said Morgan.

"Pilot to the crew, we're moving to take-off position. We'll be in assembly in a few minutes. You can test fire your guns over the English Channel."

Sgt. Gifford was thinking, *There's a lot of fire power on this B-17, a formidable fighting machine even when we're not dropping bombs. Granted, the fire power is defensive, but still lethal. We lay down .50 caliber machine gun fire from every direction. In a tightly maintained formation, this bomb group is bad news for incoming enemy fighter planes.*

"We'll be Baker-Baker in the formation," said Brick, "so be sure our right waist firing position is covered at all times. Keep a close look to the right side of the plane. We'll trust that the other planes will cover our left side. We'll be taking off number nine, so we'll have prop wash. So be ready, and secure the waist guns. There's the flag. Here we go—full rpm, full throttle, full flaps, brakes off."

The *Rachel* sped down the tarmac. The fully loaded 55,000 pound B-17 bomber continued to gain speed from its four 1,200 horsepower engines until there was enough ground speed to lift the huge fully loaded aircraft into the air. It was still at full throttle when Brick instructed Bud, "Flaps up 10, speed Bud, 130, 140, flaps up 10, 150, flaps up, 160."

Finally, the big bomber was airborne. It was now time for them to form up for the flight.

"I see the 92nd," observed Brick, "we're on their right in Baker group. All right, everybody, check your radio to make sure you're on the intercom."

During the mission, the intercom was open so everyone could hear what was happening at every crew station, providing instant communication.

"Were you guys listening to *The Bing Crosby Show* last night when Lord Hawthorne came on?" Hansford asked. "He said the Eighth Air Force was stupid to bomb in the daylight and that the Luftwaffe was going to blow us from the skies?"

Sometimes I think he's right, Thibodeaux thought to himself.

The Bing Crosby Show was one of the most popular radio shows broadcast for the troops overseas, but the Germans monitored it. They had the frequency and they could cut in whenever they wanted to. *It's kind of scary, at times, what the Germans know about us,* Brick thought to himself. *But at times, Lord Hawthorne unknowingly gives us useful information, like weather tips. If he says they'll see us at 20,000, that usually means it's overcast at 22,000.*

"Skipper," inquired Sgt. Gifford, "is that one of our Air-Sea Rescue crafts down there?"

"Yes it is, George, and he's picking up some people."

"Bombardier to pilot. Skipper, Air-Sea is circling a downed B-17 picking up the crew. It looks like the plane is about halfway beached on a little sand bar. Man, are they lucky."

"Pilot to crew, enemy coast coming up in three minutes, so be alert. Call 'em out when you see enemy fighters. We are now over enemy territory."

"Uh, oh," said Brick, "there's flak ahead from that little town. Look, they got an engine in the 92nd Group, and he's turning back. Watch him and keep him covered if he gets in trouble. He's losing altitude fast. I guess he's trying to get away from the flak. Aw man, Me-109s have jumped him."

"Pilot to bombardier. Wyman, there's something shining up under the instrument panel. Can you see what it is?"

"I'll take a look. Sir, it's a bail-out kit with the mirror sticking out"

Hansford sighed, "I can't believe it."

Wyman was thinking to himself, *Boy, it's quiet here in the nose. There must not be anything down there to protect. I'll keep my eyes open, but it's so peaceful.*

"What's that up ahead? Looks like trouble," said Bud.

"Top turret gunner to pilot. Sir, we've got bandits at one o'clock!"

"Pilot to crew, five Me-109s closing fast at one o'clock high."

The tail gunner blurted out, "I got a burst off, but no luck."

"I got off three bursts. They're turning and coming up behind us!" screamed McGuire.

"I got 'em; I got 'em! They're off of us," screamed Morgan, "and going for the short flight Baker into the 92nd Group."

"Ball turret to crew, four more Me-109s coming at six o'clock low and they're coming right up our tail pipes. Come on, you Krauts, I'm waiting for you. Hot damn, I got one! He's going down at seven o'clock."

"Pilot to crew. We're going to make a short left turn pretty soon to get around this next town. There's flak coming up to greet us. Watch our right side; we don't have protection. Here we go hard left."

"Tail gunner to crew. There's one German nut case back here trying to jump the whole formation. I gave him a burst, and he turned before he could get in too close."

"Pilot to crew. Get ready everybody; we're into it now. Bandits everywhere. Try to keep us clean. Watch out for each other. I don't ever remember seeing this many German fighters before. Keep firing boys and maybe we'll get home. Gifford, there's one coming at you."

"Ball turret to pilot. I think I got him sir. At least he was smoking when he went through the group."

"Pilot to crew. Here's the flak, so you'll get a quick rest from the fighters. Check your guns and be ready for the next round. Is anyone hurt?"

All stations reported in. All the men were okay.

"Pilot to crew. That little burst of flak must have been one of those 88s mounted on railroad cars that they mentioned in the briefing. I'm glad to see the Krauts heading for home. You can relax for a few minutes, but keep your eyes open. Gifford, come up and give us a fuel check. She seems to be eating a little heavy today."

"I can do that, sir, but you get this same idea about this same time on every mission. But I'll be right there, sir."

"Humor me, Gifford."

"Pilot to ball turret, McGuire, can you tell what's on the ground where it's burned off down there?"

"Yes, sir, it's a crash site. It looks like a B-17 at the edge of the burn. Sir, there are also five 109s taking off from a small runway."

"Thank you, McGuire, keep an eye on them."

Brick was thinking to himself, *Boy, it sure is cold up here.*

The B-17 was not pressurized or heated. Crewmen wore oxygen masks on high altitude missions, and the Fortress operated at altitudes of 18,000 to 28,000 feet. Cold, yes, very cold. Crews were exposed to temperatures that reached levels of 50 degrees below zero. Needless to say, bomber crews had more than just German fighters and flak to worry about.

Brick was also thinking, *I wish I hadn't passed on the toast and jelly at breakfast this morning. It sure would taste good right about now.*

96

BUD CARTER WAS thinking about home again while the giant bomber flew toward the target. *I guess Austin High did okay this season or the folks would have said something. I remember that Coach Reynolds had a crush on Miss Thompson. I wonder if he ever got the guts to ask her out on a date. I can't blame him. She was a looker. I would have liked to have dated her myself.*

"Pilot to top turret. Gifford, can you see what's wrong with *Chance Meeting?*"

"Yeah, Skipper, they got a bad leak in his right wing. I can see the fuel coming out."

"That's not good," Hansford lamented.

"It sure isn't, Skipper. I'm going to try and alert them by using my flashlight. They won't have enough fuel to make it home."

A few minutes went by, but it seemed longer to Brick. "Okay, he picked up my message, but they are going on to the target. I guess they figure they are better off staying with us."

"Gifford, can't they transfer what's left of that fuel to their left wing tanks and use it from there?"

"Yes, sir. They've got a good engineer, and he's got to be thinking the same way we are. I think he will."

"Pilot to radio man, Thibodeaux, what's that coming in on the radio?"

"Sir, that was an announcement about the Marines. Apparently things are going well in the Pacific."

"Thanks, Pat."

"Look at the flak coming up," said Brick, looking over at Carter.

Bud sighed, "Yeah, I see it. Did you see the German observer?"

"Yes, I did. But he bugged out. He knows what's ahead," said Brick.

"Pilot to crew. The IP is coming up in 10 minutes. Look at the flak block. We're going to a higher level. Let's see if the Krauts pick up on it."

The anti-aircraft gunners needed to know what altitude the bombers were flying for the shells to explode at the optimum level. So it was a cat and mouse game until they were on the actual bomb run. That's what the German airborne observer was trying to determine.

"Pilot to bombardier. Are you on sight?"

"Yes, sir, I have the IP in scope. Skipper, make a 10 degree left turn at the IP. I'll be taking you in so if anything happens, we'll be ready."

Wyman exclaimed, "Ye gads, look at the flak!"

"We got flak helmets, but where the hell are the flak jackets!" screamed Destafano.

"And what about the flak blankets," Gregory yelled. "Not all units have 'em and that includes us. Don't they understand how it is up here?"

Wyman's right about the flak, thought Brick, with a sigh.

How in the hell do any of us survive this shit? Carter thought.

"Watch out for each other back there, fellows," said Hansford. "And be ready to take on the fighters again when we leave the target. We're turning on the IP. You've got it, Wilson?"

"Wilson has the ball. Bomb bay door switches on. Bomb bay doors are coming open. Bomb bay doors open. All I have to do now is wait on the lead plane. This flak is unbelievable. Bombs away!"

Wyman clinched his fist and pumped his arm. "It's always an adrenalin rush when the ordinance is released. I'm a paid killer and I'm very good at my work."

Wyman had just sent ten 500-pound bombs to enemy factories below. One out of every 10 planes carried incendiary bombs. The principle purpose of incendiaries was to start fires.

"Holy shit, Skipper!" screamed Destafano over the intercom. "A piece of shrapnel just tore through the waist just behind the windows. Do you still have the elevators?"

"The elevators are a bit sloppy, but they're still working," said Brick.

Tony continued to explain the situation to Brick, "The cables are pretty frayed. I hope the hell they'll hold!"

"Calm down, Tony."

"Oh, no!' screamed Tony, into the intercom."

"What is it now?" Brick asked.

"McGuire's hit! He's in a panic. I'll be busy..."

"Bud, you better go back there and check on McGuire—and the cables."

"I'm on it, Skipper."

I wish he'd come back. I need to know the score, thought Brick.

"Skipper, McGuire's okay. There was a tear in his flight jacket and some blood. He's wounded, but we fixed him up. He'll be okay, and he can still shoot."

"Hey, that sounds good," said Brick, with relief.

"What about the cables?"

"I suggest we pray," said Bud, shaking his head.

"Great—that's just great!" said Brick, in disgust.

"Wyman, can you see that target?"

"Yes, sir, it is solid fire."

"Ball turret to pilot. We've got fighters at six o' clock low. Here they come—here they come!" His voice grew louder. "Six Me-109s are closing fast. Come on, you bastards!"

"Let 'em know you're mad," shouted Carter.

"I'm going to give them a burst! They're turning, they're turning! Stay alert, you guys."

"What the hell do you think we're doing?" screamed Gifford.

"Navigator," asked Brick, "are you keeping an eye on where we are?"

"Yes, sir, I'm reading my charts, and I recognize the country we're flying over."

"You're a good man."

Brick was thinking about food again and said, "I could stand a big plate of ham and eggs, hot biscuits, grape jelly, and butter. Boy, am I hungry."

"When you get something like that on your mind, it gets worse, not better," Bud said.

"You're mighty right about that. Well, the respite's over. Take a look, Bud. Pilot to the crew, we've got bandits coming out of the sun. You see 'em, George? They're at one o' clock high?"

"I got 'em, Skipper."

"Gregory, you've got 'em coming on the right?"

"Got 'em, sir, and I'm shooting! I had him dead to rights, but he broke off! Ball turret, do you have him?"

"Do I have him? He's on fire, he's on fire! The pilot's hitting the silk."

"George, I see *Chance Meeting* is still out there. I guess they figured out how to transfer the gasoline."

"Whew," said Brick, looking over at Bud. "I think it's finally over."

"Yeah, I think so, too."

"Okay men, you can relax for awhile," said Brick, as he drove the big bird back to England.

"PILOT TO CREW. We're at 10,000 feet so you can remove your oxygen masks now."

"But Captain, I want to keep wearing mine," said Thibodaux.

"Go ahead, you crazy Cajun."

Bud started to laugh and Brick joined in.

"Ball turret to pilot. Captain, can I get out of the turret now?"

"Oh, sure, McGuire. Get him out of there, Gifford. All of you can stand down," said Hansford. "We're definitely clear of enemy territory."

"McGuire, can you see that spot on the water straight down?" Carter asked.

"Yes, sir, it's a rubber raft and I think there's a survivor in it. Oh good, here comes Air-Sea Rescue."

"That boat must be a beautiful sight," said Bud.

"Pilot to crew. Okay, you guys all know your procedures for landing."

"Bud, fly this thing for awhile," said Brick, "I'm going back to look at those cables. I want to make sure we'll be able to make a safe landing. You got it, Bud?"

"I've got it, Skipper, go ahead."

On the way back, Brick remarked, "Boy, this walkway is narrow when you've got a parachute on. Guys, you did a great job today."

After examining some of the damage, Brick confessed, "These cables are not in good shape. But if we are real careful in our landing ..." He returned to the cockpit.

"He says the cables are not in good shape," said Destafano, rubbing his temples and squirming.

"Yeah, I'm with Tony," said Gregory. "If they snap, we're gonna crash, right?"

"And we're gonna die!" said Tony.

"We've survived the flak, the fighters, and the damn cables break?" screamed Thibodaux. "This can't happen."

McGuire and Morgan didn't say anything, but their expressions were dour. All the men moved closer to each other, as they huddled on the floor in the waist of the airplane.

"I want you guys to get a hold of yourselves. We're not going to crash—we're going to be on the ground in no time, and I'll expect all of you mullets to join me at the NCO Club for a beer," said Gifford, sternly.

"Easy for you to say," said McGuire.

"Shut up, and brace yourself for landing!"

"Pilot to crew. There's the coast and it won't be long now. I don't know about you guys, but I'm ready to get this one over."

In a short time, Hansford was back on the intercom, "All right, fellows, we'll land on as straight a pattern as we possibly can. Get yourselves in crash position just in case—and sit tight."

"Tower, this is the *Rachel* on final approach and ready to land straight ahead on number 18."

"Go ahead, *Rachel,* you're clear to land … and it's good to see you."

"Bud, don't pull back too hard on the elevators. Make it nice and easy. Touch down! We're home now, and she held together for us."

The crew in the waist began cheering and slapping each other. There were a few hugs and lots of wet eyes.

"I told you," said Sgt. Gifford.

97

FRANK MCGUIRE wrote a letter home.

Hey there, Mom and Dad,

I bring you greetings from the best damn ball turret gunner in the 91st Bomb Group, coming to you from the tranquil confines of Bassingbourn, England. We went to Germany today and it was rough, so we're all very glad to be back safe and sound and in our quarters. We're making the best of it.

There's a lot of boring routine stuff that goes on around here but there's interesting stuff that goes on as well. Someone brought in a little three month old kitten and he sort of took up residence. Everyone brings him scraps for the table so the little tyke is never hungry. As you can imagine, there are guys who like the little fellow and others who are not cat lovers. Of course, I love the little guy as you know. Well, he has a habit of crawling up on the beds after lights out, and everyone has turned in. He likes to lick your ear lobe. You might have figured out that if he licked the wrong ear lobe, he could get swatted halfway across the room.

One day I heard some barking out back. Some of those clowns had put the little cat in a pen with a mean dog and took delight in watching the cat try to defend itself. I would have none of that and I rescued the cat, much to the displeasure of some of the men. I think some of them actually wanted to see the dog tear that cat apart.

Somebody brought in some peanut butter and soda crackers. A few of the fellows were really enjoying the treat. I told them that real butter would keep the peanut butter from sticking to the roof of their mouth. Some resourceful guy produced some real butter and we tried it. Some of the guys thought it worked, but some didn't see any difference. It's always worked for me.

The last time we were on pass to London, we ate at The Mayflower. There's a clue in the name here. In 1620 a certain ship carrying certain Pilgrims left the wharf outside this very pub bound for America. That's one of the things that's so exciting for us because there's so much history all around us. Everything is old.

After dinner we were just walking around and ran smack dab into a nightclub called the Defiance. That was a good name because it had a sign that said, WE NEVER CLOSED! *We were told that meant that during the very worst of the 1940 blitz, they never shut down their operation. They had a stage show with singers and dancers. It was fun and exciting for a hillbilly like me.*

After we turned in that night, we were awakened by the sound of air raid sirens blaring. I was curious as to what was going on, so I looked outside. I could see the fingers of search lights penetrating the dark sky, and they had a German plane bracketed. The anti-aircraft batteries were blazing away, but I didn't see a hit. Eventually I went back to bed and could hear the sound of bombs exploding in the distance, but it didn't last long. The next morning we were able to observe the damage. It was bad, but didn't cover a large area. It seems strange, I guess, that we go to London on pass, to have fun and unwind, and yet the Germans are dropping bombs on the city. That's what we do. Right now, it's a pretty crazy world we live in.

Well, that's all for now. Continue to pray for me, pray for all the boys, and continue to tell me about home.

Love to you both,

Frank

98

THEY FIRST HIT the plants at Antwerp, Belgium, and then they hit the U-boat pens at Lorient, France, which they had attacked on two other occasions. The mission ordered for April 17, 1943 was Bremen, Germany.

The sergeant entered the officer's quarters and shined a flashlight in Brick's face. "Captain—Captain Hansford—wake up! It's on! You've got a mission today. Breakfast is at 0600 and the briefing is at 0645."

"Lieutenant Carter, mission today!" the sergeant repeated.

"Okay, okay, just get that flashlight out of my face," blurted Bud.

The other officers slowly but surely rolled out of their bunks and began the morning routine. "Bud, when you get your pants on, make sure the enlisted men get up."

"Sure thing, Brick."

"EGGS MAKE me want to gag," said Clark Clifford.

"Bitch, bitch, bitch," said Wyman, "give me the damn eggs."

Clifford scraped the eggs into Wyman's tray and plopped down in disgust. Wyman reached over and took his bacon as well. Clifford ate the toast, but that was it.

"Rush it up boys, we'll be late for the briefing," said Carter.

· · · · ·

"FLAK, TWELVE O'CLOCK level," said Hansford. "This penetration deep into Germany is no cake walk. We're going to catch hell!"

"Major Ellis said they had about 500 anti-aircraft guns around Bremen," said Carter.

"Thanks for reminding me, Bud," said Hansford.

"Damn it!" exclaimed McGuire.

"What's the matter, Frank?" said Hansford.

"A piece of flak hit my turret," said McGuire.

"Are you okay?" asked Hansford.

"Yes, sir, I'm okay. It glanced off, but it scared the shit out of me," said McGuire.

Hansford and Carter looked at each other and grinned. "Everybody put on their flak helmets," said Hansford, over the intercom.

"And pray," Morgan hollered.

Bud sighed, *It sure wouldn't hurt.*

"*Monkey's Uncle* calling *Rachel*," said Bill Stewart, a new radio man.

"What is it, Bill?" said Thibodeaux, a bit perturbed.

"This heavy flak, it's nothing like I expected. You guys are the lead plane. Can't Captain Hansford maybe climb out of it?" he questioned.

"Unfortunately, the answer is no. When you're on the bomb run, you have to fly straight through it or you'll get off target. It's just four more minutes."

"Just four minutes. It'll be like four hours," said Stewart, dejectedly.

"I'm cutting you off, Bill. We're not supposed to be talking like this," said Thibodeaux. He got out of his chair and crossed over to the opposite side of the *Rachel* where he could see Bill sitting at his station through the bubble. At that precise moment, a piece of flak ripped a hole in the fuselage right next to Thibodeaux's seat and started a fire on his desk with the log book as a primary victim.

If I hadn't gotten out of my chair, I think I might be dead. Maybe I should thank Stewart for saving my life, thought Thibodeaux.

"Damn it, this flak is bouncing the *Rachel* all over the place," said Carter.

"Wyman, are you ready to take control?"

"I'm ready, Skipper."

"She's all yours. You'll be flying the *Rachel* from here to the target."

"Roger," Wyman responded. The plane was still bouncing around as he tried in vain to look through the eyepiece on his sophisticated Norden bomb sight.

"Skipper, I don't think I've ever seen flak so heavy," said Carter, nervously.

Everyone on board felt the sudden jolt. "Damage report!" screamed Hansford.

"Sweet Jesus, there's a huge hole in the left wing!" shouted Destafano. "What are we gonna do, Captain?"

"Just hold on, Tony," said Hansford.

"Crap!" said Carter, looking at the gauges, "We're losing fuel like crazy."

"Gifford, get on the fuel transfer pump immediately!" Hansford shouted.

"I'm on it, Captain."

Gifford returned with bad news, "Captain, the electrics must be out on the left side. I'll have to do it by hand."

"You better give him a hand, Bud," said Hansford. "We need to save as much fuel as possible."

"Sure thing."

"Two minutes to the target," Wyman announced over the intercom, "Bomb bay doors open."

Bud Carter returned to the flight deck and climbed back into his co-pilot's seat, "Fuel transfer complete, Skipper. I think we saved most of it."

Hansford smiled, "Good, good job. Bombardier, how does that target look?"

Wyman looked through the bomb sight, raised his head and stared straight ahead for a few seconds, a bit surprised, then shook his head and reported to Captain Hansford, "The target's totally obscured."

Hansford looked at Carter, noticeably perturbed.

Bud thought to himself, *This can't be happening.*

"Thirty seconds to the target," said Wyman.

"This flak is still unbelievably heavy. Shells are bursting all over the place, but the ones right in front of us are really unnerving. I'll never get used to flying right into it. God help us to do our job, and get us home safely," said Carter.

"Wyman, we need those bombs right in the pickle barrel. Remember, the whole group is bombing on us," said Hansford.

"If I can't see the target, I can't see it!" screamed Wyman, in frustration.

"Damn!" said Hansford, looking over at Carter again, as if expecting him to offer some words of wisdom.

"How about that target, Wyman?" asked Hansford, impatiently, hoping and praying for some good news and perhaps a miracle.

Wyman sighed and looked through the sight again, "Sonofabitch, I can see it. There's a hole there—bombs away!"

Hansford and Carter looked at each other with enormous relief. Brick grinned and announced to the crew, "Okay, cowboys, we've done our job for Uncle Sam, now let's get the hell out of here."

"Bomb bay doors closing," said Wyman.

Hansford pulled back on the stick to begin a climb and leaned it to the left to start the turn.

"All right, fellows, we'll have bandits again real soon. Stay on your toes," said Brick. "But the hard part's over—I hope."

"Here they come, here they come!" shouted Morgan. "I hit him and he's smoking." As the Me-109 banked to the right, he sliced right through the tail section of *Mom's Apple Pie*. Destafano had a clear view.

"Oh, no, the tail gunner just came out and he wasn't wearing a chute."

Carter could see them from his co-pilot's window, "It's the rookies, Skipper. I don't see any parachutes and the main section is in a serious spin. She's a-goner."

"First and last mission in the same day," said Hansford. "Rotten luck. It doesn't seem fair."

Carter looked at him and said, "It's not fair—but it's not us."

Hansford sighed and nodded. He knew what Carter meant and he knew he was right. He regained his composure and spoke over the intercom, "Hey you guys, make sure your parachutes are on."

"Bandits breaking low at nine o'clock, ball turret, watch out," said Carter.

"I'm jammed up again!" screamed McGuire, as a Me-109 streaked toward him with guns blazing. Suddenly, the entire crew heard a loud noise from outside and below the plane. Gifford sensed trouble and screamed as he rushed toward the ball turret hatch. "Frank! Frank!"

Gifford hurriedly opened the two ball turret levers and was horrified to see the turret completely blown away and McGuire hanging helplessly by his safety belts, screaming hysterically. "I'm gonna die! I'm gonna die!"

"Frank, get a grip and hold on to me tight. You understand? I've got to release the safety belts and pull you inside." As the belts were released, McGuire screamed in panic.

"I've got you, Frank. You're okay, you're going to be safe," Gifford assured him as he steadily pulled him inside. Safe within the fuselage, McGuire was shaking and whimpering like a frightened child. It was understandable. He had miraculously survived a terrifying ordeal.

Gifford hugged McGuire and said, "Just relax now, you're going to be fine and we're headed home."

Suddenly, a burst of hot lead ripped through Pat Thibodeaux's station, wounding him and starting a terrible fire. His papers were helping to fuel the dangerous blaze. Now McGuire had something to take his mind off his scare.

"Grab a fire extinguisher while I tend to Thibodeaux," yelled Gifford

"Okay, the fire's out. Let me put Pat's oxygen mask back on."

"Let's unzip his flight jacket and see what's going on," said Gifford.

"Oh man, that's a nasty looking wound," said McGuire. "It looks like a bullet entered his left side."

"Right—but there's no way to determine the extent of the damage," Gifford concluded.

"PLEASE GOD, NO!" exclaimed Gifford.

"Talk to me, Sgt Gifford. What's going on?" asked Hansford.

"We just lost a big chunk out of the top of our tail section. Nobody else can see it."

"There's a fire in the number four engine!" screamed Carter.

"These people are trying to kill us," said Hansford, frantically shouting orders like the decisive leader he was, "Cut fuel! Feather prop! Fire extinguishers! Generators off!"

"The fire extinguishers are not working," said Carter. "We've got to do something quick or we'll lose the right wing!"

"You're right," said Hansford calmly. "We gotta dive—and I may need help to pull her out."

"I'm not going anywhere," Carter responded.

Hansford spoke over the command frequency, "Rachel to group. We're gonna dive to try to put out these flames in our number four engine. *Smoky Joe*, you're now the lead plane."

Brick pushed the stick over and *Rachel* began to dive, shaking and rattling from enemy flak and fighter damage, papers flying from the navigator's station, and crewmen sliding and bouncing around.

Carter and Hansford nervously watched the burning engine. "We're exceeding maximum dive speed," Carter warned, "we've got to level her out."

"No, the fire's not out," said Hansford steadfastly, "we'll wait."

"*Rachel* is gonna come apart, she's had it. We're not gonna make it this time," screamed Gregory.

Destafano slapped him across the face, "Shut up, Glenn! We're gonna be fine—we're gonna make it! *Rachel* has been in trouble before, but she always takes us home."

"I don't think *Rachel* can take it, Skipper. She's gonna come apart," said Carter, pleading.

Hansford looked at Carter and said, "Trust me, Bud, just a little bit longer."

"It's out! It's out!" screamed Carter, as Hansford pulled back on the stick. His face grimaced as *Rachel* was slow to respond. "Jump in here, Bud, I need your help."

Bud pulled back on his stick as well, urging the giant Fortress to obey. "Come on, baby, come on, *Rachel*."

Finally the airplane began to come out of the dive and eventually she was level once again, to the crew's relief.

"Damn," said Brick, looking over at Bud, "that was a bit more of a challenge than I really needed."

"I'll be honest with you, Brick, I thought we were gonna buy the farm."

"I'll be honest with you, Bud, I thought so myself."

GEORGE GIFFORD CAME forward and stood between the pilot and co-pilot. "Thibodeaux's lost a lot of blood. We're very concerned. How long until we get back to base?"

"On three engines, two to two and one-half hours," said Hansford. "What do you think, Bud?"

"I agree with you."

"I don't think Pat can last. He needs a hospital," said Gifford.

"There is one more possibility," suggested Carter, "we could bail him out."

Hansford looked at him with alarm. "Do you really consider that feasible?"

"It's been done before. Another crew did it and it worked out okay. Look, it's crawling with Germans down there. They'll pick him up and take him to a hospital. We know the Luftwaffe takes good care of airmen," Carter said.

Hansford couldn't buy it, "It will kill him."

"I agree with you, Skipper. We just can't do it. If we shove him out, I'm convinced he will die," said Gifford.

99

BACK AT THE base in England, the ground crews were anxiously waiting, shooting the breeze, some playing pitch and catch, but mostly just waiting.

"There they are," shouted a technical sergeant, as the first of the 24 B-17 bombers that had flown to Bremen were spotted approaching the field. A flare went up to notify the ambulances and fire trucks to crank up and head toward the field.

"That's eight."

"There, that's nine."

Col. Birdwell stepped out on the railed balcony that surrounded the tower and asked Major Ellis, who was looking through his binoculars, "How many so far, Cliff?"

"Nine so far. Okay, there's ten, Colonel, he just came into view."

"Who is it?"

"Can't tell yet, Colonel."

"How do they look?" he inquired.

"The ones already in look to be in good shape," Ellis responded.

"But that doesn't really tell the story, does it?"

Ellis sighed, "Not really."

■ ■ ■ ■ ■

"FEATHER THE PROP and cut the fuel," said Hansford.

"Fellows, we are now flying on two engines," said Hansford, over the intercom. "We need to lighten our load, so throw everything out that's not nailed down."

It seemed like an eternity, but finally, the English coast came into view as George Gifford entered the flight deck. He couldn't contain himself. "Man, oh man, ain't that a beautiful sight?"

"I never saw anything as beautiful," said Hansford, glancing at Carter with a grin. All three of them were smiling broadly.

Thibodeaux suddenly regained consciousness and smiled at McGuire.

That's two good signs, thought McGuire.

"Landing gear," said Hansford.

"Something's wrong," said Gifford, nervously.

"Something is wrong," said Carter, "my wheel didn't go down."

"Damn! Okay, take it back up," said Hansford calmly, "we'll make a belly landing."

Frantically working the switches, Carter concluded, "Nothing's coming up or down. The electrics must be totally out."

Hansford quickly assessed the situation and barked his decision, "Okay, then we'll lower the wheel by hand. Gifford, take Wyman and Clifford so you can take turns. And get the lead out!"

They scrambled back to the manual control, grabbed the handle, pushed it into place, and began to crank feverishly.

"Crap," said Carter, disgustedly, "now we're losing number three. How long can we fly on one engine, Skipper?"

Hansford shook his head, "I have no idea, but we're about to find out."

"WELL, WE'VE GOT 19 down out of the 24 ships we sent to Bremen," Major Ellis declared. Col. Birdwell strained his eyes, searching the sky through his binoculars for the remaining five planes, which included the lead bomber, *Rachel*.

"There's *Rachel*," said Birdwell. "Damn, it's only got one wheel down."

"GET OUT OF the way," said Wyman to Gifford, "let me spell you on the crank."

Slowly, the wheel was coming down. But they didn't know if it would be down in time and if it would lock into place. As the *Rachel* cleared the trees, everyone could see that only one wheel was down. The men on the ground knew the odds of survival for the crew would be slim. The enlisted men of the *Rachel* were huddled together in the belly of the airplane, holding hands and singing *Amazing Grace*.

They knew it would take divine intervention.

"Flaps," ordered Hansford.

"We're not going to die, and that's a promise," declared Gifford, as he summoned up more energy and cranked furiously. "That's it! We did it!" he yelled. "The gear is down and locked."

302

At almost that exact moment, *Rachel* touched down on the tarmac to the thunderous cheers of the crew—and the hundreds of men on the ground. On the flight deck, Captain Hansford managed to smile amid the sweat drops that were running down his face. Bud Carter breathed a sigh of relief as well, then laughed out loud.

COL. BIRDWELL HANDED the binoculars to Major Ellis, "Well, *Rachel* is back. It's bad for morale to lose the lead plane."

Smiling, Ellis said, "That—was close."

■ ■ ■ ■ ■

SADLY, FOUR OF the B-17s would not return. *Mom's Apple Pie, Suwannee River, Crimson Tide*, and *Darling Lily* were still in Germany.

Rachel finally rolled to a stop as fire trucks, ambulances, staff cars, and jeeps raced to her side. Sgt. Mahoney, the ground crew chief, was in one of the vehicles. He shook his head as he gazed at the pathetic, crippled, smoldering B-17 that he was responsible for.

My God, what a mess. How in the hell did she get them home? That is one great airplane. Whew, me and my guys have our work cut out for us. But we'll get the lady fixed up. Her war isn't over just yet, Sgt. Mahoney thought.

Hansford turned off all the switches in the cockpit and slumped back in his seat. He looked over at Carter who smiled and said, "Well, *Rachel* brought us home again. She's one hell of a gal. And if I may say so, sir, she has one hell of a pilot!"

"Thanks, Bud, I appreciate it. Yes, *Rachel* got us back, but she's in bad shape."

"They'll patch her up, Skipper. She'll be as good as new."

"They sure as hell better, because I'm not going to war without her," declared Hansford.

An ambulance crew carefully removed Pat Thibodeaux from the crippled airplane and quickly sped away to the base hospital. Destafano rode with him. Like *Rachel,* he would need some patching up, but he would also fly again.

Carter put his arm around Clifford, "Tell me, Clark, how are you?"

"I'm just fine, Bud," he replied, smiling broadly. "Like I told you before the flight, the fear is gone."

Bud smiled. "I'm pleased and relieved for you."

"Let's get over to the debriefing. We've got a lot to tell 'em."

"That we do, Clark, that we do."

THE LUFTWAFFE CAME out in full strength in retaliation for the Bremen raid. After April 17, German fighter attacks began to become increasingly more effective and better coordinated, and bomber losses frequently were over ten percent of the attacking force, especially whenever the Fortresses went beyond the limited radius of their fighter escorts.

The German fighters began to attack the formations from twelve o'clock high, directly head-on. They had done this before on a limited basis, but now there was a concerted effort.

The innovation was supposedly introduced by Luftwaffe Oberleutnant Egon Mayer, who had noticed that the firepower from the B-17 was weak in the nose area, with significant blind spots that neither the nose guns nor the top-turret gunner could adequately cover from the front. However, the much-publicized vulnerability to frontal attacks was due more to the lack of armor than it was to the lack of enough front-firing guns.

100

THEY MET AT the newsstand at the train station. Captain Brickley Hansford was quite a dashing figure in his perfectly fitting uniform, which was never lost on Rachel.

This time was like the others, full of excitement and anticipation. She was wearing a purple sweater with a black skirt, black beret, and black shoes. *She looks great as usual. If she's trying to rev up my engine, it's definitely working.*

"I missed you like crazy," he told her, smiling, swaying her back and forth.

"You did?" she responded, with a coy grin.

He couldn't stand it any longer and gave her a long slow kiss.

"That was very nice, Captain Hansford. You're getting pretty good at kissing."

"Hey, what's all the stuff?"

"It's food. I'd like to cook for you. I thought that would be a welcomed change of pace."

He smiled. "That's wonderful. I am very pleased."

She smiled, "I've got meat, potatoes, salad fixings, and wine." The longer she talked, the faster she talked and the more excited she became. "And I've got the makings for a Yorkshire pudding and a berry tart."

"You sound just like a British girl."

"You forget, I've been here four years now."

"You know, you have at that."

He frowned, "But where are you going to cook?"

One of my co-workers dates General Waverley. He's been invited to Ditchley House for the weekend and he's taking her. So, we have Sara's apartment."

"What is Ditchley House?" Brick asked.

"Mr. Churchill likes to get out of London on the weekends, but it's no respite. He has cabinet members, admirals, generals, and the like come in for meetings. Some come for breakfast, some for lunch, and some for dinner. It's an honor to be invited for the weekend. Ditchley House is his favorite location, and it is considered safe from the air."

Brick laughed, "You think we could get an invitation?"

She laughed, "I wouldn't count on it."

Clasping her hands together, she said, "Sara's apartment is large and quite nice, you know. It's got two bedrooms, a large living room, a full kitchen and dining room. I've been there a few times."

"How can she afford that?"

She smiled, "General Waverley."

"Ah, I understand. Well," he replied, sporting a coy smile, "it will be swell to have you fix me a meal, and tonight will be perfect. I have a surprise for you tomorrow night."

Her lovely face lit up with anticipation.

"I have arranged, through my considerable Yankee resources, for two tickets to *Hi-De-Hi* at the Palace Theatre and then a late supper at The Gamekeeper. It comes highly recommended, and it's got a good address, I'm told, Bruton Place at Berkley Square.

"That's marvelous, tickets to one of the hottest shows in town. You did well."

"Well, my darling Rachel, I like to please you."

IT RAINED, WHICH was not all that unusual. They both dropped off to sleep. Brick never got enough sleep. And the stress on missions was taking a toll. She woke before him, put on her robe, and made tea. The sound of the kettle awakened him, and she called out, "Darling, the tea is ready. Come and have a cup with me." She had taken the liberty of using Sara's fine china. "This is nice, don't you think?"

"Yes, I do," he responded with a smile. He was getting used to the tradition and it pleased Rachel, who had come to love it. In fact, she had treated him to high tea at the Dorchester Hotel. He enjoyed it rather well. "I wish we had some of those little sandwiches, cakes, and cookies."

"I have some little sugar cookies. Thanks for reminding me."

"These are good," said Brick, admiring it, before dunking it in his tea.

"CAN I HELP?" Brick inquired. She was busy in the kitchen.

"No thanks, Brick, I have it under control. Remember, I wanted to fix a meal for you. So you see, I have to do it. But you can pour me a glass of wine and see if you can find some music on the radio."

"Here you are, sweetheart," handing her the wine. "No luck finding music. I guess we'll have to make our own."

"I think we can do that, don't you?"

"Absolutely."

He thought for a moment and a big smile crossed his face, "Hey, this is just like being married. You know, an evening in, with you fixing dinner."

She didn't respond. He didn't press it.

■ ■ ■ ■ ■

SATURDAY HAD BEEN a nice day as well. They slept late and lounged around until lunchtime. Then they had fish and chips and an ale at the Sherlock Holmes Pub, and did some shopping at Harrod's where they enjoyed high tea in the late afternoon.

"I do wish you could have seen London without sand bags, bombed out buildings, and such. And a cruise on the Thames used to be so remarkable." She sighed, "But this war…"

"I love the city, sandbags and all. Anyway, you don't have to apologize for the war."

"I'm not. I was just reflecting on how it was."

"BUTTON ME UP, will you, Brick?" said Rachel, walking in from the bedroom in a tight-fitting black dress.

"Sweetheart, you look fabulous."

"Thank you."

"I'd like to roll back that clock," he lamented, as he struggled with the small covered buttons.

"I know, but we've got a big evening ahead of us and most of tomorrow. Can't we just enjoy what we have?"

"Of course, but the more of you I have the more of you I want, and my work is keeping me away."

She smiled, but again didn't comment.

"There, I'm finished," he said, gently swatting her lovely behind.

"Brick!" she responded with a laugh.

He lit a cigarette and sat down on Sara's ornate couch.

"Okay, I'm ready."

"You look stunning."

"Thanks."

•••••

SUNDAY WAS ALSO a leisurely day. They slept late again, but dressed in time for lunch at Ye Olde Mitre at 1 Ely Court. "Brick, you just happen to be in one of the most historic pubs in England."

"No fooling?"

"It was mentioned twice by William Shakespeare and was the host to Henry VIII and Catherine of Aragorn for a banquet in 1531. The pub contains a fragment of a cherry tree around which Elizabeth I danced the maypole. Frankly, it doesn't get much better than this."

"I guess not, Rachel."

A waiter appeared and inquired as to food and drinks. "Oh, Brick, I want you to try the steak and kidney pie. It's a specialty of the house."

He scrunched up his face, "Why do you care?"

"You're in England. Try some of their popular dishes."

"Okay. Say, how do you cook kidneys," he asked, naively.

"We boils the piss out of 'em, mate," said the waiter, bending over with laughter.

"I walked right into that one."

"The steak and kidneys are cooked well done in a nice gravy and then scooped into a pie crust. Then we covers that with a topping of dough, you see, just like your mum did when she made a pie."

"Okay, I get the picture."

"Tell you what, guv, if you don't likes it, I'll bring you something else with no charge."

He looked over at Rachel, "I guess I can't go wrong with a deal like that."

"I guess not."

"And for you, milady?"

"The shepherd's pie."

"And two mugs of ale," Bud suggested.

THEY RETURNED TO Sara's for the rest of the afternoon. She fixed some tea.

"You know what?"

"What?"

"I think I'm gonna make it: complete my 25 missions and go home."

"What brought that on?"

"I don't know. It just hit me. But it's good for me to be positive with the men."

"I can see that, but it sounds like you don't really believe it?"

"Oh, no, I do."

"Well, I'm relieved."

" You know what I think we should do?"

"No, but let's have it."

"Let's go to the Savoy for dinner and dancing."

She plopped down in his lap and gave him a kiss. "Captain Hansford, I think that's a lovely idea."

101

THE TARGET WAS Friedrichshafen, the largest ball bearing factory in Germany, important to the war effort. Bud Carter and Brick Hansford left the briefing, confident as usual in their ability to take the *Rachel* in harm's way and return her and her crew to the friendly soil of England. They would be in the second position in the formation.

"Just another milk run, Bud," Brick announced with a sheepish grin.

"Yeah, to be sure, a piece of cake," Bud responded, facetiously.

They flew around the northern edge of Switzerland and toward Munich to disguise their actual destination. Then they changed directions in order to hit the real target.

· · · · ·

BUD EXPLAINED IT all in the debriefing following the mission, "The 109s were like fireflies on a summer evening in Austin, Texas. Every position was firing almost simultaneously. Then that God-awful flak, you know, like you could climb out and walk on it.

"We were still on the bomb run when suddenly there was a burst close by, and shrapnel shattered the windshield on Brick's side. Metal and glass hit him in the head. Believe it or not, his eyes and face were spared major injury. Thank God for his flak helmet, that helped quite a bit. Without it, he may have been killed. Anyway, it knocked him unconscious.

"I had to take over. I asked Clark to be the first aid man. He did a swell job. Anyway, we continued on our run and dropped our eggs right in the pickle barrel. We had already turned back toward home when Brick came around. He was experiencing a red out—blood in both eyes.

"He told us he could see a little bit out of the right eye as Clifford worked on him. We were out of formation, and Kraut fighters are all over us. I could see the formation over to our left. As I turned, George Gifford got a Me-109 and immediately after that a FW 190—unbelievable. Even though we had lost an engine, Gifford's shooting allowed us to rejoin the main body where our total firepower could be brought to bear on the incoming fighter planes."

"Wow," said the debriefing officer as he tried to take down every detail.

"Brick told us his depth perception was shot," said Bud, thinking about whether there was anything else of significance. "Well, I guess that's about it."

Col. Birdwell had come over to the debriefing, which was his usual practice. He just happened to listen in on the debriefing of the *Rachel* crew. Bud explained what all had happened.

"That was a good job, Bud," said Birdwell, "hitting the target and bringing her in with Brick wounded and an inboard out of commission. I'm recommending you for a DFC."

"You rely on your training. You do your job. But, thank you, sir."

Outside, Col. Birdwell offered Bud a cigarette and took one for himself. "I've been thinking for sometime, Lieutenant Carter, that you're ready for your own ship. We've lost some experienced pilots and we could use you in the left seat. The way you handled yourself today, under intense pressure, confirmed for me what I had already been thinking. You're ready to command your own ship."

"That's very generous of you, sir. And I, too, believe I'm ready for my own command. I feel confident and fully prepared. But we've been together from the beginning and we're getting close to our 25 missions. I hope you don't think I'm ungrateful, sir, but I just want to finish up my tour of duty with the crew I started with."

"All right, Bud, I can understand that. But if you change your mind, I'll give you a good crew and a good ship, one with a chin gun."

Bud Carter smiled and saluted smartly. "Thank you, sir.

■ ■ ■ ■ ■

THE OFFICERS OF the *Rachel* were keyed up following the Friedrichshafen raid and they all headed for the officers club. Well, all but Brick.

"I hope the Skipper's gonna be okay, " said Clark Clifford.

"I think he'll be fine, but they need to be sure. We'll stand down for a time while they check him out and repair that inboard engine. I'll check on him tomorrow. Cheers," said Bud, as the boys raised their beer in unison.

"What are your plans, Clark, when this thing is over?"

"My parents own the A-Bar-A Cabins, a family oriented vacation spot, twelve miles out of Durango. It's really a swell setting— in a valley, beneath a mountain, by a trout stream. Guests can fish, hike, play horseshoes—stuff like that, really relax. Every cabin has its own grill so they can barbeque whenever they want. And there are various tours available in the area. All the units are fully equipped for cooking, so they can buy groceries in town and fix their own meals. My parents want to move back to Denver. They'll turn it over to Kathy and me to run. We'll live on the premises with our girls."

"That's sounds swell, Clark," said Bud.

"What about you, Wyman?" Bud inquired. "Got any plans for after the war?"

"My situation is a little like Clark's in that we have a family business in Taos."

"What kind of business?" asked Bud.

"We have a gallery downtown with art and sculpture. Mom is an artist, a good one, and we handle her work as well as local talent. They have no plans to retire, but they said they would make me a partner when I get back. I'm excited about that. We get a lot of tourists and we do fine."

"That sounds good," said Clifford.

"Okay, Bud, how about you?" asked Wyman.

"You fellows know about the beautiful Scarlett. Well, we've decided to tie the knot."

"No kidding?" said Clifford.

"That's right, and I want you to be the best man."

Clifford was taken aback; it was all such a surprise. "Sure, Bud, I'd be happy to stand with you."

"You need a flower boy?" Wyman asked, with a chuckle.

"I'll ask Scarlett." They laughed.

"Her parents actually asked her not to date any Yanks. She's not only dating one, she's gonna marry one, so we've got some work to do."

"Yeah, I'd say so," said Wyman, with a laugh. "And where are the nuptials going to take place and when?"

"We've actually talked about that. They will take place at St. Giles, an old church in Cheddingham, her home town. I hope the entire crew of the *Rachel* will be there. It would mean a lot to me to have my brothers in attendance."

"Are you going to take her back to America?" Clifford asked.

"I sure am, and she's fine with it. I'm sure it will be a blow to her family— but she'll have to explain that." Bud started grinning and then declared, "I'm going to get a degree from the University of Texas and become a successful high school football coach. Scarlett and I will have a boy and a girl and live happily ever after."

"Our co-pilot is decisive, I'll give him that," said Wyman. They all laughed.

102

"BRICK DIDN'T LIKE being told by the flight surgeon that he couldn't go to London with the rest of us," said Wyman.

"Brick doesn't like being told much of anything, particularly no, but it was the smart move. They just want to keep him close by so they can watch him over the weekend," Bud reasoned.

"They want him back in the cockpit next week," said Wyman.

Bud stared at Wyman a moment and said, "Col. Birdwell offered me my own ship, one of the new models with the chin gun."

"No kidding?"

"On the level. It happened after the raid on Friedrichshafen when Brick was injured."

"That's exciting and damn well deserved," said Wyman.

"I turned it down."

"Why!"

"We started out together and we've done pretty well. I told him I didn't want to break up the team, you know, destroy the chemistry. We work so well together."

"I still can't believe it," said Wyman, shaking his head.

"Listen, Wilson, if it's all the same to you, I'd just as soon you didn't mention this to anyone. I told Clark, but I don't want Brick or the crew to know."

"Sure, Bud, if that's the way you want it."

"That's the way I want it."

"Incidentally, you're in an exceptionally joyous mood, Lt. Carter," said Wilson, as the countryside flashed by the window of the train taking them to London.

"Well, seeing Scarlett always gets me in a good mood, but this weekend is sure to be something special," Bud confessed.

"I'm all ears, Bud, explain."

"You've heard of The Savoy, I suspect,"

"Of course, it's about as famous as the London Bridge, Big Ben, and the Crown Jewels.'

"I have us a room there for the next 72 hours," said Bud. "You know, lots of the pilots have stayed there and raved about it. In fact,

Brick and Rachel spent a weekend there sometime back, but for some reason, Scarlett and I never have."

"Well, Bud my boy, I'm very impressed. But why all the star treatment? You've already got the girl."

"I'm going to let that remark pass, Wilson, because I don't think you meant to be disrespectful and really make me sore!"

Wyman was taken aback, "No, Bud, I didn't mean anything."

Bud sighed, "I love her and I want to make her happy, you know, do things for her that she wouldn't ordinarily be able to do herself. And after all, junior, I get to enjoy it myself. You see, I've got this theory that you should keep things exciting all the time. Have things planned and always have something to look forward too."

"Well, I see what you mean. I've never heard that theory before. Where did you get it?"

"It's my own theory, Wilson," Bud responded, definitely perturbed.

Wyman sighed, "Maybe if I had a girl like Scarlett, I'd be spending the weekend at the Savoy."

"That's a very good point, Wilson, but there aren't any more like her."

BUD NEVER LOST his excitement at seeing Scarlett. He was crazy about his raven-haired beauty; there was no question about it. It was the same with Scarlett.

"Please explain that grin on your face. I mean, you're always happy, but there's something going on here that's different," she insisted. She grabbed the lapels of his jacket and pushed her face up close to his. "Tell me, you devil."

"Well," he said, still grinning from ear to ear.

"Tell me!"

"Okay, okay, just quit badgering me," he said with a laugh.

"Badgering?" she said.

"We're spending the weekend at the Savoy."

103

THEY ENTERED THE briefing room at 4:00 a.m. The map was covered, as usual, by a large black curtain. The men were a bit on edge to see where the red string would lead them. Ellis finally pulled the curtain so they could see the target.

"Leipzig!" said Ellis. There were a few gasps from the congregation. After the details had been covered, the crews synchronized their watches and climbed aboard the vehicles for the short hop to the flight line and their respective ships.

They taxied into position for takeoff, and Hansford pressed down hard on the brake peddles and opened the throttles all the way. The starting officer finally dropped his flag, Brick released the brakes, and they started rumbling down the runway.

"Talk to me, Bud!" said Brick.

"Fifty, sixty, eighty, one hundred, one-ten, one-twenty," said Bud, calling out the speed.

At one hundred twenty miles per hour Brick pulled back on the controls and the shaking and rattling stopped as the big overloaded Flying Fortress lifted into the air. *Rachel* was once again headed in harm's way.

As they gained speed and altitude, Bud started working the flaps up a little at a time. When the flaps were up, they started the slow turn to the left to get into formation.

"There's the lead ship circling far ahead, shooting red flares," said Bud. They kept turning inside the circle and, in a few minutes, the formation was in order and the *Rachel* took her place. Brick looked over at Bud and grinned.

"What do you say we go to Germany?" said Brick.

"Why the hell not?"

"The weather is much improved and it's good to see the sun shining brightly," said George Gifford, who had dropped down out of the top turret.

Hansford called the bombardier on the intercom. "Wyman, how do you suppose Goering has been able to explain us to Uncle Adolf?"

"I think he's probably been struggling a bit. I sure would like to be a fly on the wall."

"OKAY MEN, WE'RE in Indian country and the wagon train could be attacked at any time," said Brick. "Stay focused and call 'em out when you see 'em." About that time Bud spotted a large group of enemy fighters at 12 o'clock. They were a bit higher than their squadron.

"You better get back to your station, Giff. Look alive, fellows, I think the Krauts must have put up everything they have. I see Me-109s and 110s and Fw-190's."

Rachel was flying in the low squadron and the enemy was attacking the high squadron en mass. As they made their passes, the crew could actually see the leading edges of their wings blink red as the German 20 mm projectiles were spit out in rapid fire toward the Fortresses.

"Ships in the high squadron are catching hell," said Gifford. "They're on fire and men are bailing out. I saw a boy come out and pull his rip cord. It blossomed out beautifully at first. Then there was a bright flash of orange fire and the chute was gone. He was in free fall, kicking violently."

This is really bad stuff, Hansford thought to himself. *My God, I can see several crippled and burning B-17s which are in really bad straits.*

"*Lazy Mary* is out of control one minute and then she is flying straight. I don't know what's going on with her. There are so many white silks in the air, it looks more like a parachute drop than a bombing mission," said Brick. *We'll be damn lucky to survive this one.*

They were on their way to bomb the oil refineries at Leipzig. Now the flak was heavy. Brick went on the intercom, "Destafano, you and Gregory throw out the chaff and be quick about it."

"Right away, Captain."

The chaff was strips of aluminum foil that seemed to confuse the German radar on the flak guns. This caused them not to be as accurate. The waist gunners would tear open the foil, packed in 4x4x8 inch bundles, and throw it out by the handfuls.

"How stupid!" screamed Gregory.

"What is it, Glenn?" Hansford asked.

"The waist gunner in the ship across from us tossed out an entire bundle that caught in the air scoop of the B-17 flying behind them. It cut off the air intake and the engine shut down."

"He must be a new replacement," said Bud. "He couldn't be that stupid."

When the bombing run began, starting at the IP, all planes were to fly straight and level at a constant speed with no evasive action. The top turret gunner called the flight deck and yelled, "Skipper, we've got another ship no more than about 20 feet above us—he's got the bomb bay open! Oh no, I can see six 1,000 pound bombs hanging there just ready to be released."

Brick immediately began to take steps to alter their position.

"He just moved over out of the way!" screamed Gregory, with relief. "What in the hell is going on with this flight?"

Brick and Bud looked at each other with relief. "I think Gifford's on to something," said Bud.

The bomb run lasted approximately 30 seconds, an eternity in combat. When the lead plane dropped its bombs, black smoke was released, signaling the other ships to drop their bombs as well.

Bud was reading the gauges and looking out for flak when he saw a burst of about six or seven puffs of black smoke at exactly their altitude. A few seconds later, he and Brick saw a second burst of smoke but not as far away.

"The Krauts really have us blanketed," said Bud, shaking his head.

There was a noise and the *Rachel* reacted. "What the hell was that?" yelled Brick.

"A big piece of the nose cone Plexiglas is blown out!" screamed Wyman. "Black smoke is pouring in!"

The acrid smoke entered the cockpit along with a rush of cold air at 50 degrees below zero. "Shrapnel is hitting the ship like rocks falling on a tin roof," said Bud.

"Our bombs didn't drop!" Wyman yelled.

"Try again, Wyman!" yelled Hansford.

"I did, Captain, but no dice!"

"Keep trying! Keep trying!" Carter screamed.

The bombardier tried again, but no dice.

"Okay, the emergency bomb release worked. They're gone!"

"Oh, crap," said Wyman, "the bomb bay doors won't close!"

"Damn!" Brick exclaimed, looking at Bud, with a frown.

"Gifford, get down there and close them with the hand crank," barked Hansford.

"Yes, sir."

"What's taking so long?" Brick asked.

"Give him a chance. It's slow going with that hand crank."

"Okay, Captain, we got 'em closed. I hope you appreciate that at 20,000 feet on oxygen, it was a challenge."

"I do appreciate it, George, you're a great American."

"Bud, you better check on our navigator and bombardier."

He unhooked his oxygen hose from the main supply and attached a walk-around bottle. Then he went to check on Clifford and Wyman.

In a short time, Carter returned to the flight deck, reattached himself to the main oxygen supply, and reported what he had found. "Well, they're both okay, if you can believe it. I was fully expecting to find a mound of hamburger meat at Clifford's station. When I got down there, to my surprise, they seemed to be okay. Clifford took some shrapnel in the shoulder, but it didn't seem all that bad."

"How is his psyche?"

"He's as calm as can be. It didn't faze him."

"No kidding?"

"No kidding. Wyman didn't have a scratch. I wasn't too worried since he did his bombing."

"That's great news, Bud. I was concerned. How about taking the controls for awhile?"

"Okay, I got it, Skipper." Bud flew the ship to give Brick a break.

Soon after Brick resumed flying the *Rachel,* Bud noticed, "Oil pressure on the number three engine is 10 pounds. I'm gonna hit the feathering button to turn the leading edge of the propeller into the wind so it won't turn. Damn—I'm too late. There wasn't enough oil to feather the propeller. I recommend we cut the gasoline supply to the bum engine and turn off the ignition switch to hopefully prevent the engine from catching fire when the oil is completely gone."

"Go ahead," said Brick.

The propeller immediately started wind milling at 2,500 rpm. I'm afraid it's going to heat up and catch fire, Bud thought to himself, but didn't mention it to Brick. Luckily, it didn't happen.

They made it back to Bassingbourn without any more trouble and, on final approach, they shot a red flare indicating that they had wounded on board. An ambulance met them at the end of the landing run and took navigator Clark Clifford to the hospital. The rest of the crew went to debriefing. Bud asked Mahoney why he didn't mention that the number three engine was leaking oil.

"I swear I didn't notice it, sir."

"All right, Mahoney."

Bud sighed, *Mahoney's the best we've got and yet he missed the leak. I guess he's human and I just need to cut him some slack.*

The next day, the engineering officer jumped down Brick Hansford's throat for not getting the engine feathered before all the oil drained out of it. "That was a brand new engine we installed!" he shouted.

Brick looked him in the eye and got in his face. "Just cut the crap, Mitchell. *Rachel* is my girl, not yours. Here's the deal. You just keep fixing her, and I'll just keep flying her."

105

"THE PEOPLE IN Cheddingham don't have a good opinion of Yanks," said Scarlett, sipping her tea.

"Why would that be? I wouldn't think they'd have had that much contact with Americans," Rachel reasoned.

"They haven't. I think it's hearsay, mostly."

"That's too bad."

"I know. My folks don't think much of Americans. They don't even know I'm dating an American. They may have heart failure when I tell them I'm going to marry Bud."

Rachel laughed, "Well, that's a problem you'll have to deal with."

She thought for a minute, "I think we need to go there and let Bud meet them on his next leave."

"I think you're right about that. Bud will charm them and completely win them over."

"You know, Rachel, I don't doubt that for a minute. That's what he did to me."

Rachel smiled and nodded.

"Don't tell them you're planning to get married. Just tell them you want to bring him down to meet them, see some of the English countryside."

"That's a great idea. This is exciting. I'll look forward to it and I know he will as well."

- - - - -

"RACHEL, I WANTED to report to you on Mr. Willard Whatley and the Norwood Trading Company."

"What is it, sir?" Rachel asked, with excitement.

"Your hunch was correct. You were very clever in the way you handled Whatley and correct to tell me about it. That's exactly what I'd expect of BP people. And you were right to suspect some loose lips at BP as well. That's all I can tell you, my dear. I'm sure you understand."

She smiled and nodded.

"You have done a great service to this country as you have with your work at BP. We are grateful."

106

"DID YOU GET a look at the new B-17Gs?" Bud Carter inquired.

"Yeah, I did, and they sure look swell," said Hansford.

"They've got the chin-turret that we've all been crowing about to help defend against the head-on attacks by the Kraut fighters."

"It would sure be nice to fly one of those babies," Bud said.

"It will be great for the new crews, but I'm not going to war with a different girl. *Rachel* has always taken us there and back. We started this thing with her, and we're going to complete our tour with her." Brick declared.

"I know, I know, we all feel that way. I was just thinking out loud," said Bud.

"Did you check on Clifford?"

"The doc says he's okay."

"Is he cleared to fly?" Brick asked.

"As a matter of fact, he is."

"Good."

• • • • •

"BREAKFAST AT FIVE and briefing at six o'clock," said the sergeant, shining the offensive flashlight in Hansford's face. Brick struggled to wake up. He had never been an early riser, but the Eighth Air Force required him to go to work early. Sitting on the side of his cot, rubbing his eyes, he had no idea what this fateful day had in store for him, the crew, and the other fellows in the group.

I wonder what hellish target will be on that map in the briefing room? Hansford thought to himself. *We are learning the geography of Europe, but I do wish they'd quit shooting at us.*

He laughed and waked the other officers, and they began the usual routine. Brick shaved and had a hot shower. He hurriedly dressed in layers, as did the others, from clothes he had laid out the night before.

• • • • •

BRICK HANSFORD WAS in a fog as he drove the crew to the flight line.

The target is Schweinfurt. I can't help but wonder if we'll all still be together tonight.

He went through the checklist for pre-flight, inspecting the plane with the crew chief. *I'm here, physically doing all the things necessary, but I feel detached and totally out of my body. I have the feeling that I'm in another dimension watching what I'm doing. I'm here, but yet I'm not here. I know that we are in for another rough mission and will catch hell from fighters. We'll load additional boxes of .50 cal. ammunition, and I'll make sure everyone has their flak helmets.*

All too soon there was the green flare and they started the engines and taxied into position, checking their magnetos. Each pilot moved the throttles forward, allowing the engine noise to become like a scream. They moved down the runway and suddenly they were airborne, slightly skimming those damn trees. They climbed out and formed up at 28,000 feet.

ONCE THEY WERE in the air, Brick's personal fog lifted. The business at hand occupied everyone's mind. Soon enough they were crossing the English Channel, heading for Europe with the contrails following behind them for the Luftwaffe to see.

I love to fly the Rachel, thought Brick, *I can set the trim tabs and the plane will stay where I set it.*

This, of course, greatly reduced the amount of leg and shoulder effort, especially during formation flying, but there was the ever present turbulence, prop wash from other planes, enemy fighters, and flak. These factors required considerable physical effort in missions that took long hours to complete. The pilots learned to master techniques on sighting on the element lead, a light hand on the throttles, constant awareness of the attitude, power and position changes, trim settings, as well as relaxation. Brick smiled as he lightly gripped the controls, thinking, *The Rachel always responds well, which makes life a little easier allowing me that extra effort should calamity strike. She'll still respond with one or even two of her engines out. This girl will get me back to England, assuming there is enough of her remaining intact to keep flying.*

Suddenly, the dreaded announcement was shouted over the intercom by George Gifford in the top turret, "Bandits at nine o'clock high!" It had started—and the same message came almost simultaneously from the tail gunner and the ball turret.

THE SOUND OF a cannon shell hitting a Fortress depends on where you're located, Wyman thought to himself. *If the shell explodes close to you, there is nothing gentle and it certainly isn't a momentary tremor. It's like a giant slapping his hand on the water. There are two sounds—one from the impact—and the second from the explosion. It's like firing a shotgun into a bucket which all comes back exploding in your face.*

FOR A MOMENT, you aren't scared, thought Clark Clifford, *because your senses are dulled. Your bowels are weak, you tighten your pucker string, and your stomach shrivels up until you can figure out how much you may be hurt. It is as if you had been hit by a huge electrical shock. But thank God, today, I can handle it.*

I IMMEDIATELY FIND myself in a world alien to anything I have ever experienced, thought George Gifford. *There are 109s and 190s darting into view from everywhere. When they open fire, you suddenly see flashes of light winking at you from a distance. All at once there's a canopy of cannon shells and bombs, aerial mines and rockets exploding from everywhere. Each one of them intent on hitting us and our bomb load. We are no longer in a stately march in tight formation.*

WE TRY DESPERATLY to return to the crisp efficiency of our tight formation, thought Bud Carter, *but it is difficult to do. We slog our way through a thickening mass of exploding flame and smoke, with the equal determination of every member of the crew. We are driving ahead through jagged chunks of red hot Nazi metal.*

MY GOD, IT'S everywhere—a solid whirlwind of steel splinters, thought Tony Destafano. *It crashes into wings, engines, bulkhead, and bodies; spewing blood, tissue, intestines, and brains.*

INCOMING BANDITS ARE coming at us from every location, thought Glenn Gregory, *firing frantically with his .50 caliber machine gun from his position in the right waist. I can hear the chatter of our guns over the engine roar. Our words seem to plunge into insanity as the sounds of the battle are surrounding us, seemingly merging into an inhuman shriek. Our ship doesn't seem to be occupied by men, but rather beings from another world with strange breathing devices dangling beneath their faces.*

AS QUICKLY AS it started, thought Pat Thibodeaux, *the enemy fighters are gone. Our enemy now is the temperature that registers a minus fifty degrees and never seems to relax its vigil against us for any exposure to sensitive flesh and frostbite. And the flak will replace the machine gun fire from the bandits.*

THE ENEMY FIGHTERS broke off the attack because the Americans were getting close to the target where the anti-aircraft batteries would take over. Battle, strangely enough, made Brick Hansford hungry, and they had a few minutes before they would encounter shrapnel.

"Hey, Pat," said Hansford, "how about those sandwiches?"

"How are your teeth?"

"What do you mean?"

"Well, sir, they're frozen stiff."

"In other words, situation normal—all f---ed up!"

"That would be an affirmative, sir."

107

CENTRAL GERMANY LAY below them, and up ahead there was danger.

"I can see the first black specks of flak over the target," said Brick.

I never get used to the sheer terror of having to hold course and fly directly into the deadly metal, thought Carter.

"All positions report," said Bud.

"Tail, okay, except I'm almost out of ammo."

"I think we have plenty of extra, Morgan," said Hansford.

"Left waist okay," said Destafano, "but I lost my flak helmet somewhere."

Hansford laughed, "We'll, I'm sure it's there somewhere."

"I'm just fine, Skipper," said Gregory at the right waist.

"My side windows are screwed up," said McGuire, in the ball turret, "I can't see anything except straight ahead."

"Radio, okay," said Thibodeaux.

"I need some help when someone has time," said Gifford.

"We hear you, Giff. Hang on for a second," said Brick.

"You better check on him, Bud."

"Damn!" said Bud. Gifford's flak helmet flew off from the nearby explosion that also produced two vicious looking cracks in his canopy. He's okay, miraculously unhurt, although he had turned grey as the blood had all drained from his face.

All the gauages are still working, Hansford said to himself, *but the glass on the dials looks like someone took a hammer to 'em. The radio compass is shattered and the other radios are hanging by their connecting cords, but all seem to be working.*

Bud Carter returned to the cockpit with a report. "We're fine, Skipper, but with all the holes in this airplane, it's a miracle we're still flying and no one was hurt."

"What about Gifford?"

"It turns out that a 20 mm came through the turret, knocking out the ammo boxes on each side and tearing off his flight suit at the thigh. He has a slight red mark on one leg. It's really unbelievable.

He's lucky, but it scared him shitless. We moved new ammo boxes in and reconnected them to both guns."

Hansford hung on his every word.

"The navigator's table is shattered, but Clifford's fine and so is Wyman," said Carter.

WHEN THEY TURNED on the IP, Wilson Wyman was looking for his aiming point as the *Rachel's* controls were hooked up to the bombsight. There was a squadron ahead of them. The sky was covered with black-steel, paving a deadly roadway to Schweinfurt.

"The explosions sound as if someone is throwing rocks at us when they burst close," said Wyman. "Those German gunners are good—very good. I'd like to be somewhere else."

"Yeah," said Clifford.

German efforts to keep the B-17s from the target had failed, but the strike force was paying a tremendous price in men and machines. The stakes were high. The target below was now rapidly deteriorating into smoke and debris as strings of bombs were walking through the city.

"Bombs away!" shouted Wyman, who always felt a surge of euphoria when he had unleashed the deadly ordinance.

You can literally feel the plane lighten in little jerks as the bombs leave the bomb bay on their way to Germany, thought Clifford.

As Hansford began a wide turn to the right, Gifford remarked to Destafano, with a frown, "We're only at the halfway point."

"I'm painfully aware of that sad fact."

"Everyone is staying in close for defensive purposes. The other formations behind us look ragged and are under attack from enemy fighters," said Brick.

"The Krauts are so desperate that some of the fighters are attacking in spite of their own flak," said Bud.

The crew of the *Rachel* could see the target below and the sticks of bombs on their five mile flight to enemy soil. The target was covered with smoke, and gray dust was rising from the impact of the bombs. Thankfully, the *Rachel* was not under attack from enemy fighters.

Bud Carter looked at Hansford and said, "It seems so quiet after all we've been through. It's just so good to just hear the sound of all four of our beautiful engines and the rush of the air."

"Sounds like a symphony," said a smiling Brick Hansford.

"I hope we don't have a mission tomorrow," said Carter.

"We may catch a break in a sad way," said Hansford.

"What do you mean?"

"Well, this little trip has been very costly. You saw them going down just like I did, Bud. We've been shot up pretty badly, and some of our crews may be in bad shape—and the brass may be in shock."

Carter sighed, "It's been brutal, that's for sure, but it looks like the crew of the *Rachel* has cheated death again."

"Well, we're not home yet, but it does appear to be the case, Lt. Carter," said Hansford, with a large grin.

108

SOON THEY WERE over France, headed home, and saw enemy fighters in the distance, but for some reason they didn't attack.

"What do you make of that, Brick?" Carter inquired.

"I don't know what to think. Maybe they didn't see us or they're out of ammo or they're just as tired of fighting as we are."

Nearing home the cloud cover was up to 20,000 feet and the returning B-17s were instructed to drop down over the English Channel; then, each squadron was at liberty to proceed to their bases individually.

Soon the cold angry waters of the Channel were in sight, and they proceeded up the estuary on the east coast of England. When the smokestacks of Peterborough were in sight, they turned southwest toward home. "What a wonderful sight, and how many times in the past twelve hours have we wondered if we'd see base again?" Carter reflected.

Hansford smiled and nodded. George Gifford, the top turret gunner, had dropped down out of his position and was standing behind Carter and Hansford. He patted Hansford on the right shoulder and said, "Great job as usual, Skipper."

As they crossed the field in preparation to break into the landing pattern, they could see the ground crews, the brass outside the control tower, the meat wagons with the large red crosses painted on the tops, and the fire trucks parked along the runway. People on the ground were watching the incoming airplanes and counting the bombers, straining to read the symbols and numbers as they flew over. All at once there were red flares indicating wounded aboard, which allowed them to enter the pattern and land first. Soon it was the *Rachel's* turn, and she lined up with the runway on her final approach, crossing the boundary of the field, with the squeal of the tires hitting the tarmac.

"We made it," said Gregory, as the tail settled to the runway. All the enlisted crew, huddled together in the belly of the *Rachel,* smiled with relief.

They completed their roll and came to a stop. Brick and Bud smiled at each other. The faithful engines were silent now, and Bud turned all the switches to off. The *Rachel* had once again given them everything she had and had brought them safely home as she had done so many times before.

"You don't live and fly a Fortress for mission after mission without coming to know the airplane in the most intimate way," said Brick. "You know how well she's put together and how forgiving she is to fly. She is in our hearts, a part of us until we're finished."

"I couldn't have put it better," said Bud.

They retrieved their gear and left the plane. As they set foot on the ground, Bud saw a B-17 coming in on her belly. "Brick, you go on with the fellows to debriefing. I'm going to catch a ride over to the *Mary Ann* and check on Conway."

"Okay, Bud, go ahead." The crew of the *Rachel* boarded a truck and headed for the debriefing shack. On the way, they passed the parking and maintenance area with their waiting crews who waved and flashed the victory sign. Many of these ground crews would return to their quarters, saddened by the harsh realization that the ships they serviced were still in Germany.

Bud caught a ride with an ambulance. Fire trucks, jeeps, and staff cars were also in route to the crash scene.

Rob Conway, the skipper of the *Mary Ann*, had roomed with Bud Carter when they were in multi-engine aircraft school. They were very close friends.

When they arrived, it looked like most of the crew was out and safe. They looked pretty shook up as they all lit cigarettes and breathed a sigh of relief. Then some corpsmen pulled Billy Dale out of the ship. He was the ball turret gunner and he didn't make it. Then they brought out Conway. He wasn't dead but was groaning. *My God, you can see his brains,* Bud thought to himself, as they loaded Conway on one of the two ambulances. "Get going, you guys, get him to the hospital!" screamed Carter.

A corpsman stuck his head out the waist gunner's window and said to another corpsman, "Hand me a blanket out of the ambulance, will you? There's an entire arm in here."

Bud put his arm around the neck of Bob Nelson, the copilot, who had his head down on the wing and was pounding it with his clenched fist. "What happened up there, Bob?"

"The Fw-190s hit us hard on the first pass. That's when Conway got it. He didn't pass out. Why I don't know. But it made him a crazy man, and it was hell getting him out from under the controls."

Bud shook his head, "Who belongs to the arm?"

"That's Sgt. Skeeter Martin's arm, the top turret gunner. It was blown off too close to risk trying to bring him home."

"Where is he, then?" Bud inquired.

"I hope he's in a French hospital. We bailed him out."

"Well, you did a great job getting your cripple home. Let's get your crew over to debriefing. I think you boys could use a combat ration or two."

109

DEBRIEFINGS WERE ALWAYS grim. There were far too many of their friends who had gone down in flames, many before their very eyes. Around the debriefing table, there was a great deal of consideration given the returning crews. Questions were quietly asked. *How many fighters, types, and methods of attack? Were there any special weapons or markings? Was the flak accurate? Was it heavy?*

As the debriefing of the crew of the *Rachel* began, Captain Hansford asked if there were combat rations, which to a flier was a small bottle with a few ounces of whiskey. He was given one and asked for two more, which he threw down straight away. Then he stated matter-of-factly, to the great surprise of the others, "I had reconciled myself to the fact that I was not going to live through this one—that my number was up—that we were all going to die. I was churning inside. It was a strange sort of resignation. I knew for certain that it was only a matter of seconds or minutes."

It may have been that the others felt the same way, but they didn't say so.

This is really something, Clifford thought to himself. *I've been the one crew member, maybe the only crew member, who was terrified on every mission. Now, by the grace of God, I have overcome my fear. But the iron man, the confident indestructible Captain Brick Hansford is having doubts—is having fear. I wonder how it will affect his flying and his leadership? Time will tell.*

They found out later that during the fighter attack, the total frame just forward of the horizontal stabilizer had been totally torn apart by the deadly 20 mm rounds. Only the skin and the control cables held it together.

I have never felt fear before, Brick thought to himself, *but this Schweinfurt mission really got to me. I've never had any apprehension about a mission—any missions. But now I do and it's scaring the hell out of me. I hope it doesn't show because the crew depends on me, and I sure hope it doesn't show up in my flying and in my decisions.*

THE LOSSES OVER Schweinfurt were catastrophic—60 B-17s and 600 men out of the 376 planes that flew the mission did not return. *Bluebonnet Bell* was one of them.

THAT EVENING LORD Hawthorne was at it again. The Germans could break into Allied broadcasts whenever they felt it was advantageous. They thought this was a good time for it.

> *This is Germany calling, a special message from Berlin, Lord Hawthorne speaking. Today I bring a special message from the daring and relentless fighter pilots of the Luftwaffe to the brave B-17 crewmen of the Eighth Air Force. They send their heartfelt sympathies to the families of all the brave airmen who burned up over the skies of our beloved Fatherland. You really took a pasting today, particularly the 91ˢᵗ Bomb Group at Bassingbourn.*

Ellis banged his fist on the table, "Damn it, how do they know so much about us?"

"Look, they've been plotting their dirty deeds here in Europe since the early 1930s so no doubt they have spies everywhere and some of them probably speak perfect English," said Major Ramsey, the ground executive officer. "Some of the sorry bastards may be tossing darts and having a half and half at a local pub."

> *What on earth ever convinced you fools to conduct daylight missions?* Hawthorne continued. *It must have been your friends, the English. They gave up on the idea you know, losses were too great. So, you boys in the Eighth get to take the hits instead of the Brits. Isn't that lovely? At the rate you're losing bombers and crews, you won't be able to last much longer. But your superiors will keep sending you up, and we'll keep knocking you down. Well, good night and sweet dreams, my misguided friends.*

COL. BIRDWELL WALKED in just after Hawthorne had finished up.

"Did you hear the pep talk from Berlin?" Ellis asked.

"Yeah, I heard the sonofabitch!

110

THE GROUP DIDN'T fly the following day. The airplanes and the men were not in the best of shape. Birdwell asked Major Herbert Casey, the Group Flight Surgeon, to come to his office.

"Thanks for coming over, Doc," said Birdwell. "After Schweinfurt, I must confess that I'm concerned about my crews. How are the men holding up?"

"I could give you several answers to that question, Colonel. The reasons the men give for requesting to be excused from flying, it's all over the map. I mean, it's belly aches, migraine headaches—many complain of colds, but they don't really have colds. And that doesn't necessarily mean they've gone yellow on you, Colonel. I think they've just had a gut full of flying combat, and missions like yesterday reduce their hope of survival. My dilemma is, I don't know how much a man can take."

"The book says a man goes right up to the point where he endangers his crew and jeopardizes the mission," said Birdwell.

"Well that's just dandy. But I can't tell when that is, Colonel Birdwell. Somebody has to give me a policy, a yardstick, some way to tell when they've hit the wall. In fact, Colonel, maybe you can tell me what a maximum effort is."

"Doc, I wish I knew, but I don't. I feel that something will be developed on the order of what you're asking for. But for now, if a man can handle his airplane, handle his job, he goes."

"Well, it's not what I wanted to hear, but it's something," said Casey. He saluted and left.

THE AUGUST 17, 1943 raid on Schweinfurt would forever be referred to as *Black Thursday.*

■ ■ ■ ■ ■

"WHAT'S ON YOUR mind, Brick? You seem preoccupied," said Bud.

"Schweinfurt is part of it, I guess. We fly these missions and a new ship on its first run doesn't come back. The ship on our right takes a direct hit, and suddenly it's not there anymore. The lead ship is blown to hell and their brains and guts are all over our canopy. But we make it through every mission. We still have the same group of fellows we started out with. I'm just trying to understand it, that's all. You think there is a higher power at work here?"

Bud lit a cigarette, took a drag, and exhaled. "Yeah, I do."

"Really?"

"I come from a Baptist family, and I was saved when I was 12 years old."

"What do you mean saved?"

"I gave my heart to Jesus Christ. I belong to him and he died on the cross for me. If I die, I'll go to heaven. My faith has saved me from hell. I pray for you and the entire crew of the *Rachel,* and I know that my family back home is praying for me and so is my church."

Brick listened intently.

"I have faith that God is protecting us. I don't think I could take all this if I didn't have God."

Brick lit a cigarette as well and sighed, "We never went to church. But I am coming to believe that maybe there is a God and He does watch out for some people."

Bud smiled, "Brick, you can count on it. Maybe you should talk to a chaplain?"

"Maybe I should at that. Thanks for what you said and your encouragement."

"Hey, over here, we depend on each other for everything."

"Yeah, we sure do."

111

THE ENLISTED MEN of the *Rachel* were at the NCO Club, relaxing and talking about the time when the war would be over. They didn't do it a lot—their leaders actually counseled them not to make plans, to just concentrate on missions. They were an exceptional group of men, and they had put Schweinfurt behind them.

"I think about New York City all the time," said Destafano. "Man, I can't wait to get back there and bite into one of those choice steaks at Destafano's, the best restaurant in the Bronx. Gentleman, there are no finer steaks in the world."

"But what do you plan to do for a living?" asked Morgan.

"Destafano's is a family business—we all work there. I can do anything and everything that needs to be done. It'll be mine someday."

"What about you, Morgan?" Thibodaux asked.

"My family owns a large historic mansion in my home town of Gruene, Texas. They live in part of the house and rent out the rest of it to guests who come to our little town to dance country at Gruene Hall, sample fine chicken-fried steak, swim in the Guadalupe River, and enjoy the charm of the area. We provide a bed and full breakfast the next morning, boarding house style. We don't make a lot of money, but it pays the taxes and provides a modest living and we really enjoy it. Just like Tony, I can do anything that needs to be done, and it will be mine someday."

"Okay, Gifford, you're next," said Destafano.

"This will probably surprise you mullets, but I want to teach college. I'll go back to Pittsburg and enroll at Pitt. I want to eventually get my masters and Ph.D and teach math."

"Dr. Gifford, that sounds impressive," said Morgan.

"Okay, Louisiana, what are your postwar plans?" asked Gifford.

Thibodeaux laughed, "I am definitely going to return to the Big Easy. Man, once you've lived in New Orleans, it ruins you for anywhere else. I don't know for sure, but I'd kind of like to play piano and sing in a jazz joint."

He thought for a minute, "I might like the hotel business. I'm not as sure of my future as you fellows seem to be. But I don't really have to decide today, do I?"

"Frank McGuire from the great state of Tennessee, what do you think you'll do?" asked Morgan.

"After I get my undergraduate degree, I'd like to go to law school. I want to be a lawyer, you know, help the little guy who got screwed. I'm from Memphis, so I'd like to practice there if I can."

"Last but not least, it's my fellow waist gunner, Glenn Gregory," said Destafano.

"You guys already know I want to open a chain of hamburger joints."

"Yeah, that right," said Destafano.

Sgt. George Gifford, the senior sergeant on the *Rachel,* raised his beer bottle. He sighed and said, "Here's to us, the best damn crew in the Eighth Air Force and the finest bunch of fellows I've ever been associated with. Good luck, guys, and God bless us all." There were tears in his eyes.

THE 91st BOMB Group was standing down following the costly raid on Schweinfurt. All the men who wanted passes got them.

112

RACHEL GOT UP quietly, hoping not to disturb Brick, and put on her robe. After going to the bathroom, she retuned and sat on the side of the bed, thinking. Then she bent down and gently kissed him on the forehead, the eyes, and then the mouth. His eyes opened, and he stretched and smiled.

"Darling, you must get up," she asked sweetly.

"And why is that?"

"We're going out, remember."

"Are we?" he asked, mischievously.

"Brick, I'm starving," she insisted.

"Okay."

"Darling, what shall I wear?" she asked.

"Rachel, you always look great. Whatever you wear will be fine with me."

Brick had made reservations at the Club Bonaparte, a dinner dance establishment with a French flavor, popular with the military and the locals.

THEY CLAIMED THEIR table and started with two rounds of drinks before finally getting around to dinner. There was a female singer, French, not bad, with three male musicians. They made a lot of music for such a small group, and the dance floor was always crowded.

"I've always loved to dance with you, Brick. We're getting bumped around a bit, but it's still lovely."

Brick smiled at her warmly and held her tight, "Yes, it is. I like this place. Bud made a good recommendation."

The clientele at the club was a mixed bag: Polish, Dutch, and French military, British and American troops as well, most with dates.

"May I have another drink, please?" Rachel asked.

Brick looked around to see if he could catch the eye of a waiter; no such luck. "I'll get it," said Brick, impatiently.

"I'll try to save your place." Brick laughed. So did she.

An intoxicated but friendly Frenchman was walking around through the tables with a bottle of red wine in each hand. He approached every table and filled up every empty glass. When he saw

Rachel sitting alone he put down the bottles, sat down in Brick's chair, and proceeded to kiss her hand. When he saw Brick approaching with two drinks and a glare, he jumped up, filled her glass and shouted, "To our American friends!" Then he wisely moved himself and his bottles to another table.

"What was that about?" Brick said.

"Nothing, really, he was just happy."

She raised her glass and offered a toast, "To us—to life."

They took a sip and she said, "Dance with me."

"I'M READY FOR a change of scenery," said Rachel.

"What did you have in mind?" Brick asked.

"Do you mind if we walk a bit?"

"Not at all."

They held hands as they strolled. "You really like to walk, don't you?"

She smiled up at him, "Yes, I really do."

After about 20 minutes, she said, "I'm walked out. As a matter of fact, I'm tired out. Do you mind if we go back?"

"Look, we're right here at the Devonshire Arms. Let's have a nightcap before we head back." He was not ready to end their evening just yet.

She hesitated for a moment and then agreed.

The Devonshire Arms was a neighborhood pub. It just happened to also be a watering hole for BBC people, not that that was of any significance. After an hour or so she was beginning to fade, and they left. While in the process of hailing a cabbie, everything changed. They heard the unnerving cry of sirens, the distant drum of aircraft engines, and the muffled sound of explosions to the south. Everyone knew, from past history, that a full moon was sometimes an unwanted invitation for Fritz to come calling.

Rachel's demeanor abruptly changed. She squeezed Brick's hand, "I'm scared!"

"There's a shelter a couple of blocks down there, but we had better hurry."

"Okay, okay!"

Boy, we got here in the nick of time, he reasoned.

As they stood at the shelter entrance, the frightening roar of enemy planes came from overhead.

"You had better go inside."

"What about you?"

"I'll be there in a second."

Anti-aircraft guns began to fill the sky with deadly shrapnel, and he could definitely detect the sounds of bomb blasts. As he gazed out over the city, he saw bombs bursting like Roman candles, searchlights crisscrossing the heavens, and fires beginning to burn everywhere. Brick reacted quickly to the recognizable sound of a bomb heading his way. He hurriedly retreated inside the shelter.

"What were you doing?"

"Just watching things."

She frowned and shook her head.

As he held her tight, a deafening explosion rocked the area.

"I think they've gone now," Brick concluded.

Rachel and Brick were the last in and the first out. She cringed, "Oh, my God."

They witnessed a disturbing scene. Duchess Street, where the CBS office was located, was ablaze. Most of the adjoining streets were the same. Houses began collapsing before their eyes. Rachel gasped. The bomb that Brick felt was headed his way hit the Devonshire Arms. Dust, debris, and smoke were rising from a black hole. The Devonshire Arms was no longer there.

113

THE ANTICIPATION WAS enormous, both for Scarlett and Bud, as the clatter of the train brought them closer to her family home in Cheddingham. "How are they going to feel about all this stuff I'm bringing?" Bud questioned.

"The English people have done without for so long that I think they'll just be grateful," she reasoned.

"I hope so. I'm doing this out of the kindness of the United States Army Air Corps, which has warehouses full of supplies."

"Don't worry, darling, it will be fine." She patted him on the leg and gave him a kiss.

"Scarlett, what have you told them about me?'

"I told them you're a pilot from Austin, Texas, USA, and handsome as hell. The rest of it you can tell yourself. But I've got a feeling you're going to completely charm them."

MINNIE AND MURRAY SELLERS were eagerly waiting at the station when the train finally arrived. Bud stepped off first and helped Scarlett down, they noticed. "Scarlett, baby!" shouted Minnie as she rushed forward to embrace her daughter. Bud collected the luggage, arranged it orderly, and placed his box of Eighth Air Force rations carefully on top. By now Murray had hugged his daughter and kissed her on the forehead. Bud stood patiently, waiting his turn.

"Hey, I want you to meet Lt. Bud Carter, United States Army Air Corps."

"Lieutenant," said Murray Sellers, his hand extended.

"Mr. Sellers, it's a pleasure, sir. And please call me Bud."

"And Mrs. Sellers."

"Bud," Minnie responded, with a genuinely friendly smile. He caught her off guard when he hugged her and kissed her on the cheek. She didn't seem to mind.

"I can see where Scarlett gets her good looks, Mrs. Sellers."

Minnie smiled and blushed.

"The car's over here," said Murray, motioning in the direction of the car park.

They loaded the luggage in the trunk, but Bud kept the rations with him. Bud helped Scarlett and Minnie into the back seat and then climbed in front with Murray. "It still seems odd to me for the driver to be on the right. I haven't driven anything but a jeep since I've been over here, so I guess it doesn't matter."

Murray sped away and they chattered all the way to the house as if they had known Bud for a lifetime. It helped that the young American was uninhibited and outgoing.

They showed Bud to the guest room upstairs and he hurriedly changed into blue jeans, a belt with a large silver buckle, a soft blue work shirt, and cowboy boots.

"Look at you," said Scarlett, "I've never seen you in anything but a uniform."

Bud took his ration box into the kitchen with Scarlett following right behind. Minnie was getting organized for dinner.

"Put it here," said Scarlett, motioning toward the breakfast table. "Daddy, come in here please."

When all had gathered around, Bud said, "The United States government supplies its troops pretty well. When we are invited into the homes of the English people, we are encouraged to bring a few things to show our appreciation." He took the top off the box and started unloading. "Let's see, we have tea, jam, cheese, eggs, sugar, flour, Spam, three tins of Prince Albert smoking tobacco, and canned fruit. Actually, it's fruit cocktail with a lot of different fruits all together. I don't know if you have this product over here."

"My soul, Murray, would you look at all this?" Minnie exclaimed.

The last item was a bottle carefully wrapped in several layers of brown paper. Bud unwrapped it and handed it to Murray. He looked stunned, "Minnie, it's bourbon whiskey, Ancient Age. I do believe it's Christmas, ole girl."

"Distilled, aged, and bottled in the great state of Kentucky, USA," said Bud, proudly.

"I don't know what to say," said Minnie, "times are …"

Bud interrupted. "Don't say anything. Accept it with the appreciation of me and the 91st Bomb Group."

"Okay, fine," said Minnie.

She came close and gave him a kiss on the cheek. "That's more thanks than was necessary, but I liked it." They laughed.

"I hope you enjoy the Prince Albert, Mrs. Sellers," said Bud, laughing.

"Oh, you silly man," she said, blushing.

"Scarlett, you'll help me with supper?"

"Yes, Mom."

Murray took Bud into the living room along with the whiskey and a tin of tobacco. "Scarlett tells me you were in the First World War."

Murray perked up and after digging around in a storage area under the window sill, he produced a thick scrapbook and motioned for Bud to join him on the couch. He packed his pipe, lit it, and said, "I don't suppose it would ruin our appetite if we had a wee taste of that fine bourbon."

"No, sir, I don't think so. In fact, it might help it."

They tipped their glasses and both downed the cherished brew in one swallow. "Ah, very nice," said Murray, looking at the glass.

Bud lit a cigarette, Murray puffed on his pipe, and they got down to the pictorial review of the Great War. Bud was attentive as Murray slowly turned each page, explaining everything in detail.

"Look, Mom, they're getting on rather well, don't you think?"

Minnie peeked in the living room and a broad smile crossed her face.

"THAT WAS A wonderful meal, Mrs. Sellers, I couldn't eat another bite," Bud remarked. "Mr. Sellers, I think we need a bit more of that fine bourbon whiskey."

"You're a man after my own heart," Murray replied, with a smile, "I couldn't agree with you more."

"You men take your tobacco and whiskey in the living room. Scarlett and I will clear and join you in a bit," said Minnie.

In the kitchen, Minnie remarked, "I can see what you see in him, Scarlett. He's courteous, thoughtful—very pleasant, and bloody gorgeous."

"He's all that and more. He's a happy guy, in spite of what he's up against, and very positive. He always makes me feel better when

I'm around him." She hesitated and then spilled the beans. "I love him and he loves me. We're going to get married."

Minnie dropped a plate and broken pieces flew all over the floor.

"Is everything okay in there?" Murray asked.

"Yeah, a plate fell, that's all," said Scarlett.

Minnie was simply not prepared for that kind of announcement. But she also knew that young people in war time were grabbing life and little pleasures when and where they could.

This war will be over eventually, the Yanks will go home, and things will return to normal, Minnie thought. *Why does she have to do this?*

"Part of the reason we came down here was to tell you our plans and let you meet Bud. Oh, Mom, I love him so much. I don't want to lose him—I won't!"

Minnie continued to wash the dishes and hand them to Scarlett who dried them and put them away. "I wanted to tell you in private, Mom, and let you get used to the idea. We'll make the announcement later when we're all together in there. Please pretend you're surprised."

Tears rolled down Minnie's face. "And I suppose you'll move to America."

"That's the plan. But I'll come back for visits, and you and Dad can come to see us as well. Look, you have Joe and Ernie. It's not like I'm your only child."

"Joe and Ernie may not survive the fighting in North Africa," Minnie lamented. "And besides, you're my only girl."

Minnie turned away and looked out the kitchen window, into the darkness. Then she faced her daughter again, wiped her eyes, and hugged her. She didn't speak. She patted her on the cheek and went off into her bedroom and closed the door. Scarlett leaned up against the sink and thought about her mom and the shock she must have felt. Minnie finally returned. She looked better, smiled, and said, "Come, let's join the men."

IT WAS A very pleasant evening. Murray showed Bud his medals and Minnie dug out several scrapbooks of old family pictures. Scarlett sat on one side of Minnie and Bud on the other as her mom proudly showed her baby pictures. Bud loved it—Scarlett was embarrassed.

Later on, Scarlett played the piano and they all sang. "You know, I didn't know until tonight that Scarlett could play. She's been holding out on me."

"Listen, I don't want you to figure me out all at once."

Murray asked Bud about the Eighth Air Force and what they were doing. He told them what he could, but they understood he couldn't give them too much detail and didn't press him.

Scarlett sat on the edge of the couch, put her arm around Bud and said, "Dad, Mom, Bud and I want to be married and it would mean a lot to us if we had your blessing."

Bud looked at Scarlett and then turned toward Minnie and Murray.

"I know this is probably a huge shock to you. I can appreciate that," said Bud. "But I love her very much. I've never met a girl quite like her. In fact, I fell in love with her the first time I laid eyes on her. That doesn't happen all that often in life. It never happened in the Colonies."

Murray grinned. *In the Colonies, the Yank has a sense of humor.*

Minnie was sitting on the edge of Murray's chair. He reached up and took her hand. "I didn't mention it to Minnie, but I had a feeling that something like this was the reason you kids came down."

"Dad," she exclaimed, as if he had said something wrong.

"Quiet my girl, I'm not finished. This war makes everything different. If we weren't at war, you wouldn't be over here, Bud, and you young folks would never have met. But there is a war, and these are not ordinary times.

"Frankly, out here in Cheddingham, far removed from London and all that's going on there, I never once thought about this happening. But it did. As far as we can tell, Bud, you're a fine young man and you're getting a fine young woman."

He thought for a moment and then continued. "You have my blessing," his voice breaking, "and I hope that of your mum as well."

"Oh Dad," said Scarlett, rushing over and kissing him. Then she hugged her mother tightly. Bud walked over and shook Murray's hand and Murray squeezed it warmly. Minnie, with tears in her eyes, kissed Bud and hugged him tight. "Well," said Murray, "this calls for a drink. Minnie, fetch that bottle of fine Kentucky bourbon and four glasses."

SCARLETT TOOK PLEASURE in showing Bud her village and introducing him to the townspeople. They enjoyed sampling local fare and took long walks in the countryside. By the time they had to catch the train back to London, the Sellers had reconciled themselves to Scarlett and Bud's decision. The handsome young flier had completely won them over.

PART EIGHT

RACHEL'S FINAL MISSION

114

BRICK WAS DRAWN to Father Mathew O' Banyan. He had observed the chaplain counseling boys after interrogation, the ones traumatized by a particular mission. He had observed him at the base hospital, ministering to wounded fliers and crewmen. Brick felt O' Banyan was a sincere minister, someone he could feel comfortable with and trust.

Brick started attending Mass on the base and had had several conversations with Father O' Banyan. He found the discussions comforting and helpful. The tipping point for Brick was not a mission, but when he was on pass in London with Rachel. During a raid, the bomb that he felt was heading his way hit the Devonshire Arms. He saw the dust, the debris, and the smoke rising from a black hole where the Devonshire Arms had been.

He was struck by the realization that it was not only his buddies who were dying, it was also the citizens of London: the women, the children, the young, and the old. Death was everywhere. It was getting to him. He needed something to give him the calm assurance and peace of mind that Bud had told him about.

■ ■ ■ ■ ■

AFTER MASS, BRICK hung around until all the boys had gone.

"Father O' Banyan, do you have a minute for me?"

"Sure, Captain Hansford, what can I do for you?"

Brick sighed, "I want to become a Catholic."

"Do you know? That's a big decision, but I must admit that I'm pleased. I have been praying for you."

"Praying that I would become a Catholic?"

"No, my son, praying that God would give you peace. Well, becoming Catholic is one of life's most profound and joyous experiences. Some are blessed enough to receive this great gift while they are infants, and, over time, they recognize the enormous grace that has been bestowed on them. Others enter the Catholic fold when they are older children or adults. This tract examines the joyful process by which one becomes a Catholic. I believe you have been on that journey.

"One is brought into full communion with the Catholic Church through reception of the three sacraments of Christian initiation—baptism, confirmation, and the holy Eucharist—but the process by which one becomes a Catholic can take different forms.

"A person who is baptized in the Catholic Church becomes a Catholic at that moment. One's initiation is deepened by confirmation and the Eucharist, but one becomes a Catholic at baptism. This is true for children who are baptized Catholic. They receive the other two sacraments later. Adults can be baptized, confirmed, and receive the Eucharist at the same time.

"Those who have been validly baptized outside the Church become Catholics by making a profession of the Catholic faith and being formally received into the Church. This is normally followed immediately by confirmation and the Eucharist.

"Before a person is ready to be received into the Church, whether by baptism or by profession of faith, preparation is necessary. The amount and form of this preparation depends on the individual's circumstance. Captain Hansford, are you ready to start the process?"

"Yes, Father, I am."

"Good."

115
MISSION TWENTY-FIVE

THERE WAS THE usual chatter in the briefing room before they knew the target. Then Ellis drew the black curtain.

"Germany again!" It was uttered from all over the room.

"That's right, Germany," said Col. Birdwell, "Leipzig, to be precise—620 miles into Deutschland."

Carter glanced innocently to his left and noticed that Hansford had broken out in a heavy sweat. *He looks ashen,* thought Bud. *Could it be that the great warrior, approaching the 25th and final mission, is really scared? Frankly, I had dismissed his little speech at the debriefing after the raid on Schweinfurt. It's hard to believe. But now I am convinced that the man we have all leaned on in times of crisis is himself on the brink of a breakdown. And I remember all that bullshit about staying over here and flying missions until the war is over. Brick is definitely not the same cocky young man that he was. I really need to watch him. It's not good when your commander is about to crack.*

"You boys are going to hit their largest synthetic oil refinery. I shouldn't have to emphasize how important this target is. If we can knock out their oil supply, we can cripple the striking power of the Luftwaffe. When we invade the continent—and that day will come— we must have complete air supremacy. Can you imagine what it would be like to have thousands of our troops trapped against the Atlantic Wall, being bombed and strafed by the enemy? Well, gentlemen, that's a picture too grim to contemplate. This mission, and others that will follow, will go a long way toward helping us command the skies. I expect your best effort today, fellows, and I know I'll get it. Major Ellis will give you more details."

A movie screen was moved into place and aerial photographs of the target area were displayed. Ellis carefully pointed out areas of concern, markers to help guide them, dummy buildings, and key installations. "I'm not going to minimize the danger of this mission. This could be the toughest mission the Eighth Air Force has flown to date."

Ellis paused to let his words sink in and then turned the meeting over to Major Gene Richards, the flight leader.

"Thanks to your excellent flying, the enemy has had trouble breaking up our formations, so they're getting desperate. They will probably step up the technique of the head-on attack to try and take out the flight deck. Spitfires will cover us as far as Amsterdam and then we're on our own. That leaves us with about six critical hours over enemy territory. But maybe you'll take some comfort in knowing that you'll have company. You'll be a part of the largest force ever assembled—some 1,000 heavy bombers."

"Wow, that's incredible," said Bud Carter.

"Now, because of the sheer length of the mission, you'll be subject to more fighter attacks. We estimate that these bad boys will be coming from 80 airfields that are in striking distance of the bomber streams. So, you'll take extra rounds, but you'll still need to conserve your ammunition—no long bursts—but well timed short ones. Navigators and bombardiers will remain for additional information. The rest of you can go, and good luck."

Bud Carter stopped Richards with a request, "Any chance I can make a call to London, Major?"

"It's a total security blackout, Carter. Colonel Birdwell couldn't get an open line."

ASIDE FROM THE preflight checklist, Brick Hansford had not said a word to Carter since they woke up, which was very strange. Brick was definitely not himself.

Finally, they were in the air and at 28,000 ft. They formed up and headed for Germany. Carter looked out his window and witnessed a sight to behold. A sky full of Flying Fortresses, loaded to the limit, heading in harm's way.

"CLIFFORD, WHERE ARE WE?" Hansford inquired.

"We're over the Dutch coast, Captain," he replied.

"Okay, fellows, we're in Indian country. Look lively and call out the savages," Hansford instructed.

"Hey, Gifford, did Mahoney say anything about checking the hydraulic fluid?"

"Negative, Skipper,"

"Well, he was supposed to check it," said Hansford, disgustedly. "I forgot to ask him, I meant to ask him."

"What's the matter with you, Brick?" Carter inquired.

Hansford looked at him and frowned, but didn't answer.

"BANDITS AT FIVE o'clock high," screamed Gifford from the top turret.

"Holy shit!" yelled Destafano, "the sky is black with 'em."

Every gun position on the *Rachel* was firing like crazy. "Hey, they got Patterson," said Carter, looking out his window. "*Southern Bell* is on fire and spinning out of control. I don't see any parachutes."

"Captain, can you drop your right wing a bit? He's just sitting out there," said Gifford.

Brick Hansford did not respond. Bud knew he was screwed up, but just didn't know how bad. "You want me to take it for awhile?" Bud suggested.

"No," said Hansford, curtly.

■ ■ ■ ■ ■

"THEY SHOULD BE just north of Castle, about 40 minutes from the target," said Col. Birdwell.

"A rough 40 minutes," said Major Ellis.

"A lifetime," said Birdwell

116

"I GOT HIM, I got him," yelled Glenn Gregory, the right waist gunner.

Suddenly, one of the *Rachel's* engines was hit. "Feather number one," said Carter, looking out the window. Hansford did not respond, and Carter leaned toward him and shouted, "Feather number one, damn it!"

Hansford responded after Bud's outburst. *What in the hell is wrong with our pilot?* Bud thought to himself.

"Clifford, how close are we to the IP?" Hansford asked.

"Sixteen minutes, Captain. The lead squadron should be over it now."

"Lt. Wyman, are you ready to take over?" Hansford asked.

He frowned. "No, Captain, it's way too early." *What the hell is wrong with Hansford?*

"Okay, okay, I heard you!"

Brick Hansford, our calm, collected, indestructible leader is scared—really scared, thought Carter, staring at Hansford.

"Four 109s at five o'clock," shouted Gifford.

"Three more heading right at me," said Joe Morgan.

Bandits were coming in fast from all directions and every position was firing.

"Damn," said Carter, "the *Wicked Witch* just exploded into a million pieces."

"The fighters are breaking it off. But would you look at the flak in front of us," said Gifford.

All of a sudden, the lead ship, *Melancholy Baby*, took a direct hit and exploded. The *Rachel* flew through guts, blood, and debris. Hansford was shaking.

The German radar can tell 'em our altitude, and the gunners just set their fuses to explode right in the middle of us, Hansford thought to himself. *We don't really have a chance.*

"Gene Richards and his entire crew gone, just like that," said Carter.

"Shut up, will you! Just shut up!" screamed Hansford.

"Get a hold of yourself, Brick; we're the lead ship now. Do you want me to take it?"

"No, no, I'm in command," said Hansford.

"Then act like it. There are a lot of men and planes depending on you," said Bud, sternly.

Suddenly a Me-109 hit the *Rachel* with a sustained burst near the bomb bay and a fire broke out.

"We got fire back here, Skipper!" yelled Destafano.

"Go back there, Bud," said Hansford.

"Okay, I'll take care of it."

Carter returned to the cockpit and reported, "We're okay, Tony put the fire out. Gregory got hit in the hand and I bandaged it. He can still shoot."

"We're on the IP, five minutes to the target," said Clifford.

"Okay, Wyman, are you ready to take it?" asked Hansford.

Wyman frowned and shook his head. "Sure, why not."

Bud Carter connected the controls to the Norden bomb sight and said, "Okay, Wilson, you've got the *Rachel*."

Captain Hansford sighed and leaned back in his seat, hands in his lap. He was still shaking.

"Two minutes," said Wyman, over the intercom.

"Holy shit," said Gifford, "just look at that flak."

"Bomb bay doors open," said Wyman.

It always seems like an eternity until we drop our bomb load, thought Destafano.

"Bombs away!" yelled Wyman over the intercom.

Hansford did not react. He sat silently, quivering, staring straight ahead.

"We're lighting up the target like the Forth of July," said Bud. Hansford's demeanor did not change.

"Okay, Captain, I'm ready to give her back to you," said Wyman.

Hansford did not react for a moment, and then, he slowly took the controls. "Got it," he replied.

Suddenly, the *Rachel* was hit by flak and a warning light came on. Hansford did not react.

"Damn! What now?" said Bud, immediately leaving his co-pilot's seat to check it out. The bomb bay doors were stuck in the open position and the last bomb had not released and was still hanging in the bay. "Damn! If we get flak in the bomb bay we're dead."

"What do you want to do?" Gifford pleaded.

"We've got to do something and quick. Let's try the hand crank."

Gifford attached the crank and tried his best.

"It's no use. The doors didn't budge and the bomb is still there, still stuck."

"George, see if you can get the fuse out," said Carter.

"Okay, I'll give it a try."

"How're you doing, Gifford?"

"We're zero for two, Bud; we can't do the bomb either. The fuse is set. We'll just have to ride with it."

Carter frowned, "We can't ride with, we gotta ..." All of a sudden the bomb released.

Carter and Gifford looked at each other, both shaking their heads, perspiration flowing freely.

"I better get back to the cockpit; the captain's having some problems."

"Problems?"

"He's all screwed up, George."

George Gifford returned to his station in the top turret and wheeled it around to see what was happening. He immediately informed Captain Hansford, "I hate to be the bearer of more bad news, but a large chunk of our tail section has been blown away."

"Damn," said Hansford, "another reason she's flying so rough. Look lively, boys, it looks like the Indians are after us again. What's the status in back?"

"I've got good news and bad news, Brick," said Bud. "The bomb bay doors won't close but there was no other damage. A bomb was stuck but we worked on it, and it finally dropped."

Brick smiled at his copilot, "That's good work, Bud. You got rid of the bomb. We couldn't have that. So the bomb bay's open. It is what it is. We'll deal with it."

I don't know why, but I do believe Brick is out of the fog, back in charge, the leader he has always been, Bud thought.

They felt it and they heard it. The ball turret had taken a major hit from a Me-109. When Destafano opened the hatch, McGuire was screaming in pain. The position was becoming a very dangerous place to work.

"Lt. Carter, please come back and help me with McGuire."

"Go ahead, Bud," said Hansford, "McGuire needs you."

"All right, Skipper."

Brick's back. He's as calm as a cucumber.

"Grab him under the arms while I release his safety hooks," said Bud. "You got him?"

"I've got him."

"Okay, I'm unhooking him. Let's get him out of there."

They pulled him up and leaned him up against the fuselage. He was whimpering and groaning.

"I don't blame him for being unnerved," said Bud. "I mean, he's hanging outside the airplane by his safety belt, out there all exposed to the bandits."

"And the flak," said Gifford, "not to mention they're trying to kill him."

"Right. Let's take a look here." They tore away his pant leg.

"Oh, man, his knee is shattered. Let's put a tourniquet above the wound."

"He's really bleeding," said Gifford. "He's got wounds in the belly and chest. I'm scared, LT."

"So am I, Gifford. I'll give him a shot of morphine, which is about all we can do."

Carter returned to the flight deck, and it was in shambles. The instrument panel had been hit and he couldn't tell what was working and what wasn't. Wires and metal were hanging down from the ceiling. It looked like some shrapnel or a bullet had grazed Hansford's forehead and blood was running down his face, but he was handling it.

"McGuire's bad, Skipper, I don't think he's going to make it. We've done about all we can do."

"Take over, Bud, I'll have a look at him."

Bud smiled, *Yep, the Skipper's back.*

When Hansford reached McGuire, he was dead. He reached up and closed his eyelids. Hansford sat back and stared off into space. They were still under heavy attack from Me-109s. Glenn Gregory was firing frantically at an incoming bandit when he groaned and grabbed his throat. He dropped in his tracks, dead as a mackerel.

Twenty-four missions and my crew survived them all. This is the last one, and I've already lost two, Brick lamented.

Destafano was busy on his side of the waist and didn't realize what had happened to Gregory. No one did at that moment, except Hansford, who had seen the whole thing. He put his face in his hands for a moment. He was not a religious man, never had been. He quietly prayed out loud, "God, if you're there, we need you now. It looks like they're going to kill us all. Please save these good men."

He got to his feet and stumbled forward to the cockpit. He strapped himself in and put on his headphones.

"Are you okay, Skipper?"

"Yeah, but McGuire died and Gregory was killed," he replied, void of emotion. "I'll take it, Bud."

"Are you sure?"

"Yeah, I'm sure."

"Wyman, Gregory's dead," Brick informed him. "Go back there and take over his gun."

"Gregory's dead!" he exclaimed.

"That's right, Wilson, but we are still in a fight, and we need to have the waist covered."

"Okay, Skipper, I understand."

"WE'RE LOSING ALTITUDE," said Carter, "and number three is cutting out. It's gone."

Brick immediately spoke to the crew on the intercom, "When you can, take off your flying boots and put on your combat boots in case we have to bail out."

Men always tied their combat boots to the parachute harness just in case. They were schooled to do this in case they had to bail out over enemy territory where they might need to walk—or run.

"Clifford, where are we?" asked Hansford, calmness in his tone.

"About 40 minutes from the English coastline at our present speed."

"Clark, we're losing about 50 feet per minute," said Brick. "How does that compute?"

"It doesn't compute, Captain, we're not going to make it."

117

"BRICK, WE'RE OVER the Channel. If we're gonna jump, now would be the time to do it," said Carter.

"I know, but let's give *Rachel* a chance. She's brought us home 24 times."

"We're less than 1,500 feet; we really should get out now."

Brick sighed. Then turned to Bud, "Okay, make the call."

Carter made his way to Thibodeaux's position and said, "We're going to bail out. Call Air-Sea Rescue and give them our position."

He went back to the waist where the entire crew was assembled. "We're going to jump, fellows, but first I want you to dump all the machine guns and ammo and anything else that's not nailed down."

"WHERE THE HELL is our boat?" asked Morgan.

"There, there they are," said Gifford.

"What about McGuire and Gregory?" asked Destafano.

"Put parachutes on them and bail them out. We're not going to leave them now. We're all going home together," said Carter.

"Okay, everyone have their chutes on? Good. We're close to the water so pull your rip cord as soon as you clear the ship."

Carter returned to the cockpit, "Okay, Brick, everyone's out but you and me. We're only about 600 feet from the water. Put her on auto-pilot and let's hit the silk."

"Okay, Bud, go ahead and jump. I'm right behind you."

Carter jumped out of the plane and pulled the rip cord immediately. As he floated down he could see the crew being picked up. He almost landed on top of Wyman. They were bobbing up and down in the cold choppy water watching for Hansford's parachute.

BRICK HANSFORD WAS desperately trying to hold altitude as the White Cliffs of Dover loomed large in front of him. They would ordinarily be a beautiful and welcomed sight. At this moment, they presented an air of foreboding.

"Come on, *Rachel,* come on, baby," Hansford pleaded, "Get me up, get me up—come on, baby, get me up."

Rachel was not responding and Brick knew it. *It's no good, she can't do it.*

Brick hurried from the cockpit and out of the airplane.

"There, there's his parachute," said Carter.

The men watched in horror as the *Rachel* hit the cliffs and exploded into a jillion fiery pieces.

As the rescue boat took the cold, wet, and weary men to shore and safety, they thought about *Rachel*, how she had always brought them home.

"She deserved better, but it wasn't to be," Brick lamented. They were saddened that two of their fellow crewmen had failed to complete their 25th and final mission alive. But as men in war so often come to resolve, they were just grateful it wasn't them.

118

"OH, BRICK, I'M glad I didn't know about your last flight," Rachel lamented. "But you're okay, you're safe, you're alive. And you've done your 25 missions and you won't have to fly anymore."

Looking off into nothing, he sighed, lit a cigarette, and took a long drag. He exhaled and said, "Yeah, no more flying. Eight brave young men survived against incredible odds."

He looked at Rachel and smiled, "We were once told to quit thinking about going home, quit thinking about surviving. Just consider ourselves dead already. That way, it would be easier for us to do our jobs."

"I can't believe they really told you guys that stuff."

"Well, they did. No one could possibly know what it was like up there," he frowned, shaking his head. "Not in a million years could we explain it. You had to live it to really know."

He thought for another moment, remembering, and just started quietly talking, "We were flying in the second position in the high squadron. Bud and I were horrified as *Reluctant Virgin* exploded before our very eyes. She took a direct hit. It just disintegrated. The sky suddenly went dark as we flew through the debris from the explosion."

Tears started to slowly run down his face.

"She was there and then she wasn't. I remember Wyman screaming, 'Sweet Jesus, Mary and Joseph, there's blood and guts all over the Plexiglas.' Clifford began to gag."

Brick shook his head. The tears were heavier.

"Clifford was screaming that they were gonna kill us all. It sure as hell seemed like it."

Brick looked at Rachel through red-rimmed eyes.

"Then Clifford said, 'The thought of leaving my wife a widow with two little girls is almost unbearable.'"

Rachel frowned and put her hand on his, "Oh, baby, do you have to talk about it? It's over."

Brick had more, "Like I said, no one can possibly know what it is like unless you've been there."

He wiped away tears with his hand, "But I'll tell you this, my boys never quit thinking about going home and neither did I. I tried to stay calm, to be strong and confident for them. But what they didn't know, and what you didn't know, was that it was getting to me. You can only take so much pressure, so much dying, until you can't take it anymore. I was about to break when I turned to Father O' Banyan, one of our Catholic chaplains. He helped me cope, helped me keep my sanity."

He lit a cigarette and sighed, "Rachel, I have become Catholic."

She was taken aback. They didn't speak for a time.

"What's the matter, Rachel?"

"When you were nothing, I felt I didn't have to worry about religion. I mean, being a Jew. You see, I have been going through a similar struggle. Oh, not like you, but I've seen my share of dying too. And, I began to feel guilty about not following the teaching of my religion. I mean, my grandparents and parents were devout followers of Judaism—of all the teachings, practices, and observances"

He started to speak, but remained silent when she raised her hand.

"My parents never left Nazi Germany, and then I experienced the horrors of Poland and what they did to my people. I just felt that to honor my family, I had to return to Temple, to my faith, and my lineage. I have been going to Temple on a regular basis during the times when you were not here on leave. My problem was the separation from my parents, then college—I didn't have support around me and I just got away from it. Anyway, I'm back to being Jewish again, and it's important to me."

"I don't have an issue with that, I never have."

"Maybe not now, but it could be later."

"What are you talking about, Rachel?"

"Children."

"What about children?"

"Are we going to raise them Jewish or Catholic?"

He was deep in thought. "I love you, Rachel. I always have." He looked at her longingly, "I wanted to marry you in 1939."

"I know, but your father threatened to cut you off if you married a Jew."

Brick was taken aback. He frowned, "How do know that?"

"Paul told Katie and Katie told me. It was while we were in Stockholm, right after we had escaped Poland."

"Damn, that's embarrassing."

"It doesn't matter. That was a long time ago. Just for the record, I wouldn't have married you anyway."

Brick frowned again, "You wouldn't?"

"No, I didn't love you. I liked you, but I didn't love you."

He looked at her for a moment, a little hurt. It showed. *Come to think of it, we never spoke of love or marriage.* "I have looked death in the eye and survived. I'm a man now and I don't give a damn about what my parents think. Marry me, Rachel."

She grinned, toying with him, and asked, "What about your place in the company, and your inheritance?"

"Damn the company. Damn the inheritance. Damn it all!"

It's gratifying to know that's no longer an issue. He's a man now, that's for sure, and one hell of a man.

"I'm different, too. I survived the loss of my parents and my brother, the German invasion of Poland and I've survived the Blitz. And Brickley Hansford, I can now honestly say that I love you, too— and I'd be honored to be your wife. But before I agree to go forward, we have to settle the issue of how we would raise our children and the marriage ceremony. This is part of what I was trying to tell you about returning to my Jewish roots."

"Well, let me ask you this. If we were married, I would not object to you attending Temple if you didn't object to me attending Mass."

"That's not what I would consider ideal, but I could live with that."

"Okay, that part is resolved."

"The Jewish people have many religious holidays that are very important to the faith. I would want to observe all of them. How do you feel about that?"

"I'm okay with that as long as we could also observe Christmas."

She thought for a minute. "I can accept that."

"I guess you'd be uncomfortable with Easter?"

"Yes. I'm sorry, Brick."

"I understand. I'll celebrate on my own."

He smiled at her, "We're making progress."

"We'll see. I would want our children to go to Temple and Hebrew School."

"Come on, Rachel, that's too much to ask."

Brick lit a cigarette, he looked distraught. "Father O' Banyan and I have had many deep discussions since I have become Catholic. Naturally, raising one's children Catholic is a pretty big issue."

"A big issue with whom? The church or me?"

Brick frowned.

"And I would want a Jewish wedding ceremony."

"You want too much, Rachel."

"There it is again, Brick, the thing that always been there. I'm a Jew and you are a gentile."

119

"CAPTAIN HANSFORD, YOU and the crew of the *Rachel* have done a top notch job here in Europe. I am truly sorry for your losses on that last mission."

"I know you are, Colonel, you've been there. And we're all your boys."

"That's true, Brick."

Birdwell thought for a moment, "You've been the lead ship in a number of these raids. You're a natural leader and the men respond to you, they look up to you."

"Thank you, sir, that's kind of you to say."

"Oh, hell, Hansford, I'm not being charitable. It's the damn truth, and you're going to receive the Distinguished Flying Cross, and it's damn well deserved. That will look mighty good beside your Bronze Star and Silver Star. You've got your 25 missions and you're going home. "

This was not part of the news Brick wanted to hear.

"I don't want to go home, Colonel Birdwell. I'd like to stay here in Europe until it's over."

"I don't think the Army is going to let you do that, Captain. You and your crew have done something special. You're going home and sell war bonds for awhile, and then you'll be assigned to a training command. This war is far from over and we've got to train the kids who will continue the fight."

· · · · ·

"BABY, BIRDWELL SAYS they're sending me and my entire crew home to sell war bonds, and then we'll be assigned to a training command," Brick explained. "I'm not surprised. It makes perfectly good sense."

Rachel frowned, "That's not good."

Now, Brick frowned, "What do you mean? It sounds wonderful."

"I'm not going, Brick. I'm not leaving England until the war is over."

Brick was taken aback. He was momentarily speechless.

"Well, as Colonel Birdwell pointed out, this war is far from over. We could be fighting here in Europe for years."

"I think your colonel is right."

"Rachel, you said you loved me. You said you'd marry me. I want us to get married."

"I do love you and I do want to marry you, but we have not settled the issues of Temple, Hebrew School, and a Jewish marriage ceremony. We quit talking about it, but we didn't settle it."

Confusion reigned supreme. Brick sighed, "I'm afraid I don't understand you. The army is sending me home for the duration. I have no choice in the matter. You are making no sense."

Rachel smiled, "Darling man, I know you are confused. But I'm not leaving London until the war is over, and we are not going to get married unless we can settle our differences on children and religion. These things don't work themselves out. I'm not going to go into a marriage and hope for the best. But, you may not have serve out the rest of the war in the States."

He looked confused.

"I am going to contact Uncle Meir and see if he can help."

"Your Uncle Meir. Are you kidding?" he replied, in disbelief.

She kissed him and smiled, "Uncle Meir is well connected with the Roosevelt administration. I must remind you, Captain Hansford, that it was Uncle Meir who was responsible for getting me and Katie out of Poland. He knows the President personally."

Brick was truly speechless. Still, he couldn't help but be a bit skeptical. "This is not Poland. We were neutral at the time. The United States is in it now, and I'm in the Army Air Corps. Orders are orders."

YES, UNCLE MEIR was well connected. And yes, he knew the President personally. And yes, he knew Henry Morgenthau personally. But the real ace-in-the hole was Harry Hopkins. Meir knew him personally as well and Harry knew how much Meir had helped Roosevelt and how much the President cherished his friendship, support, and counsel.

Hopkins had proved himself with the WPA and had become close to Eleanor Roosevelt when they worked together to publicize and defend the New Deal relief programs. On May 10, 1940, after a long night and day discussing the German invasion of the Netherlands, Belgium, and Luxembourg that ended the so-called *Phony War,* Roosevelt urged the exhausted Hopkins to stay for dinner and spend the night in a second-floor White House bedroom. Hopkins did, and he would live out of that bedroom for the next three-and-a-half years. Hopkins spearheaded Lend-Lease, acted as Roosevelt's unofficial emissary to British Prime Minister Winston Churchill, and became perhaps the President's closest advisor. Yes, Meir would talk with Harry Hopkins.

· · · · ·

COLONEL BIRDWELL CALLED Brick to his office.

"Son, I've just been given some extraordinary news."

"Oh, yeah, what's that, sir?"

"You are going home to sell war bonds, but that's only for 90-days. Then you're to be sent back to the 91st Bomb Group with the rank of Major and in command of the 322nd Bombardment Squadron."

Brick was stunned.

"Well, Brickley, what do you think?"

"I'm pleased, and frankly, a bit overwhelmed."

"Frankly, you should be. So am I. You and your boys leave next Tuesday. Have a good time in the Colonies and get your ass back here as soon as possible. I need you."

Brick stood and saluted smartly. It was returned smartly.

THAT NIGHT, BRICK and Rachel had a lovely dinner at the Dorchester Hotel. Brick explained what Colonel Birdwell had said. "Frankly, I was apprehensive. But I will never again doubt what you and Meir Rosenthal can do."

She smiled, giggled, and touched his glass that had just been topped off with champagne, and said, "That would be good to remember."

"But we'll be apart for three months," Brick lamented.

"It will fly by. Now, during the 90 days you are in the States, you might want to give some serious thought to our dilemma. And I'd like your answer when you return."

Brick thought for a moment and said, "That's fair enough. We need to settle it."

"Yes, we do."

Quickly changing the subject, he said, "You know, I might just stay in the Army Air Corps. I could easily make full colonel by the end of the war. With my combat record, if I don't screw up, I could be a general officer someday. What would you think about that?"

"I think you would make a brilliant general. " *If we can have a meeting of the minds on our problem, he's going back to Buenos Aires and help me run Pampas Packing, but I don't need to tell him that right now.*

She leaned over close to him and said, "Captain Hansford, there's a great orchestra playing some wonderful music. Dance with me".

THE END

EPILOGUE

EIGHTY-EIGHT PERCENT of the Jews in Poland, the Baltic States, Germany, Austria, and Slovakia were executed. In all, the Nazis' "final solution" wiped out 67 percent, some 5,933,900, of European Jews. Adolph Hitler's misguided attempt to create a master race and a thousand-year Reich resulted in the deadliest military conflict in history. Hitler lost—but over 60 million people were killed during World War II—over 2.5 percent of the world population. Rachel Rosenthal was one of the lucky ones.

BLETCHLEY PARK'S GREATEST success was the breaking of the Germans' strategic ciphers. These complex ciphers were used to secure communications between Hitler in Berlin and his army commanders in the field. The intelligence value of breaking into these was immense. Initial efforts were manual and successful, but could not keep up with the volume of intercepts. Under Professor Max Newman, they started to devise machines to mechanize the process. This ultimately led to the design and construction of the world's first semi-programmable electronic computer. Breaking into these ciphers allowed the Allied staff, planning for the invasion of Europe, to obtain unprecedented detail of the German defenses.

The codebreakers made a vital contribution to D-Day in other ways. The breaking of the ciphers of the German Secret Intelligence Service allowed the Allies to confuse Hitler over where the invasion force was to land. Hitler's decision to hold troops and armor in reserve, away from the Normandy beaches, undoubtedly ensured the invasion's success. Rachel Rosenthal was at BP at the beginning, and she was there at the end.

THE EIGHTH AIR Force suffered substantial loses, beginning with the first official mission on July 4, 1942, until the war was over. The Eight flew 10,631 missions, lost 4,145 planes and 41,450 crewmen. Official aircraft losses do not include those aircraft that returned, but were "written off" as unrepairable. There were other losses that occurred as a result of collisions, training accidents, and the like. Ten thousand five hundred sixty-one aircraft of all types were lost in the

European Theatre of Operations along with 105,610 brave young American boys who flew in them.

The 91st Bomb Group was the first to complete 100 missions, on January 5, 1944, a truly historic accomplishment. The war could not have been won without the full deployment of America's vast air assets. Bombers crippled German industry and leveled their cities and their will to resist.

RACHEL AND BRICK married in London in December 1943 in a civil ceremony. He reached the rank of full colonel, but decided not to remain in the military after the war. They returned to Buenos Aires and the family welcomed Brick with open arms. She ran Pampas Packing, and he ran Pampas Shipping. They had a son they called Emil and a daughter named Ruth. The children went to Temple and Hebrew School. He learned to enjoy and appreciate the Jewish holidays, and she learned to enjoy Christmas.

CPSIA information can be obtained
at www.ICGtesting.com
Printed in the USA
LVOW12s0716220517
535383LV00001B/41/P